PAYING
THE
PIPER

BAEN BOOKS by DAVID DRAKE

Hammer's Slammers
The Tank Lords
Caught in the Crossfire
The Butcher's Bill
The Sharp End
Cross the Stars
Paying the Piper

RCN series
With the Lightnings
Lt. Leary, Commanding

Independent Novels and Collections
The Dragon Lord
Birds of Prey
Northworld Trilogy
Redliners
Starliner
All the Way to the Gallows
Foreign Legions (created by David Drake)
The Undesired Princess and The Enchanted Bunny
(with L. Sprague de Camp)
Lest Darkness Fall and To Bring the Light
(with L. Sprague de Camp)
Armageddon
(edited with Billie Sue Mosiman)

The General series:
The Forge (with S.M. Stirling)
The Chosen (with S.M. Stirling)
The Reformer (with S.M. Stirling)
The Tyrant (with Eric Flint)

The Belisarius series:
(with Eric Flint)
An Oblique Approach
In the Heart of Darkness
Destiny's Shield
Fortune's Stroke
The Tide of Victory

PAYING THE PIPER

DAVID DRAKE

Copyright © 2002 by David Drake. "Choosing Sides" previously appeared in *The Warmasters*, edited by Bill Fawcett.

A Baen Books Original

Baen Publishing Enterprises
P.O. Box 1403
Riverdale, NY 10471
www.baen.com

ISBN: 0-7434-3547-8

Cover art by Larry Elmore

First printing, July 2002

Library of Congress Cataloging-in-Publication Data
Drake, David.
    Paying the piper / by David Drake.
        p. cm.
    "A Baen Books original"—T.p. verso.
    ISBN 0-7434-3547-8
    1. Life on other planets—Fiction. 2. Space warfare—Fiction. I. Title.

PS3554.RI96 P39 2002
813'.54—dc21

2002018522

Distributed by Simon & Schuster
1230 Avenue of the Americas
New York, NY 10020

Production by Windhaven Press, Auburn, NH
Printed in the United States of America

10 9 8 7 6 5 4 3 2 1

DEDICATION

To Larry Barnthouse, who long ago as
another 96C2L94 was missed by all the
same bullets that missed me.

ACKNOWLEDGMENTS

This book involved computer adventures unusual even for me, The Man Who Kills Computers. (Three dead within two weeks.) My son Jonathan, Mark Van Name, Karen Zimmerman, Allyn Vogel, and my wife Jo, were of particular importance in making it possible for me to continue working.

This book required a lot of attention by Dan Breen, my first reader. I'm very fortunate to have him.

A BACKGROUND NOTE

I've always found it easier to use real settings and cultures than to invent my own. No matter how good a writer's imagination, the six or seven millennia of available human history can do a better job of creating backgrounds.

More than ten years ago I finally took the advice my friends Jim Baen and Mark Van Name had been giving me and did an afterword, explaining where I got the details of the book I'd just completed. I'd resisted this, feeling that it was bad art—the book should explain itself—and anyway, it was unnecessary. It was obvious to any reader that I was using historical and mythological backgrounds, so why should I bother to tell them?

It still may be bad art, and I may have been correct about readers in general seeing what I was doing without me telling them explicitly, but reviewers suddenly discovered that my fiction utilizes literary, historical and mythological material. I've kept up the practice, though generally not with straight Military SF like the Hammer series—but in this case I thought it might be useful, because the background I've used is from a backwater of history.

The Eastern Mediterranean at the end of the 3rd century BC was a very complex region. The three empires founded by the successors of Alexander the Great were collapsing. They were locally powerful, but none was a superpower. Usurpers and secessionists complicated their politics.

Leagues of city states—the Achaeans and Aetolians in Greece proper, others in Asia Minor—had their own interests. New kingdoms, particularly that of Pergamum, were growing at the expense of their neighbors, and barbarians—both Celtic and Illyrian—were becoming regional powers instead of merely raiding and moving on.

Rome was still in the wings but the violent morass would shortly draw her in, ending both the chaos and her own status as a republic. (The region's enormous wealth and complexity, in my opinion, inexorably turned Rome into an empire.)

I adapted this setting for *Paying the Piper*. The general background is that of the war between Rhodes and Byzantium, ostensibly over freedom of navigation. It was about as stupid a conflict as you're likely to find, during which the real principals licked their lips and chuckled while well-meaning idealists wrecked their own societies in pursuit of unobtainable goals by improper means. Much of the military detail is drawn from the campaigns of Phillip the Fifth and his allies against the Aetolian League, particularly the campaign of 219 BC which culminated in Phillip's capture of Psophis.

I guess it isn't out of place to add one comment about the study of history. Knowing a good deal about how cultures interacted in the past allows one to predict how they will interact in the present, so I'm rarely surprised by the daily news. But I regret to say that this understanding doesn't appear to make me happier.

Dave Drake
david-drake.com

CONTENTS

CHOOSING SIDES

The driver of the lead combat car revved his fans to lift the bow when he reached the bottom of the starship's steep boarding ramp. The gale whirling from under the car's skirts rocked Lieutenant Arne Huber forward into the second vehicle—his own *Fencing Master*, still locked to the deck because a turnbuckle had kinked when the ship unexpectedly tilted on the soft ground.

Huber was twenty-five standard years old, shorter than average and fit without being impressively muscular. He wore a commo helmet now, but the short-cropped hair beneath it was as black as the pupils of his eyes.

Sighing, he pushed himself up from *Fencing Master*'s bow slope. His head hurt the way it always did just after star-travel—which meant worse than it did any other time in his life. Even without the howling fans of *Foghorn*, the lead car, his ears would be roaring in time with his pulse.

None of the troopers in Huber's platoon were in much better shape, and he didn't guess the starship's crew were more than nominal themselves. The disorientation from star travel, like a hangover, didn't stop hurting just because it'd become familiar.

"Look!" said Sergeant Deseau, shouting so that the three starship crewmen could hear him over the fans' screaming. "If you don't have us free in a minute flat, starting *now*, I'm going to shoot the cursed thing off and you can worry about the damage to your cursed deck without me to watch you. Do you understand?"

1

Two more spacers were squeezing through the maze of vehicles and equipment in the hold, carrying a power tool between them. This sort of problem can't have been unique to *Fencing Master*.

Huber put his hand on Deseau's shoulder. "Let's get out of the way and let them fix this, Sarge," he said, speaking through the helmet intercom so that he didn't have to raise his voice. Shouting put people's backs up, even if you didn't mean anything by it except that it was hard to hear. "Let's take a look at Plattner's World."

They turned together and walked to the open hatch. Deseau was glad enough to step away from the problem.

The freighter which had brought Platoon F-3, Arne Huber's command, to Plattner's World had a number rather than a name: KPZ 9719. It was much smaller than the vessels which usually carried the men and vehicles of Hammer's Regiment, but even so it virtually overwhelmed the facilities here at Rhodesville. The ship had set down normally, but one of the outriggers then sank an additional meter into the soil. The lurch had flung everybody who'd already unstrapped against the bulkheads and jammed *Fencing Master* in place, blocking two additional combat cars behind it in the hold.

Huber chuckled. That made his head throb, but it throbbed already. Deseau gave him a sour look.

"It's a good thing we hadn't freed the cars before the outrigger gave," Huber explained. "Bad enough people bouncing off the walls; at least we didn't have thirty-tonne combat cars doing it too."

"I don't see why we're landing in a cow pasture anyway," Deseau muttered. "Isn't there a real spaceport somewhere on this bloody tree-farm of a planet?"

"Yeah, there is," Huber said dryly. "The trouble is, it's in Solace. The people the United Cities are hiring us to fight."

The briefing cubes were available to everybody in the Slammers, but Sergeant Deseau was like most of the enlisted personnel—and no few of the officers—in spending the time between deployments finding other ways to entertain himself. It was a reasonable enough attitude. Mercenaries tended to be pragmatists. Knowledge of the local culture wasn't a factor when a planet hired mercenary soldiers, nor did it increase the gunmen's chances of survival.

Deseau spit toward the ground, either a comment or just a way of clearing phlegm from his throat. Huber's mouth felt like somebody'd scrubbed a rusty pot, then used the same wad of steel wool to scour his mouth and tongue.

"Let's hope we capture Solace fast so we don't lose half our supplies in the mud," Deseau said. "This place'll be a swamp the first time it rains."

KPZ 9719 had come down on the field serving the dirigibles which connected Rhodesville with the other communities on Plattner's World—and particularly with the spaceport at Solace in the central highlands. The field's surface was graveled, but there were more soft spots than the one the starship's outrigger had stabbed down through. Deseau was right about what wet weather would bring.

The starship sat on the southern edge of the kilometer-square field. On the north side opposite them were a one-story brick terminal with an attached control tower, and a dozen warehouses with walls and trusses of plastic extrusion. Those few buildings comprised the entire port facilities.

Tractors were positioning lowboys under the corrugated metal shipping containers slung beneath the 300-meter-long dirigible now unloading at the east end of the field. A second dirigible had dropped its incoming cargo and was easing westward against a mild breeze, heading for the mooring mast where it would tether. The rank of outbound shipping containers there waited to be slung in place of the food and merchandise the United Cities imported. The containers had been painted a variety of colors, but rust now provided the most uniform livery.

A third dirigible was in the center of the field, its props turning just fast enough to hold it steady. The four shipping containers hanging from its belly occasionally kicked up dust as they touched the ground. A port official stood in an open-topped jitney with a flashing red light. He was screaming through a bullhorn at the dirigible's forward cockpit, but the crew there seemed to be ignoring him.

Trooper Learoyd, *Fencing Master*'s right wing gunner—Huber chose to ride at the left gun, with Deseau in the vehicle commander's post in the center—joined them at the hatch. He was stocky, pale, and almost bald even though he was younger than Huber by several years. He looked out and said, "What's worth having a war about this place?"

"There's people on it," Deseau said with a sharp laugh. "That's all the reason you need for a war, snake. You ought to know that by now."

According to the briefing cubes, Rhodesville had a permanent population of 50,000; the residents provided light manufacturing and services for the Moss-hunters coursing thousands of square kilometers of the surrounding forest. Only a few houses were visible from the port. The community wound through the forest, constructed under the trees instead of clearing them for construction. The forest was the wealth of Plattner's World, and the settlers acted as though they understood that fact.

"There's a fungus that's a parasite on the trees here," Huber explained. "They call it Moss because it grows in patches of gray tendrils from the trunks. It's the source of an anti-aging drug. The processing's done offworld, but there's enough money in the business that even the rangers who gather the Moss have aircars and better holodecks than you'd find in most homes on Friesland."

"Well I'll be," Learoyd said, though he didn't sound excited. He rubbed his temples, as if trying to squeeze the pain out through his eyesockets.

Deseau spat again. "So long as they've got enough set by to pay our wages," he said. "I'd like a good, long war this time, because if I never board a ship again it'll be too soon."

The third dirigible was drifting sideways. Huber wouldn't have been sure except for the official in the jitney; he suddenly dropped back into his seat and drove forward to keep from being crushed by the underslung cargo containers. The official stopped again and got out of his vehicle, running back toward the dirigible with his fists raised overhead in fury.

Huber looked over his shoulder to see how the spacers were making out with the turnbuckle. The tool they'd brought, a cart with chucks on extensible arms, wasn't working. Well, that was par for the course.

Trooper Kolbe sat in the driver's compartment, his chin bar resting on the hatch coaming. His faceshield was down, presenting an opaque surface to the outside world. Kolbe could have been using the helmet's infrared, light-amplification, or sonic imaging to improve his view of the dimly lit hold, but Huber suspected the driver was simply hiding the fact that his eyes were closed.

Kolbe needn't have been so discreet. If Huber hadn't thought he ought to set an example, he'd have been leaning his forehead against *Fencing Master*'s cool iridium bow slope and wishing he didn't hurt so much.

Platoon Sergeant Jellicoe was at the arms locker, issuing troopers their personal weapons. Jellicoe seemed as dispassionate as the hull of her combat car, but Trooper Coblentz, handing out the weapons as the sergeant checked them off, looked like he'd died several weeks ago.

Unless and until Colonel Hammer ordered otherwise, troopers on a contract world were required to go armed at all times. Revised orders were generally issued within hours of landing; troopers barhopping in rear areas with submachine guns and 2-cm shoulder weapons made the Regiment's local employers nervous, and rightly so.

On Plattner's World the Slammers had to land at six sites scattered across the United Cities, a nation that was mostly forest. None of the available landing fields was large enough to take the monster starships on which the Regiment preferred to travel, and only the administrative capital, Benjamin, could handle more than one twenty-vehicle company at a time. Chances were that even off-duty troopers would be operating in full combat gear for longer than usual.

"What's that gas-bag doing?" Deseau asked. "What do they fill 'em with here, anyway? If it's hydrogen and it usually is . . ."

Foghorn had shut down, well clear of the starship's ramp. Her four crewmen were shifting their gear out of the open-topped fighting compartment and onto the splinter shield of beryllium net overhead. A Slammers' vehicle on combat deployment looked like a bag lady's cart; the crew knew that the only things they could count on having were what they carried with them. Tanks and combat cars could shift position by over 500 klicks in a day, smashing the flank or rear of an enemy who didn't even know he was threatened; but logistics support couldn't follow the fighting vehicles as they stabbed through hostile territory.

"Aide, unit," Huber said, cueing his commo helmet's AI to the band all F-3 used in common. "Tatzig, pull around where that dirigible isn't going to hit you. Something's wrong with the bloody thing and the locals aren't doing much of a job of sorting it out."

Sergeant Tatzig looked up. He grunted an order to his driver, then replied over the unit push, *"Roger, will do."*

There was a clang from the hold. A spacer had just hit the turnbuckle with a heavy hammer.

A huge, hollow metallic racket sounded from the field; the dirigible had dropped its four shipping containers. The instant the big metal boxes hit the ground, the sides facing the starship fell open. Three of them did, anyway: the fourth container opened halfway, then stuck.

The containers were full of armed men wearing uniforms of chameleon cloth that mimicked the hue of whatever it was close to. The troops looked like pools of shadow from which slugthrowers and anti-armor missiles protruded.

"Incoming!" Huber screamed. "We're under attack!"

One of the attacking soldiers had a buzzbomb, a shoulder-launched missile, already aimed at Huber's face. He fired. Huber reacted by instinct, grabbing his two companions and throwing himself down the ramp instead of back into the open hold.

The missile howled overhead and detonated on *Fencing Master*'s bow. White fire filled the universe for an instant. The blast made the ramp jump, flipping Huber from his belly to his right side. He got up. He was seeing double, but he could see; details didn't matter at times like this.

The attack had obviously been carefully planned, but things went wrong for the hostiles as sure as they had for Huber and his troopers. The buzzbomber had launched early instead of stepping away from the shipping container as he should've done. The steel box caught the missile's backblast and reflected it onto the shooter and those of his fellows who hadn't jumped clear. They spun out of the container, screaming as flames licked from their tattered uniforms.

A dozen automatic weapons raked *Foghorn*, killing Tatzig and his crewmen instantly. The attackers' weapons used electromagnets to accelerate heavy-metal slugs down the bore at hypersonic velocity. When slugs hit the car's iridium armor, they ricocheted as neon streaks that were brilliant even in sunlight.

Slugs that hit troopers chewed their bodies into a mist of blood and bone.

The starship's hold was full of roiling white smoke, harsh as a wood rasp on the back of Huber's throat in the instant before his helmet slapped filters down over his nostrils. The buzzbomb had hit *Fencing Master*'s bow slope at an angle. Its shaped-charge warhead had gouged a long trough across the armor instead of punching through into the car's vitals. There was no sign of Kolbe.

The tie-down, jammed turnbuckle and all, had vanished in the explosion. Two pairs of legs lay beside the vehicle. They'd probably belonged to spacers rather than Huber's troopers, but the blast had blown the victims' clothing off at the same time it pureed their heads and torsos.

Slugs snapped through the starship's hatchway, clanging and howling as they ricocheted deeper into the hold. Huber mounted *Fencing Master*'s bow slope with a jump and a quick step. He dabbed a hand down and the blast-heated armor burned him. He'd have blisters in the morning, if he lived that long.

Huber thought the driver's compartment was empty, but Kolbe's body from the shoulders on down had slumped onto the floor. Huber bent through the hatch and grabbed him. The driver's right arm came off when Huber tugged.

Huber screamed in frustration and threw the limb out of the vehicle, then got a double grip on Kolbe's equipment belt and hauled him up by it. Bracing his elbows for leverage, Huber pulled the driver's torso and thighs over the coaming and let gravity do the rest. The body slithered down the bow, making room for Huber inside. The compartment was too tight to share with a corpse and still be able to drive.

Kolbe had raised the seat so that he could sit with his head out of the vehicle. Huber dropped it because he wanted the compartment's full-sized displays instead of the miniature versions his faceshield would provide. The slugs whipping around the hold would've been a consideration if he'd had time to think about it, but right now he had more important things on his mind than whether he was going to be alive in the next millisecond.

"All Fox elements!" he shouted, his helmet still cued to the unit push. Half a dozen troopers were talking at the same time; Huber didn't know if anybody would hear the order, but they were mostly veterans and ought to react the right way without a lieutenant telling them what that was. "Bring your cars on line and engage the enemy!"

Arne Huber was F-3's platoon leader, not a driver, but right now the most critical task the platoon faced was getting the damaged, crewless, combat car out of the way of the two vehicles behind it. With *Fencing Master* blocking the hatch, the attackers would wipe out the platoon like so many bugs in a killing bottle. Huber was the closest trooper to the job, so he was doing it.

The fusion bottle that powered the vehicle was on line. Eight powerful fans in nacelles under *Fencing Master*'s hull sucked in outside air and filled the steel-skirted plenum chamber at pressure sufficient to lift the car's thirty tonnes. Kolbe had switched the fans on but left them spinning at idle, their blades set at zero incidence, while the spacers freed the turnbuckle.

Huber palmed the combined throttles forward while his thumb adjusted blade incidence in concert. As the fusion bottle fed more power to the nacelles, the blades tilted on their axes so that they drove the air rather than merely cutting it. Fan speed remained roughly constant, but *Fencing Master* shifted greasily as her skirts began to lift from the freighter's deck.

A second buzzbomb hit the bow.

For an instant, Huber's mind went as blank as the white glare of the blast. The shock curtains in the driver's compartment expanded, and his helmet did as much as physics allowed to save his head. Despite that, his brain sloshed in his skull.

He came around as the shock curtains shrank back to their ready state. He didn't know who or where he was. The display screen before him was a gray, roiling mass. He switched the control to thermal imaging by trained reflex and saw armed figures rising from the ground to rush the open hatch.

I'm Arne Huber. We're being attacked.

His right hand was on the throttles; the fans were howling. He twisted the grip, angling the nacelles back so that their thrust pushed the combat car instead of just lifting it. *Fencing Master*'s bow skirt screeched on the deck, braking the vehicle's forward motion beyond the ability of the fans to drive it.

The second warhead had opened the plenum chamber like a ration packet. The fan-driven air rushed out through the hole instead of raising the vehicle as it was meant to do.

The attackers had thrown themselves flat so that the missile wouldn't scythe them down also. Three of them reached the base of the ramp, then paused and opened fire. Dazzling streaks crisscrossed the hold, and the *whang* of slugs hitting the *Fencing Master*'s iridium armor was loud even over the roar of the fans.

Huber decoupled the front four nacelles and tilted them vertical again. He shoved the throttle through the gate, feeding full emergency power to the fans. The windings would burn out in a few minutes under this overload, but right now Huber wouldn't bet he or anybody in his platoon would be alive then to know.

Fencing Master's ruined bow lifted on thrust alone. Not high, not even a finger's breadth, but enough to free the skirt from the decking and allow the rear nacelles to shove her forward. Staggering like a drunken ox, the car lurched from the hold and onto the ramp. Her bow dragged again, but this time the fans had gravity to aid them. She accelerated toward the field, scraping up a fountain of red sparks from either side of her hull.

The attackers tried to jump out of the way. Huber didn't know and didn't much care what happened to them when they disappeared below the level of the sensor pickups feeding *Fencing Master*'s main screen. A few gunmen more or less didn't matter; Huber's problem was to get this car clear of the ramp so that *Flame Farter* and *Floosie*, still aboard the freighter, could deploy and deal with the enemy.

Fencing Master reached the bottom of the ramp and drove a trench through the gravel before shuddering to a halt. The shock curtains swathed Huber again; he'd have disengaged the system if he'd had time for nonessentials after the machine's well-meant swaddling clothes freed him. Skewing the stern nacelles slightly to port, he pivoted *Fencing Master* around her bow and rocked free of the rut.

The air above him sizzled with ozone and cyan light: two of the tribarrels in the car's fighting compartment had opened up on the enemy. Somebody'd managed to board while Huber was putting the vehicle in motion. *Fencing Master* was a combat unit again.

There must've been about forty of the attackers all told, ten to each of the shipping containers. Half were now bunched near *Foghorn* or between that car and the starship's ramp. Huber switched *Fencing Master*'s Automatic Defense System live, then used the manual override to trigger three segments.

The ADS was a groove around the car's hull, just above the skirts. It was packed with plastic explosive and faced with barrel-shaped osmium pellets. When the system was engaged, sensors triggered segments of the explosive to send blasts of pellets out to meet and disrupt an incoming missile.

Fired manually, each segment acted as a huge shotgun. The clanging explosions chopped into cat food everyone who stood within ten meters of *Fencing Master*. Huber got a whiff of sweetly-poisonous explosive residues as his nose filters closed again. The screaming fans sucked away the smoke before he could switch back to thermal imaging.

An attacker aboard *Foghorn* had seen the danger in time to duck into the fighting compartment; the pellets scarred the car's armor but didn't penetrate it. The attacker rose, pointing his slugthrower down at the hatch Huber hadn't had time to close. A tribarrel from *Fencing Master* decapitated the hostile.

A powergun converted a few precisely aligned copper atoms into energy which it directed down the weapon's mirror-polished iridium bore. Each light-swift bolt continued in a straight line to its target, however distant, and released its energy as heat in a cyan flash. A 2-cm round like those the tribarrels fired could turn a man's torso into steam and fire; the 20-cm bolt from a tank's main gun could split a mountain.

One of the shipping containers was still jammed halfway open. Soldiers were climbing out like worms squirming up the sides of a bait can. Two raised their weapons when they saw a tribarrel slewing in their direction. Ravening light slashed across them, flinging their maimed bodies into the air. The steel container flashed into white fireballs every time a bolt hit it.

Huber's ears were numb. It looked like the fighting was over, but he was afraid to shut down *Fencing Master*'s fans just in case he was wrong; it was easier to keep the car up than it'd be to raise her again from a dead halt. He did back off the throttles slightly to bring the fans down out of the red zone, though. The bow skirt tapped and rose repeatedly, like a chicken drinking.

Flame Farter pulled into the freighter's hatchway and dipped to slide down the ramp under full control. Platoon Sergeant Jellicoe was behind the central tribarrel. She'd commandeered the leading car when the shooting started rather than wait for her own *Floosie* to follow out of the hold.

Jellicoe fired at something out of sight beyond the shipping containers. Huber touched the menu, importing the view from Jellicoe's gunsight and expanding it to a quarter of his screen.

Three attackers stood with their hands in the air; their weapons were on the gravel behind them. Jellicoe had plowed up the ground alongside to make sure they weren't going to change their minds.

Mercenaries fought for money, not principle. The Slammers and their peers took prisoners as a matter of policy, encouraging their opponents toward the same professional ideal.

Enemies who killed captured Slammers could expect to be slaughtered man, woman and child; down to the last kitten that mewled in their burning homes.

"Bloody Hell . . ." Huber muttered. He raised the seat to look out at the shattered landscape with his own eyes, though the filters still muffled his nostrils.

Haze blurred the landing field. It was a mix of ozone from powergun bolts and the coils of the slug-throwers, burning paint and burning uniforms, and gases from superheated disks that had held the copper atoms in alignment: empties ejected from the tribarrels. Some of the victims were fat enough that their flesh burned also.

The dirigible that'd carried the attackers into position now fled north as fast as the dozen engines podded on outriggers could push it. That wasn't very fast, even with the help of the breeze to swing the big vessel's bow; they couldn't possibly escape.

Huber wondered for a moment how he could contact the dirigible's crew and order them to set down or be destroyed. Plattner's World probably had emergency frequencies, but the data hadn't been downloaded to F-3's data banks yet.

Sergeant Jellicoe raked the dirigible's cabin with her tribarrel. The light-metal structure went up like fireworks in the cyan bolts. An instant later all eight gunners in the platoon were firing, and the driver of *Floosie* was shooting a pistol with one hand as he steered his car down the ramp with the other.

"Cease fire!" Huber shouted, not that it was going to make the Devil's bit of difference. "Unit, cease fire *now!*"

The dirigible was too big for the powerguns to destroy instantly, but the bolts had stripped away swathes of the outer shell and ruptured the ballonets within. Deseau had guessed right: the dirigible got its lift from hydrogen, the lightest gas and cheap enough to dump and replace after every voyage so that the ballonets didn't fill with condensed water over time.

The downside was the way it burned.

Flames as pale and blue as a drowned woman's flesh licked from the ballonets, engulfing the middle of the great vessel. The motors continued to drive forward, but the stern started to swing down as fire sawed the airship in half. The skeleton of open girders showed momentarily, then burned away.

"Oh bloody buggering Hell!" Huber said. He idled *Fencing Master*'s fans and stood up on the seat. "*Hell!*"

"What's the matter, sir?" Learoyd asked. He'd lost his helmet, but he and Sergeant Deseau both were at their combat stations. The tribarrels spun in use, rotating a fresh bore up to fire while the other two cooled. Even so the barrels still glowed yellow from their long bursts. "They were hostiles too, the good Lord knows."

"*They* were," Huber said grimly. "But the folks living around here are the ones who've hired us."

The remaining ballonets in the dirigible's bow exploded simultaneously, flinging blobs of burning metal hundreds of meters away. Fires sprang up from the treetops, crackling and spewing further showers of sparks.

Huber heard a siren wind from somewhere deep in the forest community. It wasn't going to do a lot of good.

The dirigible's stern, roaring like a blast furnace, struck the terminal building. Some of those inside ran out; they were probably screaming, but Huber couldn't hear them over the sound of the inferno. One fellow had actually gotten twenty meters from the door when the mass of airship and building exploded, engulfing him in flames. He was a carbonized husk when they sucked back an instant later.

Huber sighed. That pretty well put a cap on the day, he figured.

Base Alpha—regimental headquarters on every world that hired the Slammers was Base Alpha—was a raw wasteland bulldozed from several hectares of forest. The clay was deep red when freshly turned, russet when it dried by itself to a form of porous rock, and oddly purple when mixed with plasticizer to form the roadways and building foundations of the camp.

The aircar and driver that'd brought Huber from Rhodesville to Base Alpha were both local, though the woman driving had a cap with a red ball insignia and the words

LOGISTICS SECTION
HAMMER'S REGIMENT

marking her as a Slammers' contract employee. Colonel Hammer brought his own combat personnel and equipment to each deployment, but much of the Regiment's logistics tail was procured for the operation. Supplies and the infrastructure to transport them usually came from what the hiring state had available.

Huber stopped in front of the building marked PROVOST MARSHAL and straightened his equipment belt. The guards, one of them in a gun jeep mounting a tribarrel, watched him in the anonymity of mirrored faceshields. The tribarrel remained centered on Huber's midriff as he approached.

The orders recalling Lieutenant Arne Huber from F-3 directed him to report to the Provost Marshal's office on arrival at Base Alpha. Huber had left his gear with the clerk at the Transient Barracks—he wasn't going to report to the Regiment's hatchetman with a dufflebag and two footlockers—but he hadn't taken time to be assigned a billet. There was a good chance—fifty-fifty, Huber guessed—that he wouldn't be a member of the Slammers when the present interview concluded.

He felt cold inside. He'd known the possibilities the instant he saw the first bolts rake the dirigible, but the terse recall message that followed his report had still made his guts churn.

Nothing to be done about it now. Nothing to be done about it since Sergeant Jellicoe shifted her aim to the dirigible and thumbed her butterfly trigger.

"Lieutenant Huber reporting to the Provost Marshal, as ordered," he said to the sergeant commanding the squad of guards.

"You're on the list," the sergeant said without inflexion. He and the rest of his squad were from A Company; they were the Regiment's police, wearing a stylized gorget as their collar flash. In some mercenary outfits the field police were called Chain Dogs from the gorget; in the Slammers they were the White Mice. "You can leave your weapons with me and go on in."

"Right," said Huber, though the order surprised him. He unslung his belt with the holstered pistol, then handed over the powerknife clipped to a trouser pocket as well.

"He's clean," said a guard standing at the read-out from a detection frame. The sergeant nodded Huber forward.

The Slammers were used to people wanting to kill them. Major Joachim Steuben, the Regiment's Provost Marshal, was obviously used to the Slammers themselves wanting to kill *him*.

Huber opened the door and entered. The building was a standard one-story new-build with walls of stabilized earth and a roof of plastic extrusion. It was a temporary structure so far as the Slammers were concerned, but it'd still be here generations later unless the locals chose to knock it down.

It was crude, ugly, and as solid as bedrock. You could use it as an analogy for the Slammers' methods, if you wanted to.

The door facing the end of the hallway was open. A trim, boyishly handsome man sat at a console there; he was looking toward Huber through his holographic display. If it weren't for the eyes, you might have guessed the fellow was a clerk. . . .

Huber strode down the hall, staring straight ahead. Some of the side doors were open also, but he didn't look into them. He wondered if this was how it felt to be a rabbit facing a snake.

I'm not a rabbit. But if half the stories told about him were true, Joachim Steuben was a snake for sure.

Before Huber could raise his hand to knock on the door jamb, the man behind the desk said, "Come in, Lieutenant; and close it behind you."

A holographic landscape covered the walls of Joachim Steuben's office; flowers poked through brightly lit snow, with rugged slopes in the background. The illusion was seamless and probably very expensive.

"You know why you're here, Huber?" Steuben asked. Everything about the little man was expensive: his manicure, his tailored uniform of natural silk, and the richly chased pistol in a cut-away holster high on his right hip.

The only chair in the office was the one behind Steuben's console.

"I'm here because of the ratfuck at Rhodesville, sir," Huber said. He held himself at attention, though the major's attitude wasn't so much formal as playfully catlike.

Instead of staring at the wall over Steuben's shoulder, Huber met the major's eyes directly. If he hadn't, he'd have been giving in to fear. Because Major Joachim Steuben scared the crap out of him.

"Close enough," Steuben said as though he didn't much care. "What's your excuse?"

"Sir!" Huber said, truly shocked this time. "No excuse, *sir.*"

It was the Nieuw Friesland Military Academy answer, and

it was the right answer this time beyond question. Platoon F-3's commander had started to disembark his unit without waiting to issue sidearms and to cycle ammunition for the vehicles' tribarrels up from their storage magazines. Five troopers had died, a sixth had lost her left arm to a ricocheting slug, and it was the Lord's mercy alone that kept the damage from being worse.

Steuben raised an eyebrow and smiled faintly. His console's holographic display was only a shimmer of light from the back side, so Huber didn't know whether the major was really viewing something—Huber's file? A stress read-out?— or if he just left it up to make the interviewee more uncomfortable.

Which would be a pretty good trick, as uncomfortable as Huber felt even before he entered the office.

"A fair number of people in the United Cities think it'd be a mistake to go to war with Solace, Huber," Steuben said calmly. "They want to use the way you gutted Rhodesville as an excuse to cancel the Regiment's contract and go back to peaceful negotiation with Solace over port fees. Do you have any comment about that?"

Huber licked his lips. "Sir," he said, "everything my platoon did at Rhodesville was by my direct order. No blame whatever should attach to any of my troopers."

Steuben laughed. It was a horrible sound, a madman's titter. "Goodness," he said. "An officer who has complete control of his troops while he's driving a damaged combat car? You're quite a paragon, Lieutenant."

Huber licked his lips again. He had to pull his eyes back to meet Steuben's. *Like looking at a cobra. . . .*

"For the time being," the major continued, suddenly businesslike and almost bored, "you've been transferred to command of Logistics Section, Lieutenant Huber. Your office is in Benjamin proper, not Base Alpha here, because most of your personnel are locals. You have a cadre of six or so troopers, all of them deadlined for one reason or another."

He laughed again. "None of the others have burned down a friendly community, however," he added.

"Yes sir," Huber said. He felt dizzy with relief. He'd thought he was out. He'd been pretending he didn't, but he'd walked into this office believing he'd suddenly become a civilian again, with no friends and no future.

Major Steuben shut down his display and stood. He was a small man with broad shoulders for his size and a wasp waist. From any distance, the word "pretty" was the one you'd pick to describe him. Only if you were close enough to see Steuben's eyes did you think of snakes and death walking on two legs. . . .

"I don't have any problem with what you did in Rhodesville, Lieutenant," Steuben said quietly. "But I don't have a problem with a lot of things that seem to bother other people. If the Colonel told me to, I'd shoot you down where you stand instead of transferring you to Log Section. And it wouldn't bother me at all."

He smiled. "Do you understand?"

"Yes sir," Huber said. "I understand."

"Lieutenant Basime was a friend of yours at the Academy, I believe," Steuben said with another of his changes of direction. "She's acting head of our signals liaison with the UC now. Drop in and see her before you report to Log Section. She can fill you in on the background you'll need to operate here in the rear."

He waved a negligent hand. "You're dismissed, Lieutenant," he said. "Close the door behind you."

Huber swung the panel hard—too hard. It slipped out of his hands and slammed.

Major Steuben's terrible laugh followed him back down the hallway.

The ten-place aircar that ferried Huber into Benjamin had six other passengers aboard when it left Base Alpha: three troopers going into town on leave, and three local citizens returning from business dealings with the Regiment. Each trio kept to itself, which was fine with Arne Huber. He wasn't sure what'd happened in Joachim Steuben's office, whether it had all been playacting or if Steuben had really been testing him.

A test Huber'd passed, in that case; seeing as he was not only alive, he'd been transferred into a slot that normally went to a captain. But he wasn't sure, of that or anything else.

He was the only passenger remaining when the car reached

its depot, what had been a public school with a sports arena in back. The freshly painted sign out front read

BENJAMIN LIAISON OFFICE
HAMMER'S REGIMENT

with a red lion rampant on a gold field. The driver set the car down by the sign, then lifted away to the arena to shut down as soon as Huber had gotten his luggage off the seat beside him.

Would the local have been more helpfully polite if he'd known Huber was his new boss? Huber smiled faintly. He was too wrung out, from the firefight and now from the interview with Major Steuben, to really care that a direct subordinate had just dumped him out on the pavement.

He bent to shoulder the dufflebag's strap. "We'll watch it for you, sir!" called one of the guards on the front steps. They were alert and fully armed, but they seemed relaxed compared to the White Mice guarding the Provost Marshal's office at Base Alpha.

The troopers of F-3 had been relaxed when they started to disembark, too. Huber winced, wondering how long he was going to remember the feel of Kolbe's body slipping through his fingers like a half-filled waterbed. For the rest of his life, he supposed.

Gratefully he left his gear behind as he mounted the stone steps to the front doors. The four troopers were from G Company, wearing their dismounted kit and carrying 2-cm shoulder weapons. Their two combat cars and the remaining crew members were parked at opposite ends of the arena with their tribarrels elevated on air-defense duty. They'd track anything that came over the horizon, whether aircraft or artillery shell, and blast it if required.

"Where's the signals office, Sergeant?" Huber asked the trooper who'd offered to watch his gear.

"All the way down and to the left, ground floor," the fellow said. "Ah, sir? You're Lieutenant Huber?"

"Yeah, I am," Huber said, suddenly cold. The name tape above his left breast pocket was too faded to read; the fellow must have recognized his face.

"It's an honor to meet you, sir," the sergeant said. "You

saved everybody's ass at Rhodesville. We all watched the imagery."

For a moment Huber frowned, thinking that the man was being sarcastic. But he wasn't, and the other troopers were nodding agreement.

"Thank you, Sergeant," he said. His voice wanted to tremble, but he didn't let it. "That isn't the way it looked from where I was sitting, but I appreciate your viewpoint on the business."

Huber went inside quickly, before anybody else could speak. He was as shocked as if the guards had suddenly stripped off their uniforms and started dancing around him. Their words didn't belong in the world of Arne Huber's mind.

Dungaree-clad locals under the direction of a Slammers sergeant were bringing cartloads of files up the back stairs, two on each cart. When they got inside, they rolled them down the hallway to the big room on the right marked CAFETERIA. It was a clerical office now; the tables were arranged back to back and held data consoles manned by locals.

Huber moved to the left to let the carts get past. The sergeant turned from shouting at somebody in the six-wheeled truck outside and saw him. He looked like he was going to speak, but Huber ducked into the door with the recent SIGNALS LIAISON sign before he could.

Huber could have understood it if troopers turned their backs on him and whispered: five dead in a matter of seconds was a heavy loss for a single platoon. That wasn't what was happening.

Lieutenant Adria Basime—Doll to her friends—was bent over the desk of a warrant leader by the door, pointing out something on his console. She saw Huber and brightened. "Arne!" she said. "Come back to my office! My broom closet, more like, but it's got a door. Tory, have me those numbers when I come out, right?"

"Right, El-Tee," agreed the warrant leader. Even Huber, who'd never seen the fellow before, could read the relief in his expression. "Just a couple minutes, that's all I need."

There were a dozen consoles in the outer office, only half of them occupied. Three of the personnel present were Slammers, the others locals.

"I've got ten more people under me," Doll explained as she closed the door of the inner office behind her. "They're out trying to set up nets that we can at least pretend are secure. Plattner's World has a curst good commo network—they'd just about have to, as spread out as the population is. The trouble is, it *all* goes through Solace."

Doll's office wasn't huge, but it compared favorably with the enclosed box of a command car, let alone the amount of space there was in the fighting compartment of a combat car like *Fencing Master*. All a matter of what you've gotten used to, Huber supposed. Doll gestured him to a chair and took the one beside it instead of seating herself behind the console.

"What're you here for, Arne?" she asked. "Did you debrief to the Colonel in person?"

"I thought they were pulling me back to cashier me," Huber said carefully. "I didn't need Major Steuben to tell me how much damage we did to Rhodesville in the firefight. Apparently the locals want to void our contract for that."

Doll frowned. She was petite and strikingly pretty, even in a service uniform. She wore her hair short, but it fluffed like a dazzle of blonde sunlight when she wasn't wearing a commo helmet.

"Some of them maybe do," she said. "The government's in it all the way now, though. They can't back down unless they want to risk not only losing their places but likely being tried for treason if the peace party gets into power."

"Well, I'm transferred to run local transport," Huber said. He felt better already for talking to Doll. She came from a powerful family on Nieuw Friesland and had a keen political sense. If she said Huber hadn't jeopardized the Regiment's contract, that was the gospel truth. "They had to get me out of the field after the way I screwed up, after all."

"Screwed up?" Doll said in surprise. "You guys got ambushed by a company of Harris's Commando while you were still aboard the ship that brought you. You not only saved your platoon, you wiped out the kill team pretty much single-handedly, the way *I* heard it."

"That's not—" Huber said; and as he spoke, his mind flashed him a shard of memory, his finger selecting three segments of the Automatic Defense System and the *Whang!*

as they fired simultaneously. He hadn't been thinking of the bunched infantry as human beings, just as a problem to be solved like the jammed turnbuckle. They were figures on his display; and after he'd fired the ADS, they were no longer a problem.

"Via," he whispered. "There must've been twenty of them. . . ."

Huber had killed before, but he hadn't thought of what he'd done in Rhodesville as killing until Doll stated the obvious. He'd been thinking of other things.

"Yeah, well . . ." he said, looking toward the window. "Given the way they caught us with our pants down, things went as well as they could. But we *were* caught. I was caught."

Huber shrugged, forced a smile, and looked at his friend. "Major Steuben said you could give me a rundown on my new section, Doll. The people, I mean. I called up the roster on my helmet on the way here, but they were mostly locals and there's nothing beyond date of hire."

"I can tell you about Hera Graciano," Doll said with a grin. "She's your deputy, and she put the section together before the Regiment's combat assets started to arrive. For what it's worth, it seemed to me she was running things by herself even on the days Captain Cassutt was in the office."

The grin grew broader. She went on, "That wasn't many days, from what I saw. And he's on administrative leave right now."

"I'm glad there'll be one of us who knows the job, then," Huber said, feeling a rush of relief that surprised him. Apparently while his conscious mind was telling him how lucky he was to be alive and still a member of the Regiment, his guts were worried about handling a rear echelon job in which his only background was a three-month rotation in the Academy four years earlier.

"Her father's Agis Graciano," Doll said. "He's Minister of Trade for the UC at the moment, but the ruling party shifts ministries around without changing anything important. He was Chief Lawgiver when the motion to hire the Slammers passed, and he's very much the head of the war party."

Huber frowned as he ran through the possibilities. It was

good to have a competent deputy, but a deputy who'd gotten in the habit of running things herself *and* who had political connections could be a problem in herself. And there was one more thing. . . .

"Does the lady get along with her father?" he asked. "Because I know sometimes that can be a worse problem than strangers ever thought of having."

Doll laughed cheerfully. "Hera lives with her father," she said. "They're very close. It's the elder brother, Patroklos, who's the problem. He's in the Senate too, and he'd say it was midnight if his father claimed it was noon."

Her face hardened as she added, "Patroklos is somebody I'd be looking at if I wanted to know how Harris's Commando learned exactly when a single platoon was going to land at Rhodesville, but that's not my job. You shouldn't have any trouble with him now that you're in Log Section."

"Thanks, Doll," Huber said as he rose to his feet. "I guess I'd better check the section out myself now. They're on the second floor?"

"Right," Doll said as she stood up also. "Two things more, though. Your senior non-com, Sergeant Tranter? He's a technical specialist and he's curst good at it. He's helped me a couple times here, finding equipment and getting it to work. The only reason he's not still in field maintenance is he lost a leg when a jack slipped and the new one spasms anytime the temperature gets below minus five."

"That's good to know," Huber said. "And the other thing?"

Doll's grin was back, broader than ever before. "Mistress Graciano is a real stunner, trooper," she said. "And she wasn't a bit interested when *I* tried to chat her up, so I figure that means a handsome young hero like you is in with a chance."

Huber gave his buddy a hug. They were both laughing as they walked back into the outer office.

Instead of a stenciled legend, the words LOGISTICS SECTION over the doorway were of brass letters on a background of bleached hardwood. Huber heard shuffling within the room as he reached the top of the stairs, then silence. He frowned and had to resist the impulse to fold back the flap of his pistol holster before he opened the door.

"All rise for Lieutenant Huber!" bellowed the non-com standing in front of the console nearest the doorway. He had curly red hair and a fluffy moustache the full width of his face. There wasn't a boot on his mechanical left leg, so Huber didn't need the name tape over the man's left breast to identify him as Sergeant Tranter.

There were ten consoles in the main room but almost a score of people, and they'd been standing before Tranter gave his order. Beside Tranter stood a wispy Slammers trooper; his left arm below the sleeve of his khakis was covered with a rash which Huber hoped to the good Lord's mercy wasn't contagious. The others were local civilians, and the black-haired young woman who stepped forward offering her hand was just as impressive as Adria said she was.

"I'm glad you made it, Lieutenant Huber," she said in a voice as pleasantly sexy as the rest of her. "I'm your deputy, Hera Graciano."

"Ma'am," Huber said, shaking the woman's hand gingerly. Was he supposed to have kissed it? There might be something in the briefing cubes that he'd missed, but he doubted they went into local culture at this social level. It wasn't the sort of thing the commander of a line platoon was likely to need.

"Sergeant Tranter, sir," said the non-com. He didn't salute; saluting wasn't part of the Slammers' protocol, where all deployments were to combat zones and the main thing a salute did was target the recipient for any snipers in the vicinity. "This is Trooper Bayes, he's helping me go over the vehicles we're offered for hire."

Hera looked ready to step in and introduce her staff too. Huber raised his hand to forestall her.

"Please?" he said to get attention. "Before I try to memorize names, Deputy Graciano, could you give me a quick rundown of where the section is and where it's supposed to be?"

He flashed the roomful of people an embarrassed smile. "I intend to carry my weight, but an hour ago I couldn't have told you anything about Log Section beyond that there probably was one."

"Of course," Hera said. "We can use your office—" she nodded to a connecting door "—or mine," this time indicating a cubicle set off from the rest of the room by waist-high paneling.

"We'll use yours," Huber said, because he was pretty sure from what he'd heard about Captain Cassutt that useful information was going to be in the deputy's office instead. "Oh— and I don't have quarters, yet. Is there a billeting officer here or—?"

"I'll take care of it, sir," Tranter said. "Do we need to go pick up your baggage too?"

"It's out in front of the building," Huber said. "I—"

"Right," said Tranter. "Come on, Bayes. Sir, you'll be in Building Five in back of the vehicle park. They're temporaries but they're pretty nice, and engineering threw us up a nice bulletproof wall around the whole compound. Just in case—which I guess I *don't* have to explain to you."

Chuckling at the reference to Rhodesville, the two troopers left the room. Huber smiled too. It was gallows humor, sure; but if you couldn't laugh at grim jokes, you weren't going to laugh very much on service with the Slammers.

And it wasn't that Tranter didn't have personal experience with disaster. The nonskid sole of his mechanical foot thumped the floor with a note distinct from that of the boot on his right foot.

"I'm impressed by Sergeant Tranter," Hera said in a low voice as she stepped into her alcove after Huber. Though it seemed open to the rest of the room, a sonic distorter kept conversations within the cubicle private by canceling any sounds that crossed the invisible barrier. "As a matter of fact, I'm impressed by all the, ah, soldiers assigned to this section. I'd assumed that because they weren't fit for regular duties. . . ."

"Ma'am," Huber said, hearing the unmeant chill in his voice. "We're the Slammers. It's not just that everybody in the Regiment's a volunteer—that's true of a lot of merc outfits. We're the best. We've got the best equipment, we get the best pay, and we've got our pick of recruits. People who don't do the job they're assigned to because they don't feel like it, they go someplace else. By their choice or by the Colonel's."

"I'm sorry," the woman said. "I didn't mean . . ."

Her voice trailed off. She *had* meant she expected people on medical profile to slack off while they were on temporary assignment to ash and trash jobs.

Huber gave an embarrassed chuckle. He felt like an idiot to've come on like a regimental recruiter to somebody who was trying to offer praise.

"Ma'am," he said, "I was out of line. I just mean the folks who stay in the Slammers are professionals. Sergeant Tranter, now—he could retire on full pay. If he didn't, it's because he wants to stay with the Regiment. And I'd venture a guess—"

Made more vivid by Huber's own sudden vision of being cast out of the Slammers.

"—that it's because he's grown to like being around other professionals, other people who do their job *because* it's their job. You don't find a lot of that in the outside world."

She looked at him without expression. "No," she said, "you don't. Well, Lieutenant Huber, again I'm glad for your arrival. And if it's agreeable to you, I prefer 'Hera' to 'ma'am' or 'Deputy Graciano.' But of course it's up to you as section head to decide on the etiquette."

"Hera's fine and so's Arne," Huber said in relief. "And ah—Hera? About Captain Cassutt?"

She gestured to affect disinterest.

"No, you deserve to hear," Huber said, "after the way I got up on my haunches. Cassutt had a bad time the deployment before this one. It wasn't his fault, mostly at any rate, but he got pulled out of the line."

The same way I did, but Huber didn't say that.

"He's off on leave, now," he continued. "He'll either dry out or he'll *be* out. If he's forcibly retired, his pension will keep him in booze as long as his liver lasts—but he won't be anywhere he's going to screw up the business of the Regiment."

"I . . ." Hera said. There was no way of telling what the thought she'd smothered unspoken was. "I see that. Ah, here's the transport that I've either purchased or contracted for, based on volume requirements sent me by the regimental prep section. If you'd like to go over them . . . ?"

She'd set her holographic projector on a 360-degree display so that they both could read the data from their different angles. Huber checked the list of tonnage per unit per day, in combat and in reserve, then the parallel columns giving vehicles and payloads. Those last figures floored him.

"Ma'am?" he said, careting the anomaly with his light wand. "Hera, I mean, these numbers—oh! They're dirigibles?"

She nodded warily. "Yes, we use dirigibles for most heavy lifting," she explained. "They're as fast as ground vehicles even on good roads, and we don't have many good surface roads on Plattner's World."

She frowned and corrected herself, "In the Outer States, that is. Solace has roads and a monorail system for collecting farm produce."

"I don't have anything against dirigibles in general," Huber said, then said with the emphasis of having remembered, "*Hera*. But in a war zone they're—"

He kept his voice steady with effort as his mind replayed a vision of the dirigible crashing into Rhodesville's brick-faced terminal building and erupting like a volcano.

"—too vulnerable. We'll need ground transport, or—how about surface effect cargo carriers? Do you have them here? They look like airplanes, but their wings just compress the air between them and the ground instead of really flying."

"I don't see how that could work over a forest," Hera said tartly—and neither did Huber, when he thought about it. "And as for vulnerable, trucks are vulnerable too if they're attacked, aren't they?"

"A truck isn't carrying five hundred tonnes for a single powergun bolt to light up," Huber said, careful to keep his voice neutral. "And it's not chugging along fifty or a hundred meters in the air where it's a target for a gunner clear in the next state if he knows what he's doing."

He shook his head in memory. "Which some of them will," he added. "If Solace hired Harris's Commando, they'll get a good outfit for air defense too."

Hera didn't move for a moment. Her hands on the display controller in her lap could've been carved from a grainless wood. Then she said, "Yes, if we . . . ."

Her fingers caressed the controller. The display shifted like a waterfall; Huber could watch the data, but they meant nothing to him at the speed they cascaded across the air-projected holograms.

"Yes . . ." Hera repeated, then looked up beaming. "There isn't anything like enough ground transport available in the UC alone, but if the other Outer States send us what *they* have, we should be able to meet your needs. Though roads . . ."

"We can use dirigibles to stage supplies to forward depots," Huber said, leaning forward reflexively though the data still didn't mean a cursed thing to him. "We'll need a topo display and for that matter a battle plan to know where, but—"

"Can you do that?" Hera said, also excited by breaking through a barrier she hadn't known of a few moments before. "The map and the battle plan?"

Huber laughed out loud—for the first time since Rhodesville, he guessed. "The topo display's easy," he said, "but lieutenants don't plan regimental operations by themselves. I'll forward what we have to the S-3, the Operations Officer, and his shop'll fill us in when they know more."

He locked his faceshield down and used the helmet's internal processor to sort for the address of the Log Section Deputy's console, then transfer the Regiment's full topographic file on Plattner's World to it. The commo helmet had both the storage and processing power to handle the task alone, but given where they were and the size of the file, Huber let Central in Base Alpha do the job.

He raised his faceshield and saw Hera disconnecting from a voice call. "Oh!" he said. "I'm sorry, I didn't explain—"

"I assumed you were doing your job," she said with a smile that exalted a face already beautiful. "And I can't tell you how reassuring it is to, ah, work for someone who can do that."

She gestured to the phone. "That's what I've been doing too," she said. "I just talked to my father. He's . . ."

She waved a hand in a small circle as if churning a pile of words.

"I've been told who he is," Huber said, saving Hera the embarrassment of explaining that Agis Graciano was the most important single person in the state which had employed the Slammers.

"Good," Hera said with a grateful nod. "When I said we can get ground transport from the other Outer States, I didn't mean that I could commandeer it myself. Father has connections; he'll use them. It'll have to be made to look like a business transaction, even though the other states are helping to fund the UC's stand against the tyranny of Solace."

Huber nodded acknowledgment. He knew better than to discuss politics with anybody, especially a local like Hera Graciano. It wasn't that he didn't understand political science and history: the Academy had an extensive mandatory curriculum in both subjects.

The problem was that the locals always wanted to talk about the rightness of their position. By the time they'd hired Hammer's Slammers, the only right that mattered rode behind iridium armor.

"Ah, Arne?" Hera said. "It's going to be two hours, maybe three, before father gets back to me. We've certainly got enough work to occupy us till then—"

Their wry grins mirrored one another.

"—but do you have dinner plans for tonight?"

"Ma'am," Huber said in surprise, "I don't know any more about rations than I did about billeting."

The thought made him turn his head. Sergeant Tranter was back; he gave Huber the high sign. The locals still in the office buried their expressions quickly in their consoles; they'd obviously been covertly watching Hera and their new chief the instant before.

"As a matter of fact, I haven't eaten anything yet today," Huber continued to his deputy. "Hera. I didn't have an appetite before my meeting with Major Steuben."

Hera's face changed. "I've met Major Steuben," she said without expression.

Huber nodded understandingly. "I told you we were the best the UC could hire," he said. "Joachim Steuben is better at his job than anybody else I've heard of. But because of what his job is, he's an uncomfortable person to be around for most people."

For everybody who wasn't a conscienceless killer; but Huber didn't say that aloud.

"Yes," Hera said, agreeing with more than the spoken words. "Well, what I was saying—can I take you out to dinner tonight,

Lieutenant? You've kept me from making a terrible mistake with the dirigibles, and I'd like to thank you."

"I'd be honored," Huber said, perfectly truthful and for a wonder suppressing his urge to explain he was just doing his job. She knew that, and if she wanted to go to dinner with him, that was fine. He didn't guess it much mattered who paid, not judging from the off-planet dress suit she was wearing even here at work.

"When you say 'trucks,'" he resumed, "what're we talking about? Five-tonners or little utility haulers?"

Hera Graciano was *very* attractive. And if Arne Huber didn't keep his mind on his business, he was going to start blushing.

The restaurant was quite obviously expensive. Huber could afford to eat here on his salary, but he probably wouldn't have chosen to.

"Well, I suppose you could say there was significant opposition to confronting Solace," Hera said, frowning toward a point beyond Huber's shoulder as she concentrated on the past. "Some people are always afraid to stand up for their rights, that's inevitable. But the vote in our Senate to hire your Regiment was overwhelming as soon as we determined that the other Outer States would contribute to the charges. My brother's faction only mustered nineteen votes out of the hundred, with seven abstentions."

Wooden beams supported the restaurant's domed ceiling. Their curves were natural, and the polished branches which carried the light fixtures seemed to grow from the wall paneling. The food was excellent—boned rabbit in a bed of pungent leaves, Huber thought, but he'd learned on his first deployment never to ask what went into a dish he found tasty.

His only quibble was with the music: to him it sounded like the wind blowing over a roof missing a number of tiles. The muted keening didn't get in the way of him talking with Hera, and her voice was just as pleasant as the rest of the package.

"And all your income, the income of the Outer States," Huber said, "comes from gathering the raw Moss? There's no diversification?"

"The factories refining the *Pseudofistus thalopsis* extract into Thalderol base are in Solace," she said, gesturing with her left hand as she held her glass poised in her right. "That isn't the problem, though: we could build refineries in the Outer States quite easily. We'd have to import technicians for the first few years, but there'd be plenty of other planets ready to help us."

"But . . . ?" said Huber, sipping his own wine. It was pale yellow, though that might have been a product of the beads of light on the branch tips which illuminated the room. They pulsed slowly and were color-balanced to mimic candle-flames.

"But we couldn't build a spaceport capable of handling starships the size of those that now land at Solace," Hera explained. "It's not just the expense, though that's bad enough. The port at Solace is built on a sandstone plate. There's no comparable expanse of bedrock anywhere in the Outer States. An artificial substrate that could support three-hundred kilotonne freighters is beyond possibility."

"I've seen the problems of bringing even small ships down in the UC," Huber said with studied calm. "Though I suppose there's better ports than Rhodesville's."

Hera sniffed. "Better," she said, "but not much better. And of course even the refined base is a high-volume cargo, so transportation costs go up steeply on small hulls."

The dining room had about twenty tables, most of them occupied by expensively dressed locals. The aircar Hera'd brought him here in was built on Nonesuch; it had an agate-faced dashboard and showed a number of other luxury details. She'd parked adjacent to the restaurant, in a tree-shaded lot where the other vehicles were of comparable quality.

Huber wore his newest service uniform, one of three he'd brought on the deployment. The Regiment had a dress uniform, but he'd never bothered to invest in one. Even if he *had* owned such a thing it'd be back in his permanent billet on Nieuw Friesland, since a platoon leader in the field had less space for personal effects than he had formal dinner occasions.

Huber's commo helmet was in his quarters, but his

holstered pistol knocked against the arm of the chair he sat in. The Colonel hadn't issued a revised weapons policy for Plattner's World yet; and even if he had, Huber would probably have stuck his 1-cm powergun in a cargo pocket even if he couldn't carry it openly. He'd felt naked in Rhodesville when he saw the buzzbomb swing in his direction and he couldn't do anything but duck.

"Ten months ago . . ." Hera went on. "Ah, that's seven months standard. Ten months ago, Solace raised landing fees five percent. The buyers, Nonesuch and the other planets buying our base and processing it to Thalderol, refused to raise the price they'd pay. We in the Outer States, the people who actually do the work, were left to make up the difference out of our pockets!"

It didn't look like Hera had spent much of her life ranging the forest and gathering Moss, but Huber wouldn't have needed his history courses to know that politicians generally said "we" when they meant "you." The funny thing was, they generally didn't see there was a difference.

That wasn't a point a Slammers officer raised with a well-placed member of the state which had hired the Regiment. Aloud he said, "But you do have multiple markets for your drugs? For your base, I mean?"

"Nonesuch takes about half the total," Hera said, nodding agreement. "The rest goes to about a dozen other planets, some more than others. The final processing takes temperature and vibration control beyond anything we could do on Plattner's World. Building a second spaceport would be easier."

She paused, looking at her wine, then across at Huber again. "The government of Nonesuch has been very supportive," she said carefully. "They couldn't get directly involved, but they helped to make the arrangements that led to our hiring Hammer's Regiment."

"But they wouldn't simply raise their payments for Thalderol base?" Huber said, keeping his tone empty of everything but mild curiosity.

"Where would it stop?" Hera blazed. "If those vultures on Solace learn that they can get away with extortion, they'll keep turning the screws!"

Based on what Huber knew about the price of anti-aging

drugs, he didn't think a five-percent boost in the cost of raw materials was going to make a lot of difference, but he didn't need to get into that. There was more going on than he saw; more going on than Hera was willing to tell him, that was obvious; and probably a lot more going on than even she knew.

None of that mattered. The result of all those unseen wheels whirling was that Colonel Hammer had a lucrative contract, and Lieutenant Arne Huber was spending the evening with a very attractive woman.

"My brother claims that even with other states defraying the costs, the UC is taking all the military risk itself," Hera continued. "But somebody has to have the courage to take a stand! When the other states see Solace back down, they'll be quick enough to step up beside us and claim credit!"

"It didn't seem when I arrived . . ." Huber said, the chill in his guts cooling his tone more than he'd intended. "That backing down was the way Solace was planning to play it."

He smiled, hoping that would make his words sound less like the flat disagreement that he felt. Hera was smart and competent, but she was turning her face from the reality the ambush at Rhodesville would've proved to a half-wit. It wasn't what she wanted to believe, so she was using her fine intellect to prove a lie.

"Well then, if they persist—" she said, but broke off as the waiter approached the table.

"More wine, sir and madam?" he asked. "Or perhaps you've changed your mind about dessert?"

The outside door opened, drawing Huber's eyes and those of the waiter. It was late for customers, though the restaurant hadn't started dimming the lights.

"Patroklos!" Hera said, her head turning because Huber's had. "What are you doing here?"

Not coming for dinner, that was for sure. Senator Patroklos Graciano was a good twenty years older than his sister. He was a beefy man, not fat but heavier than he'd have been if he were a manual laborer. His features were regular, handsome even, but they showed no resemblance whatever to Hera's.

Huber wondered if the two children had different mothers,

but that wasn't the question at the top of his mind just this instant. He got to his feet; smoothly, he thought, but he heard the chair go over behind him with a crash on the hardwood floor and he didn't care about *that* either.

"What am I doing here?" Patroklos said. He had a trained voice; he used its volume to fill the domed restaurant. "I'm not entertaining the butcher who destroyed Rhodesville, that's one thing! Are you part of the mercenaries' price, dear sister? Your body as an earnest for the bodies of all the women of the United Cities?"

Chairs were scuffling all over the room; a pair of diners edged toward the service area since Patroklos stood in front of the outside door. There were two waiters and the female manager looking on, but they'd obviously decided to leave the business to the principals involved for now.

Huber was as sure as he could be that there wasn't going to be trouble—worse trouble—here unless something went badly wrong. Patroklos wasn't nearly as angry as he sounded, and he'd come into the restaurant by himself. If his body-guards had been with him—Patroklos was the sort who had bodyguards—it would've been a different matter.

"Patroklos, you're drunk!" Hera said. He wasn't drunk, but maybe Hera didn't see her brother's real plan. "Get out of here and stop degrading the family name!"

She hadn't gotten up at the first shouting. Now that Patroklos was only arm's length away, she was trapped between the table and her brother's presence.

Huber thought of walking around to join her, but that might start things moving in the wrong direction. From the corners of his eyes he could see that others of the remaining customers were eyeing him with hard faces. The "butcher of Rhodesville" line had probably struck a chord even with people who didn't support Patroklos' position on the Regiment as a whole.

"Degrade the family name?" Patroklos shouted. "A fine concern for a camp follower!"

Huber scraped the table back and toward his left side, spilling a wine glass and some flatware onto the floor. Freed from its presence, Hera jumped to her feet and retreated to where Huber stood. He swung her behind him with his left arm.

That wasn't entirely chivalry. Huber wasn't worried about her brother, but the chance of somebody throwing a bottle at him from behind was another matter.

If I'd known there was going to be a brawl, I'd have asked for a table by the wall. He grinned at the thought; and that was probably the right thing to do, because Patroklos' mouth—open for another bellow—closed abruptly.

The Slammers didn't spend a lot of training time on unarmed combat: people didn't hire the Regiment for special operations, they wanted an armored spearhead that could punch through any shield the other guy raised. Huber wasn't sure that barehanded he could put this older, less fit man away since the fellow outweighed him by double, but he wasn't going to try. Huber would use a chair with the four legs out like spearpoints and then finish the job with his boots. . . .

"Fine, hide behind your murderer for now, you whore!" Patroklos said, but his voice wasn't as forceful as before. He eased his body backward though as yet without shifting his feet. "You'll have nowhere to hide when the citizens of our glorious state realize the madness into which you and our father have thrown them!"

Patroklos backed quickly, then jerked the door open and stomped out into the night. The last glance he threw over his shoulder seemed more speculative than angry or afraid.

"Ma'am!" Huber said, turning his head a few degrees to face the manager without ever letting his eyes leave the empty doorway. "Get our bill ready ASAP, will you?"

"Maria, put it on my account!" Hera said. She swept the room with her gaze. In the same clear, cold voice she went on, "I won't bother apologizing for my brother, but I hope his display won't encourage others into drunken boorishness!"

She's noticed the temper of the onlookers too, Huber thought. Stepping quickly, he led the girl between tables Patroklos had emptied with his advance. They went out the front door.

The night air was warm and full of unfamiliar scents. A track of dust along the street and the howl of an aircar accelerating—though by now out of sight—indicated how and where Patroklos had departed. There were no pedestrians or other vehicles; the buildings across the street were offices over stores, closed and dark at this hour.

Huber sneezed. Hera whirled with a stark expression.

"Just dust," he explained. He rubbed the back of his hand over his eyes. "Or maybe the tree pollen, that's all. Nothing important."

He felt like a puppeteer pulling the strings of a body that'd once been his but was now an empty shell. The thing that walked and talked like Arne Huber didn't have a soul for the moment; that'd been burned out by the adrenaline flooding him in the restaurant a few moments ago. The emotionless intellect floating over Huber's quivering body was bemused by the world it observed.

"I can't explain my brother's behavior!" Hera said. She walked with her head down, snarling the words to her feet. "He's angry because father remarried—there's no other reason for what he does!"

Huber didn't speak. He didn't care about the internal politics of the Graciano clan, and the girl was only vaguely aware of his presence anyway. She was working out her emotions while he dealt with his. They were different people, so their methods were different.

It hadn't been a lucky night, but things could've been worse. Just as at Rhodesville . . .

They stepped around the corner of the building into the parking lot. Things got worse.

There were at least a dozen of them, maybe more, waiting among the cars. They started forward when Huber and the girl appeared. They had clubs; maybe some of them had guns besides. The light on the pole overhead concealed features instead of revealing them.

"Who are you?" Hera called in a voice of clear command. "Attendant! Where's the lot attendant?"

"Get back into the restaurant," Huber said. "*Now!*"

He grabbed the girl's shoulder with his left hand and swung her behind him, a more brutal repetition of what he'd done with her earlier. Patroklos had been posturing in the restaurant. These thugs of his, though—this was meant for real.

Huber thumbed open his holster flap and drew his pistol. He held it muzzle-down by his thigh for the moment.

"He's got a gun!" said one of the shadowy figures in a rising whisper. That was a good sign; it meant they hadn't figured on their victim being armed.

"Shut up, Lefty!" another voice snarled.

The pistol had a ten-round magazine. Huber knew how to use the weapon, but if these guys were really serious he wouldn't be able to put down more than two or three of them before it turned into work for clubs and knives. . . .

Huber backed a step, hoping Hera had done as he ordered; hoping also that there wasn't another gang of them waiting at the restaurant door to close the escape route. If Huber got around the corner again, he could either wait and shoot every face that appeared or he could run like Hell was on his heels. Running was the better choice, but he didn't think—

"Easy now," said the second voice. "Now, all to—"

A big aircar—it might've been the one that ferried Huber from Base Alpha to Benjamin—came down the street in a scream of fans. It hit hard, lifting a doughnut of dust from the unpaved surface. That wasn't a bad landing, it was a combat insertion where speed counted and grace just got you killed.

Half the score of men filling the back of the vehicle wore khaki uniforms; they unassed the bouncing aircar with the ease of training and experience. The civilians were clumsier, but they were only a step or two behind when the Slammers tore into the local thugs with pipes, wrenches, and lengths of reinforcing rod.

"Run for it!" shouted the voice that'd given the orders before. He was preaching to the converted; none of his gang had stayed around to argue with the rescue party. Huber stood where he was, now holding the pistol beside his ear.

"Arne!" Doll Basime called. "This way, fast!"

She stood in the vehicle's open cab, her sub-machine gun ready but not pointed. Sergeant Tranter was at the rear of the aircar; he had a 2-cm shoulder weapon. Both wore their faceshields down, probably using light-enhanced viewing. If a thug had decided to turn it into a gunfight, he and his buddies were going to learn what a *real* gunfight was like.

Huber ran for the truck. He heard screams from the parking

lot; thumps followed by crackling meant that some of the expensive aircars were going to have body damage from being used as trampolines by troops in combat boots.

That didn't even begin to bother Huber. He remembered the eyes on him in the restaurant.

"Recall! Recall! Recall!" bellowed the loudspeaker built into Tranter's commo helmet. The other troopers had helmet intercoms, but the civilians didn't.

"How'd you get the word, Doll?" Huber said as he jumped into the back of the vehicle, just behind Basime. Another of the party had been driving; the cab would be crowded even with two.

Doll was too busy doing her job to answer him. Her throat worked as she snarled an order over the intercom, though with the faceshield down her helmet muted the words to a shadow.

Sirens sounded from several directions. They were coming closer.

The rescue party piled into the back of the truck. Two Slammers and a civilian remained in the parking lot, putting the boot in with methodical savagery. Their victim was out of sight behind the parked cars. One of the thugs must've tried to make a fight out of it—that, or he'd hit somebody while flailing about in panic.

"Move it, Bayes!" Tranter called.

Huber pointed his pistol skyward and fired. The *thump!* and blue flash both reflected from overhanging foliage. For a moment the bolt was as striking as the blast from a tank's main gun. The three stragglers looked up in palpable shock, then ran to join their fellows.

Huber hung over the truck's sidewall to make sure Hera was all right. She wasn't in sight, so she'd probably gotten back into the restaurant. If she hadn't, well, better the local cops look into it than that the cops spend their energy discussing matters with the rescue party. *That* was a situation that could go really wrong fast.

The fans roared. Kelso, a civilian clerk from Log Section, was in the driver's seat. From the way the vehicle'd nosed in, Huber'd guessed a trooper was at the controls.

The aircar slid forward, gathering speed but staying within a centimeter of the gravel. Faces staring from the restaurant's front windows vanished as the car roared by in cascades of dust and pebbles.

Only when the vehicle had reached 90 kph and the end of the block did Kelso lift it out of ground effect. He banked *hard* through a stand of towering trees.

Huber could still hear sirens, but they didn't seem to be approaching nearly as fast as a moment before. Witnesses being what they were, Huber's single pistol shot had probably been described as a tank battle.

Doll put her hand on Huber's shoulder. Raising her faceshield she shouted over the windrush, "That was a little too close on the timing, Arne. Sorry about that."

"It was perfect, Doll," he shouted back. The aircar was racketing along at the best speed it could manage with the present overload. That was too fast for comfort in an open vehicle, but torn metal showed where the folding top had been ripped off in a hurry to lower the gross weight. "Perfect execution, too. What brought you?"

They were heading in the direction of the Liaison Office, staying just over the treetops. Kelso had his running lights off. Red strobes high in the sky marked the emergency vehicles easing gingerly toward the summons.

"That's a funny thing," Doll said, her pretty face scrunched into a frown. "Every trooper billeted at Base Benjamin got an alert, saying a trooper needed help—and if there was shooting, the best result would be courts martial for everybody involved. It gave coordinates that turned out to be you. We hauled ass till we got here."

She shrugged. "Sergeant Tranter invited some civilian drivers from Log Section, too. I guess there was a card game going when the call came."

"But who gave the alert?" Huber said. "Did the—"

He'd started to ask if the restaurant manager had called it in; that was dumb, so he swallowed the final words. There hadn't been time for a civilian to get an alarm through the regimental net.

"There was no attribution," Basime said. She lifted her helmet and ran a hand through her short hair; it was gleaming with sweat. "That means it had to come from Base Alpha; and it had to be a secure sector besides, not the regular Signals Office."

"The White Mice?" Huber said. That was the only possible source, but . . . "But if it was them, why didn't they
respond themselves?"

"You're asking me?" Doll said. She grinned, but the
released strain had aged her by years. She'd known she was
risking her career—and life—to respond to the call.

"I will say, though," she added quietly, "that whoever put
out the alarm seems to be a friend of yours. And that's better
than having him for an enemy."

"Yeah," said Huber. Through the windscreen he could see
the converted school and the temporary buildings behind
it. Kelso throttled back.

Much better to have him for a friend; because the people
whom Joachim Steuben considered enemies usually didn't
live long enough to worry about it.

This time Huber had his equipment belt unbuckled and
his knife in his hand before he stepped out of the four-
place aircar in which Sergeant Tranter had brought him
to the Provost Marshal's office. The sky of Plattner's
World had an omnipresent high overcast; it muted what
would otherwise be an unpleasantly brilliant sun and was
turning the present dawn above Base Alpha into gorgeous
pastels.

Tranter had shut down the car in the street. He sat with
his arms crossed, staring into the mirrored faceshields of
the White Mice on guard.

The guards didn't care, but the trivial defiance made Tranter
feel better; and Huber felt a little better also. He wasn't completely alone this time as he reported as ordered to Major
Steuben.

"Go on through, Lieutenant," said the faceless guard who
took Huber's weapons. "He's waiting for you."

Huber walked down the hall to the office at the end. The
door was open again, but this time Steuben dimmed his
holographic display as Huber approached. The major even
smiled, though that was one of those things that you didn't
necessarily want to take as a good omen.

"Close the door behind you, Lieutenant," Steuben said as
Huber raised his hand to knock. "I want to discuss what
happened last night. How would you—"

He waited till the panel closed behind Huber's weight; it was a much sturdier door than it looked from the thin plastic sheathing on the outside.

"—describe the event?"

"Sir," Huber said. He didn't know what Steuben expected him to say. The truth might get some good people into difficulties, so in a flat voice he lied, "I was eating with my deputy in a restaurant she'd chosen. When we went out to get into her aircar, we were set on by thugs who'd been breaking into cars. Fortunately some off-duty troopers were passing nearby and came to our aid. My deputy went home in her own vehicle—"

He sure hoped she had. He didn't have a home number to call Hera at, and the summons waiting at Huber's billets to see the Provost Marshal at 0600 precluded Huber from waiting to meet Hera when she arrived at office.

"—and I returned to my quarters with the fellows who'd rescued us."

"Want to comment on the shooting?" Steuben asked with a raised eyebrow. "The use of powerguns in the middle of Benjamin?"

"Sir," Huber said, looking straight into the hard brown eyes of Colonel Hammer's hatchetman, "I didn't notice any shooting. I believe the business was handled with fists alone, though some of the thugs may have had clubs."

Steuben reached into his shirt pocket and came out with a thin plastic disk. He flipped it to Huber, who snatched it out of the air. It was the pitted gray matrix which had held copper atoms in place in a powergun's bore; a 1-cm empty, fired by a pistol or sub-machine gun.

Specifically, fired from Huber's pistol.

"Sir, I don't have anything useful to say about this," Huber said. The bastard across the desk could only kill him once, so there wasn't any point in going back now. "If it came from the scene of the fight, it must have been fired after we left there."

"It's old news, Lieutenant," Steuben said, "and we won't worry about it. If there had been a shooting incident . . . let's say, if you'd shot one or more citizens of the UC, you'd have been dismissed from the Regiment. It's very possible that you'd have been turned over to the local authorities for trial. Our contract with the UC really *is* in the balance as a result of what happened at Rhodesville."

"Then I'm glad there wasn't any shooting, sir," Huber said. "I intend to stay inside the Liaison Office for the foreseeable future so that there won't be a repetition."

The holographic scenes on the major's wall weren't still images as Huber had thought the first time he'd seen them. What had initially been a tiny dot above the horizon had grown during the interview to a creature flying at a great height above the snowfields.

Steuben giggled. Huber felt his face freeze in a rictus of horror.

"Aren't you going to tell me it isn't fair, Lieutenant?" the major said. "Or perhaps you'd like to tell me that you're an innocent victim whom I'm making the scapegoat for political reasons?"

For the first time since the the ambush at Rhodesville, Huber felt angry instead of being frightened or sick to his stomach. "Sir, you know it's not fair," he said, much louder than he'd allowed his voice to range before in this room. "Why should I waste my breath or your time? And why should you waste *my* time?"

"I take your point, Lieutenant," the major said. He rose to his feet; gracefully as everything he did was graceful. He was a small man, almost childlike; he was smiling now with the same curved lips as a serpent's. "You're dismissed to your duties—unless perhaps there's something you'd like to ask me?"

Huber started to turn to the door, then paused with a frown. "Sir?" he said. "How many people could have given Harris's Commando—given Solace—accurate information as to when a single platoon was landing at Rhodesville?"

"Besides members of the Regiment itself?" Steuben said, his reptilian smile a trifle wider. Huber nodded tersely. He wasn't sure if the question was serious, so he treated it as though it was.

"A handful of people within the UC government certainly knew," the major said. "A larger number, also people within the government or with connections to it, could probably have gotten the information unattributably. But it wasn't something that was being discussed on the streets of Rhodesville, if that's what you meant."

"Yes sir," said Huber. "That's what I meant."

He went out the door, closing it behind him as he'd been told to do the first time he'd left Major Steuben's presence. It was good to have the heavy panel between him and the man in that room.

He walked quickly. There was a lot of work waiting in Log Section; and there was another job as well, a task for the officer who'd been commanding platoon F-3 when it landed at Rhodesville.

Huber hadn't forgotten Kolbe or the crew of *Foghorn*; and he hadn't forgotten what he owed their memory.

Hera Graciano arrived at Log Section half an hour after Huber and the sergeant got back from Base Alpha, well before the staff was expected to show up for work. She stepped in, looking surprised to find the Slammers at their consoles.

"I rearranged things a bit." Huber said with a grin. "I moved my desk into the main office here; I figure we can use Captain Cassutt's office for a break room or something, hey?"

"Well, if you like . . ." Hera said. "But I don't think . . ."

"If they see me . . ." Huber explained quietly. Sergeant Tranter watched with the care of an enlisted man who knows that the whims of his superiors may mean his job or his life. "Then it's easier for them to believe we're all part of the same team. Given the number of factions in the UC right at the moment, I'd like there to be a core of locals who figure I'm on whatever their side is."

"I'm very sorry about last night!" Hera said, bowing her head in the first real confusion Huber had noticed in her demeanor. She crossed the room quickly without glancing at Tranter by the door. "That isn't normal, even for my brother. I think something's gone wrong with him, badly wrong."

"Any one you walk away from," Huber said brightly. He was immensely relieved to learn that Hera was all right, but he *really* didn't want to discuss either last night or the wider situation with her. "I'm paid to take risks, after all. Let's let it drop, shall we?"

"Yes," she said, settling herself behind her desk. Her expression was a mixture of relief and puzzlement. "Yes, of course."

Hera hadn't powered up the privacy shield as yet, so Huber could add smilingly, "By the way—does the UC have a central population registry? An office that tracks everybody?"

"What?" Hera said in amazement. "No, of course not! I mean, do other planets have that sort of thing? We have a voter's list, is that what you mean?"

"Some places are more centralized, yeah," Huber said, thinking of the cradle to grave oversight that the Frisian government kept on its citizens. Those who stayed on the planet, at least; which was maybe a reason to join a mercenary company, though the Colonel kept a pretty close eye on his troopers as well.

Through the White Mice . . .

"No matter," he continued. "Would you download a list of all the Regiment's local employees and their home addresses to me before you get onto your own work, Hera? It may be in this console I inherited from the good captain, but I sure haven't been able to locate it."

"Yes, of course . . ." she said, bringing her console live. She seemed grateful for an excuse to look away from Huber. Last night had been a real embarrassment to her.

One more thing to thank her brother for. It was pretty minor compared to the rest of what Huber suspected Patroklos was involved in, though.

Other clerks were coming in to the office; perhaps merely to make a good impression on the new director, but maybe they'd heard about the business last night and hoped to get more gossip. Huber grinned blandly and set to work with the file that appeared in his transfer box.

The business of the day proceeded. Log Section had been running perfectly well without Huber for the past three weeks, but as more starships landed—three in one mad hour at the relatively large field here in Benjamin, and four more during the day at other members of the United Cities—there were frequent calls to the Officer in Command of Log Section. None of the Slammers calling wanted to talk to a wog: they wanted a *real* officer wearing the lion rampant of the

Regiment. They were fresh out of stardrive, with headaches and tempers to match.

Huber fielded the calls. He almost never knew the answer to the angry questions himself, but he dumped quick summaries to Hera through his console while holding the speaker on the line. As a general rule she had the answer for him—a vehicle dispatched, a storage warehouse located, or a staff member on the way to the scene—in a minute or less. When it was going to take longer, that warning appeared on Huber's console and he calmed the caller down as best he could.

Not everybody wanted to calm down. An artillery lieutenant shouted, "Look, are you going to stop being a dickheaded pissant and get my bloody hog out of the marsh you had us land in?"

Huber shouted back, "Look, redleg, when my platoon drove out of the ship there was a kill-team from Harris's Commando waiting for us. We managed. If you fools can't avoid a hole in the ground, then don't expect a lot of sympathy here! Now, I say again—there's a maintenance and recovery platoon due in Youngblood's Vale tomorrow and I'll vector the recovery vehicle to you people in Henessey ASAP. If you'd prefer to keep saying you want me to drag heavy equipment out of my ass because your driver's blind, you can talk to an open line!"

There was a pause, then, "Roger, we'll wait. Two-Ay-Six out."

One thing a soldier learns by surviving any length of time in a war zone is that you use whatever you've got available. Huber smiled grimly.

In between the work of the Log Section, he played with the data he was gathering on his other job. Huber didn't have the sort of mind that leaped instantly to the right answer to complex questions. He worked things over mentally, turning the bits and fitting them first this way, then another. It was a lot like doing jigsaw puzzles. At the end of the process there was an answer, and he guessed he'd be working on it till he found what the answer was.

Hera left for lunch. She invited Huber but didn't argue when he turned her down, and she didn't argue either when he insisted she go on as she'd planned instead of staying in the office because he was staying. Huber knew as well as the next guy how important it was to get some time away from the place you were working; otherwise you could lock yourself down tighter than happened to most prisoners.

It didn't apply to him, of course. He was too busy to worry about where his butt happened to be located at the moment.

The Regiment already employed more than three hundred UC citizens. There'd be over a thousand by the time the deployment was complete, and that was without counting the number of recreation personnel hired to deal with the off-duty requirements of the combat troopers. On a place like Plattner's World most of that last group would be freelance, but the Colonel would set up and staff official brothels if the free market didn't appear to him to be up to the job.

Central Repair was one of the larger employers of local personnel. CR was where heavily damaged vehicles were brought: for repair if possible, for stripping and scrapping if it weren't. Line maintenance was mostly done at company level, but at battalion in the case of major drive-train components; Central Repair dealt with more serious or complex problems.

Fencing Master was thus far the Regiment's only serious battle damage on Plattner's World, but there were plenty of things that could go wrong with complex vehicles transiting between star systems. Furthermore, there were a dozen blowers deadlined from the previous contract. They'd been shipped to Plattner's World for repair instead of being held behind and repaired in place.

Late in the day, Huber got around to checking addresses. There were many groupings of employees who gave the same home address. That didn't concern him. Besides members of the same family all working in the booming new industry, war, many of the personnel came into Benjamin from outlying locations. Those transients lived in apartments or rooming houses here in the city.

Three of the mechanics in Central Repair lived at what the voter registration records—forwarded to Huber by Doll Basime; he didn't go through Hera to get them—listed as the address of Senator Patroklos Graciano. *That* was a matter for concern.

Huber looked around the office. Hera was out of the room; off to the latrine, he supposed. That made things a little simpler. Kelso, the local who'd driven the rescue vehicle the night before, looked up and caught his eye. Huber gestured him over, into the area of the privacy screen.

"Sir?" Kelso said brightly. His thin blond hair made him look younger than he probably was; close up Huber guessed the fellow was thirty standard years old. Kelso dressed a little more formally than most of the staff and he seemed to want very much to please. *Looking for a permanent billet with the Regiment,* Huber guessed; which was all right with Huber, and just might work out.

"I've got three names and lists of former employers here," Huber said, running hardcopy of the employment applications as he spoke. "I want you to check these out— just go around to the listed employers and ask about the people. I'm not looking for anything formal. If the boss isn't in—"

He handed the three flimsies to Kelso.

"—but the desk clerk remembers them, that's fine. Take one of the section jeeps, and I'd rather have the information sooner than later."

"Sir, it's pretty late . . ." Kelso said with a concerned expression. "Should I chase people down at their homes if the business is closed, or—"

Huber thought for a moment, then laughed. "No, nothing like that," he said. "But if you can get me the data before tomorrow midday, I'd appreciate it."

"You can count on me, sir!" the fellow said. Holding the hardcopy in his hand, he trotted past the consoles—some of them empty; it *was* getting late—and out the door just as Hera returned.

They passed; she glanced questioningly from the disappearing local and then to Huber. Huber waved cheerfully and immediately bent to his console, calling up information on the Officer in Charge of Central Repair. Hera might have asked what was going on with Kelso if Huber hadn't made it pointedly clear that he was busy.

Which he was, of course, but it bothered him to treat her this way. Well, it'd bother her worse if he told her what he was doing; and there was also the risk that . . .

Say it: the risk that this bright, competent, woman, attractive in all respects—would be loyal to her brother if push came to shove, instead of being loyal to the regiment of off-planet killers she happened to be working for at the moment. Surviving in a combat environment meant taking as few risks as possible, because the ones you couldn't avoid were plenty bad enough.

CR was at present under the command of Senior Warrant Leader Edlinger; Buck Edlinger to his friends, and Huber knew him well enough from previous deployments to be in that number. Instead of doing a data transmission through the console, Huber made a voice call. It took a moment for Edlinger to answer; he didn't sound pleased as he snarled, "Edlinger, and who couldn't bloody wait for me to call back, tell me!"

"Arne Huber, Buck," Huber replied calmly. He'd been shouted at before—and worse. Edlinger'd been squeezed into a place too tight for him to wear his commo helmet, and he wasn't best pleased to be dragged out of there to take a voice call slugged URGENT. "I've got a problem that may turn out to be your problem too. Are your people working round the clock right now?"

"Via!" Edlinger said. "No, not by a long ways. You're in Log Section now, Huber? What're you about to drop on us? Did a shipload of blowers come down hard?"

"Nothing like that, Buck," Huber said. Edlinger must have checked Huber's status when *Fencing Master* came in for repair. "I want to check what three of your locals've been working on, and I want to check it when the locals and their friends aren't around."

"What d'ye know about maintenance oversight, Huber?" Edlinger said; not exactly hostile, but not as friendly as he'd have been if it hadn't seemed an outsider was moving in on his territory.

"I know squat," Huber said, "but I've got a tech here, Sergeant Tranter, who you gave curst good fitness reports to back when when he worked for you. And you can help, Buck—I'd just as soon you did. But this isn't a joke."

That was the Lord's truth. This could be much worse than a company of armored vehicles getting bent in a starship crash.

"You got Tranter?" Edlinger said. "Oh, that's okay, then. Look, Huber, I can have everybody out of here by twenty hundred hours if that suits you. Okay?"

"That's great, Buck," Huber said, nodding in an enthusiasm that Edlinger couldn't see over a standard regimental voice-only transmission. "We'll be there at twenty hundred hours."

"Hey Huber?" Edlinger added as he started to break the connection.

"Right?"

"Can you tell me who you're worried about, or do I have to guess?"

That was a fair question. "Their names are Galieni, Osorio, and Triulski," Huber said, reading them off the display in front of him. "Do they ring a bell?"

Edlinger snorted something between disgust and real concern. "Ring a bell?" he said. "You bet they do. They're the best wrenches I've been able to find. I'd recommend them all for permanent status in the Regiment if they wanted to join."

Huber grimaced. "Yeah, I thought it might be like that," he said.

"And Huber?" Edlinger added. "One more thing. You wanted to know what they're working on? That's easy. They're putting your old blower, *Fencing Master*, back together. She'll go out late tomorrow the way things are getting on."

When Tranter came in with Bayes, the sergeant laughing as the trooper gestured in the air, Huber cued his helmet intercom and said, "Sarge? Come talk to me in my little garden of silence, will you?"

A console with regimental programming like Hera Graciano's could eavesdrop on intercom transmissions unless Huber went to more effort on encryption than he wanted to. It was simpler and less obtrusive to use voice and the privacy screen that was already in place around his area of the office.

Tranter patted Bayes on the shoulder and sauntered over to the lieutenant as though the idea was his alone rather than a response to a summons. Huber was becoming more and more impressed with the way Tranter picked up on things without need for them to be said. Sometimes Huber wasn't sure exactly what he'd say if he did have to explain.

"Do we have a problem, El-Tee?" Tranter asked as he bent over the console, resting his knuckles on the flat surface beside the holographic display.

Huber noticed the "we." He grinned. "We're going maybe to solve one before it crops up, Sarge," he said. "Are you up to poking around in a combat car tonight?"

"I guess," Tranter said, unexpectedly guarded. "Ah—what would it be we're looking for, El-Tee? Booze? Drugs?"

Huber burst out laughing when he understood Tranter's concern. "Via, Sarge!" he said. "You've been on field deployments, haven't you? All that stuff belongs, and so does anything else that helps a trooper get through the nights he's not going to get through any other way. No, I'm looking for stuff that our people didn't put there. I don't know what it'll be; but I do know that if something's there, I want to know what it is. Okay?"

Tranter beamed as he straightened up. "Hey, a chance to be a wrench again instead of pushing electrons? You got it, boss!"

"Pick me up at the front of the building at a quarter of eight, then," Huber said. "We need to be at Central Repair on the hour—I've cleared it with the chief. Oh, and Tranter?"

"Sir?" The sergeant looked . . . not worried exactly, but wary. He wasn't going to ask what was going on; but something was and though he seemed to trust Huber, a veteran non-com knows just how disastrously wrong officers' bright ideas are capable of going.

"Don't talk about it," Huber said. "And you know that gun you were holding last night? Think you could look one up for me?"

"Roger that, sir!" Tranter said, perfectly cheerful again. "Or if you'd rather have a sub-machine gun?"

Huber shook his head. "I want something with authority," he explained. "I don't think there's a chance in a million we'll have somebody try to pull something while we're flying between here and Central Repair tonight . . . but I do think that if it happens, I'm going to make sure we're the car still in the air at the end of it."

Chuckling in bright good humor, the sergeant returned to his console. The other clerks looked at him, but Hera was watching Huber instead.

Huber cued his intercom and said, "What's the latest on the ground transport situation, Hera? Did your father come through?"

The best way to conceal the rest of what was going on was to bury it in the work of Log Section; and the fact that quite a lot of work was getting done that way was a nice bonus.

Central Repair was a block of six warehouses in the north-central district of Benjamin. Engineer Section had thrown up a wall of plasticized earth around the complex as a basic precaution, but the location was neither secure nor really defensible despite the infantry company and platoon of combat cars stationed there.

Tranter brought the four-place aircar down at CR's entrance gate. They were tracked all the way by a tribarrel of the combat car there—*Flesh Hook*, another F Company vehicle—and, for as long as the aircar was above the horizon, by the guns of two more cars within the compound. Huber would've been just as happy to ride to Repair in a Regimental-standard air-cushion jeep, but Tranter was proud of being able to drive an aircar. There were plenty of them in Log Section's inventory since they were the normal means of civilian transportation on Plattner's World.

Tranter wasn't a good aircar driver—he was too heavy-handed, trying to outguess the AI—and there was always the chance that a trooper on guard would decide the car wobbling toward the compound was hostile despite Huber's extreme care to check in with detachment control. Still, Tranter was investing his time and maybe more to satisfy his section leader's whim; the least the section leader could do was let him show off what he fondly imagined were his talents.

The car bumped hard on the gravel apron in front of Central Repair. The gate was open, but *Flesh Hook* had parked to block the entrance. Huber raised his faceshield and said, "Lieutenant Huber, Log Section, to see Chief Edlinger. He's expecting me."

"Good to see you, El-Tee," called the trooper behind the front tribarrel. The driver watched from his hatch, but the two wing guns were unmanned; they continued to search the sky in air defense mode under detachment control. "You guys earned your pay at Rhodesville, didn't you? Curst glad it was you and not us in F-2."

"I don't know that I feel the same way," Huber said; but even if he'd shouted, he couldn't have been heard over the rising howl of drive fans as the combat car shifted sideways to open the passage. Tranter drove through the gate in surface effect.

Central Repair would've been much safer against external attack if it had been located within Base Alpha. It remained separate because of the greater risk of having so many local personnel—well over a hundred if combat operations persisted for any length of time—inside the Regimental HQ. Losing Central Repair would be a serious blow to the Regiment; the sort of damage a saboteur could do within Base Alpha wouldn't be survivable.

The warehouses had been placed following the curve of the land instead of being aligned on a grid pattern. Tranter followed the access road meandering past the front of the buildings. Three of them were empty, held against future need. The sliding doors of the fourth from the gate were closed, but light streamed out of the pedestrian entrance set beside them.

Three troopers looked down from the warehouse roof as Tranter pulled the aircar over. Huber waved at them with his left hand; he held the 2-cm powergun in his right.

Chief Edlinger met them at the door. "Good to see you again, Huber," he said. "Tranter, you need a hand?"

"I haven't forgotten how to carry a toolchest, Chief," the sergeant said, lifting his equipment out of the back of the car with a grunt. And of course he hadn't, but his mechanical leg didn't bend the way the one he'd been born with had; balance was tricky with such a heavy weight.

Huber had offered help when they got into the car. If Tranter wanted to prove he could move a toolchest or do any other curst thing he wanted without help, then more power to him.

"I appreciate this, Buck," Huber said as he entered the

warehouse. The air within was chilly and had overtones of lubricant and ozone; it was a place which only tolerated human beings. "I'd like there not to be a problem, but—"

"But you think there is," Edlinger completed grimly. He was a wiry little man whose sandy hair was more gray than not; he'd rolled his sleeves up, showing the tattoos covering both arms. Time and ingrained grease had blurred their patterns. If even the chief could identify the designs, he'd have to do it from memory.

Huber laughed wryly. "I think so enough that if we don't find something, I'll worry more," he admitted. "I won't believe it isn't there, just that we didn't find it."

"That looks like the lady," Tranter said, striding purposefully across the cracked concrete floor. There were two other combat cars in the workshop, but *Fencing Master* wore like a flag across her bow slope the marks of the buzzbomb and the welding repairs. Iridium was named for Iris, the goddess of the rainbow, because of the range of beautiful colors that heat spread across the metal.

Tranter and the chief spent the next two hours taking off panels, running diagnostics, and sending fiber optic filaments up passages that Huber hadn't known were parts of a combat car's structure. He stayed clear, sitting mostly on an empty forty-liter lubricant container. The techs worked with the natural rhythm of men who'd worked together often in the past; they spoke in a verbal shorthand, and they never got in one another's way.

It struck Huber that the chief must really have regretted losing Tranter from his section. Huber hadn't known the sergeant very long, and *he'd* bloody well miss him if something happened.

"Hel-*lo*, what have we here?" Tranter called, his voice echoing out of the iridium cavern into which he'd crawled. He'd removed a hull access plate beneath the driver's compartment; only his feet showed outside the opening. "Chief, what d'ye make of this? I'm sending it on channel seven."

Huber locked his faceshield down and cued it to the imagery Tranter's probe was picking up. He had no context for what he was looking at: a series of chips were set in a board bracketed between iridium bulkheads. On the bottom of the board was an additional chip, attached to the circuits on the other side with hair-fine wires.

"Hang on, I've got the catalog," Edlinger replied. They were using lapel mikes because their commo helmets were too bulky for some of the spaces they were slipping into. "Can you give me more magnification? Are those two reds, a blue and a . . ."

"Purple and white, chief," Tranter said. "The fourth line's a purple and white."

"Roger that," said Edlinger. "A simple control circuit, sonny. Probably made on Sonderby, wouldn't you say?"

A dozen chips flashed up on Huber's faceshield beside the real-time image, matches that the chief's AI had found in a catalog of parts and equipment. They could've been yea many mirror images as far as Huber could tell, but the techs and their electronics apparently found minute differences among them.

"Galieni said he'd been trained on Sonderby," Edlinger added in a somber voice. "I don't doubt that he was, but I'd be willing to bet that it wasn't Southern Cross Spacelines that hired him when he left school."

The original image blanked as Sergeant Tranter squirmed back out of the equipment bay. Huber raised his faceshield as the chief walked around from the other side of the car.

"All right," said Huber. "What does it do? Is it a bomb?"

"It isn't a bomb, El-Tee," Tranter said, squatting for a moment before he got to his feet. "It's a control circuit, and it's been added to the air defense board. It's got an antenna wire out through the chanel for the running lights—that's how I noticed it."

"They could've set it to switch off the guns when somebody sent a coded radio signal, Huber," Edlinger added. "That's the most likely plan, though it depends on exactly where on the board they were plugged in. I'm not sure we can tell with just the maintenance manuals I've got here."

"I've got a better guess than that, Buck," Huber said, standing and feeling his gut contract. "Shutting the guns off wouldn't be a disaster if it just affected one car in a platoon. What if that chip locked all three tribarrels on full automatic fire in the middle of Benjamin? What do you suppose would happen to the houses for a klick in every direction?"

"Bloody hell," Tranter muttered.

Huber nodded. "Yeah, that's exactly what would happen: bloody hell. And coming on top of Rhodesville, the UC government'd cancel the Regiment's contract so fast we'd be off-planet with our heads swimming before we knew what happened."

The technicians looked at one another, then back to Huber. "What do we do now, El-Tee?" Tranter asked.

"Have you disconnected the chip?" Huber asked.

"You bet!" Tranter said with a frown of amazement. "I cut both leads as soon as I saw them. Whatever the thing was, I knew it didn't belong."

"Then we shut things up and I go talk to Major Steuben in the morning," Huber said. "I'd do it now, but—"

He grinned with wry honesty.

"—not only do I think it'll keep, I *don't* think I'm in any shape to talk to the major before I've had a good night's sleep."

Sergeant Tranter rubbed the back of his neck with his knuckles. "And maybe a stiff drink or two, hey El-Tee?" he said. "Which I'm going to share with you, if you don't mind."

"I'm buying for both of you for what you've done tonight," Huber said, thinking of the coming interview. "And I just wish you could carry it the rest of the way with the major, but that's my job. . . ."

Major Steuben wasn't available through the regimental net at dawn plus thirty, at noon, or at any of the other times Huber checked for him into mid afternoon. Huber didn't leave a message—he was sure Steuben would learn about the calls as soon as he wanted to know—and it didn't even cross his mind to talk to some other member of the White Mice. Little as Huber liked the major, this was no time to bring a subordinate up to speed on the problem. He began to wonder if he was going to reach Steuben before 1800 hours, close of business for the regular staff.

Huber smiled at his own presumption; he'd gotten to think that Steuben would be there any time he wanted him—

because the major had been in his office the times he summoned Huber. Why his mind should've reversed the pattern was just one of those mysteries of human arrogance, Huber supposed. It wasn't like Log Section didn't have work to do, after all.

Now that more crews and vehicles were on the ground, the Regiment was setting up a second operations base outside Arbor Palisades, the second-largest of the United Cities and located on the northeast border with Solace. Two platoons from L Troop plus support vehicles would be leaving Base Alpha tonight for the new location. Huber with the approval of the S-3 shop had decided to send a column of thirty wheeled vehicles along with them. The civilian trucks could've moved on their own—the UC and Solace weren't at war despite the level of tension—but it gave both the troopers and the civilian drivers practice in convoy techniques.

"Via, El-Tee," Sergeant Tranter said, shaking his head in amusement. "You better not let anybody in L Troop catch you in a dark alley. The trip'll take 'em four times as long and be about that much rougher per hour besides."

"Right," said Huber. "And nobody's shooting at them. Which won't be the case if we have to do it for real, as we bloody well will when those trucks start supplying forward bases inside Solace territory as soon as the balloon goes up."

Huber didn't take lunch, though he gnawed ration bars at his desk. Most people claimed the bars tasted like compressed sawdust, but Huber found them to have a series of subtle flavors. They were bland, sure, but bland wasn't such a bad thing. The commander of a line platoon had enough excitement in his life without needing it in his food.

At random moments throughout the day, Huber checked in with the Provost Marshal's office. At 1530 hours instead of a machine voice announcing, "Unavailable," Major Steuben himself said, "Go ahead."

"Sir!" Huber said. His brain disconnected but he'd rehearsed his approach often enough in his head to blurt it out now: "May I see you ASAP with some information about the Rhodesville ambush?"

"If by 'as soon as possible' you mean in fifteen minutes,

Lieutenant . . ." Steuben said. He had a pleasant voice, a modulated tenor as smooth and civilized as his appearance; and as deceptive, of course. "Then you may, yes."

"Sir, on the way, sir!" Huber said, standing and breaking the connection.

"Tranter!" he shouted across the room as he rounded his console; he snatched the 2-cm powergun slung from the back of his chair. "I need to be in front of Major Steuben in fifteen minutes! That means an aircar, and I don't even pretend to drive the cursed things."

Huber waved at Hera as he followed the sergeant out the door. "I'll be back when I'm back," he said. "I don't expect to be long."

The good Lord knew he *hoped* it wouldn't be long.

He and Tranter didn't talk much on the short flight from Benjamin to Base Alpha. The sergeant turned his head toward his passenger a couple times, but he didn't speak. Huber was concentrating on the open triangle formed by his hands lying in his lap. He was aware of Tranter's regard, but he really needed to compose himself before he brought this to Major Steuben.

This time when Huber got out of the car in front of the Provost Marshal's, he reflexively scooped the 2-cm shoulder weapon from the butt-cup holding it upright beside his seat. If he'd been thinking he'd have left the heavy weapon in the vehicle, but since he was holding it anyway he passed it to the watching guard along with his pistol and knife.

"Expecting some excitement, Lieutenant?" said the man behind the mirrored faceshield as he took the weapons.

"What would a desk jockey like me know about excitement?" Huber said cheerfully as he opened the main door.

He wondered about his comment as he strode down the hallway. It struck him that it was the first interaction he'd had with the guards that wasn't strictly professional. As with so much of his life since he'd landed on Plattner's World, Huber had the feeling that he was running downhill in the darkness and the only thing that was going to save him was pure dumb luck.

Major Steuben nodded him into the office. Huber closed the door behind him and without preamble said, "Sir! Three of the techs in Central Repair are living at Senator Graciano's townhouse. That is, Patroklos Graciano, the—"

"I know who Patroklos Graciano is," Steuben said through his cold smile. "Continue."

"Right," said Huber. He was blurting what he knew in the baldest fashion possible. He understood Major Steuben too well to want to exchange empty pleasantries with the man. "We checked—Chief Edlinger and a former tech in my section, that is—checked the combat car they were working on. There's an extra control chip in the air defense board with an antenna for external inputs. I think it was meant to send the tribarrels berserk while the car was in the middle of Benjamin."

"You've disconnected the chip?" Steuben said. For a moment there was a spark from something very hard glinting in his voice.

"Yes sir, but that's all we've done thus far," Huber said. His muscles were tight across his rib cage and his tongue seemed to be chipping out the words. In a firefight he wouldn't have been this tense, because he'd have known the rules. . . .

"Good," said the major, smoothly unconcerned again. "You've properly reported the matter and your suspicions, Lieutenant. Now go back to your duties in Logistics and take no more action on the matter. Do you understand?"

Huber felt the anger rise in his throat. "No sir," he said. He spoke in a normal voice, maybe even a little quieter than usual. "I don't understand at all. Senator Graciano is certainly a traitor, probably the traitor who set up me and my platoon at Rhodesville. We can't leave him out there, looking for another place to slide the knife into us. One more chance may be just the one he needed!"

Steuben didn't rise, but he leaned forward very slightly in his seat. He wore his 1-cm pistol in a cutaway holster high on his right hip. Inlays of platinum, gold, and rich violet gold-uranium alloy decorated the weapon's receiver, but the pistol was still as deadly as the service weapon Huber had left with the guards outside the building.

And the dapper little man who wore it was far more deadly than Huber had ever thought of being.

"You've shown initiative, Lieutenant," Steuben said.

"Because of that, I'm going to politely point something out to you instead of treating your insolence as I normally would: even if everything you believe regarding Senator Graciano is true, he remains *Senator* Graciano. He has a large following in the United Cities and is in some ways more influential in the remainder of the Outer States than any other UC politician, his father included. Probably the best way to boost his standing still further would be for off-planet mercenaries to accuse him of being a traitor."

"Sir, I lost friends at Rhodesville!" Huber said.

"Then you were lucky to have friends to begin with, Lieutenant," the major said, rising to his feet. "Friendship is an experience I've never shared. Now *get* back to Log Section and your duties. Or submit your resignation from the Regiment, which I assure you will be accepted at the moment you offer it."

Huber's lips were dry. He didn't speak.

"I asked you before if you understood," Steuben said, his left fingertips resting lightly on the desk top. "You chose to discuss the matter. Now the only thing for you to understand is this: you will go back to your duties in Log Section, or you will resign. *Do* you understand?"

"Sir!" Huber said. "May I return to my duties now?"

"Dismissed, Lieutenant," the major said. "And Lieutenant? I don't expect to see you again until I summon you."

As Huber walked down the hallway, his back to the door he'd closed behind him, he kept thinking, *It's in the hands of the people who ought to be handling it. It's none of my business any more.*

The trouble was, he knew that at the level of Steuben and Colonel Hammer it was a political problem. Political problems were generally best solved by compromise and quiet neglect.

Huber didn't think he'd ever be able to chalk up the sound of Kolbe's body squishing down *Fencing Master*'s bow slope to political expedience, though.

"Got any plans for tonight, El-Tee?" Sergeant Tranter asked as he followed Huber up the stairs to Log Section. "There's a game on in the maintenance shed."

The paint on the stairwell walls had been rubbed at the height of children's shoulders; it was a reminder of what the building had been. Whether it'd ever be a school again depended on how well the Slammers performed. If things went wrong, the Outer States—at least the United Cities— would be paying reparations to Solace that'd preclude luxuries like public schooling.

"I'm thinking about throwing darts into a target," Huber muttered. "And don't ask whose picture I'm thinking of using for the target!"

Hera wasn't at her desk. In her absence and Huber's, a senior clerk named Farinelli was in titular charge—and he obviously had no idea of how to deal with the two armed Slammers who stood before his console. Their backs were to the door and the remainder of the staring locals.

"Can I help you gentle—" Huber began, politely but with a sharp undertone. A stranger listening could have guessed that he didn't much like aggrieved troopers making personal visits to Log Section when a call or data transmission would get the facts into his hands without disrupting the office. Midway in Huber's question, the troopers turned.

"Deseau!" Huber said. "And you, Learoyd! Say, they didn't reassign you guys too, did they?"

The troopers smiled gratefully, though Learoyd knuckled his bald scalp in embarrassment and wouldn't meet Huber's eyes. "Nothing like that, Lieutenant," the sergeant said. "We're here to take *Fencing Master* back to the unit as soon as they assign us a couple bodies from the Replacement Depot. I figured you wouldn't mind if we stopped in and saw how you were making out."

From the way Deseau spoke and Learoyd acted, they weren't at all sure that Huber *wouldn't* mind. They were line troopers, neither of them with any formal education; the only civilians they were comfortable with were whores and bartenders. It must have been a shock to come looking for the lieutenant who'd been one of them and find themselves in an office full of well-dressed locals who stared as if they were poisonous snakes.

Huber thought suddenly of the ropes of 2-cm bolts sending the dirigible down in fiery destruction over Rhodesville. There was never a poisonous snake as dangerous as either of these two men; or as Arne Huber, who *was* after all one of them.

"Mind?" he said. "I'm delighted! Sergeant Tranter—"

Huber took his men by either hand and raised his voice as his eyes swept the office. "Everybody? These are two of the people who kept me alive at the sharp end: my blower captain Sergeant Deseau and Trooper Learoyd, my right wing gunner. That won't mean much to you civilians, but you can understand when I say I wouldn't have survived landing on Plattner's World if it weren't for these men!"

Learoyd muttered something to his shoes, but he looked pleased. Deseau's expression didn't change, but he didn't seem to mind either.

"Do you have plans for tonight?" Huber asked. "Ah, Sergeant Tranter? Do you think we could find these men a billet here in the compound?" He switched his eyes back to Deseau and Learoyd, continuing, "There's usually a card game, and I think I can promise something to drink."

"And if he couldn't get you booze, I can," Tranter said cheerfully. "Sure, we can put you guys up. It's best the El-Tee not go wandering around, but you won't miss Benjamin."

"If I never see Warrant Leader Niscombe," Learoyd said to his boots, "it'll be too soon."

"Niscombe runs the enlisted side of Transient Depot, sir," Deseau explained. "He figures that something bad'll happen if he lets folks passing through from field duty just rest and relax. He'll find a lot of little jobs for us if we bunk there."

"Something bad'll happen to Niscombe if he ever shows his face out in the field," Learoyd muttered with a venom Huber hadn't expected to hear in that trooper's voice. "Which he won't do, you can be sure of that."

"Right," said Huber. "I'll send a temporary duty request for the two of you through channels, but for now consider yourselves at liberty."

He glanced at Hera's empty desk. "Ah, does anybody know when Deputy Graciano's due back?" he asked the room in a raised voice.

Everybody stared at him; nobody answered the question, though. It struck Huber that all this was out of the locals' previous experience with the Slammers. When Captain Cassutt was director, there hadn't been troopers with personal weapons standing in the middle of the office.

"Sir?" said Kelso from the back of the room.

"What?" said Huber. "Via, if you know something, spit it out!"

"Yessir," said Kelso, swallowing. "Ah, I don't know when the deputy's coming back, but she went out as soon as I gave her the information you requested, sir."

"Information?" Huber repeated. For a moment he didn't know what the local was talking about; nonetheless his stomach slid toward the bottom of an icy pit.

Then he remembered. "You mean the previous employment data."

"Yessir!" said Kelso, more brightly this time. "None of those techs had worked at the places they put down. Not a soul remembered any one of the three!"

Huber opened his mouth to ask another question, but he really didn't have to. He'd given Kelso the full applications including the applicants' home addresses. That's what Hera had seen, and she wouldn't have had to check to recognize the address of her brother's townhouse. The fact that the men's listed employment records were phony would be a red flag to anybody with brains enough to feed themselves.

"What's the matter, sir?" Tranter said.

"I screwed up," Huber said. His face must've gone white; he felt cold all over. "It's nobody's fault but mine."

Hera could've gone to her father with the information; she could've gone to the civil authorities—though Huber wasn't sure the United Cities had security police in the fashion that larger states generally did; or she could even have gone to Colonel Hammer. Any of those choices would have been fine. The possibility that scared Huber, though, was that instead—

His helmet pinged him with an URGENT call. Huber wasn't in a platoon and company net, so the sound was unexpected. He locked down his faceshield to mute the conversation and said, "Fox three-six, go ahead!"

In his surprise—and fear—he'd given his old call signal. Somebody else was leader of platoon F-3 nowadays.

"*Arne, this is Doll,*" said Lieutenant Basime's voice. "*We don't exactly monitor the civil police here, but we* are *a signals liaison section. Ah—"*

"Say it!" Huber snapped.

"There was a police call just now," Doll said mildly. She was a solid lady, well able to stand up for her rights and smart enough to know when that wasn't the best choice. *"There's an aircar down west of town. The driver and sole occupant is dead. Initial report is that it's your deputy, Hera Graciano."*

"Right," said Huber. He felt calm again, much as he'd been as he watched the stern of the blazing dirigible slide slowly into the terminal building. The past was the past; now there were only the consequences to deal with. "Can you download the coordinates of the crash site?"

"You've got 'em," Doll said. There was an icon Huber hadn't noticed in the terrain box on his faceshield. *"Anything more I can do, snake?"*

"Negative, Doll," Huber said. "I'll take it from here. Three-six out."

He broke the connection and raised his faceshield. "Trouble, El-Tee?" said Sergeant Tranter. Tranter had been in the field, but he didn't have a line trooper's instincts. Deseau and Learoyd stood facing outward from their former platoon leader; their feet were spread and their sub-machine guns slanted in front of them. They weren't aiming at anything, not threatening anybody; but they hadn't had to ask if there was trouble, and they were ready to deal in their own way with anything that showed itself.

The civilian clerks looked terrified, as they well should have been.

"Tranter, I need a ride," Huber said. "West of town there's been an aircar crash. I'll transfer the coordinates to the car's navigation system."

"We're coming along," Deseau said. He continued to watch half the room and the doorway, while the trooper watched the clerks on the other side. "Learoyd and me."

"You go relax," Huber said in a tight voice. "This is Log Section business, not yours."

"Fuck that," said Deseau. "You said we're at liberty. Fine, we're at liberty to come with you."

"Right," said Huber. He was still holding his big shoulder

weapon; he hadn't had time to put it down since he entered the office. "You—Farinelli? You're in charge till I get back." He thought for a moment and added, "Or you hear that I've been replaced."

"But Director Huber!" the clerk said. "What if Deputy Graciano comes back?"

"She won't," Huber snarled. Then to his men he added, "Come on, troopers. Let's roll!"

"She was up about a thousand meters," said the cop. He was a young fellow in a blue jacket and red trousers with a blue stripe down the seam. For all that he was determined not to be cowed by the heavily armed mercenaries, he behaved politely instead of blustering to show his authority. "She had the top down and wasn't belted in, so she came out the first time the car tumbled."

It was probably chance then that the body and the vehicle had hit the ground within fifty meters of one another, Huber realized. Hera had gone through tree-branches face-first, hit the ground, and then bounced over to lie on her back. Her features were distorted, but he could've identified her easily if the UC policeman had been concerned about that; he wasn't.

There was almost no blood. The dent in the center of her forehead had spilled considerable gore over Hera's face, but that had been dry when the branches slashed her and wiped much of it off. Huber was no pathologist, but he'd seen death often and in a variety of forms. Hera Graciano had been dead for some length of time before her body hit the ground.

"Why did the car tumble?" Tranter said, kneeling to check the underside of the crumpled vehicle. It'd nosed in, then fallen back on its underside with its broken frame cocked up like an inverted V. "There's an air turbine that deploys when you run outa fuel. It generates enough juice to keep your control gyro spinning."

"You're friends of the lady?" the cop asked. He was expecting backup, but the Slammers had arrived almost as soon as he did himself. He seemed puzzled, which Huber was willing to grant him the right to be.

But it was a really good thing for the cop that he hadn't

decided to throw his weight around. Huber wasn't in a mood
for it; and while he wasn't sure how Sergeant Tranter would
react, he knew that the two troopers from *Fencing Master*
would obey without question if their lieutenant told them
to blow the local's brains out.

"She was my deputy," Huber said. "She worked for the
Regiment in a civilian capacity."

"Somebody whacked the turbine with a heavy hammer,"
Tranter said, rising from where he knelt. "That's why it's
still stuck in the cradle."

He pulled at an access plate on the wreck's quarter panel.
It didn't come till he took a multitool from his belt and
gave the warped plastic a calculated blow.

The local policeman looked at the sky again and fingered
his lapel communicator. He didn't try to prod the dispatcher,
though. "There was an anonymous call that the car had been
circling up here and just dropped outa the sky," he explained.
"D'ye suppose it was maybe, well . . . suicide?"

"No," said Huber. "I don't think that."

"That's good," said the cop, misunderstanding completely.
"Because you guys might not know it, but this lady was from
a bloody important family here in the UC. I don't want to
get caught in some kinda scandal, if you see what I mean."

"I see what you mean," Huber said. His eyes drifted across
Tranter for a moment, then resumed scanning their surroundings. They were within ten klicks of the center of Benjamin,
but the forest was unbroken. Trees on Plattner's World had
enough chlorophyll in their bark to look deep green from
a distance. Their branches twisted like snakes, but the leaves
were individually tiny and stuck on the twigs like a child's
drawing.

The cop grimaced. "I wish the Commander Miltianas
would get the lead outa his pants and take over here," he
went on. "Of course, he probably doesn't want to be mixed
up in this either—but curse it, it's what they're paying him
the big bucks for, right?"

"There's four fuel cells in this model," Tranter said, his
head inside the vehicle's stern section. "The back three are
disconnected and there's a puncture in the forward cell."

He straightened, looking puzzled and concerned. "El-Tee,"
he said. "It looks to me like—"

"Drop the subject for now, Sergeant," Huber said. He gestured to their own vehicle, a ten-place bus rather than the little runabout Tranter had used to ferry Huber alone. Four troopers in combat gear would've been a crowd and a burden for the smaller car. "We'll talk on the way back to the office."

"But—" said Tranter.

Deseau rapped the side of Tranter's commo helmet with his knuckles. "Hey!" Deseau said. "He's the man, right? He just gave you an order!"

Tranter looked startled, then nodded in embarrassment and trotted for the bus. There were three aircars approaching fast from Benjamin. Two had red strobe lights flashing, but they weren't running their sirens.

Huber turned to the cop. "Thanks for letting us look over the site," he said. "We'll leave you to your business now. And we'll get back to our own."

"Yeah, right," said the local man with a worried frown. "I sure hope I don't wind up holding the bucket on this one. A death like this can be a lot of trouble!"

"You got that right," Huber muttered as he got into the cab with Tranter. The tech already had the fans live; now he boosted power and wobbled into the air, narrowly missing a line of trees.

Kelso would have done a better job driving, but this was no longer business for civilians. Huber locked his faceshield down.

"Unit, switch to intercom," he ordered. Nobody but the three men in the car with him could hear the discussion without a lot of decryption equipment and skill. "Tranter, I'm leaving you in the circuit, but I'm not expecting you to get involved. You'll have to keep your mouth shut, that's all. Can you handle that?"

"Fuck not being involved," Tranter said. His hands were tight on the control yoke and his eyes were straight ahead; a degree of hurt sounded in his voice. *"I knew the deputy better than you did, sir. She was a good boss; and anyway, she was one of ours even if she didn't wear the uniform. Which I do."*

"Right," said Huber. "Deseau and Learoyd, you don't know the background. I figure her brother killed her or one of his thugs did. It was probably an accident, but maybe not. She'd have gone to see him, threatening to tell the world he was an agent for Solace. She maybe even guessed he'd set up the ambush at Rhodesville."

Sergeant Deseau made a sound loud enough to trip the intercom. In something like a normal voice he went on, *"We gonna take care of him, then?"*

"He's got a lot of pull," Huber warned. "I went to Major Steuben about him and got told to mind my own business. It's going to make real waves if somebody from the Regiment takes him out. *Real* waves, about as bad as it gets."

"El-Tee?" Learoyd said, frustration so evident in his tone that Huber could visualize the trooper trying to knuckle his bald scalp through his commo helmet. *"Just tell us what to do, right? That's your job. Don't worry about me and Frenchie doing ours."*

Learoyd was correct, of course. He had a simple approach of necessity, and he cut through all the nonsense that smarter people wrapped themselves up with.

"Right," Huber repeated. "There'll be a gang of thugs at the guy's townhouse, and they'll have guns available even if they aren't going out on the street with them just yet. It could be that he'd got a squad of Harris's Commando on premises. I doubt it because of the risk to him if it comes out, but we've got to figure we're going up against people who know what they're doing."

He paused, arranging his next words. The aircar was over Benjamin now, but Tranter was taking them in a wide circuit of the suburbs where the tree cover was almost as complete as over the virgin forest beyond.

"For that reason," Huber said, "I figure to borrow *Fencing Master* for the operation. There's a detachment leaving Central Repair for Base Alpha tonight. We'll tag onto the back and trail off when we're close to the bastard's compound. If we can, we'll duck back to CR when we're done—but I *don't* expect to get away with this, troops."

"I been shot at before," Deseau said calmly. *"I can't see anything worse'n that that's going to happen if they catch us."*

Learoyd didn't bother to speak. Huber heard the *clack* as the trooper withdrew his sub-machine gun's loading tube, then locked it back home in the receiver. Like he'd said, he was getting ready to do his part of the job.

"Sergeant Tranter," Huber said, turning to the tech beside him. "Now that you know what we're talking about, I think it'd be a good night for you to spend playing cards back at the billets. You're a curst good man, but this really isn't your line of work."

Tranter's face was red with suppressed emotion. *"Guess you'll need a driver, right?"* he snapped. *"Guess I've driven the Lord's great plenty of combat cars, shifting them around for repair. I guess it bloody well is my line of work. Sir."*

"Well in that case, troopers . . ." Huber said. "We'll leave our billets for Central Repair at twenty hundred. Start time for the draft is twenty-one hundred, but they'll be late. That'll make the timing about right."

Tranter muttered, *"Roger,"* Deseau grunted, and Learoyd said as little as he usually did. There wasn't a lot *to* say at this point.

Huber wasn't frightened; it was all over but the consequences.

Senator Patroklos Graciano was about to learn the consequences of fucking with Hammer's Slammers.

The racket of drive fans made every joint in the girder-framed warehouse rattle and sing. There were two other combat cars besides *Fencing Master*; all three thirty-tonne monsters were powered up, their fans supporting them on bubbles of pressurized air. From the way the interior lights danced, some of the overhead fixtures were likely to be sucked down into the intakes unless the cars either shut down or drove out shortly.

"Are they going to get this bloody show on the road?" Sergeant Deseau muttered. His faceshield was raised and he wasn't using intercom. Huber wouldn't have understood the words had he not been looking into Deseau's face and watching his lips move.

"Can it!" Huber snapped. "Take care of your own end and keep your mouth shut."

Deseau grimaced agreement and faced front again. They were all nervous. Well, three of them were, at any rate; Learoyd seemed about as calm as he'd been a couple hours before, when he'd been methodically loading spare magazines for his sub-machine gun.

"*Seven Red, this is Green One,*" ordered the detachment commander—an artillery captain who happened to be the senior officer in the temporary unit. If the move had been more serious than the five kilometers between Central Repair and Base Alpha, the detachment would've been under the control of a line officer regardless of rank. "*Pull into place behind Five Blue. Eight Red, follow Seven. Unit, prepare to move out. Green One out.*"

"Tranter, slide in behind the second blower," Huber ordered. "Don't push up their ass, just keep normal interval so it looks like we belong."

Chief Edlinger had put Huber and his men on the list for admission to Central Repair, but that was easily explained if it needed to be. The chief didn't know what Huber planned— just that it wasn't something he *ought* to know more about. The detachment commander didn't know even that: he was in the self-propelled gun at the head of the column. The eight vehicles leaving for Base Alpha included two tanks, four combat cars, the detachment commander's hog, and a repair vehicle with a crane and a powered bed that could lift a combat car. The crews didn't know one another, and nobody would wonder or even notice that a fifth car had joined the procession.

The lead car jerked toward the open door. The driver, inexperienced or jumpy from the long wait, canted his nacelles too suddenly. The bow skirt dipped and scraped a shrieking line of sparks along the concrete floor until the car bounced over the threshold and into the open air.

The second car followed with greater care but the same lack of skill, rising nearly a hand's-breadth above the ground. The skirts spilled air in a roar around their whole circuit. The car wallowed; when the driver nudged his controls forward Huber thought for a moment the vehicle was going to slide into the jamb of the sliding door.

"*They've got newbie crews,*" Tranter said scornfully. "*Via, I could do better than that with my eyes closed!*"

"I'll settle for you keeping your eyes open and not attracting attention," Huber said tightly. "Move out, Trooper."

Fencing Master slid gracefully through the doorway and

into the warm night. The skirts ticked once on the door track, but that wasn't worth mentioning.

"*Let's keep him, El-Tee,*" Deseau said with a chuckle. "*He's as good as Kolbe was, and a curst sight better than I ever thought of being as a driver.*"

"Keep your mind on the present job, didn't I tell you?" Huber snapped. "I don't think any of us need to plan for a future much beyond tonight."

Deseau laughed. Huber supposed that was as good a response as any.

Plattner's World had seen moons, but none of them were big enough to provide useful illumination. The pole lights placed for security when these were warehouses threw bright pools at the front of each building, but that just made the night darker when *Fencing Master* moved between them. Huber locked down his faceshield and switched to light enhancement, though he knew he lost depth perception that way.

The rocket howitzer at the head of the column started to negotiate the gate to the compound, then stopped. The tank immediately following very nearly drove up its stern.

There was something wrong with the response of the hog's drive fans, or at any rate the captain thought there was. He began arguing off-net with Repair's Charge of Quarters, a senior sergeant who replied calmly, "*Sir, you can bring it back and park it in the shop if you like, but I don't have authority to roust a technician at this hour on a non-emergency problem.*"

The CQ kept saying the same thing. So did the captain, though he varied the words a bit.

Huber listened for a moment to make sure that what was going on didn't affect him, then switched to intercom. "They'll get it sorted out in a bit," he said to his crew. "The blowers are straight out of the shops and half the crews are newbies. Nothing to worry about."

"*Who's worried?*" Deseau said. He stretched at his central gun station, then turned and grinned at Huber.

They were all wearing body armor, even Tranter. The bulky ceramic clamshells crowded the fighting compartment even without the personal gear and extra ammo that'd pack the vehicle on a line deployment.

Learoyd could've been a statue placed at the right wing gun. He didn't fidget with the weapon or with the sub-machine gun slung across his chest. Though his body was motionless, his helmet would be scanning the terrain and careting movement onto his lowered faceshield. If one of the highlights was a hostile pointing a weapon in the direc-tion of *Fencing Master*—and anybody pointing a weapon at *Fencing Master* was hostile, in Learoyd's opinion and Huber's as well—his tribarrel would light the night with cyan destruction.

"*Unit, we're moving,*" the captain announced in a dis-gruntled tone. As he spoke, the hog shifted forward again. Metal rang as the drivers of other vehicles in the column struggled to react to the sudden change from stasis to movement. Skirts were stuttering up and down on the roadway of stabilized earth. *You get lulled into patterns in no time at all. . . .*

Huber brought up a terrain display in the box welded to the pintle supporting his tribarrel. *Fencing Master* didn't have the sensor and communications suite of a proper com-mand car, but it did have an additional package that allowed the platoon leader to project displays instead of taking all his information through the visor of his commo helmet.

The column got moving in fits and starts; a combat car *did* run into the back of the tank preceding it. Huber's helmet damped the sound, but the whole fab-ric of *Fencing Master* shivered in sympathy to the impact of a thirty-tonne hammer hitting a hundred-and-seventy-tonne anvil.

"*Via, that'll hold us up for the next three hours!*" Sergeant Deseau snarled. "*We'll be lucky if we get away before bloody dawn!*"

Huber thought the same. Instead the detachment com-mander just growled, "*Unit, hold your intervals,*" as his vehicle proceeded down the road on the set course.

"*Dumb bastard,*" Deseau muttered. "*Dicked around all that time for nothing, and now he's going to put the hammer down and string the column out to make up the time he lost.*"

That was close enough to Huber's appreciation of what

was going on that he didn't bother telling the sergeant to shut up. He grinned beneath his faceshield. Under the circumstances, a lieutenant couldn't claim to have any authority over the enlisted men with him except what they chose to give him freely.

The tank got moving again smoothly; *its* driver at least knew how to handle his massive vehicle. Tanks weren't really clumsy, and given the right terrain and enough time they were hellaciously fast; but the inertia of so many tonnes of metal required the driver to plan her maneuvers a very long way ahead.

The collision hadn't sprung the skirts of the following combat car, so it was able to proceed also. Its driver kept a good hundred and fifty meters between his vehicle's dented bow slope and the tank's stern. The rest of the column trailed the three leaders out of Central Repair and into the nighted city beyond.

Tranter lifted *Fencing Master*'s skirts with a greasy wobble, then set the car sliding forward. They passed the guard blower at the gate and turned left. Huber waved at the trooper in the fighting compartment; he—or she—waved back, more bored than not.

"Tranter, when we make the corner up ahead," Huber ordered, "cut your headlights and running lights. Can you drive using just your visor's enhancement?"

"*Roger*," the driver said calmly. Behind them the guard vehicle was pulling back across the compound's gateway; ahead, the last of the cars in the detachment proper slid awkwardly around an elbow in the broad freight road leading west and eventually out of Benjamin.

Even here in the center of the administrative capital of the UC, there were more trees than houses. The locals built narrow structures three or four stories high, with parking for aircars either beneath the support pilings or on rooftop landing pads. Most of the windows were dark, but occasionally they lighted as armored vehicles howled slowly by on columns of air.

Even without lights, *Fencing Master* wasn't going to pass unnoticed in Senator Graciano's neighborhood of expensive residences. This'd have to be a quick in and out; or at least a quick in.

Tranter was keeping a rock-solid fifty-meter interval between him and the stern of Red Eight. He seemed to judge what the driver ahead would do well before that fellow acted.

"Start opening the distance, Tranter," Huber said, judging their position on the terrain display against the quivering running lights of Red Eight. "We'll peel off to the right at the intersection half a kay west of our present position. As soon as Red Eight's out of sight, goose it hard. We've got eighteen hundred meters to cover, and I want to be there before they have time to react to the sound of our fans."

"*Roger*," Tranter said. He still didn't sound nervous; maybe he was concentrating on his driving.

And maybe the technician didn't really understand what was about to happen. Well, there were a lot of cases where intellectual understanding fell well short of emotional realities.

Fencing Master slowed almost imperceptibly; the fan note didn't change, but Tranter cocked the nacelles toward the vertical so that their thrust was spent more on lifting the car than driving it forward. Red Eight ahead had gained another fifty meters by the time its lights shifted angle, then glittered randomly through the trees of a grove that the road twisted behind.

"Here we go, Tranter," Huber warned, though the driver obviously had everything under control. "Easy right turn, then get on—"

Fencing Master was already swinging; Tranter dragged the right skirt, not in error but because the direct friction of steel against gravel was hugely more effective at transferring momentum than a fluid coupling of compressed air. As the combat car straightened onto a much narrower street than the route they'd been following from Repair, the headlights of four ten-wheeled trucks flooded over them. An air cushion jeep pulled out squarely in front of the combat car.

"*Blood and bleeding Martyrs!*" somebody screamed over the intercom, and the voice might've been Huber's own. Tranter lifted *Fencing Master*'s bow, dumping air and dropping the skirts back onto the road. The bang jolted the teeth of everybody aboard and rattled the transoms of nearby houses.

The combat car hopped forward despite the impact. They'd have overrun the jeep sure as sunrise if its driver hadn't been a real pro as well. The lighter vehicle lifted on the gust from *Fencing Master*'s plenum chamber, surfing the bow wave and bouncing down the other side on its own flexible skirts.

A trim figure stood beside the jeep's driver, touching the top of the windscreen for balance but not locked to it in a deathgrip the way most people would've been while riding a bucking jeep upright. The fellow's faceshield was raised; to make himself easy to identify, Huber assumed, but the glittering pistol in his cutaway holster was enough to do that.

"Lock your tribarrels in carry position!" Huber shouted to his men. As he spoke, he slapped the pintle catch with his left hand and rotated the barrels of his heavy automatic weapon skyward. "That's Major Steuben, and we won't get two mistakes!"

Tranter never quite lost control of *Fencing Master*, but it wasn't till the third jounce that he actually brought the car to rest. Each impact blasted a doughnut of dust and grit from the road; Huber's nose filters swung down and saved him from the worst of it, but his eyes watered. The jeep stayed just ahead of them, then curved back when the bigger vehicle halted.

The trucks—they had civilian markings and weren't from the Logistics Section inventory—moved up on either side of the combat car, two and two. They were stake-beds; a dozen troopers lined the back of each, their weapons ready for anybody in *Fencing Master* to make the wrong move.

That wasn't going to happen: Huber and his men were veterans; they knew what was survivable.

"*Bloody fucking hell,*" Deseau whispered. He kept his hands in sight and raised at his sides.

"*Get out, all four of you,*" Major Steuben ordered through the commo helmets. He sounded amused. "*Leave your guns behind.*"

Huber slung his 2-cm weapon over the raised tribarrel, then unbuckled his equipment belt and hung it on the big gun also. He paused and looked, really *looked*, at the White Mice watching *Fencing Master* and her crew through the sights of their weapons. They wore ordinary Slammers combat gear—helmets, body armor, and uniforms—but the only powergun in the whole platoon was the pistol on Major

Steuben's hip. The rest of the unit carried electromagnetic slug-throwers and buzzbombs.

"Unit," Huber ordered, "let me do the talking."

He raised himself to the edge of the fighting compartment's armor, then swung his legs over in a practiced motion. His boots clanged down on the top of the plenum chamber. Starting with the coaming as a hand-hold, he let himself slide along the curve of the skirts to the ground.

Deseau and Learoyd were dismounting with similar ease, but Tranter—awkward in body armor—was having more difficulty in the bow. The technician also hadn't taken off his holstered pistol; he'd probably forgotten he was wearing it.

Huber opened his mouth to call a warning. Before he could, Steuben said, *"Sergeant Tranter, I'd appreciate it if you'd drop your equipment belt before you step to the ground. It'll save me the trouble of shooting you."*

He tittered and added, *"Not that it would be a great deal of trouble."*

Startled, Tranter undid the belt. He wobbled on the hatch coaming, then lost his balance. He and the belt slipped down the bow in opposite directions, though Tranter was able to keep from landing on his face by dabbing a hand to the ground.

Huber stepped briskly toward the jeep, stopping two paces away. He threw what was as close to an Academy salute as he could come after five years in the field.

"Sir!" he said. Steuben stood above him by the height of the jeep's plenum chamber. "The men with me had no idea what was going on. I ordered them to accompany me on a test drive of the repaired vehicle."

"Fuck that," Deseau said, swaggering to Huber's side. "We were going to put paid to the bastards that set us up and got our buddies killed. Somebody in the Regiment's got to show some balls, after all."

He spit into the dust beside him. Deseau had the bravado of a lot of little men; his pride was worth more to him than his life just now.

Joachim Steuben, no taller than Deseau flat-footed, giggled at him.

Learoyd walked up on Deseau's other side. He'd taken his helmet off and was rubbing his scalp. Sergeant Tranter, his eyes wide open and unblinking, joined Learoyd at the end of the rank.

"What did you think was going to happen when a Slammers combat car killed a senior UC official and destroyed his house, Lieutenant?" Steuben asked. The anger in his tone was all the more terrible because his eyes were utterly dispassionate. "Didn't it occur to you that other officials, even those who opposed the victim, would decide that Hammer's Regiment was more dangerous to its employers than it was to the enemy?"

"I'm not a politician, sir," Huber said. He was trembling, not with fear—he was beyond fear—but with hope. "I don't know what would happen afterwards."

"Not a politician?" Steuben's voice sneered while his eyes laughed with anticipation. "You were about to carry out a political act, weren't you? You do understand that, don't you?"

"Yes sir, I do understand," Huber said. The four trucks that surrounded *Fencing Master* had turned off their lights, though their diesel engines rattled at idle. The jeep's headlights fell on Huber and his men, then reflected from the combat car's iridium armor; they stood in almost shadowless illumination.

"Is there anything you want to say before I decide what I'm going to do with you, Lieutenant?" Steuben said with a lilt like the curve of a cat's tongue.

"Sir," Huber said. His muscles were trembling and his mind hung outside his body, watching what was going on with detached interest. "I'd like to accompany you and your troops on the operation you've planned. It may not be necessary to discipline me afterward."

"You mean it won't be possible to discipline you if you get your head blown off," the major said. He laughed again with a terrible humor that had nothing human in it. "Yes, that's a point."

"El-Tee?" said Learoyd. "Where are you going? Can I come?"

Huber looked toward the trooper. "They're carrying non-issue weapons, Learoyd," he said. He didn't know if he was explaining to Deseau and Tranter at the same time. "Probably the hardware we captured at Rhodesville. They're going to take out Graciano just like we planned, but they're going to do it in a way that doesn't point straight back at the Regiment."

"I shot off my mouth when I shouldn't've, Major," Deseau said. "I do that a lot. I'm sorry."

Huber blinked. He couldn't have been more surprised if his sergeant had started chanting nursery rhymes.

Deseau cleared his throat and added, "Ah, Major? We carried an EM slugthrower in the car for a while till we ran out of ammo for it. The penetration was handy sometimes. Anyway, we're checked out on hardware like what I see there in the back of your jeep."

"So," Steuben said very softly. "You understand the situation, *gentlemen*, but do you also understand the rules of an operation like this? There will be no prisoners, and there will be no survivors in the target location."

"I understand," Huber said; because he did.

"Works for me," said Deseau. Learoyd knuckled his skull again; he probably didn't realize he'd been asked a question.

"We're going to kill everybody in the senator's house, Learoyd," Huber said, leaning forward to catch the trooper's eyes.

"Right," said Learoyd. He put his helmet back on.

"Caxton," Major Steuben said to his driver, "issue slug-throwers to these three troopers. Sergeant Tranter?"

Tranter stiffened to attention.

"You'll drive the combat car here back to Central Repair," Steuben said. "And forget completely about what's happened tonight."

"Sir!" said Tranter. His eyes were focused into the empty night past Steuben's pistol holster. "I can drive a truck, and I guess you got people here—"

He nodded to the truck beside him, its bed lined with blank-faced troopers.

"—who can drive *Fencing Master*. Sir, I deserve to be in on this!"

Joachim Steuben giggled again. "Deserve?" he said. "The only thing any of us deserve, Sergeant, is to die; which I'm sure we all will before long."

He looked toward the cab of an idling truck and said in a whipcrack voice, "Gieseking, Sergeant Tranter here is going to drive your vehicle. Take the combat car back to Central Repair and wait there for someone to pick you up."

Huber took the weapon Steuben's driver handed him. It was a sub-machine gun, lighter than its powergun equivalent but longer as well. It'd do for the job, though.

And so would Arne Huber.

Major Steuben's jeep led two trucks down the street at the speed of a fast walk. Their lights were out, and sound of their idling engines was slight enough to be lost in the breeze to those sleeping in the houses to either side.

Huber and the men from *Fencing Master* rode in the bed of the first truck; Sergeant Tranter was driving. The only difference between the line troopers and the White Mice around them was that the latter wore no insignia; Huber, Deseau, and Learoyd had rank and branch buttons on the collars. Everyone's faceshield was down and opaque.

In this wealthy suburb, the individual structures—houses and outbuildings—were of the same tall, narrow design as those of lesser districts, but these were grouped within compounds. Road transport in Benjamin was almost completely limited to delivery vehicles, so the two-meter walls were for privacy rather than protection. Most were wooden, but the one surrounding the residence of Patroklos Graciano was brick on a stone foundation like the main house.

Huber muttered a command to the AI in his helmet, cueing the situation map in a fifty percent overlay. He could still see—or aim—through the faceshield on which terrain features and icons of the forty-six men in the combat team were projected.

The other two trucks had gone around to the back street—not really parallel, the way things were laid out in Benjamin, but still a route that permitted those squads to approach the compound from the rear. They were already in position, waiting for anybody who tried to escape in that direction. The squads in front would carry out the assault by themselves unless something went badly wrong.

Few lights were on in the houses the trucks crawled past; the Graciano compound was an exception. The whole fourth floor of the main building was bright, and the separate structure where the servants lived had many lighted windows as well.

The gate to the Graciano compound was of steel or wrought iron, three meters high and wide enough to pass even trucks the size of those carrying the assault force if the leaves were open. As they very shortly would be . . .

An alert flashed red at the upper right-hand corner of Huber's visor; the truck braked to a gentle halt. The light went green.

Huber and all but three of the troopers ducked, leaning the tops of their helmets against the side of the truck. The three still standing launched buzzbombs with snarling roars that ended with white flashes. The hollow *bang*s would've been deafening were it not for the helmets' damping. Gusts of hot exhaust buffeted the kneeling men, but they were out of the direct backblast. The second truck loosed a similar volley.

Two missiles hit the gate pillars, shattering them into clouds of mortar and pulverized brick. The leaves dangled crazily, their weight barely supported by the lowest of the three sets of hinges on either side. Tranter cramped his steering wheel and accelerated as hard as the truck's big diesel would allow.

The rest of the buzzbombs had gone through lighted windows of both structures and exploded within. The servants' quarters were wood. A gush of red flames followed the initial blast at the ground floor, a sign that the fuel for the oven in the kitchen had ignited.

Tranter hit the leaning gates and smashed them down. He roared into the courtyard, knocking over a fountain on the way, and pulled up screeching in front of the ornamental porch.

The truck's tailgate was already open. Huber was the first man out, leaping to the gravel with Deseau beside him and Learoyd following with the first of the squad of White Mice. The ground glittered with shards of glass blown from all the windows.

A buzzbomb had hit the front door; the missile must've been fired moments after the initial volley or the gate would've been in the way. The doorpanel was wood veneer over a steel core, but a shaped-charge warhead designed to punch through a tank's turret had blown it off its hinges.

Scores of fires burned in the entrance hall. White-hot metal had sprayed the big room, overwhelming the retardant which impregnated the paneling. Huber's nose filters flipped into place as he ran for the staircase; his faceshield was already on infrared, displaying his surroundings in false color. If fire raised the background temperature too high for infrared to discriminate properly, he'd switch to sonic imaging—but he wasn't coming out till he'd completed his mission. . . .

There were two bodies in the hall. Parts of two bodies, at any rate; the bigger chunks of door armor had spun through them like buzzsaws. They were wearing uniforms of some sort; guards, Huber assumed. One of them had a slugthrower but the other's severed right arm still gripped a 2-cm powergun.

The stairs curved from both sides of the entrance to a railed mezzanine at the top. Huber's visor careted movement as he started up. Before he could swing his sub-machine gun onto the target, a trooper behind him with a better angle shredded it and several balustrades with a short burst.

The staircase was for show; the owner and guests used the elevator running in a filigree shaft in the center of the dwelling. It started down from the top floor when Huber reached the mezzanine, which was appointed for formal entertainments. He couldn't see anything but the solid bottom of the cage. He put a burst into it, chewing the embossed design, but he didn't think his sub-machine gun's light pellets were penetrating.

One of the White Mice standing at the outside door put seven slugs from his heavy shoulder weapon through the cage the long way. One of them hit the drive motor and ricocheted, flinging parts up through the floor at an angle complementary to that of the projectile. The elevator stopped; a woman's arm flopped out of the metal lacework.

Huber jerked open the door to the narrow stairwell leading upward from the mezzanine. A pudgy servant in garishly-patterned pajamas almost ran into him. Huber shot the fellow through the body and shoved him out of the way. The servant continued screaming for the moment until Deseau, a step behind his lieutenant, ripped a burst through the dying man's head.

Huber ran up the stairs, feeling the weight and constriction of his body armor and also the filters that kept him from breathing freely. Platoon leaders in the combat car companies didn't spend a lot of time climbing stairwells in the normal course of their business, but he'd asked for the job.

The door to the third floor was closed. Huber ignored it as he rounded the landing and started up the last flight. Teams of White Mice would clear the lower floors and the basement; the men from F-3 were tasked with the senator's suite at the top of the building.

The door at the stairhead was ajar. Huber fired through the gap while he was still below the level of the floor. As he'd expected, that drew a pistol shot—from a powergun—though it hit the inside of the panel instead of slapping the stairwell.

"Learoyd!" Huber shouted. He crouched, swapping his submachine gun's magazine for a full one from his bandolier. Deseau would cover him if somebody burst out of the door. "Gren—"

Before he finished the word, Learoyd spun a bomb the size of a walnut up through the narrow opening. Huber had seen the trooper knock birds off limbs ten meters high; this was no test at all for him.

The grenade blew the door shut with a bright flash that to the naked eye would've been blue. The bomb's capacitors dumped their charge through an osmium wire. Electrical grenades had very little fragmentation effect, but their sudden energy release was both physically and mentally shattering for anybody close to the blast. Huber rose to his feet, leaped the final steps to the landing, and kicked the door open again. He went in shooting.

For the first instant he didn't have a target, just the need to disconcert anybody who hadn't lost his nerve when the grenade went off. The carpet of the sitting room beyond was on fire. A man lay in the middle of it, screaming and beating the floor with the butt of his pistol. Huber's burst stitched him from the middle of one shoulderblade to the other. The man flopped like a fish on dry land, then shuddered silent.

There was a doorway ahead of Huber and another to the right, toward the back of the building. Huber went straight, into a small foyer around the elevator shaft. The top of the cage remained just above floor level.

Huber jerked open the door across the foyer. The room beyond was a mass of flame. It'd been a bedroom, and the buzzbomb had ignited all the fabric. Huber slammed the door again. His hands were singed; and only his faceshield had saved his eyes and lungs from the fire's shriveling touch.

At the back of the foyer was a window onto the grounds; concussion from the warhead going off in the bedroom had blown out the casement an instant before it slammed the connecting door. Through the empty window, Huber heard the lift fans of an aircar spin up.

He jumped to the opening. To his right a closed car with polarized windows sat on a pad cantilevered off the back of the building, trembling as its driver built up speed in the fan blades. It was a large vehicle, capable of carrying six in comfort. The front passenger door was open and a uniformed man leaned out of it, firing a heavy slugthrower back toward the sitting room. The aluminum skirts that propelled the osmium projectiles vaporized in the dense magnetic flux, blazing as white muzzle flashes in Huber's thermal vision.

Huber aimed between the hinge side of the car door and the jamb, then shot the guard in the neck and head. The fellow sprang forward like a headless chicken, flinging his gun away with nerveless hands.

The aircar lifted, the door swinging closed from momentum. Huber fired, starring the windscreen but not penetrating it. Deseau and Learoyd were in the doorway now, pocking the car's thick plastic side-panels; their sub-machine guns couldn't do real damage.

The car half-pivoted as its driver prepared to dive off the edge of the platform and use gravity to speed his escape. A buzzbomb detonated on the underside of the bow, flipping the vehicle over onto its back. The instant the warhead hit, Huber saw a spear of molten metal stab through the car's roof in a white dazzle. The driver would've been in direct line with the explosion-formed hypersonic jet.

The blast rocked Huber away from the window, but the

car had taken the direct impact and the building had protected him from the worst of the remainder. Deseau and
Learoyd, running toward the vehicle when the warhead went
off, bounced into the wall behind them and now lay sprawled
on the deck. Learoyd had managed to hang onto his sub-
machine gun; Deseau patted the tiles numbly, trying to find
his again.

A man crawled out of the overturned car. The right side
of his face was bloody, but Huber recognized Senator
Patroklos Graciano.

The senator stood with a look of desperation on his face.
Huber braced his left elbow on the window opening and
laid his ring sight at the base of Graciano's throat. He fired
a short burst, flinging the man backward. Tufts of beard
trimmed by the pellets swirled in the air, falling more slowly
than the corpse.

There were figures still moving in the car. A stunningly
beautiful woman tried to squirm out, hampered by the
necklaces and jewel-glittering rings she clutched to her
breasts with both hands. She wore a diaphanous shift that
accentuated rather than hid her body, but on her a gunnysack
would've been provocative.

Huber aimed. She looked up at him, her elbows on the
chest of her lover so freshly dead that his corpse still
shuddered. A powergun bolt blew out her left eyesocket and
lifted the top of her skull. Her arms straightened convulsively, scattering the jewelry across the landing platform.

Major Steuben stood in the doorway from the sitting room,
his pistol in his delicate right hand. His faceshield was raised
and he was smiling.

The girl still in the car was probably a maid. She opened
her mouth to scream when she saw her mistress die. The
second pistol bolt snapped between her perfect teeth and
nearly decapitated her. Her body thrashed wildly in the
passenger compartment.

Learoyd was getting to his feet. Steuben grabbed the collar
of Deseau's clamshell armor and jerked the sergeant upright;
the major must have muscles like steel cables under his trim
exterior. The muzzle of the powergun in his other hand was
a white-hot circle.

He turned toward Huber, looking out of the adjacent

window, and shouted, "Come along, Lieutenant. We've taken care of our little problem and it's time to leave now."

Huber met them in the sitting room. Steuben waved him toward the stairwell. Sergeant Deseau still walked like a drunk, so Huber grabbed his arm in a fireman's carry and half-lifted, half-dragged the man to the trucks. Every floor of the building was burning. The major was the last man out.

In all the cacophony—the screams and the blasts and the weeping desperation—that Arne Huber had heard in the past few minutes, there was only one sound that would haunt his future nightmares. That was Joachim Steuben's laughter as he blew a girl's head off.

If I buy the farm here on Plattner's World, Huber thought as he walked toward the open door of Major Steuben's office, *they're going to have to name this the Lieutenant Arne C. Huber Memorial Hallway.*

There's never a bad time for humor in a war zone. This was a better time than most.

"Come in and close the door, Lieutenant," Steuben said as Huber raised his hand to knock on the jamb. "And *don't*, if you please, attempt to salute me ever again. You're not very good at it."

Huber obeyed meekly. The major was working behind a live display, entering data on the touchpad lying on his wooden desk. It wasn't a game this time: Steuben was finishing a task before he got on to the business who'd just walked in his door.

He shut down the display and met Huber's eyes. He smiled; Huber didn't try to smile back.

"This will be brief, Lieutenant," Steuben said. "The United Cities are in a state of war with Solace, or will be when the Senate meets in a few hours. There's been a second attack within UC territory by mercenaries in Solace pay. This one was directed against Senator Patroklos Graciano here in Benjamin."

Steuben quirked a smile. "It was quite a horrific scene, according to reports of the event," he went on. "Graciano and his whole household were killed."

Huber looked at the man across the desk, remembering the same smile lighted by the flash of a powergun. "If I may ask, sir?" he said. "Why did the, ah, mercenaries attack that particular senator?"

"It's believed that the Solace authorities had made an attempt to turn the poor fellow against his own people," the major said blandly. "Graciano had gathered a great deal of information about Solace plans and was about to make a full report to the Senate. The attack forestalled him, but as a result of such blatant aggression even the former peace party in the Senate is unanimous in supporting military action against Solace."

I wonder how many of the senators believe the official story, Huber thought, *and how many are afraid they'll go the same way as Patroklos Graciano if they continue to get in the way of the Regiment's contract?*

Well, it didn't really matter. Like he'd told Major Steuben last night, he wasn't a politician. Aloud he said, "I see, sir."

"None of that matters to you, of course," Steuben continued. "I called you here to say that a review of your actions at Rhodesville the day you landed has determined that you behaved properly and in accordance with the best traditions of the Regiment."

He giggled. "You may even get a medal out of it, Lieutenant."

Huber's mouth was dry; for a moment he didn't trust himself to speak. Then he said, "Ah, sir? Does this mean that I'm being returned to my platoon?"

Steuben looked up at Huber. He smiled. "Well, Lieutenant," he said, "that's the reason I called you here in person instead of just informing you of the investigation outcome through channels. How would you like a transfer to A Company? You'd stay at the same rank, but you probably know already that the pay in A Company is better than the same grade levels in line units."

"A Company?" Huber repeated. He couldn't have heard right. "The White Mice, you mean?"

"Yes, Lieutenant," Steuben said. His face didn't change in a definable way, but his smile was suddenly very hard. "The White Mice. The company under my personal command."

"I don't . . ." Huber said, then realized that among the things he didn't know was how to end the sentence he'd begun. He let his voice trail off.

"Recent events have demonstrated that you're smart and that you're willing to use your initiative," the major said. His fingers were tented before him, but his wrists didn't quite rest on the touchpad beneath them.

The smile became amused again. He added, "Also, you can handle a gun. You'll have ample opportunity to exercise all these abilities in A Company, I assure you."

"Sir . . ." said Huber's lips. He was watching from outside himself again. "I don't think I have enough . . ."

This time he stopped, not because he didn't know how to finish the sentence but because he thought of Steuben's hell-lit smile the night before. The words choked in his throat.

"Ruthlessness, you were perhaps going to say, Lieutenant?" the major said with his cat's-tongue lilt. "Oh, I think you'll do. I'm a good judge of that sort of thing, you know."

He giggled again. "You're dismissed for now," Steuben said. "Go back to Logistics—you'll have to break in your replacement no matter what you decide. But rest assured, you'll be hearing from me again."

Arne Huber's soul watched his body walking back down the hallway. Even his mind was numb, and despite the closed door behind him he continued to hear laughter.

THE POLITICAL PROCESS

The air above *Fencing Master* sizzled just beyond the visual range; some of the farm's defenders were using lasers that operated in the low-ultraviolet. Lieutenant Arne Huber sighted his tribarrel through his visor's thirty percent mask of the battlefield terrain and the units engaged. He swung the muzzles forward to aim past Sergeant Deseau's left elbow and gunshield.

If Huber fired at the present angle, the powerful 2-cm bolts would singe Deseau's sleeve and his neck below the flare of his commo helmet. He wouldn't do that unless the risk to his sergeant was worth it—though worse things had happened to Deseau during his fifteen years in Hammer's Slammers.

"Fox Three-one," Huber said; his helmet's artificial intelligence cued *Foghorn*, another of the four combat cars in platoon F-3. "Ready to go? Fox Six over."

A rocket gun from somewhere in the Solace defenses fired three times, its coughing ignition followed an instant later by the *snap-p-p!* of the multiple projectiles going supersonic. At least one of the heavy-metal slugs punched more than a hole in the air: the *clang* against armor would have been audible kilometers away. No way to tell who'd been hit or how badly; and no time to worry about it now anyway.

"*Roger, Six, we're ready!*" cried Sergeant Nagano, *Foghorn*'s commander. He didn't sound scared, but his voice was an octave higher than usual with excitement. "*Three-one out!*"

Huber figured Nagano had a right to be excited. Via, he had a right to be scared.

"Costunna, pull forward," Huber ordered his own driver, a newbie who'd replaced the man whom a buzzbomb had decapitated. "Three-one, rush 'em!"

The Northern Star Farm was a network of corn fields crisscrossed by concrete-lined irrigation canals. In the center were more than twenty single-story buildings: barns, equipment sheds, and barracks for the work force. The layout was typical of the large agricultural complexes with which the nation of Solace produced food not only for her own citizens but for all the residents of Plattner's World—when Solace wasn't at war with the Outer States, at any rate.

Technically, only the United Cities were at war with Solace at the moment. Everybody knew that the other five Outer States were helping fund the cost of hiring Hammer's Regiment, but Solace couldn't afford not to look the other way.

The civilians had fled, driving off in wagons pulled by the farm's tractors. The buildings and canals remained as a strongpoint where a battalion of Solace Militia and a company of off-planet mercenaries defended howitzers with the range to loft shells deep into the UC. Colonel Hammer had sent Task Force Sangrela, one platoon each of tanks, combat cars, and infantry, to eliminate the problem.

Fencing Master began to vibrate as Costunna brought up the speed of the eight powerful fans which pressurized the plenum chamber and lifted the combat car for frictionless passage over the ground. The thirty-tonne vehicle didn't slide forward, however. "Go, Costunna!" Huber screamed. "Go! Go! G—"

Finally *Fencing Master* pulled up from the swale in which she'd sheltered during her approach to the target. Huber's helmet careted movement all along the canal slanting across their front at thirty degrees to their course: Solace Militiamen rising to fire at *Foghorn*, which was already in plain sight.

If the two cars had broken cover together as Huber planned, *Foghorn* wouldn't have looked like the lone target in a shooting gallery. Swearing desperately, he hosed the lip of the canal with his tribarrel. Deseau, Learoyd at

Fencing Master's right wing gun, and *Foghorn*'s three gunners fired also, but the other car sparkled like a short circuit as slugs struck her iridium armor.

In Huber's holographic sight picture, dark-uniformed Militiamen turned with horrified looks as they tried to shift the heavy rocket guns they wore harnessed to their shoulders. They'd been so focused on *Foghorn* that the appearance of another combat car two hundred meters away took them completely by surprise.

Fencing Master's forward motion and the angle of the canal helped Huber traverse the target simply by holding his thumbs on the tribarrel's trigger. The 2-centimeter weapon's barrel cluster rotated as it sent copper ions blasting at the speed of light down each iridium bore in turn. The bolts burned metal, shattered concrete in flares of glass and white-hot quicklime, and blew humans apart in gushes of steam. An arm spun thirty meters into the air, trailing smoke from its burning sleeve.

One of the D Company tanks on overwatch to the west fired its main gun twice, not toward the canal but into the interior of the farm where anti-armor weapons were showing themselves to engage the combat cars. An orange flash blew out the sidewalls of a barn; three seconds later, the shock of that enormous secondary explosion made water dance in the irrigation canals.

The surviving Militiamen ducked to cover. *Foghorn* had stalled for a moment, but she was bucking forward again now. Huber cleared the terrain mask from his faceshield to let his eyes and the helmet AI concentrate on nearby motion, his potential targets. He didn't worry about the heavier weapons that might be locking in on *Fencing Master* from long range; that was the business of the tanks—and of the Gods, if you believed in them, which right at the moment Huber couldn't even pretend to do.

A slug penetrated the plenum chamber on the right side of the bow, struck a nacelle inside—the fan howled momentarily, then died; blue sparks sprayed from a portside intake duct and the hair on Huber's arm stood up—and punched out from the left rear in a flash of burning steel. Costunna screamed, *"Port three's out!"*

The air was sharp with ozone. Huber's nose filters kept

the ions from searing his lungs, but the skin of his throat and wrists prickled.

"Drive on!" Huber shouted.

You didn't have to believe in Gods to believe in Hell.

Instead of a square grid, Northern Star's canal system formed a honeycomb of hexagons three hundred meters across each flat. *Fencing Master* slid to where three canals joined and halted as planned. Costunna had adequate mechanical skills and took orders well enough, he just seemed to lack an instinct for what was important. Huber had a straight view down the length of the shallow trough slanting north-northeast from his side. Solace Militiamen— some of them dead, some of them hunching in terror; a few raising weapons to confront the howling monster that had driven down on them—were dark blurs against the white concrete and the trickle of sunbright water.

Huber fired, his bolts shredding targets and glancing from the canal walls in white gouts. Deseau was firing also, and from *Fencing Master*'s starboard wing Learoyd ripped the canal intersecting at a southeastern angle. *Foghorn*'s left gun was raking that canal in the opposite direction.

It was dangerous having two cars firing pretty much toward one another—if either of the gunners raised his muzzles too far, he'd blow divots out of the friendly vehicle—but this was a battle. If safety'd been the Slammers' first concern, they'd all have stayed in bed this morning.

A bullet from the central complex ricocheted off *Fencing Master*'s bow slope, denting the armor and impact-heating it to a shimmering rainbow. Further rounds clipped cornstalks and spewed up little geysers of black dirt.

Sergeant Deseau shouted a curse and grabbed his right wrist momentarily, but he had his hands back on the tribarrel's spade grips before Huber could ask if he was all right. The slug that hit the bow had probably sprayed him with bits of white-hot iridium; nothing serious.

The two automatic mortars accompanying the infantry chugged a salvo of white phosphorus from the swale where *Fencing Master* had waited among the knee-high corn. The Willy Pete lifted in ragged mushrooms above the courtyard building where the farm's workforce ate and gathered for social events.

The roofs slanted down toward the interior; Militiamen with automatic weapons had been using the inner slopes as firing positions. The shellbursts trailed tendrils up, then downward. From a distance they had a glowing white beauty, but Huber knew what a rain of blazing phosphorous did where it landed. Bits continued burning all the way through a human body unless somebody picked them out of the flesh one at a time.

Solace troops leaped to their feet, desperate to escape the shower of death. The other two-car section of Huber's platoon, *Floosie* and *Flame Farter* under Platoon Sergeant Jellicoe, were waiting to the south of the complex for those targets to appear. Their tribarrels lashed the Militiamen, killing most and completely breaking the survivors' will to resist.

"Costunna, get us across the canal!" Huber ordered. He didn't feel the instant response he'd expected—the driver should've been tense on his throttles, ready to angle the car down this side of the channel and up the other with his fans on emergency power—so he added in a snarl, "Move it, man! Move it *now!*"

The tanks were firing methodically, punching holes in the sides of buildings with each 20-cm bolt from their main guns. Walls blew up and inward at every cyan impact, leaving openings more than a meter in diameter. The tanks weren't trying to destroy the structures—a pile of broken concrete made a better nest for enemy snipers than a standing building—but they were providing entrances for infantry assault.

The infantry, twenty-seven troopers under Captain Sangrela himself—the task force commander wasn't going to hang back when his own people were at the sharp end—were belly-down on their one-man skimmers, making the final rush toward the complex from the south,. A heavy laser lifted above the wall of a cow byre to the southeast and started to track them. Two D Company tanks on overwatch had been waiting for it. The laser vanished in a cyan crossfire before it could rake the infantry line.

Costunna shoved his control yoke forward. *Fencing Master* scraped and sparked her skirts over the lip of the canal, then down into the watercourse, spraying water in a fog to either side. Instead of building speed and quickly angling up the opposite wall, the driver continued to roar along the main channel.

"Costunna!" Huber screamed. He leaned forward, trying to see the man, but the driver's hatch was closed. "Via, man! Cut right! Get us up out of here!"

Foghorn was stalled, unable to climb up from the canal. Her fans and skirts had taken a serious hammering while she advanced alone toward the Solace position. *Fencing Master* was nowhere near that badly damaged, but Costunna seemed unwilling or emotionally unable to turn back toward the guns that'd targeted him before.

And until he did, neither of the cars in Huber's section could support the infantry at the moment they needed it most. The tribarrels were unable to shoot through the haze surrounding *Fencing Master*; the water droplets would absorb the bolts as surely as a brick wall or a meter of armor plate could do.

Captain Sangrela was bellowing furious orders over the command channel, but Huber didn't need to be told there was a problem. He opened his mouth to shout at Costunna again because he couldn't think of anything else to do. Before he got the words out, Deseau snarled over the intercom, *"Costunna, get us the fuck outa this ditch or I'll stick my gun up your ass before I pull the trigger!"*

Maybe it was the threat, maybe it was realizing that the car's bumping was its skirts hitting the bodies of Militiamen before smearing them into the concrete. Whatever the reason, Costunna twisted his yoke convulsively. *Fencing Master* lurched from the canal, her plenum chamber shrieking over the concrete coping.

Three white flares burst over the central complex, a signal that the surviving mercenaries wanted to surrender. They were probably broadcasting on one of the general purpose frequencies as well, but you couldn't trust radio in a battle. Powerguns and drive fans both kicked out seas of RF trash, so even commands could be lost or distorted in the middle of a battle. A moment after the flares went up, four soldiers in mottled battledress came out of a smoldering barn with their hands in the air.

"Fox Three elements cease fire!" Huber ordered. He didn't

raise the muzzles of his tribarrel, but he took his hands off the grips. If some trooper got trigger happy now with those easy targets, it'd be the difference between peaceful surrender and a last-ditch defense that meant a lot more Slammers' casualties before it was over. "Stop shooting *now*! Three-six out."

Captain Sangrela was shouting much the same thing over the common task force push also, and Huber figured Lieutenant Mitzi Trogon echoed the words to her four D Company tanks. A powergun snapped a single shot into the bright sky: an infantryman trying to put his weapon on safe while he steered his tiny skimmer had managed to shoot instead.

No serious harm done: the rest of the mercenary company emerged from dugouts and the concrete buildings. They'd been armed with crew-served lasers, bulky weapons but effective even against tanks when they were close enough. Rather than bull straight in, Captain Sangrela had used F-3's combat cars to draw the lasers into sight where the tanks could vaporize them from a safe three kilometers away. Arne Huber understood the logic and he trusted the skill of Mitzi's gunners about as far as he trusted anybody, but he'd known who was going to catch it if something went wrong.

"Costunna, pull around to the tramhead," he ordered, frowning. The main thing that'd gone wrong this time had been with *Fencing Master*'s driver, and that was Arne Huber's responsibility.

Most of the single continent of Plattner's World was accessible only by aircar or dirigible. The trees covering the coastal lowlands were parasitized by "Moss," a fungus which in turn was the source of an anti-aging drug. The forests were therefore more valuable than almost anything that would have replaced them on other planets, highways and railroads included.

The exception was Solace, the state comprising the central highlands. There the soil supported Terran grains and produce, but native trees which grew in the drier climate were stunted and free of the Moss. Solace had become the granary of Plattner's World, and its bedrock supported the only starport on the planet which could accept the largest interstellar freighters.

A network of monorail tramways connected Solace's collective farms with Bezant, the capital, from which giant dirigibles distributed food and manufactured goods to the Outer States. They brought back Moss, *Pseudofistus thalopsis*, which factories on Solace turned into Thalderol base and shipped off-planet for final processing.

In theory one might have thought that the huge profits from Thalderol meant that the inhabitants of Plattner's World lived with one another in wealthy harmony. Mercenary soldiers, even Academy-trained officers like Arne Huber, learned about human nature in a practical school: the riches of Plattner's World just meant people could hire better talent to fight for them. When Solace raised port dues by five percent and the buyers refused to pay more for Thalderol base, the Outer States had hired Hammer's Slammers to reverse the increase.

"Fox Three-six, this is Charlie Six!" Captain Sangrela called abruptly. *"The mercs have surrendered but the locals are planning to break out to the north in their aircars. Cut 'em off, will you? I don't want a massacre, but I'm curst if I want to fight 'em again either! Six out."*

Sangrela was obviously using signals intelligence; it was probably forwarded to him as task force commander by Central, Slammers headquarters at Base Alpha far to the rear. The locals didn't understand what they were up against, of course. The tanks on high ground to the south could track and vaporize even fast-moving aircars at a greater distance than the eye could see: there was no escape from a battlefield they overwatched.

But a volley of 20-cm bolts wasn't a threat, it was a massacre just as Sangrela had said. The Slammers took prisoners wherever possible: that encouraged their opponents to do the same. Needlessly converting several hundred locals into steam and carbonized bone, on the other hand, was likely to have a bad result the next time a trooper got in over his head and wanted to surrender.

"Cancel that, Costunna!" Huber said, setting his faceshield left-handed to caret the electromagnetic signatures of aircar fans revving up. Two equipment sheds on the north side of the complex became a forest of red highlights as the AI obeyed. If they were as full of vehicles as the carets implied, there was a score of large aircars in each. "Get us around north of the buildings—but stay away from the canal, right? Goose it!"

The sheds were aligned east-west and had overhead doors the length of both long sides. As Huber spoke, all twelve of the north-side doors began to rise.

"Guns!" Huber shouted over the intercom to the men with him in the fighting compartment. "Aim low, don't kill anybody you don't have to! Costunna, get *on* it!"

Fencing Master finally started to accelerate. The car was five hundred meters from the west sidewall of the nearer shed, almost twice that from the far end of the other one. The tribarrels were effective at many times that distance, but it was beyond the range at which you could expect delicate shooting from a moving vehicle. It'd be what it'd be.

An aircar with room for twenty soldiers or two tonnes of cargo nosed out of the nearer shed. Huber laid his holographic sights on it, letting the aircar's forward motion pull it through his rope of vividly cyan bolts. The plastic quarterpanel exploded in a red fireball, flipping the car onto its right side in the path of the identical vehicle pulling out of the adjacent bay. They collided, and the second car also overturned.

A third truck started from the near end of the shed and pitched nose-high as the driver tried to vault the line of powergun bolts. He didn't have enough speed. The bow slammed back into the ground, breaking the vehicle's frame and hurling passengers twenty meters from the wreck.

If Costunna had known his job better, he'd have slewed *Fencing Master* so that her bow pointed thirty degrees to starboard of her axis of movement. Because he didn't—*and Via! Sure he was a newbie but didn't he know any cursed thing?*—Huber stopped firing when Sgt Deseau's gunshield masked his point of aim.

Deseau and Learoyd didn't need help anyway. The gunners punched three-round bursts into each truck that showed its bow past the side of the sheds. Though the bolts couldn't penetrate even an aircar's light body, the energy they liberated vaporized the sheathing in blasts with the impact of falling anvils, slamming the targets in the opposite direction.

Aircars skidded, bounced, and overturned. None of them got properly airborne.

Huber swung his tribarrel onto the canal half a klick to the north, intending to cover the troops who'd been using it as a trench like their fellows in the stretch Huber's section had overrun. None of them showed themselves, let alone fired at *Fencing Master*.

A pair of gleaming troughs reaching from the south to just short of the canal's inner lip indicated why: while Huber concentrated on the equipment sheds, two D Company tanks had warned the hidden Militiamen of what'd happen to them if they continued to make a fight of it. The main-gun bolts had converted all the silica in the ground they struck to molten glass, spraying it over those huddled in the canal. The flashes and concussion must have been enormous, but Huber hadn't been aware of it while it was happening.

Huber glanced to his right, past the two gunners hunched over their tribarrels. The crown of red markers on his faceshield collapsed as he looked. The surviving vehicles were shutting down; the only fan motors still racing were in the wrecks whose drivers weren't able to obey the order to switch off.

Deseau fired into the bow of a motionless truck, visible now because *Fencing Master* was crossing the front of the nearer shed. The molded plastic flared red, blooming into a meters-wide bubble that hung shimmering for several seconds in front of the building.

"Guns, cease fire!" Huber ordered. "They're surrendering, boys. Cease fire!"

Via! He hoped he was right because there was the Lord's own plenty of locals, coming out of the equipment sheds and rising from the canals on the other side of *Fencing Master*. The troops in the sheds must've been the crews for the howitzers dug into pits in the center of the complex. There the guns were safe from the sniping tanks, but they hadn't been able to threaten the assault force with direct fire either. The commander must have pulled the crews under cover, knowing the artillerymen would've been no better than targets if he'd tried to use them as infantry against the oncoming mercenaries.

The nearest friendly unit was *Foghorn*, just managing to work out of the channel where she'd been stuck. Maybe some of Captain Sangrela's troopers were still advancing from the south, but Huber guessed most of those figured to let *Fencing Master* learn what the locals intended before putting themselves in the middle of things. Huber couldn't say he blamed them.

Costunna slowed the car, then brought it to a halt with the fans idling. Huber'd been about to order him to do that, but the driver shouldn't have made the decision on his own. Well, Costunna was business for another time—though the time was going to come pretty cursed soon.

A middle-aged man limped toward *Fencing Master* with his helmet in his left hand. He looked haggard, and the left side of his face and shoulder were covered with soot. A younger man hovered at his side. The glowing muzzles of Learoyd's tribarrel terrified the aide, but the older officer didn't appear to notice the gun aimed point blank at them.

"I am Colonel Apollonio Priamedes," he said. His voice was raw with emotion and the mix of ozone and combustion products that fouled the atmosphere; the Solace Militia didn't have nose filters or gas masks that Huber could see. "I was in command here. I have ordered my men to lay down their weapons and surrender. May I expect that we will be treated honorably as prisoners of war?"

Huber raised his faceshield. His fingers were claws, cramping from their grip on his tribarrel.

"Yes sir," Huber said, "you sure can."

And the Solace colonel couldn't possibly be more relieved by the end of this business than Lieutenant Arne Huber was.

When the resupply and maintenance convoy radioed, they'd estimated they were still fifteen minutes out from Northern Star. If they'd get on the stick they could cut their arrival time by two-thirds. Huber supposed the commander was afraid stragglers from the garrison would ambush his mostly soft-skinned vehicles. That was a reasonable concern—*if* you hadn't seen how completely the assault had broken the Solace Militiamen.

When the convoy arrived Task Force Sangrela could stand

down and let the newcomers take care of security, but right now everybody was on alert. The eight combat vehicles were just west of the building complex, laagered bows-outward so that their weapons threatened all points of the compass. The jeep-mounted mortars were dug in at the center. Two infantry squads were in pits between the vehicles, while the remainder of the platoon was spread in fire teams around the two relatively-undamaged buildings into which the prisoners had been herded.

Sangrela had ordered each car to send a man to help guard the prisoners. Normally Huber would've complained—F-3 had carried out the assault pretty much by itself, after all—but he was just as glad for an excuse to send Costunna off. Learoyd was in the driver's compartment now with the fans on idle. The squat, balding trooper wasn't the Regiment's best driver, but you never had to worry about his instincts in a firefight.

Nights here on the edge of the highlands were clearer than under the hazy atmosphere of the United Cities. Arne Huber could see the stars for the first time since he'd landed on Plattner's World.

They made him feel more lonely, of course. The one thing that hadn't changed during Huber's childhood on Nieuw Friesland was the general pattern of the night sky. Since he'd joined the Slammers, he couldn't even count on that.

He smiled wryly. "El-Tee?" Sergeant Deseau said, catching the expression.

"Change is growth, Frenchie," Huber said. "Have you ever been told that?"

"Not so's I recall," the sergeant said, rubbing the side of his neck with his knuckles. "Think they're going to leave us here to garrison the place?"

The slug that splashed the bow slope had peppered Deseau between the bottom of his faceshield and the top of his clamshell body armor. He knew that a slightly bigger chunk might have ripped his throat out, just as he knew that he was going to be sweating in the plenum chamber tomorrow, when he helped Maintenance replace the fan that'd been shot away. Both facts were part of the job.

Huber could hear the convoy now over *Fencing Master*'s humming nacelles. The incoming vehicles, mostly air-cushion trucks but with a section of combat cars for escort, kept their fans spinning at high speed in case they had to move fast.

"Charlie Six to all units," said a tense voice on the common task force channel. *"Eleven vehicles, I repeat one-one vehicles, entering the perimeter at vector one-seven-zero. They will show—"*

A pause during which the signals officer waited for Captain Sangrela's last-instant decision.

"—blue. Charlie Six out."

As he spoke, the darkness to the southeast of the laager lit with quivering azure spikes: static discharges from the antennas of the incoming convoy. Huber didn't bother to count them: there'd be eleven. Electronic identification was foolproof or almost foolproof; but soldiers were humans, not machines, and they liked to have confirmation from their own eyes as well as from a readout.

Captain Sangrela walked forward, holding a blue marker wand in his left hand. The troops between the armored vehicles rose and moved to the center of the laager where they wouldn't be driven over. The newcomers would be parking between the vehicles of Task Force Sangrela.

If the units spent the night in two separate laagers they risked a mutal firefight, especially if the enemy was smart enough to slip into the gap and shoot toward both camps in turn. The Solace Militia probably didn't have that standard of skill, but some of mercenaries Solace had hired certainly did. Soldiers, even the Slammers, could get killed easily enough without taking needless chances.

The convoy came in, lighted only by its static discharges. Huber could've switched his faceshield to thermal imaging or light-amplification if he'd wanted to see clearly—that's how the drivers were maneuvering their big vehicles into place—but he was afraid he'd drop into a reverie if he surrounded himself with an electronic cocoon. He still felt numb from reaction to the assault.

"El-Tee, that combat car's from A Company," Deseau said, one hand resting idly on the grip of his tribarrel. He was using helmet intercom because the howls of incoming vehicles would've overwhelmed his voice even if he'd shouted at the top of his lungs. *"So's the infantry riding*

on the back of them wrenchmobiles. When did the White Mice start pulling convoy security?"

Huber's mind kept playing back the moment *Fencing Master* had lurched into position above the canal so he could rake it with his tribarrel. In his memory there was only equipment and empty uniforms in the sun-struck channel. No men at all . . .

"You've got me, Frenchie," Huber said. He should've noticed that himself.

A Company—the White Mice, though Huber didn't know where the name came from—was the Regiment's field police, under the command of Major Joachim Steuben. The White Mice weren't all murderous sociopaths; but Major Steuben was, and the troopers of A Company who still had consciences didn't let them get in the way of carrying out the orders Steuben gave.

"*Officers to the command car ASAP,*" a female voice ordered without bothering to identify herself. "*All units shut down, maintaining sensor watch and normal guard rosters. Regiment Three-three out.*"

Huber felt his face freeze. Regiment Three-three was the signalman for the Slammers' S-3, the operations officer. What was Major Pritchard doing out here?

Though his presence explained why the White Mice were escorting the convoy, that was for sure.

Resupply was aboard six air-cushion trucks. They could keep up with the combat vehicles on any terrain, but their only armor was thin plating around the cab. Besides them the convoy included two combat cars for escort and two recovery vehicles—wrenchmobiles—which could lift a crippled car in the bed between their fore and aft nacelles. For this run the beds had been screened with woven-wire fencing, so that the twenty A Company infantrymen aboard each wouldn't bounce out no matter how rough the ride.

The last member of the convoy was a command vehicle. Its high, thinly armored box replaced the fighting compartment and held more signal and sensor equipment than would fit in a standard combat car. It backed between *Fencing Master* and the tank to Huber's left, then shut down; the rear wall lowered to form a ramp with a whine of hydraulic pumps.

"Well, you don't got far to go, El-Tee," Deseau said judiciously. He rubbed his neck again. *"What d'ye suppose is going on?"*

"I'll let you know," Huber said as he swung his legs out of the fighting compartment and stood for a moment on the bulge of the plenum chamber. He gripped the frame of the bustle rack left-handed, then slid down the steel skirt with the skill of long practice.

His right hand held a sub-machine gun, the butt resting on his pelvis. It fired the same 1-cm charges as the Slammers pistols, but it was fully automatic.

Deseau sounded like he didn't expect to like the answer his lieutenant came back with. That was fair, because Huber didn't think he was going to like it either.

Captain Sangrela, looking older than Huber remembered him being at the start of the operation, had just shaken hands with Pritchard at the bottom of the ramp. Mitzi Trogon, built like one of her tanks and at least as hard, was climbing down from *Dinkybob* on the other side of the command track from *Fencing Master*. She was a good officer to serve with—*if* you were able to do your job to her standards.

"Lieutenant Myers's on the way from the prisoner guard in the farm buildings," Sangrela explained to Pritchard as Huber joined them. The buzz of a skimmer was faintly audible, wavering with the breeze but seeming to come closer. "I moved us half a klick out before laagering for the night so we wouldn't have hostiles in the middle of us if they got loose or some curst thing."

This was the first time Huber had seen Major Danny Pritchard in the field; body armor made the S-3 seem bigger than he did addressing the Regiment from a podium. His normal expression was a smile, so he looked younger than his probable real age of thirty-eight or so Standard Years. He'd come up through the ranks, and the pistol he wore over his clamshell in a shoulder rig wasn't just for show.

A woman wearing a jumpsuit uniform of a style Huber hadn't seen before—it wasn't United Cities garb, and it *sure* wasn't Slammers—had arrived in the car with Pritchard but now waited at the top of the ramp. She responded to Huber's grin with a guarded nod. She was trimly attractive, very alert, and—if Arne Huber was any judge of people—plenty tough as well.

Pritchard looked to his right and said, "Good to see you again, Mitzi," in a cheerful voice. Turning to Huber he went on, warmly enough but with the touch of reserve proper between near strangers, "Lieutenant Huber? Good to meet you."

Lieutenant Myers' skimmer buzzed to a halt beside them, kicking dirt over everybody's feet. Sangrela glared at the infantry platoon leader who now acted as the task force's executive officer.

"Sorry," Myers muttered as he got to his feet. He was a lanky, nervous man who seemed to do his job all right but never would let well enough alone. "I was, I mean—"

"Can it, Lieutenant!" Sangrela said in a tone Huber wouldn't have wanted anyone using to him. To Pritchard he continued apologetically, "Sir, all my officers are now present."

Pritchard quirked a smile. "I guess we'll fit inside," he said, stepping back into the command car and gesturing the others to follow. The roof hatch forward was open; from the inside, all Huber could see of Pritchard's signals officer was the lower half of her body standing on the full-function seat now acting as a firing step. "Not for privacy, but the imagery's going to be sharper if we use the car."

Huber unlatched his body armor and shrugged it off before he climbed into the compartment. Mitzi wasn't wearing hers anyway—she said she bumped often enough in a tank turret as it was. Lieutenant Myers saw Huber strip, started to follow suit, then froze for a moment with the expression of a bunny in the headlights. He was the last to enter, and even then only when Sangrela gestured him angrily forward.

The compartment was smaller than it looked from the outside because the sidewalls were fifteen centimeters thick with electronics. There were fold-down seats at the three touchplate consoles on each side, blandly neutral at this moment because nobody'd chosen the function they were to control.

"Right," said Pritchard when they were all inside. "Officially the government of United Cities has hired the Regiment to support it in its tariff discussions with the government of Solace. Unofficially, everybody on the planet knows that the other five of the Outer States are helping the UC pay our hire."

Huber suspected that not all the Slammers—and not even all the officers here in the S-3's command car—knew or cared who was paying the Slammers. It wasn't their job to know, and a lot of the troopers didn't want to clutter up their minds with things that didn't matter. It might get in the way of stuff that helped them stay alive. . . .

"The government of the Point," Pritchard continued, "that's the state on the north of the continent—"

A map of the sole continent of Plattner's World bloomed in front of Huber. Everyone in the compartment would see an identical image, no matter where they stood. Though an air-projected hologram, it was as sharp as if it had been carved from agate.

A pale beige overlay identified UC territory on the contour display; as Pritchard spoke, an elongated diamond of the map went greenish: a promontory in the north balanced by a southward-tapering wedge which ended at the central mass of Solace. The Point and the United Cities were directly across the continent from one another.

"—is fully supportive of the UC position. Melinda Riker Grayle, a politician who's not in the government but who has a considerable following among the Moss rangers who collect the raw material for the anti-aging drug—"

The image of a stern-looking woman, well into middle age, replaced the map. She wouldn't have been beautiful even thirty years before, but she was handsome in her way and she glared out at the world with a strength that was evident even in hologram.

"—opposes the government in this. She argues that supporting the Regiment lays the Point open to Solace attack, and that the Regiment couldn't do anything to help the Point in such an event."

Huber nodded. It seemed to him that the only thing protecting the "neutral" Outer States from Solace attack was the fact that Solace needed both the Moss they shipped to Solace for processing and the market they provided for Solace produce. For that matter, everybody knew that part of the Moss shipped from the neutral states came from the UC, and that food and manufactures from Solace found their way back to the UC by the same route.

Pritchard grinned. He had a pleasant face, but his expression now made Huber realize that Colonel Hammer's operations officer had to be just as ruthless as Joachim Steuben in his different way.

"Task Force Sangrela's going to prove Grayle's wrong," he said. "You're going to run from here straight to the Point and be in the capital, Midway, before any civilians even know you're coming."

His grin tightened fractionally. "I wish I could say the same about the Solace military," he added, "but their surveillance equipment's better than that. We're all leaving the satellites up because our employers need them. We can hope they won't have time to mount a real counter to the move, though."

"Blood and Martyrs!" Lieutenant Myers muttered.

"How's my infantry supposed to keep up?" asked Captain Sangrela in a more reasoned version of what was probably the same concern. "That's fourteen hundred kilometers by the shortest practical route—"

Either he'd cued his helmet AI with the question, or he was a better off-the-cuff estimator than Huber ever thought of being.

"—and we're not going to do that in skimmers without taking breaks the cars 'n panzers won't need."

Slammers infantry could travel long distances on their skimmers, recharging their batteries on the move by hooking up to the fusion bottles of the armored fighting vehicles. What they couldn't do was change off drivers the way their heavy brethren would.

Pritchard nodded. "The recovery vehicles that just arrived will go along with you on the run," he said. "Off-duty troops'll ride in the boxes the A Company infantry arrived in. There'll be a convoy of wheeled trucks here tomorrow for the prisoners; the White Mice will ride back in them as guards and escort."

Huber frowned. "What happens if a car's too badly damaged to move under its own power, though?" he asked. Battle damage wasn't the only thing that could cripple a vehicle on a long run over rough country, but a montage of explosions and dazzling flashes danced through Huber's memory as he spoke the words. "The wrenchmobiles can't carry twenty troops and a car besides."

"If a car's damaged that bad," Pritchard said, "you blow her in place, report a combat loss, and move on."

He turned to Mitzi Trogon and continued, "You do the same thing if it's a tank. No hauling cripples along, no leaving other units behind to guard the ones that have to drop out. This mission is more important than the hardware. Understood?"

Everybody nodded grimly.

What Arne Huber understood was that on a mission of this priority, the troops involved were items of hardware also. Colonel Hammer wouldn't throw them away, but their personal wellbeing and survival weren't his first concern either.

"My people plotted a route for you," the S-3 resumed. The electronics projected a yellow line—more jagged than snaky—across the holographic continent. More than a third of the route was within the russet central block of Solace territory, though that probably didn't matter: the task force was going to be a target anywhere the enemy could catch it, whether or not that was in theoretically neutral territory.

Captain Sangrela's face went even bleaker than it'd been a moment before. Pritchard saw the expression and grinned reassuringly. "No, you're not required to follow it," he said. "I know as well as the next guy that what looks like a good idea from satellite imagery isn't necessarily something I want to drive a tank over. Make any modifications you see fit to—but this is a starting point, in more ways than one."

Sangrela nodded, relaxing noticeably. Huber did too, though he was only fully conscious of the momentary knot in his guts when it released. It was good to know that despite the political importance of this mission, the troops on the ground wouldn't have Regimental Command trying to run things from Base Alpha. That'd have been a sure way to get killed.

Mind, if Solace reacted as quickly as the Slammers themselves would respond to a similar opportunity, the mission was still a recipe for disaster.

"What're we going to find when we get to the Point?" Lieutenant Myers asked. "You say there's opposition in the backwoods. Are we going to have to look out for local snipers when we get to—"

He grinned harshly.

"—friendly territory?"

"I'll let our guest field that one," Pritchard said with a tip of his hand toward the woman in the jumpsuit beside him. "Troops, this is Captain Mauricia Orichos of the Point Gendarmery, their army. Captain Orichos?"

"We're not an army," Orichos said. Her pleasant, throaty voice complemented her cheerfully cynical smile. "The job of the Gendarmery is primarily to prevent outsiders from harvesting our Moss. Without paying taxes on it, that is."

She let that sink in for a moment, then continued, "My own job is a little different, however. You might say that I'm head of the state security section. I contacted my opposite number in your regiment—"

Which means Joachim Steuben. Huber hoped he kept his reaction from reaching his facial muscles.

"—and asked for help. The situation is beyond what the Gendarmery, what the Point, can handle by itself."

The map had vanished when Orichos began to speak. Now in its place the car projected first the close-up of Melinda Grayle speaking, then drew back to an image of her audience—a long plaza holding several thousand people: mostly male, mostly armed. Mostly drunk as well, or Huber missed his bet.

"Generally," Orichos continued, "Grayle's supporters—they call themselves the Freedom Party—have stayed in the backlands. They've got a base and supposedly stores of heavy weapons on Bulstrode Bay—"

The map returned briefly, this time with a caret noting an indentation on the west coast of the peninsula, near the tip.

"—which is completely illegal, of course, but we—the government—weren't in any position to investigate it thoroughly." Her smile quirked again. "It seemed to me that most members of the government were concerned that we'd find the rumors were true and they wouldn't be able to stick their heads in the sand any more."

Huber and the other Slammers smiled back at her. Cynicism about official cowardice was cheap, but mercenary soldiers gathered more supporting evidence for the belief than many people did.

The image of Grayle appeared again, but this time the point of view drew back even farther than before. The crowd itself shrank to the center of the field. On all sides were the two- and three-story buildings typical of Plattner's World, set within a forest which had been thinned but not cleared. This was a city. It was larger by far than Benjamin, the administrative capital of the UC.

"Two weeks ago," Orichos said, "Grayle ordered her followers to join her in Midway—and come armed. Her Freedom Party has its headquarters directly across the Axis, Midway's central boulevard, from the Assembly Building. They've been holding rallies every day in the street. This was the first, but they've gotten bigger."

"And you can't stop them?" Captain Sangrela asked. He tried to keep his voice neutral, but Huber could hear the tone of disapproval.

Orichos had probably heard it also, because she replied with noticeable sharpness, "Apart from the ordinary members of the Freedom Party, Captain, there are some ten thousand so-called Volunteers who train in military tactics and who're considerably better armed than the Gendarmery— as well as outnumbering us two to one. I *am* doing something about them: I'm calling in your Regiment to aid the Point with a show of force."

"Captain Sangrela was merely curious, Mauricia," Pritchard said mildly, though his smile wasn't so much mild as dismissive of anything as trivial as status and honor. "Task Force Sangrela's arrival in Midway will prove Mistress Grayle was wrong about the Slammers being unable to reach the Point in a hurry . . . and if a more robust show turns out to be necessary, that's possible as well."

The imagery vanished. Pritchard looked across the arc of officers, his eyes meeting those of each in turn. In that moment he reminded Huber of a bird of prey.

"Troopers," he said, "route and intelligence assessments have been downloaded to all members of your force. The resupply convoy brought a full maintenance platoon; they'll be working on your equipment overnight so you can get some sleep. I recommend you brief your personnel and turn in immediately. You've got quite a run ahead of you starting tomorrow."

"Blood and Martyrs!" Lieutenant Myers repeated. "That's not *half* the truth!"

Huber waited for Sangrela and Myers to clear the doorway, then started out. Offering politely to let Mitzi precede him would've at best been a joke—at worst she'd have kicked him in the balls—and he didn't feel much like joking.

"Lieutenant Huber?" Pritchard called. He turned his head. "Walk with me for a moment, will you?"

"Sir," Huber said in muted agreement. He stepped down the ramp and put his clamshell on as he waited for the major to follow Mitzi out of the command car. For a moment his eyes started to adapt to darkness; then the first of several banks of lights lit the Night Defensive Position. The scarred iridium hulls reflected ghostly shadows in all directions.

Huber didn't know why the S-3 wanted to talk to him out of Captain Orichos' hearing; the thought made him uncomfortable. Things a soldier doesn't know are very likely to kill him.

Pritchard gestured them into the passage between his command car and Mitzi's tank, *Dinkybob*. He didn't speak till they were past the bows of the outward-facing blowers. A crew was already at work on *Fencing Master*; across the laager, a recovery vehicle had winched *Foghorn*'s bow up at a thirty-degree angle so that a squad of mechanics could start switching out the several damaged nacelles for new ones. Power wrenches and occasionally a diamond saw tore the night like sonic lightning.

"Two things, Lieutenant," Pritchard said when they were beyond the bright pool from the floodlights. He faced the night, his back to the NDP. "First, I was surprised to see you were back with F-3. I had the impression that you'd applied for a transfer?"

Ah. "No sir," Huber said, looking toward the horizon instead of turning toward the major. "Major Steuben offered me a position in A Company. I considered it, but I decided to turn him down."

"I see," said Pritchard. "May I ask why? Because I'll tell you frankly, I don't know of a single case in which Joachim offered an officer's slot to someone who didn't prove capable of doing the job."

"I'm not surprised, sir," Huber said, smiling faintly. "It was because I was pretty sure I *could* handle the work that I passed. I decided that I didn't want to live with the person I'd be then."

Pritchard laughed. "I can't say I'm sorry to hear that, Huber," he said. "What are your ambitions then? Because I've looked at your record—"

He faced Huber, drawing the younger man's eyes toward him. They couldn't see one another's expressions in the darkness, but the gesture was significant.

"—and I don't believe you're *not* ambitious."

"Sir . . ." Huber said. He was willing to tell the truth, but right in this moment he wasn't sure what the truth *was*. "Sir, I figure to stay with F-3 and do a good job until a captaincy opens up in one of the line companies. Or I buy the farm, of course. And after that, we'll see."

Pritchard laughed again. Huber thought there was wistfulness in the sound along with the humor, but he didn't know the S-3 well enough to judge his moods. "Let's go back to your car and get you settled in," he said.

"Yes, sir," Huber said, turning obediently. "But you said there were two things, sir?"

"Hey, there you are, El-Tee!" Sergeant Deseau bellowed as he saw Huber reentering the haze of light. "Come look what the cat dragged in! It's Tranter, and he says he's back with us for the operation!"

"I saw from the after-action review that you were going to need a replacement driver," Pritchard said in a low voice. "You've worked with Sergeant Tranter before and I believe you found him a satisfactory driver—"

"Frenchie says he's the best driver he ever served with," Huber said. "I say that too, but Frenchie's got a hell of a lot more experience than I do."

"—so I had him transferred from Logistics Section to F-3."

Huber strode forward to greet the red-haired sergeant he

knew from his brief stint in Log Section. Suddenly remembering where he was—and who he'd just turned his back on—he stopped and faced the major again.

"Sorry, sir," he muttered. "I—I mean, I've been sweating making the run tomorrow short a crewman, and there was no way I was going to have Costunna on my car or in my platoon. I was . . . Well, thank you, I really appreciate it."

"Colonel Hammer and I are asking you and the rest of the task force to do a difficult job, Lieutenant," Major Danny Pritchard said. This time his smile was simple and genuine. "I hope you can depend on us to do whatever we can to help you."

He clasped Huber's right hand and added, "Now, go give your troopers a pep talk and then get some rest. It's going to be your last chance to do that for a bloody long time."

Unless I buy the farm, Huber repeated mentally; but he didn't worry near as much about dying as he had about carrying out tomorrow's operation with his car a crewman short.

The Command and Control module housed in the box welded to Huber's gun mount projected ten holographic beads above *Fencing Master*'s fighting compartment. Call-Sign Sierra—the four tanks, four combat cars, and two recovery vehicles of Task Force Sangrela—was ready to roll.

If Huber'd wanted to go up an increment, the display would've added separate dots for the vehicle crews, the infantry platoon, and the air-cushion jeep carrying the task force commander with additional signals and sensor equipment. He didn't need that now, though he'd raise the sensitivity when the scout section—one car and a fire-team of infantry on skimmers—moved out ahead.

Huber gestured to the display and said over the two-way link he'd set with Captain Orichos' borrowed commo helmet, "We're on track, Captain. Another two minutes."

Sergeant Tranter ran up his fans, keeping the blade incidence fine so that they didn't develop any lift. Huber heard the note change minusculely as the driver adjusted settings, bringing the replacement nacelle into perfect balance with the other seven.

Sergeant Deseau nodded approvingly, chopping the lip of the armor with his hand and then pointing forward to indicate the driver's compartment. Trooper Learoyd didn't react. He usually didn't react, except to do his job; which he did very well, though Huber had met cocker spaniels he guessed had greater intellectual capacity than Learoyd.

The fighting compartment was crowded with Orichos sharing the space with the three men of the combat crew, but Via! it was always crowded. A slim woman who wasn't wearing body armor—her choice, and Huber thought it was a bad one—didn't take up as much room as the cooler of beer they'd strapped onto the back of the bustle rack when they took her aboard. They weren't using overhead cover for the combat cars here on Plattner's World because they were generally operating in heavy forest.

"Wouldn't your helmet show that information?" Orichos asked, tapping the side of the one Huber had borrowed for her from a mechanic when he learned she'd be travelling in his car. She didn't need it so much for communications as for the sound damping it provided. A run like the one planned would jelly the brains of anybody making it without protection from all the shrieks, hums and roars they'd get in an open combat car.

"Sierra Six to Sierra," Captain Sangrela. *"White Section—"* the scouts *"—move out. Over."*

The lead car, *Foghorn*, was already off the ground on fan thrust. Its driver nudged his control yoke forward, sending the thirty-tonne vehicle toward the northwest in a billow of dust. *Foghorn*'s skirts plowed a broad path through the young corn.

Four infantrymen on skimmers lifted when the combat car moved. For a moment they flew parallel to the bigger vehicle, just out of the turbulent air squirting beneath the plenum chamber; then they moved out ahead by 150 meters, spreading to cover a half-klick frontage. *Foghorn*'s sensor suite covered the infantry while they ranged ahead on their light mounts to discover the sort of terrain problems that didn't show up on satellite.

"I can access everything Central's got in its data banks here on my faceshield," Huber replied to Orichos, thinking about her gray eyes behind her faceshield. She'd smiled at him when he offered her the helmet. "I like to keep it for stuff with immediate combat significance, though."

He grinned through his visor and added, "Sometimes it's more important that I'm *Fencing Master*'s left wing gunner than that I command Platoon F-3."

The scouts patrolled a klick ahead of whichever vehicle was leading the main body. The combat cars and infantry would rotate through White Section every hour under the present conditions, more frequently if the terrain got challenging.

Huber had picked Sergeant Nagano's car to start out in the lead because it'd been so badly battered at Northern Star. If last night's massive repairs weren't going to hold up, Huber wanted to know about it now—by daylight and long before the enemy started reacting to Task Force Sangrela.

"*Sierra Six to Sierra*," Sangrela ordered in a hoarsely taut voice. "*Red Section—*" the main body, with *Fencing Master* leading two tanks, followed by the recovery vehicles and the last two tanks "*—move out. Over.*"

"That's us, Tranter," Huber ordered on the intercom channel. "Hold us at thirty kph until the whole section's under way, got that?"

They planned to average sixty kph on the run, putting them in Midway exactly twenty-four hours from this moment, including breaks to switch drivers and the stretches of bad terrain that'd hold down their speed. Ordinarily on this sort of smooth ground they'd have belted along at the best speed the infantry could manage on skimmers, close to 100 kph. Sierra had to build speed gradually, however, or the vehicles would scatter themselves too widely to support each other in event of enemy action.

Which was certain to come; more certain than any trooper in Task Force Sangrela could be of seeing the next sunrise.

Sergeant Tranter brought *Fencing Master* up from a dead halt as smoothly as if he were twisting a rheostat. He'd been a maintenance technician, so he'd learned to drive armored vehicles by shifting them—frequently badly damaged—around one another in the tight confines of maintenance parks. He'd stopped being a tech when a hydraulic jack blew out, dropping a tank's skirts to a concrete pad and pinching his right leg off as suddenly as lightning.

The mechanical leg was in most respects as good as the original one, but in serious cold the organic/electrical interface degraded enough to send the limb into spasms. The Regiment had offered Tranter the choice of retirement on full pay or a rear-echelon job he could do in a heated building. He'd chosen the latter, a berth in Logistics Section.

Summer temperatures on Plattner's World never dropped below the level of mildly chilly. If Regimental command was willing to make an exception, there was nobody Arne Huber would've preferred driving his car than Tranter.

Huber looked over his shoulder, twisting his body at the waist because the clamshell armor stiffened his neck and upper torso. The lead tank, *Dinkybob,* lifted to follow thirty meters behind *Fencing Master.* Mitzi's driver echeloned the big vehicle slightly to the right of Tranter's line to stay out of the combat car's dust. That was fine on a grain-field like this, but pretty soon Task Force Sangrela would be winding through hillside scrub where the big vehicles'd feel lucky to have one route.

Well, troopers got used to dust pretty quick. The only thing they knew better was mud. . . . The commo helmets had nose filters that dropped down automatically and static charges to keep their faceshields clear, but on a run like this Huber knew to expect a faintly gritty feeling every time he blinked. The ration bars he ate on the move would crunch, too.

The tribarrels were sealed against dust—until you had to use them. It didn't take much grit seeping down the ejection port to jam mechanisms as precise as those in the interior of an automatic weapon.

Captain Orichos swayed awkwardly, uncertain of what she could safely grab or sit on. She was familiar with aircars and thought this would be the same. She hadn't realized that terrain affected the ride of air cushion vehicles—not as much as it affected wheels and treads, but still a great deal.

She caught Huber's glance and waved a hand in frustration. "*I'd expected the floor to vibrate,*" she said. "*But the jolting—what does that? I didn't feel anything like that when I rode here with Major Pritchard.*"

Huber grinned. "You rode here in a convoy travelling at the speed of heavily loaded supply vehicles, with the number two man in the Slammers aboard. Sierra has different priorities. Even on these fields, the front skirt digs in every time there's a little dip or rise in the ground. It'll get a lot worse when we start working along the sides of the foothills we're scheduled to hit pretty soon."

"*Then it's always like this?*" she asked. Deliberately she lifted her faceshield, squinting slightly against the wind blast. She quirked the wry smile he'd seen the night before as she discussed the moral courage of elected officials.

"No, not always," Huber said, raising his own shield to give Orichos a much broader smile than the one he'd been wearing before. "Sometimes they're shooting at us, Captain."

"*Sierra Six to Sierra,*" Captain Sangrela said. "*Blue Section, move out.*"

Blue Section was the two remaining combat cars under Platoon Sergeant Jellicoe. They'd follow the main body at a kilometer's distance, extending the column's sensor range to the rear by that much. There wasn't a high likelihood that the enemy would sweep up on the task force from behind, but some of the mercenary units Solace was known to have hired had equipment with sufficient performance to manage it.

The cars in Blue Section would rotate at the same intervals as the scouts did. Either Huber or Jellicoe would be at the front or rear of the column—but never both at the same end.

"*Then I guess I'd better get used to it, hadn't I?*" Orichos said. She spread her left hand over her eyes to shield them as she surveyed the terrain. She added, "*Have you been with Hammer's Slammers long, Lieutenant?*"

"Five years," Huber said, facing forward and lowering his faceshield so that Orichos could do the same. "I entered the Military Academy on Nieuw Friesland with the intention of enlisting in the Regiment when I graduated . . . and I did."

The scouts were already into the gullied scrubland that the task force would grind through for the first half of the route. Central had timed the departure from Northern Star so that Sierra would be in pitch darkness while it navigated the last of the foothills south of Point territory where forests resumed.

Until the task force set off, the enemy would assume the

Slammers intended to return to UC territory after capturing Northern Star. It'd take the Solace command time to react when they realized the Slammers' real intent. The most dangerous ambush sites were in the foothills; by waiting till noon to set off, the task force would have the advantage of the Regiment's more sophisticated night vision equipment in that last stretch which the enemy might reach in time to block them.

Huber hoped the Colonel was right; but then, he hoped a lot of things, and his tribarrel was ready to take care of whatever reality threw at them. You couldn't always blast your way through problems, but the ability to out-slug the other fellow never stopped being an advantage.

"Do you know much about the political structure of the Point, Lieutenant?" Orichos asked. Since her voice came through the commo helmet, she could've been standing anywhere on the planet—but Huber was very much aware of her presence beside and just behind him.

"Not a thing, ma'am," he admitted. "I studied the United Cities some from the briefing cubes because they were hiring us, but I didn't look at the rest of you folks."

He touched the controller with his left hand, projecting an image remoted from *Foghorn* into the air before him. The scout car was bulling through brush already. The stems were wiry enough to spring back after *Foghorn* passed, but they were too thin to be a barrier to a thirty-tonne vehicle.

He hoped what he'd just said didn't sound too much like, "I'm not interested in you dumb wogs;" which wasn't true for Arne Huber himself but pretty well summed up the attitude of a lot of Slammers, officers as well as line troopers like Sergeant Deseau. Trooper Learoyd wasn't likely to have thoughts so abstract.

"Midway's the only city in the Point," Orichos said. *"We're not like Trenchard or the UC where there's half a dozen places each as big as the next. There's a quarter million people in Midway, and no town as big as a thousand in all the rest of the country."*

"So about a third of your population's in the one city," Huber said. He hadn't *studied* the Point, not like you'd really mean studied; but he'd checked the basic statistics on Plattner's World, sure. "I guess there's a lot of trouble between people in Midway and the rest of the country, then?"

"*There wasn't any trouble at all before Melinda Grayle came along!*" snapped Captain Orichos, her very vehemence proving that she was lying. "*She started stirring up the Moss rangers ten years ago. All she's interested in is power for herself.*"

Not unlikely, Arne Huber thought. Of course, Melinda Grayle wasn't the only politician you could say that about; and she maybe wasn't the only politician in the Point you could say it about, either.

"*Grayle claims that the votes in the last election were falsified and that she should've been elected Speaker of the Assembly,*" Orichos went on. "*She's threatening to take by force what she claims her Freedom Party lost by fraud. Everybody knows that the reason most Assemblymen are residents of Midway is because Moss rangers can't be bothered to vote!*"

"Ma'am," said Arne Huber, "I wouldn't know about that. But if the lady thinks she's going to use force while we're in Midway—"

He turned his head toward her again and patted the receiver of his tribarrel.

"—then she'll have another think coming. Because force is something I do know about."

"*Amen to that, El-Tee,*" said Frenchie Deseau. He didn't raise his voice on the intercom, but his words had the timbre of feeding time in the lion house.

It was four hours to dawn; the sky was a hazy overcast through which only the brightest stars winked. The car's vibration and buffeting wind of passage—seventy kph, a little more or a little less—drew the strength out of the troopers who'd been subjected to it for the past half day.

Huber sat cross-legged beside the left gun, watching the shimmering holographic display. He was too low to look out of the fighting compartment from here, but the range of inputs from *Fencing Master*'s sensors should provide more warning that than his eyes could even during daylight.

Body heat, CO_2 exhalations, and even the bioelectrical field which every living creature created were grist for the sensors to process. They scanned the gullied slopes a full three kilometers ahead, noting small animals sleeping in burrows and the scaly, warm-blooded night-flyers of Plattner's World which curvetted in the skies above.

Tranter was sleeping—was curled up, anyway—under the right wing gun on a layer of ammo boxes. Orichos squatted behind him with her back to the armor, looking as miserable as a drenched kitten. Learoyd had just taken over the driving chores from Deseau, awake but barely as he hunched over the forward tribarrel. Huber didn't worry about how the sergeant'd react to an alarm—Deseau was enough of a veteran and a warrior both to lay fire on a target in a sound sleep—but he certainly wasn't going to *raise* the alarm.

That would be Arne Huber's job. As platoon leader he wasn't taking a turn driving, but neither did he catch catnaps like the rest of the crew between stints in the driver's compartment. *Fencing Master* was the combat car in White Section during this leg, so Huber had the sensor suite on high sensitivity.

Task Force Sangrela was running the part of the route which Solace forces might have been able to reach for an ambush. Central hadn't warned of enemy movement, but there could've been troops already in place in the region. Technically they were still within Solace territory, not that anybody was likely to stand on a technicality during wartime.

"*Bloody fuckin' hell,*" Sergeant Deseau growled over the intercom. He clung to the grips of his tribarrel as though he'd have fallen without them to hold onto . . . which he might well have done. High-speed driving over rough terrain at night was a ten-tenths activity, many times worse than the grueling business of surviving the ride in the fighting compartment. "*I wish somebody'd just shoot at us for a break from this bloody grind.*"

"There's nobody around to shoot, Frenchie," Huber said; and as he spoke, he saw he was wrong.

Keying the emergency channel with the manual controller he'd been using to switch between sensor modes, Huber said, "White Six to Sierra, we've got locals waiting for us ahead. It's six-three, repeat six-three—" the display threw up the numbers in the corner; he sure wasn't going to have counted the blips overlaying the terrain map that fast "—personnel, no equipment signatures. Looks like dispersed infantry with personal weapons only."

A company of infantry with small arms would be plenty to wipe out White Section if they'd driven straight into the ambush. Mind, knowing about the ambush didn't mean there was no risk remaining, especially to the scouts on point.

"Sierra, this is Sierra Six," Captain Sangrela snapped. His voice sounded sleep-strangled, but he'd responded instantly to the alert. *"Throttle back to twenty, repeat two-zero, kay-pee-aitch. Charlie Four-six—"* The sergeant commanding the infantry of White Section *"—take your team ahead while they're listening to the cars and see if you can get a sight of what we're dealing with. Six out."*

Deseau, now wakeful as a stooping hawk, stretched his right leg backwards without looking. He kicked Tranter hard on the buttocks, bringing him out of the fetal doze as the alarm call had failed to do.

Swaying, drunk with fatigue, Tranter took his place behind the right gun. He didn't look confident there.

"Charlie Four-six," responded a female voice without a lot of obvious enthusiasm. On Huber's display, the four beads of the skimmer-mounted fire team curved to the right, up the slope the column was paralleling. *"Roger."*

Instead of throttling back when Sangrela ordered them to cut speed, Learoyd adjusted his nacelles toward the vertical. The fans' sonic signature remained the same, but the blades were spending most of their effort in lifting *Fencing Master*'s skirts off the ground instead of driving her forward. The car slowed without informing the listening enemy of the change.

Huber rose to his feet and gripped the tribarrel. The task force commander had taken operational control of White Section, so Huber's primary task was to lay fire on any hostiles who showed themselves in his sector.

"Fox Three-one, come up to my starboard side," he ordered. Sergeant Tranter was a fine driver and a first-rate mechanic, but he may never have fired a tribarrel since his basic combat qualification course in recruit school. Huber wanted more than two guns on line if they were about to go into action against an infantry company.

"*Roger, Three-six,*" Sergeant Nagano responded. The display icon indicating his combat car disengaged from the front of the main body and began to close the kilometer gap separating it from *Fencing Master.*

Captain Sangrela must have seen *Foghorn* move as well as overhearing Huber's order on the command channel; he chose to say nothing. Sensibly, he was leaving the immediate tactical disposition to the man on the ground.

Mauricia Orichos stood erect, her back against the rear coaming of the fighting compartment. She didn't ask questions when the troopers around her obviously needed to focus on other things, but she looked about her alertly, like a grackle in a grain field.

Huber noticed that she didn't draw the pistol from her belt holster. To Orichos' mind it was an insignia of rank, not a weapon.

Huber switched his faceshield to thermal imaging. It wouldn't give him as good a general picture of his surroundings, but it was better for targeting at night than light amplification would be. He couldn't see the cold light of the holographic display, so he projected the data as a thirty percent mask over the faceshield's ghostly infrared landscape.

The dots representing the mounted infantrymen approached the upper end of a ravine in which the combat car's sensors saw more than a dozen hostiles waiting under cover. From their angle, the four Slammers would be able to rake the gully and turn it into an abattoir. The enemy gave no indication of being aware of the troopers.

When *Fencing Master* slowed, the dust her fans had been raising caught up with her. Yellow-gray grit swirled down the intake gratings on top of the plenum chamber and settled over the troops in the fighting compartment; the back of Huber's neck tickled.

He felt taut. He wasn't nervous, but he was trying to spread his mind to cover everything around him. The task was beyond human ability, as part of Arne Huber's soap-bubble thin consciousness was well aware.

The fire team leader started laughing over the command push. The sound was wholly unexpected—and because of that, more disconcerting than a burst of shots.

"Charlie Four-six, report!" Captain Sangrela snarled. He sounded angry enough to have slapped his subordinate if she'd been within arm's length. Huber wouldn't have blamed him. . . .

"Imagery coming, sir," the sergeant replied; suppressing her laughter, but only barely.

Huber raised his visor and used the Command and Control box to project the view from the sergeant's helmet where everybody in the car could see it. The hologram of a sheep stared quizzically at him. Behind the nearest animal stretched a hillside panorama of sheep turning their heads and a startled boy holding a long bamboo pole.

"Sierra Six to Sierra," Captain Sangrela said in a neutral tone. *"Resume previous order of march. Out."*

Fencing Master lurched as Learoyd adjusted his nacelles again. The bow skirts gouged a divot of the loose soil, but the car's forward motion blew it behind them.

"Blood and Martyrs!" said Sergeant Deseau. *"Curst if I'm not ready to blast a few a' them sheep just for the fright they give me!"*

"Save your ammo, Frenchie," Huber said. "I guess we'll have plenty of things to kill before this mission's over."

The sun was an hour above the horizon, Task Force Sangrela had been in the fringe forest for longer than that. *Fencing Master* was in the trail position, last of the ten vehicles. *Foghorn* was a hundred meters ahead where Huber could've caught glimpses of her iridium hull if he'd tried.

He didn't bother. His job was to check the sensor suite, oriented now to the rear, and that was more than enough to occupy the few brain cells still working in his numb mind.

Tranter was driving again; the ride was noticeably smoother than either of the troopers could've managed, even when they were fresh. Learoyd was curled beneath his tribarrel, asleep and apparently as comfortable as he'd have been back in barracks.

Because they were in the drag position in the column, Deseau wasn't at his forward-facing tribarrel. Instead he crouched in the corner behind Huber, cradling a 2-cm shoulder weapon in the crook of his arm. It fired the same round as the tribarrels, but it was self-loading instead of being fully automatic. A single 2-cm charge in the right place was enough to put paid to most targets.

Mauricia Orichos had sunk into herself, seated between Learoyd's head and Deseau across the rear of the fighting compartment. She didn't look any more animated than a lichen on a rock. Huber knew how she felt: the constant vibration reduced mind and body alike to jelly.

This run'd get over, or Arne Huber would die. Either'd be an acceptable change.

A red light pulsed at the upper left corner of the display. Fully alert, Huber straightened and locked his faceshield down. "Frenchie," he snapped. "Take over on the sensors!"

Huber cued the summons, turning his faceshield into a virtual conference room. He sat at a holographic plotting table with the other task force officers—Mitzi Trogon blinked into the net an instant after Huber did; Myers and Captain Sangrela were already there—and Colonel Hammer himself.

The imagery wavered. It was never fuzzy, but often it had a certain over-sharpness as the computer called up stock visuals when the transmitted data were insufficient.

To prevent jamming and possible corruption, Central was communicating with the task force in tight-beam transmissions bounced from cosmic ray ionization tracks. The Regiment's signals equipment used the most advanced processors and algorithms in the human universe to adjust for breaks and distortion. Even so, links to vehicles moving at speed beneath scattered vegetation were bound to be flawed.

"There's a battalion of the Wolverines on the way to block you," the Colonel said without preamble. "We operated alongside them once—Sangrela, you probably remember on Redwood?"

"Roger that," Sangrela said, rubbing his chin with the knuckles of his left fist. "Anti-tank specialists, aren't they?"

"Right, and they're good," Hammer agreed. The only time Huber'd seen the small, stocky man without his helmet, he'd been surprised that the sandy hair was thinning; nothing else about the Colonel's face and smooth, muscular movements hinted at age. "They're tasked to set up a hedge of gunpits across our route."

Imagery on the plotting table—a holographic representation of a holographic representation, indistinct but adequate for this moment—showed a terrain map. Red dots blinked across a ten-kilometer stretch to form a serrated line: a rank of interlocking strong points.

Hammer smiled grimly. "We couldn't have broken the Wolverines' encryption any more than they could break ours," he said. "But they passed the information to the Solace authorities, and that's a different matter."

The smile—and it'd never been one of enthusiastic joy—froze back into the previous hard lines. "Which doesn't solve our problem. Your problem in particular, since each of those positions is a 5-cm high intensity weapon with ten men for crew and close-in defense. They aren't mobile—the teams're being lifted in by air, two to a cargo hauler. The trucks have light armor but they won't dare come anywhere close to point of contact. I'm doing the briefing because Operations is looking for alternative routes so you can skirt them. Shooting your way through would take too long and cost too much."

"Sir?" said Huber. His mind was working on a glacially smooth surface divorced from the vibration he still felt through his separated body. "They're still en route, aren't they?"

"Roger," the Colonel said, his eyes pinning Huber like a pair of calipers. He had a presence, even in virtual reality, far beyond what his small form should've projected.

"If I put one or two of my cars on high ground, the hostiles'll have to land short of where they plan to set up," Huber said. "We can hold 'em down until the rest of Sierra's clear, then catch up."

Without poring over a terrain map Huber couldn't have determined where to site his cars, and even then there were plenty of people better at that sort of thing than he was. The principle of it, though, and the certainty that there was a way to do it—that he had. His tribarrels would be effective against thin-skinned aircars at twenty klicks or even greater range. The hostiles wouldn't dare try to bull through the combat cars.

What the Wolverines *would* do, almost certainly, was surround the detached cars and eliminate them in default of the bigger catch they'd hoped to make. They'd be willing to accept the detachment's surrender, but Huber figured he'd try to break out. He could hope that at least one of the two cars—he had to use two, he couldn't be sure of driving the hostiles to the ground with only one—would get clear.

A 5-cm high-intensity round could penetrate even a tank's frontal armor. A hit on a combat car would vaporize the front half of the vehicle.

"No!" said Mitzi Trogon unexpectedly. "Huber's got a good idea, but we don't want to send his little fellows to do the job. Sir, find a firing position for my panzers and screw this business of scaring the hostiles to ground. I'll blow 'em to hell 'n gone before they know they've been targeted!"

"By the *Lord*," Colonel Hammer said in a tone of rasping delight. "Roger that! Go back to your duties, troopers. I'll be back with you as soon as I've brought Operations up to speed."

The virtual conference room vanished so suddenly that Huber jumped with the shock. The change made him feel as though he'd dropped into ice water instead of just returning to the world in which his body rode a combat car toward a powerful enemy.

"*What's the word, El-Tee?*" Deseau said, his voice sharp. He sat cross-legged at Huber's feet with his 2-cm weapon upright, its butt on his left knee. His eyes were on the sensor display.

"Fox Three, this is Fox Three-six," Huber said, cueing the platoon push instead of answering Frenchie on the intercom channel. "There's an anti-tank battalion headed out to block us. They probably figure to hold us while Solace command comes up with a way to do a more permanent job. Lieutenant Trogon and Central between 'em are planning to put the hostiles in touch with some 20-cm bolts before they get anywhere close to the rest of us. Hold what you got for now, and keep your fingers crossed. Out."

"*Is there going to be a battle, then, Lieutenant?*" a voice asked. Gears slipped a moment before meshing in Huber's mind. Captain Orichos had spoken; she was standing upright with her eyes on him, her faceshield raised. Orichos looked calm but alert. Vibrant as her face now was, she seemed brightly attractive instead of the haggard, aged derelict she'd looked before the alarm.

Learoyd stood at his tribarrel, scanning the scattered forest to starboard. None of the trees were more than wrist-thick, though the tufts of flowers at the tips of some branches showed they were adults. The leading vehicles, the tanks and especially the broad-beamed recovery vehicles, had to break a path where the stunted forest was densest.

Closer to the coast where the soil and rainfall were better, the overarching canopy would keep the understory clear. The task force'd have to skirt the trees there, however; not even a tank could smash down a meter-thick trunk without damaging itself in the process. . . .

"Not a battle, no," Huber said over the intercom. "If things work out, the hostiles won't get anywhere near us. If things don't, we'll still go around them rather than shooting our way through. That may mean worse problems down the road, but we'll deal with that when it happens."

As Huber spoke, he cued his AI to project a terrain and status map in a seventy percent mask across the upper left quadrant of his faceshield. His helmet with all Central's resources on tap could provide him with whatever information he might need. What electronics *couldn't* do was to stop time while he tried to absorb all that maybe-necessary information.

In a crisis, making no decision is the worst possible decision. A shrunken map that he could see through to shoot if he had to was a better choice than trying to know everything.

"Is it gonna work, El-Tee?" Deseau asked, still watching the sensor display. He cocked his head to the left so that he could scratch his neck with his right little finger.

Instead of saying, "Who the fuck knows?" which a sudden rush of fatigue brought to his mind, Huber treated the question as a classroom exercise at the Academy.

"Yeah," he said, "I think it maybe will, Frenchie. The Wolverines, that's who's coming, they know what a big powergun can do as well as we do—but knowing it and *knowing* it, that's different. If Sierra just keeps rolling along, they're going to forget that a tank can hit 'em any time there's a line of sight between them and a main gun's bore. A surprise like that's likely to make the survivors sit tight and take stock for long enough that we can get by the place they planned to hold us."

"That's good," Deseau said. *"Because I saw what a battery of the Wolverines did to a government armored regiment on Redwood. Bugger me if I want to fight 'em if we can get by without it."*

"Sierra, this is Sierra Six," said Captain Sangrela, sounding hoarse but animated. *"Delta elements, execute the orders downloaded to you from Central. Remaining Sierra elements, hold to the march plan. We're not going to do anything to alert the other side. Estimated time to action is thirty-nine, that's three-niner, minutes. Six out."*

"Fox Three-six, roger," Huber said, his words merging with the responses of Sierra's other two platoon leaders.

He stretched his arms, over his head and then behind him, bending forward at the waist. It was going to feel good to get the clamshell off; it itched like an ant colony had taken up residence.

Always assuming he lived long enough to get to a place he didn't need body armor, of course. But he did assume that, soldiers always assumed that.

Arne Huber grinned behind his faceshield. And it was always true—until the day it wasn't true.

The task force had slowed again to switch assignments. *Fencing Master* was now at the head of the main body, *Foghorn* and a fire team of infantry who'd jumped their skimmers off the maintenance vehicle where they'd been resting were scouting a klick in the lead, and Sergeant Jellicoe's section trailed to the rear.

Huber smiled grimly behind the anonymity of his faceshield. "Resting" wasn't a good word to describe what the infantry was going through, jolting around in the back of a wrenchmobile. Though this was a hard ride for the troops in the armored vehicles, it was a lot worse for the infantry. But Via! every soul in the Slammers was a volunteer.

They were climbing a slope of harder rock than most of the surroundings—a spine of sandstone from which time had worn away the limestone overburden. The top was bald except for patches of wiry grass and a few saplings whose roots had found purchase in a crack. A fresh scar across the stone showed where *Foghorn* had dragged her skirts.

"*Sierra, thirty seconds to execute!*" snapped Captain Sangrela over the general push.

Huber rested his left hand on the receiver of his tribarrel and looked over his shoulder. Fifty meters behind *Fencing Master*, *Dinkybob*, a massive iridium tortoise, snorted up the slight rise. The tank's hatches were buttoned up; as Huber watched, the turret swung to starboard. The squat 20-cm main gun elevated very slightly.

Mauricia Orichos raised her faceshield to watch the tank. Huber reached over her shoulder and clicked the protection back over her eyes. "Not now!" he said sharply. "Aide—"

As Huber voice-cued his AI, he manually keyed the pad over Orichos' right ear to link her helmet to his.

"—import targeting from Delta Two-six."

With the final word, Huber viewed not his immediate surroundings but the sight picture from the gunnery screen of the huge tank just behind him. It was at high magnification, so high that it had the glassy smoothness of images heavily retouched by the computer to sharpen them.

Five waves of large aircars skimmed undulating, almost barren, terrain. There were four vehicles in the leading ranks and three in the final, all echeloned right. They'd just crossed a ridgeline and were nosing down to cross a shallow valley.

Dinkybob's sight pipper settled over the lead vehicle in the left file. Instead of being a solid orange ball, the reticle was crosshatched to indicate that the fire-control computer was auto-targeting just as it would do in air defense mode.

The cyan flash of the main gun stabbed across Huber's bare skin like a separate needle every millimeter. It would've been instantly blinding to anyone looking toward it without a faceshield's polarizing protection. The crash of heated air—louder than an equally close thunderbolt—shook *Fencing Master*. Deseau, jounced from his squat, sprawled across Huber's feet.

The center of the targeted aircar erupted in blue flame. The bow and a fragment of the stern tumbled out of the sky, spilling such of the contents as hadn't been carbonized by the blast.

Dinkybob continued to fire, ripping the formation as

quickly as her gun mechanism could cycle fresh loads into the chamber. Trogon was burning out her barrel by shooting without giving the bore time to cool between rounds. For the people in *Fencing Master*'s fighting compartment, the volley was like being whipped by a scorpion's tail.

For the Wolverines at the other end, it was a brief glimpse of Hell.

A tank hit at that range—eighty-one kilometers distant— might have shrugged off the bolt with damage only to its external sensors and its running gear. It was impossible for a vehicle that had to fly with a heavy cargo the way the Wolverines' trucks did to be armored like a tank. Each bolt scattered its target in a fireball of its own burning structure.

Dinkybob was nearing the edge of the bald patch, but *Doomsayer* was immediately behind. For an instant both 20-cm guns fired in tight syncopation; then *Fencing Master* drove into heavy forest, *Dinkybob* passed out of its targeting window, and even *Doomsayer*'s main gun ceased firing. Huber's heartbeat throbbed in the silence.

The summons wobbled at the corner of Huber's faceshield. He cued it, dropping into the virtual conference room again.

Colonel Hammer looked around the circle of Sierra officers. "That's fourteen out of nineteen trucks destroyed," he said, "and two of the others grounded hard enough to break as best we can tell by satellite."

Hammer grinned like a shark. "Task accomplished, troopers. Complete the rest of the mission the same way and there'll be a lot of promotions out of this business. Dismissed!"

Arne Huber swayed in the rumbling fighting compartment of his combat car, thinking about what the Colonel had just said. Promotion—maybe.

But if they didn't complete the mission, very probably death. Well, the Slammers were all volunteers. . . .

The muzzle of *Dinkybob*'s main gun had cooled from white to a red so deep it was mostly a shimmer in the air around the hot metal. Mitzi's turret hatch was open, dribbling a trail of gray haze. A plastic matrix held the copper atoms in alignment for release as plasma down the powergun's bore; the smoke was the last of the breakdown products from the recent shooting.

An alert wobbled on the upper right corner of Huber's faceshield. He crooked his left little finger, one of six ways he could cue the icon. It was a download-only channel, information from Central for Sierra Six. Huber and the other task force officers were brought into the circuit to listen but not to comment.

"Sierra, this is Operations Three-four-one," said the voice from somewhere back in Base Alpha. *"Solace command is pissed about what you did to the Wolverines. They've ordered a fire mission by all batteries that can range you. You'll have to take care of your own air defense. Any questions? Over."*

Though voice-only, the increasingly thick foliage overhead attenuated the transmission to sexlessness. On this side of the ridge, the task force was descending into healthy coastal forest.

"What do you mean 'all batteries'?" Captain Sangrela asked. He sounded more irritable than concerned. *"Is this a real problem? Over."*

"Negative on a real problem," Central replied calmly. It was easy to be calm in Base Alpha, of course. *"There's two, maybe three off-planet batteries with rocket howitzers and carrier shells. We'll get you time and vector data as soon as they fire, but you'll have plenty of room to pop them before the carriers separate. Besides that, the Solace Militia has thirty or forty conventional tubes that can range you with rocket assisted rounds, but they won't have any payload to speak of after what the booster rocket requires. I repeat, you'll have full data soonest. Over"*

"Roger, Sierra out," Sangrela said. *"Break, Fox Three-six—"*

The signal now was coming through the task force command channel.

"—that puts it on your cars. Is there going to be any problem? Over."

"No problem, Six," Huber said curtly. "Just give me a minute to plan. Out."

He raised his faceshield and brought up a terrain display through the Command and Control box. On cue the AI highlighted the locations on or near Sierra's forward track which provided a line of sight toward the arc of territory where the hostile guns might be sited.

The display used a violet overlay to mark ranges of thirty

klicks and above; the hue moved down the spectrum as the range closed. Points from which a tribarrel could reach out five kilometers—as close as Huber was willing to let the sophisticated carrier shells get—were green.

A single carrier shell held a load of between three and several scores of bomblets, each with its own target-seeking head. When the carrier round opened to release them, the difficulties of defense went up by an order of magnitude.

Sergeant Tranter had traded jobs with Deseau. He turned from the forward tribarrel and asked, *"Whatcha got, El-Tee?"*

"Watch your sector!" Huber snapped in a blaze of frustration.

He'd apologize later. Tranter was a good driver and a great man to have on your team, but he was a technician and not—till this run—a combat crewman. He didn't know by reflex that Huber was busy with something that likely meant all their lives if he did it wrong. Had Tranter realized that, he'd have kept his mouth shut.

The display showed what Huber expected but didn't like to see: there were very few places along Sierra's planned route that would let the tribarrels range out ten klicks, and even those were points. The combat cars wouldn't be able to protect the column on the fly. They'd have to set up on the few patches where the ground was higher and relatively clear of vegetation.

Huber straightened. Learoyd scanned the car's starboard flank with the bored certainty of a machine; Sergeant Tranter was as rigid as a statue at the forward gun—*Via! I didn't mean to bite his head off*—and Captain Orichos was trying to watch all directions like a bird who's heard a cat she can't see.

"Sierra, this is Fox Three-six," Huber said. "When Central gives us an alert, the C and C box'll choose the best overwatch position and direct the nearest car to it. The rest of Sierra'll bypass that car, which'll leapfrog forward when it comes out of air defense mode. It may be that there'll be more than one car at a time out of the column. Three-six out."

There was a series of Rogers from the other officers. Huber hadn't bothered to run the plan by Sierra Six before delivering it to the whole unit. Sangrela'd tasked him with the solution of the problem, and it was something that an infantry officer didn't have much experience with anyway.

"What happens if the bad guys're waiting out in the woods, El-Tee?" Deseau asked over the intercom from the driver's compartment. He had the hatch open so that he could drive with his head out in the breeze. *"With the guns locked on air defense, a lone car's pretty much dead meat, right?"*

"The same thing that happens if you fall out a window drunk, Frenchie," Huber said with a quiver of irritation. Did Deseau think that hadn't occurred to him? But there wasn't any choice. With only four cars, he couldn't detach a second unit to guard the one on air defense. "Either you get up and go on, or you don't."

"Yeah, that's about what I figured," Deseau said. He sighed. *"You don't suppose me 'n Tranter could trade off again, do you?"*

"Negative," said Huber. "We've got to keep moving."

He too would like to have Frenchie in the fighting compartment, watching their surroundings with his shoulder weapon while the gunnery computer aimed the tribarrels skyward. Huber'd like a lot of things, but he was a veteran. He'd make do with what he had.

The alert from Central overrode F-3's helmet AIs, filling ninety percent of each faceshield with fire control data and relegating previous tasks to a box in the center. Huber flicked his helmet back to Sierra status in a thirty percent mask over the forest around him and ordered, "Fox Three-three, execute."

Not that Sergeant Jellicoe needed his okay. Her car, *Floosie*, had already steered to the right of the column's track and was pulling up a rise. *Flame Farter* would be alone in the drag position until *Floosie* rejoined, and *Floosie* would be very much alone.

"A Rangemaster battery's sent us a salvo of 200-mm shells," Huber explained over the intercom. "The battery's sited at one-thirty degrees from us, so Jellicoe's breaking out of line for a moment to take care of the incoming. The Rangemasters're a good enough outfit, but there's next to no chance that anything'll get past *Floosie*."

He was speaking mostly for Orichos' benefit; *Fencing Master*'s crew probably understood the situation as well as their lieutenant did. Well, Deseau and Tranter understood; Learoyd understood the little he needed to understand.

Mauricia Orichos nodded appreciatively, then quirked Huber a smile. *"It's like being a baby again,"* she said. *"I know there's a lot going on, but I don't understand any of it."*

Her smile grew marginally harder; she no longer looked haggard. She added, *"We'll be back in my element soon."*

Huber switched his helmet to remote, importing fire control imagery from *Floosie*. As an afterthought, he restored the link to Orichos' helmet also.

The display was blank until Huber stuttered up three orders of magnitude. At such high gain there was a tiny quiver that even the Slammers' electronics couldn't fully damp.

The shell, twenty centimeters in diameter and almost two meters long, was a blurred dash in the four-bar reticle to which Jellicoe had set her sights. The image jumped minusculely as a tribarrel's recoil jiggled the platform. Several cyan dots, vivid even at that range, intersected the shell.

The target ruptured in a red flash and a puff of dirty black smoke. Two more shells exploded into black rags in the sky around it; a fourth followed an instant later as one of the car's tribarrels made a double. Bomblets from the last shell detonated around the initial burst in a white sparkle.

Huber thought he heard the distance-delayed thumping of *Floosie*'s guns, but he was probably wrong. Loud though they were up close, the sound of 2-cm discharges several klicks away would've been lost in *Fencing Master*'s intake roar. As for the shellbursts, they wouldn't have been visible to unaided eyes even if the column had a clear view of the sky to the southeast.

Huber cleared his and Orichos' faceshield. "They'll keep on firing for a while," he said, speaking through the intercom but keeping eye contact with the local, the only person in the car who'd be interested. "The thing is, cargo shells're expensive to make and they have to be brought in from off-planet. If Solace command wants to waste them like this, they can be our guests. There could be a time the tribarrels'd have their usual work to do, and we wouldn't want to worry then about firecracker rounds going off overhead."

"*Fox Three-three rejoining column,*" Jellicoe said in a tone of mild satisfaction. Sure it was shooting fish in a barrel; and true, neither she nor her crew had touched their triggers while the gunnery computer took care of business . . . but it was still a nice bag of fish. "*Out.*"

"*Three indig batteries have opened fire,*" Central announced. "*Seventeen tubes. None of the rounds are going to come close enough to worry about, so proceed on course as planned. Over.*"

Tranter straightened, stretched, and then turned enough to meet Huber's eyes. He ventured a weak grin; Huber clasped Tranter's arm, closing the file on their previous short exchange.

From the driver's compartment Deseau called, "*Hey El-Tee? See if you can find us something t' shoot at, will you? I don't want my tribarrel growing shut like an old maid's cunt.*"

He laughed.

Before Huber could speak, Central broke in with, "*Six rounds incoming from vector oh-nine-three. Fox Three-six respond. Over.*"

A terrain display appeared on the upper left quadrant of his faceshield with a short, crooked red line reaching left toward the spot Central had picked for *Fencing Master*'s firing position.

"Roger, Central," Huber said, swaying as Deseau pulled into a ravine. It was filled with feathery bushes that crumpled beneath *Fencing Master*'s bow skirts. The car rocked violently on the rough climb.

"*Well, it's a start,*" said Frenchie. He kept his voice bright, but Huber could hear the strain; this wasn't easy driving, not for anybody. "*But you know, it's been a bitch of a run. I'm looking forward to getting back behind my gun where I can maybe kill some of the bastards who put us through it.*"

Deseau laughed. Huber didn't join him, but he noticed that Captain Orichos wore a broad, grim smile.

"*Sierra, we got buildings up here!*" called an unfamiliar voice. Huber's AI slugged the speaker as one of the scouting infantry. "*By the Lord, we do! There's more of 'em! We finally made it!*"

"*Ermanez, get off the push!*" Captain Sangrela snapped. They were all punchy, fatigued in mind and body alike. "*White Section, hold in place. Blue Section, close up as soon as you can without running any civilians down. These're friendlies, remember! Six out.*"

"Six, this is Fox Three-six," Huber said. He twisted and leaned sideways to look off the stern of the car, past Captain Orichos. As he expected, the commander's jeep was on its way forward. The light vehicle wobbled furiously in the turbulent air spurting beneath the skirts of the wrenchmobiles and tanks it was passing. "I'm moving into the lead in place of Sergeant Nagano. All right? Over."

"*Roger, Three-six,*" Sangrela said. Huber watched the jeep lift airborne and plop down again hard enough to pogo on its flexible skirts. The message paused for a grunt. Sangrela went on, "*Three-six, I'm dismounting all the infantry. I'm putting two squads up front with you for outriders. Out.*"

"Fox Three-one," Huber said, cueing *Foghorn* ahead of him with the scouts, "halt at a wide spot and let me in ahead of you. Three-six out."

He could see *Foghorn*. For nearly eight hundred kilometers the column had been picking its way through trees. Suddenly they'd exited the forest onto a boulevard broad enough that even the wide recovery vehicles could've driven down it two abreast. The buildings to either side were three and four story wood-framed structures, but they had much wider street frontage than those of the United Cities. In the UC, Huber'd had the feeling he was standing in a field of towers rather than houses.

A few pedestrians walked between buildings and a scattering of high-wheeled jitneys bounced and wavered along the street. There was no other traffic. Despite its width the road wasn't surfaced. At the moment it was rutted and dusty, but a rainstorm would turn it into a sea of mud.

Captain Orichos took a hand-held communicator from a belt pouch, stuck a throat mike against her larynx—it adhered to the skin of her neck, but it hadn't clung to her fingers— and lifted the commo helmet enough to slip earphones under. As she entered codes on the handset, her eyes remained on the road ahead.

The scouts waited as ordered, the four infantrymen beside

their skimmers to the left of *Foghorn*. They looked ragged and filthy—Huber glanced down at himself, his jacket sleeves a rusty color from the road grime, and grinned wearily— but they held their weapons with the easy care of veterans ready for whatever happened next.

Tranter throttled back and adjusted his nacelles to slow gently to a halt. He steered to bring *Fencing Master* up on *Foghorn's* starboard side without fishtailing or dragging a jolting dust storm with the skirts.

The thought made Huber look over his shoulder. He trusted Sergeant Tranter to be able to drive safely, no matter how tired. The tank immediately behind them weighed 170 tonnes and its driver had probably had less rest than the car crewmen. Some of the infantry could drive and had been spelling the two-man crews of the tanks, but there was still a real chance that whoever was at *Dinkybob's* control yoke wouldn't notice that the vehicles ahead were stopped.

Orichos lowered her communicator and looked at Huber. *"You'll be camping on the grounds of the Assembly Building straight ahead,"* she said over the intercom. *"I informed my superiors that you were on the way. We can proceed immediately."*

Can we indeed? Huber thought. He didn't let the irritation reach his face; it'd been a hard run for all of them. Instead of responding to Orichos, he said, "Sierra Six, this is Fox Three-six. The indig officer riding with me says that that we can go straight on in to the Assembly Building and set up around it. Do you have any direction for me? Over."

The jeep pulled alongside *Fencing Master.* Captain Sangrela sat braced in the passenger seat, his holographic display a shimmer before him as he looked up at Huber. *"Via, yes!"* he snarled. *"Let's get to where we're going so we can bloody dismount! Move out, Three-six. Sierra Six out."*

Dinkybob had managed to slow to a halt. So did the vehicles following, though as Huber looked back he noticed one of the later tanks swing wide to the left when its driver awoke to the fact that he was in danger of overrunning whoever was stopped ahead of him.

"Roger, Six," Huber said, keeping his tone even. "Three-six out. Break. Tranter, start on up the street. Keep it at twenty kph and—"

"And don't run over any locals," he'd started to say, but there wasn't any risk of that. The words would've done nothing but shown his own ill-temper.

"—and maybe we'll have a chance to rest pretty quick."

Huber's muscles were so wobbly that he wasn't sure he'd be able to walk any distance when he got down from the combat car. The clamshell had chafed him over the shoulders, his hip bones, and at several points on his rib cage. He itched everywhere, especially the skin of his hands and throat; they'd been exposed to the ozone, cartridge gases, and iridium vaporized from the gunbores when the tribarrels raked incoming shells from the sky.

Fencing Master lifted and started forward, building speed to an easy lope. The roadway was smooth, a welcome relief from the slopes and outcrops they'd been navigating for the last long while. Dust billowed from beneath the skirts, a vast gulp initially but settling into a wake that rolled out to either side.

Even before the recovery vehicles had halted, the infantrymen pitched off to port and starboard on their skimmers. The infantry platoon, C-1, had left the jeep-mounted tribarrels of its Heavy Weapons Squad behind in Base Alpha. The gun jeeps weren't needed for the original mission, the capture of Northern Star Farm, because there the infantry was to operate in close conjunction with combat cars in open country. The soft-skinned jeeps would be easy targets for an enemy and wouldn't add appreciably to the firepower of the task force.

Here in a city, gun jeeps would look a lot more useful that the pair of automatic mortars Sierra *did* have along; but they'd make do. They always did.

More aircars appeared, circling above the column instead of buzzing from place to place across the sky. The Slammers' sudden appearance had taken the city by surprise, but now the citizens were reacting like wasps around an opened hive.

Deseau looked up and muttered a curse. His hand tightened on his tribarrel's grip, raising the muzzles minutely before Huber touched his arm.

Huber leaned close and said, "They're friendly, Frenchie."

"Says you!" Deseau snarled, but he lowered the big gun again.

Huber coughed. "I'm surprised the streets here are so wide, Captain Orichos," he said, looking at the local officer again. With *Fencing Master* idling along like this he could've spoken to her also without using the intercom, but he didn't see any reason to. "In the United Cities, even the boulevards twist around under the trees."

"*This street—the Axis—is wide,*" Orichos explained. "*We don't have a separate landing ground here at Midway. The warehouses where the rangers sell their Moss are on both sides—*"

She gestured.

"*—here, so the dirigibles from Solace set down in front of the establishment they're trading with. They unload goods, mostly from the spaceport, of course—then they lift off again with the bales of Moss.*"

Now that Orichos had told him the adjacent buildings were warehouses, Huber could see the outside elevators on each one and the doors at each story wide enough to take corrugated steel shipping containers which would then be shifted within by an overhead suspension system. The windows were narrow, providing light and ventilation, but with no concern for the view out them.

Orichos' face blanked. She turned her head away from Huber and began talking into her communicator again.

Huber locked his faceshield down and concentrated on the terrain to the left front of his vehicle. That was the area his tribarrel'd be responsible for if the task force was suddenly ambushed . . . which they wouldn't be, of course, but his irritation with the local officer cooled when he thought about a hose of cyan bolts lashing the buildings *Fencing Master* slid past.

Chances were Orichos would inform him of whatever crisis had called her attention away. Besides, it was a near certainty that the signals equipment in Sangrela's jeep could break whatever encryption system the Point Gendarmery was using if Huber really thought the task force needed to know. . . .

Which he didn't. He was just in a bad mood from the long run.

Captain Orichos lowered the communicator and said, "*Lieutenant Huber, there's a problem. Grayle's gotten word of your arrival. She's ordered her supporters to gather in the Axis in front of the Freedom Party offices. There's already hundreds of them there, blocking the street. There may be thousands by the time we arrive."*

Even if there'd been no previous contact between Solace and the Freedom Party, somebody there had certainly given Grayle a heads-up when they realized where Task Force Sangrela was bound. Grayle probably wasn't pro-Solace, but they were both opposed to the Point's present government.

At the word "problem," Huber had cut Sierra Six into the intercom channel. Orichos looked startled when Sangrela rather than Huber replied, *"Are they armed, then? Do we have to shoot our way through? Six over."*

"Via, no!" Orichos cried in horror. *"A bloodbath would do exactly what Grayle hopes! Everybody'd turn against you mercenaries and the government! These are just people standing in the street!"*

In the distance ahead of *Fencing Master* stood the stone Assembly Building on a terraced hillside. A quick flash of Huber's map display showed him that the Axis circled the building and continued its broad way northward.

Huber's eyes narrowed. The map also emphasized that Midway was a large city compared to most of the places the Slammers operated. A company-sized task force would drown in a place this big if it turned hostile. And gunning down a few hundred citizens in the street would be a good way to make the hundreds of *thousands* of survivors hostile. . . .

"Well, bloody Hell, woman!" Captain Sangrela said. His jeep had pulled alongside *Fencing Master* and he was glaring up at Orichos. *"If it's a job for the police, get your bloody police on it, will you? You don't expect us to idle here in the middle of the bloody street, do you? Or do you? Six over."*

"Captain Sangrela, I'm very sorry for the delay but we're working on it," Orichos said. *Fencing Master* continued to rumble on, twenty meters behind the screen of skimmer-mounted infantry. *"We didn't expect Grayle to react so quickly. Most of the crowd in the street are the Freedom Volunteers, the party's militia, and there's too many of them for the Gendarmery manpower we've got available at the moment. Over."*

She realizes she's on a net, not the car's intercom, and she's following proper commo protocol, Huber noticed with a grin.

"*Well, what use will waiting do, Captain?*" Sangrela demanded. "*Look, is there a back way around? Because if the idea was for the Regiment to make a show of force, having a bunch of yahoos stop us in our tracks is going to send a bloody wrong signal! What about us putting a few shots over their heads? Six over.*"

Huber touched Orichos' arm to silence her before she could answer. He said, "Six, this is Fox Three-six. Put me out front and the panzers right behind me. Get the infantry outa the way, back on the recovery vehicles'd be the best place— they can't do any good without shooting and that's what we're trying to avoid. Three-six over."

"*You can handle this, Three-six?*" Sangrela said. Captain Orichos was searching Huber's face, her expression blankly concerned. "*Because if you can, go with it. Six over.*"

"I've got a driver who can handle it, sir," Huber said. "Three-six out. Break—" cutting Captain Sangrela out of the circuit again "—Tranter, on a road surface like this, I'll bet my left nut you can spray enough rock and grit off the bow to clear us a path and still keep us moving forward. What d'ye say?"

"*I'd say you needn't worry about disappointing your girl-friend, El-Tee,*" Tranter replied cheerfully. He laughed. "*Just watch our dust!*"

The infantry ahead of *Fencing Master* turned and circled back, obeying Sangrela's command on the C-1 unit push. Lieutenant Myers was on one of the skimmers; he looked at Huber as he slid past. *Dinkybob* closed up so that the gap between the tank and *Fencing Master*'s rear skirt was only about five meters. That'd probably be safe when both vehicles were moving at a slow walk—but if something *did* go wrong, the tank'd send Huber's car cannoning forward like a billiard ball.

Huber could easily see the mob filling the street without raising his faceshield's magnification. He didn't want to do that: he needed all the peripheral vision he had and probably then some.

Aircars kept arriving at the back of the crowd, adding to

the numbers already present. Many were big vehicles marked in red with the logo of a broken chain, capable of carrying twenty passengers. It looked to Huber as though they were ferrying people from outlying locations and going back empty for more.

Sergeant Deseau must've thought the same thing, because he leaned back from his tribarrel and shouted, "Hey El-Tee? I bet I could scatter those jokers right fast if I popped a couple of trucks while they was overhead."

"That's a big negative, Sergeant," Huber said, hoping he sounded sufficiently disapproving. He'd been thinking the same thing himself, and Deseau probably knew him well enough to be sure of that.

Though that did raise another thought. The sky above Task Force Sangrela was full of aircars jockeying for position. So far as Huber could tell they were simply civilians who wanted to watch what was going on, but some might be members of Grayle's militia with guns or grenades.

Besides, there was a fair chance that cars might collide and crash down on the column. The trees bordering the Axis constrained the aerial spectators into a relatively narrow channel, so they kept dropping lower to get a good view.

"Captain Orichos," Huber said. "I understand you can't deal with the mob on the ground, but can't you Gendarmes do something about the idiots buzzing around overhead? ASAP."

Orichos gave him a hard look, then nodded and spoke into her communicator. A pair of gun-metal gray aircars with blue triangles bow and stern had been paralleling the column at the fringes of the civilian vehicles. They immediately began bellowing through loudspeakers. The words were unintelligible over the intake roar of *Fencing Master*'s fans, but the aircars overhead edged away reluctantly.

Apparently to speed the process, a Gendarme aimed his electromagnetic carbine skyward and fired a burst. The civilian cars dived away in a panic.

That was bad enough, though the actual collisions were minor and didn't knock anybody out of the air. It would've been much worse if Huber hadn't caught Deseau as the sergeant reacted to *shots fired* in the fashion any bloody fool should've expected, by swinging his tribarrel onto the threat.

"Captain Orichos?" Huber said. "Shooting is a really bad idea. No matter who's doing it. All right?"

Orichos nodded with a guarded expression; she didn't like the implied reprimand, but it was obviously well-founded. She snapped a further series of orders into the communicator.

Two men in jumpsuits like the one Orichos wore—hers was now gray/yellow/red from grit it'd picked up during the run—looked over the side of the aircar to the right of the column. Deseau gave them the finger. The face of the cop who'd fired the carbine went black with anger. Orichos shouted into her communicator and the police vehicle rose quickly to a hundred meters.

"Sorry," Orichos muttered over the intercom. Huber shrugged noncommittally.

Fencing Master's bow slope was well within half a klick of the mob. Looking forward, his left hand on the tribarrel's receiver and his right at his side instead of on the spade grip, Deseau said, *"Some a' them got guns, El-Tee. What do we do if they start shooting? Just take it?"*

"Crew," Huber said, "Nobody shoots till I do. Break. Six, this is Fox Three-six. If we start taking serious fire, my people aren't going to stand here and be targets. Are we clear on that? Over."

"Roger Three-six," Sangrela said. *"Delta Two-six—"* Lieutenant Trogon *"—if Fox Three-six opens fire, put a couple main gun rounds at his point of aim. Break. Sierra, Fox Three-six and Delta Two-six will do all the shooting till I tell you otherwise. Six out."*

"Roger, Three-six out," Huber said. He was keyed up and felt as though he should be standing on the balls of his feet. Myers and Mitzi Trogon responded curtly as well.

Dinkybob slid to the left of *Fencing Master*'s track. Trogon was buttoned up in the turret. She'd elevated the 20-cm main gun to forty-five degrees for safety when the column entered an inhabited area; now she lowered it in line with the mob ahead. A crust of iridium redeposited from the bore made the muzzle look grimy.

If *Dinkybob* fired from close behind, the side-scatter from the burned-out gun was going to be curst uncomfortable in *Fencing Master*'s fighting compartment. But then, it was going to be curst uncomfortable regardless if this turned into a firefight.

The mob watched the column come on. Tranter closed the driver's hatch. He'd been throttling back gradually, so by now *Fencing Master* was advancing no faster than a promenading couple. Huber and the troopers with him in the fighting compartment looked out through polarized faceshields as they aimed their forward-facing tribarrels. Normally the wing gunners'd be covering the flanks—and the good Lord knew, there might be snipers in the buildings, tall dwellings now instead of warehouses, to either side. The rest of the task force was going to have to deal with that threat, because *Fencing Master* had really immediate problems to her front.

Huber'd hoped the crowd'd scatter when the shouting civilians saw the huge vehicles coming at them, but they were holding steady. The front rank was of rough-looking men—almost all of them were men—with clubs. They didn't have uniforms, but each of them and many of those behind wore red sweatbands. Banners with the red logo on a black ground waved from several places in the midst of the group.

Huber's eyes narrowed. Those in front didn't have guns, but many of the ones standing at the back of the crowd carried short-barreled slugthrowers much like the Gendarmery's. You wouldn't often have call for a long-range weapon in the forests of Plattner's World, but at anything up to two hundred meters those carbines were as deadly as a powergun.

The trucks which'd been ferrying people in now landed in line across the Axis, forming a barrier behind the crowd. Grayle was doing everything she could to prevent her demonstration from melting away before the roaring bulk of the armored vehicles.

A good half of the mob was shouting and waving their fists in the air, often holding a club or a bludgeon. The other half seemed more scared than not, but they were in it now and knew there was no easy way out.

"*What d'ye guess, El-Tee?*" Deseau said. "*Maybe three thousand of 'em?*"

"Maybe more," Huber said. "Just stay calm and let Tranter do the work. Ready, Sarge?"

"*Roger that, sir,*" Sergeant Tranter said, brightly cheerful. "*Any time you say.*"

It'd been a worse run for Tranter than for the line troopers—they were used to the hammering, or at least to some degree of it. Now at last Tranter was in his element, moving a combat car in precise, minuscule increments. As a repair technician, he'd regularly shifted cars and tanks in crowded maintenance parks where the tolerances were much tighter than anything combat troops dealt with in the field.

"Execute, then!" Huber said.

Huber felt the fans speed up through the soles of his feet; *Fencing Master* shivered. The crowd was shouting in unison, "*Free-dom! Free-dom!*" Compared to the intake roar, the sound of so many voices was no more than bird cries against the boom of the surf.

A dozen meters from the crowd, Tranter tilted the nacelles vertical and brought the fans up to maximum output so that the car drifted to a quivering halt. *Dinkybob* continued sliding forward till its bow slope overlapped *Fencing Master*'s stern. If they'd been directly in line, there'd have been a collision.

While *Fencing Master* balanced in place, dust and grit billowed out all around beneath her lifted skirts. Some flew toward the crowd, forcing the thugs in the front rank to cover their faces or turn their heads away.

"Watch the guys in the back!" Huber ordered, gripping the tribarrel with his thumbs deliberately lifted clear of the butterfly trigger. "Watch for anybody aiming at us!"

With the skill of a ballerina, Tranter cocked the two bow nacelles forward at the same time as he angled the six other fans slightly to the rear. The blast from the bow nacelles dug like a firehose into the gravel roadway, then sprayed the spoil into the crowd with the energy required to float thirty tonnes of combat vehicle.

The crowd broke. Those in the direct blast could no more stand against it than they could've swum through an avalanche. Spun away, battered away—some of the gravel was the size of a clenched fist—frightened away; blind from the dust and deafened by the howling air, they drove against those behind them.

The rout was as sudden and certain as the collapse of

a house of cards. Tranter adjusted his throttles with the care of a chemist titrating a solution. The thugs at the front and the gunmen at the rear were no threat compared to the iridium sandstorm that ground forward, minutely but inexorably.

Dinkybob held station at *Fencing Master*'s left flank, her mass even more of a threat than the gape of her main gun's pitted bore. She and the tank echeloned to the right behind her, *Doomsayer*, were buttoned up. There was nothing human about any of them, not even the mirrored facelessness of the gunners behind the combat car's tribarrels.

When panic started the crowd running, it continued till there was nothing left but the sort of detritus a flood throws up at the edge of its channel: clothing, clubs, papers of all manner and fashions, whirling in the wind from beneath *Fencing Master*'s steel skirts. A few bodies lay in the street as well: people who'd been trampled, people who'd been squeezed breathless; probably a few who'd fainted.

Tranter cut his fan speed, adjusting the nacelles in parallel again to bring *Fencing Master* back into normal operation. They resumed forward movement at a walking pace.

Arne Huber relaxed for the first time in . . . well, he wasn't sure how long. He raised his faceshield and rubbed his eyes with the back of his hand.

"Good job, Tranter," he said. "Now, park us in the grounds of that building up there on the mound."

"*Roger, El-Tee*," the driver said. "*Ah, how about the landscaping, sir?*"

"*Fuck the landscaping!*" said Sergeant Deseau.

Huber looked over his shoulder at Captain Orichos. She stood with the communicator in her hand but she wasn't speaking into it. Huber grinned and said, "Frenchie's right, Tranter. The bushes can take their chances."

He took a deep breath and looked at the dust and debris in front of them. "The good Lord knows the rest of us just did," he added.

The second recovery vehicle backed carefully into position between *Fencing Master* and a tank, grunting and whining through her intake ducts. Her rear skirts pinched up turf which her fans fired forward out of the plenum chamber in a black spray. The driver shut down, and for the first time since Task Force Sangrela's arrival there was relative peace in the center of Midway.

"Can we stand down now, El-Tee?" Deseau asked, turning to face Huber. People in the street were staring up at the mercenaries while others looked down from circling aircars, but they were simply interested spectators. Some onlookers might have belonged to the mob that scattered half an hour earlier, but if so they'd thrown away their weapons and hidden their red headbands. Certainly they were no present threat.

"Fox, this is Fox Three-six," Huber said, making a general answer to Frenchie's personal question. "Stand down, troopers. One man in the fighting compartment, the rest on thirty second standby. I don't know how long we'll be halting here, but at least break out the shelter tarps. Three-six out."

"Learoyd, you've got first watch," Frenchie said. "In two hours I'll relieve you. Tranter, give me a hand with the tarp and the coolers."

Captain Orichos had vanished into the Assembly Building as soon as *Fencing Master* settled onto the terraced mound. To Huber's surprise, a stream of chauffeured aircars had begun to arrive while Task Force Sangrela was setting up a defensive position around the pillared stone building. The civilian vehicles landed in the street and disgorged one or two expensively dressed passengers apiece, then lifted away in a flurry of dust.

The new arrivals walked up the steps—three flights with landings between on the terraces—and entered the building. Some eyed the armored vehicles with obvious interest; others, just as obviously, averted their eyes as if from dung or a corpse.

Captain Sangrela had spaced his vehicles bows outward like spokes on a wheel. Because there were only ten vehicles, they had to back onto the uppermost terrace in order to be close enough for mutual support; even so there was a twenty-meter gap between the flank of one unit and the next. The infantry were using power augers to dig two-man pits above and behind the armored circle.

Huber unlatched his body armor to loosen it, but he didn't

strip it off quite yet. Tranter and Deseau stood behind *Fencing Master*, releasing the tie-downs that held gear to the bustle rack. Huber leaned out of the fighting compartment to steady a beer cooler with his hand till the troopers on the ground were ready to take the weight.

Trooper Learoyd raised his helmet and rubbed his scalp; he was in his early twenties but already nearly bald. "Hey El-Tee?" he said. "Are all them people behind us friendlies? Because if they're not . . . ?"

"I don't think they're going to shoot at us, Learoyd," Huber said. "I won't say I think they're friendly, though."

That was particularly true of the group now walking across the Axis toward where *Fencing Master* was grounded. There were three principals, a woman with two men flanking her at a half step behind to either side. Each wore a white blouse and kilt with a bright red sash and cummerbund. Before and behind that trio were squads of toughs with red sweatbands, some of those who'd been at the front and rear of the mob half an hour before. Now they weren't carrying weapons, at least openly.

They'd come from a walled compound across the Axis where it circled the Assembly Building. The outer walls were plasticized earth cast with a dye that Huber supposed was meant to be bright red. Because the soil was yellowish, the mixture had the bilious color of a sunburned Han.

There were two four-story buildings within—wood-sheathed and painted red—and two more domed roofs which the three-meter walls would've hidden from ground level. *Fencing Master* had a good view down into the compound, however.

Mauricia Orichos came out of the Assembly Building, pausing briefly to speak with a man entering. His cape of gossamer fabric shimmered repeatedly up through the spectrum on a three-minute cycle.

The conversation over, Orichos walked purposefully toward Captain Sangrela who was bent over the commo unit on the back of his jeep. His driver was inflating a two-man tent.

"El-Tee?" Learoyd said. "Is that the woman who's making all the trouble?"

He meant the head of the three dignitaries in white and

red, now climbing the steps. "Right," Huber said, a little surprised that Learoyd had volunteered what amounted to a political observation. "That's Melinda Riker Grayle."

Grayle moved with an athleticism that hadn't come through in the hologram of her haranguing the crowd. Those images must have been taken right here: Grayle speaking from the steps of the Assembly Building to a crowd larger than the one *Fencing Master* had just scattered.

"But I still shouldn't shoot her, that's right?" Learoyd said, his voice troubled.

"Blood and Martyrs!" Huber said. "Negative, don't shoot her, Learoyd!"

Grayle wasn't one of those who averted her eyes from the armored vehicles. She noticed Huber's attention and glared back at him like a bird of prey. Her hair was in short curls. Judging from Grayle's complexion she'd once been a redhead, but she'd let her hair go naturally gray.

She and her companions—including the escort—stalked through the tall doors of embossed bronze into the Assembly Building. Learoyd sighed and said, "Yeah, that's what I figured."

Huber looked at him hard. Nobody but Learoyd would've considered shooting the leader of the opposition dead in the middle of the city, with the whole country watching through video links. Nobody but simple-minded Herbert Learoyd; but you know, it might not have been such a bad idea after all. . . .

"*Fox Three-six to me ASAP!*" Captain Sangrela ordered. Huber glanced over. Beside Sangrela stood Orichos, wearing a gray beret in place of the commo helmet she'd left behind on *Fencing Master*. She looked very cool and alert: her hands were crossed behind her at the waist. "*Six out.*"

"No rest for the wicked," Huber murmured, but he couldn't say he was sorry for the summons. "Fox, this is Fox Three-six. Sergeant Jellicoe will take acting command of the platoon till I return. Three-six out."

Huber snugged the sling of his 2-cm weapon, then swung out of the fighting compartment. He balanced for a moment on the bulging plenum chamber before half jumping, half sliding to the ground. The landing was softer than he'd expected because his boots dug into the black loam of what had been a flowerbed.

"You gonna be all right, El-Tee?" Sergeant Tranter asked. Despite the hard run they'd just completed, Tranter managed to look as though he'd stepped off a recruiting poster.

"Sure he is!" said Deseau who'd by contrast be scruffy the day they buried him in an open coffin. Right now you might guess he'd been dragged behind *Fencing Master* instead of riding in her. "Hey, there's nobody around this place that the Slammers need to worry about, right?"

"I'll let you know, Frenchie," Huber said. He walked toward the captain wearing a grin, wry but genuine.

Now that Huber's world no longer quivered with the harmonics of the drive fans, he was coming alive again. He guessed he knew how a toad felt when the first rains of autumn allowed it to break out of the summer-baked clay of a water hole.

"Sir?" he said to Sangrela. Huber hadn't known the captain well before the operation began, but he'd been impressed by what he'd seen thus far. A lot of times infantry officers didn't have much feel for how to use armored vehicles. Officers from the vehicle companies probably didn't do any better with infantry, but that wasn't Huber's problem.

"Captain Orichos wants you with her inside there," Sangrela said, indicating the Assembly Building with a curt jerk of his head. He didn't look happy about the situation. "Our orders are to cooperate with the Point authorities, so that's what you're going to do."

"The Speaker's called an extraordinary meeting of the Assembly to deal with the crisis," Captain Orichos said, sounding conciliatory if not apologetic. "I'm to address them. I'd like you with me, Lieutenant, as a representative of Hammer's Regiment."

Me rather than Sangrela, Huber thought. "Sure," he said aloud. "Do I need to say anything?"

"No, Lieutenant," Orichos said. "Your presence really says all that's necessary. Your armed presence."

Well, that's clear enough, Huber thought. He said, "All right, I'm ready when you are."

Orichos turned, nodding him to follow. "When we get inside, the ushers will direct us to the gallery upstairs," she said. "Ignore them; we'll wait in the anteroom until Speaker Nestilrode recognizes me. When he does, you'll come with me to the podium."

Huber shrugged. Parliamentary procedure, especially on somebody else's planet, wasn't a matter of great concern to him. "Who all's going to be in there?" he said, gesturing left-handed to the approaching doorway. The stairway up from the street was limestone, but the building's plinth and the attached steps were of dense black granite.

"Most assemblymen will be present," Orichos said. "Many are afraid, but they've been warned that this is the government's only chance of safety and that they won't be allowed to compromise it. If necessary—"

She looked sidelong at Huber.

"—members of the Gendarmery would escort a sufficient number of assemblymen here to make up a quorum. Whether they wanted to come or not."

Huber grinned, then sobered again. It was easy—and satisfying—to mock cowardly politicians, but in fairness they weren't people who'd signed on for armed conflict. You could be brave enough in the ordinary sense and still not want to enter a building surrounded by tanks and professional killers.

"The only people in the gallery . . ." Orichos continued. "Will be the goons, the so-called Volunteers, who you saw enter with the Grayle and her Freedom Party colleagues. Those few are just bodyguards, but there'd have been hundreds packing the seats if it weren't for your arrival."

A porch of the same hard black stone as the plinth loomed above them. Just inside the doorway stood a man and a woman in embroidered tunics, presumably the ushers.

A mural on the wall of the semi-circular anteroom depicted an idealized Moss ranger on the right and an equally heroic female mechanic on the left. Stairs slanted upward from either side.

"We'll wait here," Orichos said curtly to the male usher. He and his colleague looked doubtful, but they didn't argue. Huber's big powergun drew their quick glances the way the view of a nude woman might have tempted a modest man, but they said nothing about the weapon.

Huber stood beside the jamb and looked through the inner

doorway. Save for the anteroom, the ground floor of the Assembly Building was given over to a single chamber paneled in carved wood. Desks in ranks curved around three sides, each row rising above the one before it. It didn't look to Huber as though half of the places were occupied, but presumably enough assemblymen for the purpose were present.

The entrance was on the fourth side. Facing the desks to the right of the doorway was a railed enclosure with seats for a dozen members; all but one of them were filled. To the left was a raised lectern at which an old man in a black robe was saying, "By virtue of the powers granted me as Speaker, I have called this extraordinary session. . . ."

Orichos leaned close to Huber. "The cabinet," she whispered, nodding toward the enclosure.

The ordinary assemblymen sitting in the arcs of desks were staring at Huber and Orichos instead of watching the Speaker. Even some of the cabinet members stole furtive glances over their shoulders, though they faced front quickly when they caught Huber's eye.

Melinda Grayle and her two companions were almost alone on the Speaker's side of the room. The men appeared ill at ease, but Grayle's expression was sneeringly dismissive as she eyed the doorway.

Huber couldn't see the gallery from where he stood; that meant it must be directly overhead. The Volunteers'd be staring at his back if he went to the podium with Orichos. Staring at, and maybe aiming . . .

Well, Huber hadn't joined the Slammers because he was looking for a risk-free life. He grinned; but he also latched his clamshell again.

The Speaker continued reading from a lighted screen set into the lectern before him. He stumbled frequently over the words. This may have been the first time he'd had occasion to invoke these emergency powers, and he was probably just as nervous as most of the assemblymen.

"I'd think some of the public would want to watch," Huber said into Captain Orichos' ear. "Is everybody in the Point afraid of his shadow?"

Orichos looked at him sharply. "Of course not!" she said. "The proceedings are broadcast to the whole country by satellite! The gallery only holds a few hundred people;

it'd be full normally, but by citizens indulging their whim rather than because they needed to be present to know what the Assembly was doing. Half the population lives in individual households scattered throughout the forest anyway."

Huber nodded, his eyes on the Assembly beyond. He hadn't meant to step on the woman's toes, but he should've known his comment would do just that. He must be nervous too.

"Therefore . . ." the Speaker said, his voice gaining new life as he reached the end of the set formula; the constitutions of most colonies had been drafted by settlers with little education but a fierce desire to make things "sound right" by using high-flown language. "Invoking the special powers granted the Speaker in the present emergency, I hereby call Captain Mauricia Orichos of the Gendarmery to address the Assembly."

Melinda Riker Grayle rose to her feet. "I protest!" she said. She filled the hall as effectively with her unamplified voice as the Speaker had moments before using a concealed public address system. "This is a business for the citizens of the Point, not for the self-serving bureaucracy which rigged the last—"

Speaker Nestilrode stabbed a control on the lectern with his bony index finger.

"—elec—" Grayle said. Her voice cut off abruptly; her lips continued to move. The Assembly Building had a *very* sophisticated audio system. The Speaker had clamped a sonic distorter around Grayle, not for privacy as it'd be used for in an office but to shut her up.

"The member from Bulstrode Borough is out of order," Nestilrode said with a touch of venom in his dry voice. "The chair recognizes Captain Orichos."

Orichos stepped forward purposefully. Huber followed at her heel like a well-trained dog. The patrol sling held his 2-cm weapon muzzle-forward. His hand was on the grip, though his index finger lay along the receiver instead of through the trigger guard.

His faceshield was down. For the moment he left it clear instead of polarizing the surface to those trying to look at him.

Orichos mounted the podium. The Speaker edged sideways to let her by, but there wasn't even possibly room for Huber wearing his body armor. He stood below the Gendarmery officer instead, surveying the Assembly.

"Honored Personages," Orichos said in a tone that combined dignity with considerable forcefulness. "As many of you know, my department is responsible for information about our foreign enemies and potential enemies. While pursuing sources in the Solace government, we came upon conclusive proof that Assemblyman Grayle of Bulstrode Borough takes the pay of Solace in exchange for sowing discord within the Point."

Grayle jumped to her feet, shouting silently. The older of her male colleagues rose also, but the younger man—a blond fellow in his thirties with a neat moustache and goatee—was noticeably slower to get up. His eyes flicked from Orichos to Grayle, as nervous when they rested on his own leader as when he looked at the Gendarmery officer.

"Based on this report," Orichos continued as though oblivious of the capering Freedom Party officials, "I have applied for and been granted a warrant by the Chief Justice of the High Court to search the premises of the Freedom Party in order to corroborate our information. Due to the delicacy of the situation, I'm informing the Assembly before taking action."

Grayle's older colleague was a rougher sort than the handsome blond on her other side. She extended an arm to keep him from climbing over his desk to reach the floor. Grayle's blue eyes never left Orichos and the Speaker on the podium.

She sat down again, gesturing her colleagues with her. Her face was red, but she stared at Orichos with sneering contempt, not anger. She touched a button in her desk; a spiral of coherent orange light appeared above her head.

Orichos nodded meaningfully to the Speaker. Nestilrode leaned forward, touched the muting switch, and said, "The chair recognizes the member from Bulstrode."

Still seated, Grayle said, "That's not just a lie but a bloody lie. As Captain Orichos knows well, my party is funded entirely by the contributions of the Moss rangers on whom the nation's economy is based. There are no documents in our party headquarters or anywhere else to support these lies!"

Grayle turned so that her gaze swept the hostile assemblymen to her left and behind her. Some met her eyes; most did not. "I will not have the machinery of the law perverted to allow lying bureaucrats to plant false documents in our party offices. The so-called search has no other purpose. If that's what you intend, *Captain*, you'll have to shoot your way in—or use the mercenaries you've hired at a true cost equal to the national budget for three full years!"

Her eyes locked Huber's with almost physical force. The blond man to her left was cringing back in his chair, looking at an empty corner of the chamber with an anguished expression.

Captain Orichos gestured the Speaker aside again. "We have no desire to plant anything in the Freedom Party files," she said, "nor would we even need to disturb the normal office routine. Will the member from Bulstrode permit me and one aide to search her files in her presence, with the entire exercise being broadcast live to the citizens of the Point?"

The older man snarled something toward Grayle. She shushed him with a gesture, though the chamber's electronics had swallowed the words.

Grayle stood. She pointed her index finger at Orichos. "You'll be showing this live over the regular governmental channel?" she said. "And you'll search in the presence of me and my fellow party members?"

"Yes," said Orichos, nodding without expression. "The only concern I and my department have is that the truth come out. If our sources in Solace have misled us, then I will be the first to apologize to you and your colleagues."

Grayle slammed her fist down on her desk. "By the Lord's bleeding wounds!" she said. "That's *just* what you'll do."

She stepped sideways toward the aisle leading out. "Come on, then," she added. "We'll take care of that now—and then we'll discuss the cost of these alien murderers you've saddled the Point with!"

"You'll come with me into the Freedom Party headquarters, Lieutenant," Orichos murmured as they watched Melinda Grayle and her henchmen stride out of the chamber. Their bodyguards were trampling down the stairs from the gallery to join them. The remaining assemblymen were either rigid in their seats or whispering in small cliques.

"All right," said Huber. "Sierra, this is Fox Three-six. I'll be accompanying the liaison officer into the red buildings across the way. If anything pops, you'll know where to come and get me. Three-six out."

"*Roger that, Three-six,*" growled Captain Sangrela. "*Six out.*"

Huber looked at the Gendarmery captain. "Why me?" he said.

"Let's go," Orichos said, nodding to the doorway. "A recording team from the Speaker's staff is joining us outside."

They went out. The ushers were backed against the walls, watching Huber and Orichos with silent concern.

"I want you rather than someone from the Point . . ." Orichos said, showing that she wasn't ignoring Huber's question after all. "Because Grayle knows that her Volunteers outnumber the Gendarmery by several times. Your regiment's an unknown quantity, so she'll be less inclined to resort to violence."

Huber noticed that she said, " . . . the Gendarmery . . ." rather than " . . . from my organization. . . ." Orichos was a member of the police force only as a matter of administrative convenience. In their own self-image, intelligence personnel are a breed apart—and generally a law unto themselves as well.

Two black-haired young women waited on the porch with lens wands and satchels of recording equipment. One technician was plumpish with a broad mouth, the other razor thin with three vertical blue lines on her right cheek. Huber couldn't tell whether the marks were tattoos or makeup.

Grayle and her entourage were walking back across the Axis to their compound. The older male was speaking into a hand communicator as he gestured forcefully with the other arm. The compound gates were open; the squad waiting there wore red headbands and carried carbines openly.

"Come along," Orichos said to the recording technicians as she strode past and started down the steps. They fell in behind obediently, looking excited but not frightened. They obviously didn't have any conception of what they were about to get into.

Trooper Learoyd waved from *Fencing Master*; Huber nodded in response. He was operating on trained reflex now. His intellect had dug itself a hole from which it viewed its surroundings in puling terror, but the part of him that was a soldier remained fully functional.

If things broke wrong, Task Force Sangrela couldn't get Huber out of the Freedom Party headquarters. The whole Regiment in line couldn't do that, though it could pulverize the buildings and everybody in them easily enough.

That wouldn't help Huber while he *was* inside. He wasn't going to fight his way out through the hundreds—at least—of armed Volunteers inside with him, either. Well, it'd be what it'd be. . . .

On the lowest of the three terrace landings, Orichos turned her head and said, "This is of course dangerous, Lieutenant; but I don't want you to imagine that it's a suicide mission."

Huber shrugged. "It doesn't matter what I think," he said. "It's my job."

Oddly enough, the words brought him a degree of comfort. They reminded him that he was here by choice, however dangerous "here" turned out to be. And by the Lord—Arne Huber couldn't clear out the compound alone, but if push came to shove the Volunteers who took him down'd know they'd been in a fight.

The road surface was more irregular than it'd seemed while Huber was riding over it in a combat car; repeatedly his foot slipped in a rut or scuffed a ridge he hadn't noticed because his attention was where it belonged, on the armed guards waiting for him in the gateway. He imagined taking this same route while mounted on *Fencing Master*. The thought made him grin, and maybe because of that expression the solid phalanx of Volunteers parted to let Huber and his companions through without jostling.

Orichos looked over her shoulder and said, "Begin recording now," to the technicians.

The thin one sniffed and replied tartly, "We've been recording since you came out of the building, ma'am. We have orders from our supervisor."

Orichos nodded without evident emotion. Huber wondered if she were nervous or if like him she was following by rote the path she'd planned while there was time for cool reflection.

They entered the compound. Melinda Grayle stood with the older male assemblyman in the doorway of the building ten meters ahead of them. Grayle was still in the white and red outfit she'd come from the Assembly with, but her companion had changed into black battledress set off by a red headband; he carried a carbine and wore a powergun in a belt holster.

Huber didn't see the blond assemblyman. He might be inside the building, of course. Aircars, mostly battered-looking private vehicles—the large trucks were garaged in an annex outside the walls—filled the grounds within the compound. They were parked so tightly that except for the path between the gate and the central building, anyone walking across the tract would have to worm his way through and sometimes over cars.

The people they'd flown into the city watched Orichos and her companions from the buildings and from the cars themselves. Everyone Huber saw was armed, and they were trying to look tough. For most of them, that didn't require a great deal of effort.

"All right, madam snoop," Grayle said to Orichos. "You're here now. How do you intend to proceed?"

"We'll go directly to the file room adjacent to your personal office on the fourth floor, Assemblyman Grayle," Orichos said calmly. "If there's no record of wrongdoing there, you'll have my apologies and we'll leave immediately."

Grayle's eyes narrowed; she looked angry but not, if Huber read her correctly, afraid. "I'll have your apology *and* your resignation, Captain," she said. "And you'll be lucky if there's not a libel suit as well!"

"Just as you please," Orichos said. She didn't look concerned either.

Grayle turned on her heel and strode into the building. Orichos followed immediately instead of waiting for the permission that wasn't going to come. Huber gestured the recorders ahead of him and brought up the rear. He didn't bother trying to watch behind him; he knew he'd see an armed mob, and it wasn't going to make him feel any more comfortable.

The two girls now looked nervous. They were walking so close together so that they occasionally bumped elbows. They'd started to understand. . . .

There were two elevators in the wall to the right of the doorway. Grayle gestured to them with her left hand and said sardonically, "Take your pick, snooper."

"We'll take the one that goes to the fourth floor," Orichos replied in a mild tone, stepping in front of Grayle and pressing the call button for the cage farther from the door.

Grayle's face went carefully neutral, but the male assemblyman with her said, "Hey, how does she—"

"Shut up, Fewsett!" Grayle said. Her voice didn't rise, but the snarl in it brought a look of surprise and anger to her subordinate's face. He cocked his right hand back, then gaped in blank horror at what he'd been about to do.

Grayle ignored him, pushing past Orichos to enter the elevator before the delegation from the Assembly could do so. Fewsett followed; other Volunteers would have done so as well, but there simply wasn't room on what was meant as a private car for the highest officials.

Huber grinned without humor. He didn't doubt that there'd be a sufficiency of gunmen already waiting for them upstairs.

The elevator rose smoothly but with a repetitive squeak to which the plump recording technician winced in synchrony. The thinner girl took her hand and squeezed it tightly. The contact seemed to help; at any rate, the twitches immediately became less pronounced.

The elevator stopped. What had been the back of the cage opened into an office appointed like a throne room. A large stuffed chair with gilt upholstery stood on a dais behind an agate-topped desk. Behind it was a wood-framed triptych of heroic figures created not by an artist but by a technician using stock imagery. Highlights on the pictures' glossy surface veiled them; a good result.

Even urban structures on Plattner's World tended to be tall and narrow, slipped in among the trees that were the source of the planet's considerable income. This high-ceilinged office was half the building's top floor; even so, another dozen people besides the six waiting gunmen would've filled the space left over by the desk and throne. They'd have had to stand, because there was no other chair in the room.

Grayle and her henchman got out first as they had entered. Fewsett immediately began to talk in a guttural whisper to the leader of the waiting squad, a slender man with tattoos and a serpentine copper bracelet.

Captain Orichos led the way to the small door at the side of the throne room; Huber brought up the rear. Through it was a paneled hallway with a stairwell at the far end and a doorway on the left side. Another squad of guards waited in the hall.

"Back, if you please!" Orichos said, gesturing at the guards. She opened the side door and entered the file room beyond.

Huber gave the gunmen a wry smile. They didn't know what was going on any better than he himself did. That didn't make him and the Volunteers brothers, but it was a good enough illustration of a soldier's life to amuse him.

There was no one in the file room; five-drawer cabinets circled the walls, leaving only an aisle in the middle. Though the Freedom Party was as technically advanced as the rest of Plattner's World, hardcopy remained a necessary backup to electronic files and ultimately more secure than any form of information linked directly to the outside world.

"Assemblyman Grayle?" Orichos said to the woman watching from the doorway. "Would you or a deputy please join us before I begin examining your files? Although the whole nation is witness to the proceedings—"

The thin technician's face was frozen, her mouth slightly open; she held her wand rigidly upright where it recorded events in a sphere around her. The other technician huddled against a back corner, leaning on her wand as though it were a cane. Huber supposed it was doing an adequate job of recording the parts of the file room that were blocked from her companion's lenses.

"—I'd like someone in whom you have confidence to be present to ensure that I'm merely examining files, not adding anything to them."

"By the Lord, you'd *better* not be adding stuff!" Fewsett growled. He added, presumably to some of the gunmen, "Come on, boys."

Grayle stepped in herself. Huber squeezed against the cabinets behind him to allow her to get by if she wanted, but she merely gave him a sneer. "Go ahead!" she said. "You'll find nothing because there's nothing to find."

Fewsett crowded in behind Grayle and touched her shoulder to move her back. She slapped his hand without looking around. More Volunteers stacked into the doorway; those in front pushed back against their fellows to the rear to keep from being shoved into Fewsett's massive figure.

Orichos nodded, then turned to a cabinet midway down the row. "Let the record show that I am at a cabinet marked Finance," she said, and opened the second drawer from the top.

Huber stood with his head cocked so that though he mainly faced the Freedom Party officials, he could still watch Orichos out of the corner of his eye. Grayle's expression was one of iron disdain; Fewsett glared past her with a mixture of anger and frustration.

"Bring the wand closer," Orichos snapped to the plump recorder. When there was no reaction, Orichos lifted the girl's arm and placed the lens wand on the edge of the drawer. In a dry, mechanical voice Orichos continued, "I am removing a file marked Special."

"What is this?" Grayle said on a rising note. She tried to look behind her but the way was filled with gunmen. "Where's Patronus? Why isn't he here?"

Orichos displayed her empty right hand to the lens wand, then reached into the drawer and brought out a folder with a red tab. She spread her left hand in plain sight also, then opened the folder.

Fewsett turned and bellowed, "Get that bastard Patronus here now! He's the fucking party treasurer. We need him *now*!"

Huber didn't move except to slide his finger into the trigger guard. He'd figured how the business was going to play out, but he didn't know quite the exact time.

Or whether he'd survive it.

"The folder holds a list of amounts and dates," Orichos said. "It purports to be records—"

The lens wand slipped off the drawer; the plump technician had curled her arms around herself, sunk into a personal world light-years away from this terror. In a sudden break from her detached calm, Orichos looked at the girl and screamed, "Hold that bloody thing up or I'll have you executed for treason!"

The thin technician tilted her wand closer to the open drawer. She didn't look toward Orichos.

"This is fake!" Grayle said. "It's been planted! There's no—"

"Purports to be a record," Orichos resumed in a louder voice, "of payments—"

"—truth in it at all!"

"—by the Interior Ministry of the Government of Solace to the Freedom Party!"

Grayle turned to get out of the file room. Fewsett knocked her back accidentally as he raised his carbine. Huber fired from the hip. His 2-cm bolt hit Fewsett in the upper chest, vaporizing most of the big man's torso in a thunderclap. The shockwave slammed Huber against a file cabinet and knocked the Volunteers in the doorway off their feet.

A Volunteer tried to aim his carbine, or maybe he was just flailing his arms for support. The powergun's cyan flash would've blinded anybody seeing it close-up without the protection of a polarizing faceshield like Huber's. He fired twice more, clearing the doorway save for a scatter of body parts. A blast-severed head flew past Huber, driven by vaporized body fluids.

The thin technician screamed and flung down her wand. It wobbled behind her on its flex as she sprang through the doorway Huber was trying to slam shut with his left hand. Two or more gunmen riddled her before she took a second step into the hallway. She thrashed backward, but Huber threw all his weight against the panel. It latched despite the obstructions.

A burst of shots whanged into the door from the outside. The panel was metal-cored, but concentrated gunfire would peck through it before long. For that matter there must be somebody in the gang outside with the key to the door's snap lock.

"Don't shoot, you idiots!" Melinda Riker Grayle screamed. "Don't shoot or you'll kill me!"

Huber glanced behind him. Grayle sprawled on the floor. Captain Orichos lay on top of her, twisting back her left arm and holding a pistol to Grayle's neck.

The plump technician sat on the floor with her legs splayed, crying uncontrollably. The room was hot—oven hot, heated by the three heavy-caliber powergun discharges in its narrow confines.

When a bolt liberated its energy in a human body, it turned the tissues to steam with explosive suddenness. The file room's walls, the ceiling, and the people within were all covered with a mist of blood. Huber's hands were red, and there was a sticky film across his faceshield that the static charge hadn't been able to repel. He flipped the shield up and out of the way.

The stench of cooked flesh and of the wastes voided when Fewsett's sphincters spasmed in death was stomach-churning, even for Huber who'd smelled it before. Some things you never get used to. . . .

Captain Orichos raised herself to her knees, still pointing her pistol at the assemblyman. She patted the floor with her left hand till she found the lens wand and raised it vertical again. Grayle twisted to look back into the bore of the pistol.

"Assemblyman Grayle!" Orichos said. "You stand convicted of treason by your own records and by your failed attempt to use force against the agents of the Assembly!"

"That's a lie!" Grayle said in a hoarse voice. "You planted that file!"

Several voices were jabbering at Huber through his commo helmet; at least one of them seemed to be from Base Alpha. He locked out all incoming channels and concentrated on the door in case the Volunteers tried to rush it. The muzzle of his powergun was cooling from yellow to bright orange.

"In order to prevent bloodshed among citizens . . ." Orichos continued as though her prisoner hadn't spoken. She was facing Grayle over the gunsights, but Huber noted that her eyes weren't focused anywhere in this world. "I'm offering you, in the name of the citizens of the Point, a chance to go into exile. You and all your fellow conspirators will have one hour to leave Midway and six hours to leave the Point. After that time, you will be considered criminals and dealt with according to law."

"You faked that so-called evidence," Grayle said, "and you faked the vote count to steal the last election from the

Freedom Party! You're the criminals! You're thieves, and you're bankrupting the state by hiring these mercenaries!"

"Assemblyman Grayle!" Orichos said. She jerked her weight backward to balance her as she stood. She held the wand in her left hand like a torch, and the pistol slanted down toward her prisoner's face. "Do you accept my offer, made in the presence of the entire citizenry of the Point?"

"Better take the offer, lady," Huber said. Ozone from the 2-cm bolts had flayed his throat, making his voice a rasp that he wouldn't have recognized himself. "Whatever else happens, I guarantee you're not going to leave here alive any other way."

Grayle looked at him. Her eyes slid downward to the floor on which she lay. Fewsett's head, severed when his chest exploded, stared back at her from a hand's breadth away. She jumped to her feet, forgetting the threat of Orichos' pistol.

"It's all a lie!" Grayle said. She got control of her breathing and went on, "But I don't have any choice. All right—we'll leave Midway, but I'm agreeing under duress. You have no legal right to expel us!"

"You out there in the hall?" Huber shouted. He figured the Volunteers, a lot of them anyway, would be watching the broadcast along with the rest of the citizens, but the gunmen just outside the door might be an exception. "I'm going to open the door. The first one through it's going to be your leader, Assemblyman Grayle. But be clear on this— you've got a deal with your government and your Gendarmery. You don't have a deal with me personally. If anybody sticks his head into this room, I'm going to blow him to atoms just like I did a lot of his buddies a moment ago. Got it?"

Nobody answered. Huber thought he heard the sound of boots running down the staircase. Grayle was poised like a roach caught by the light, momentarily frozen.

"Captain Orichos?" Huber said.

"Yes, open the door," Orichos said.

Instead of reaching, Huber kicked out with his right boot and sprung the latch. The panel bounced open. The hallway was empty.

Grayle jumped through so quickly that she slid on the

blood pooling from the dead technician's body. She caught herself on the wall and ran toward the stairs, leaving a handprint on the wall behind her.

Nothing else moved for over a minute.

Huber let out his breath. He switched his helmet back to RECEIVE mode and said, "Fox Three-six to Sierra. We're holding our present position on the fourth floor of the Freedom Party headquarters until somebody comes to fetch us out. And give me plenty of warning before you show yourselves, people, because I'm as jumpy as I've ever been in my life!"

Captain Sangrela's driver had bounced his jeep up the Assembly Building steps and parked it under the porch. The officers and senior sergeants of Task Force Sangrela stood on the patterned stone, listening to the holographic image of Danny Pritchard speaking from Base Alpha.

Around them the citizens of Midway noisily celebrated their release from Freedom Party domination. In the street below whirled a round dance with hundreds of participants. A fiddler stood on a raised platform in the middle of the circle; beside him, occasionally crowding his elbow, gyrated a young woman wearing only briefs. Huber didn't think she was professional—just exuberant and very happy. As far up and down the Axis as Huber could see there were similar dances as well as free buffets, speakers on makeshift podiums, and crowds of people drinking and singing in good fellowship.

"The Volunteers are gathering at their base on Bulstrode Bay on the northern coast," said Danny Pritchard's holographic image. "They call it Fort Freedom, and it's going to be a tough nut to crack."

Aircars spun and swooped overhead, often with sirens blaring. The drivers were as excited and as generally drunk as the people in the street. Huber had seen two collisions and heard a worse one that sent a car crashing to the ground on the other side of the Mound.

"Why us, sir?" Captain Sangrela asked. His voice was calm, but the way his hands tightly gripped the opposite elbows indicated his tension.

"Because you can, Captain," Pritchard said simply.

"Because we can't leave ten thousand armed enemies in a state whose support we need. And because the locals can't do it themselves—"

He grinned harshly.

"—which is generally why people hire the Slammers, right?"

The Gendarmery had been conspicuous by its absence during the events of the afternoon. Now the Point's gray-uniformed police were out in force, though they seemed more to be showing themselves than making an effort to control the good-natured partying that was going on. The Gendarmes on foot patrol carried only pistols; those in the cruising aircars may have had carbines but they weren't showing them.

"Ten *thousand* of 'em, sir?" said C-1's platoon sergeant, a rangy man named Dunsterville. He sounded incredulous rather than afraid at what he'd heard. "You mean the guys with red sweatbands?"

"The Volunteers, yes," Pritchard agreed with a grim nod. "You won't have to deal with all of them—indeed, that's why we've decided to move on Fort Freedom immediately. We expect that at least half of Grayle's Volunteers will decide to stay home in the woods if they know that joining her means facing tanks. If we withdraw from the Point and the Volunteers don't have anybody to worry about except the locals, then they'll everyone of them march back into Midway and this time loot the place."

When Pritchard said, "we've decided," he meant Colonel Hammer and his regimental command group. The "we" who'd be carrying out the operation meant Call-Sign Sierra, ten vehicles and less than a hundred troopers under Captain Sangrela. Huber was a volunteer, and he knew that the senior officers had all been at the sharp end in their day too . . . but Via! Fifty to one was curst long odds!

"Here's a plan of Fort Freedom," Pritchard continued. The image of his body disappeared, leaving his head hovering above a sharply circular embayment viewed from the south at an apparent downward angle of forty-five degrees. The sea had cut away the northern third of the rock walls and filled the interior. "Bulstrode Bay's an ancient volcano. The walls average a hundred meters high and are about that thick at the base. There's normal housing inside of the crater, but the Volunteers have also tunneled extensively into the walls."

"Have they got artillery?" Huber asked. He was still trying to get his head around the notion of going up against five *thousand* armed hostiles . . . or maybe ten thousand after all, because staff estimates were just that, estimates, and Sierra would be facing real guns.

"The Volunteers don't have an indirect fire capacity so far as we can tell," Pritchard said, nodding at a good question. "Not even mortars. What they *do* have—"

The holographic image transformed itself into a gun carriage mounting eight stubby iridium barrels locked together in two banks; each tube had its own ammo feed. The chassis was on two wheels with a trail for towing the weapon rather than being self-powered.

"—are calliopes. We've traced a lot of twenty purchased by Grayle's agents nine months ago, and it's possible that there've been others besides."

Calliopes, multi-barreled 2- or 3-cm powerguns, provided many mercenary units with the air defense that the Slammers handled through their own armored vehicles. The weapons were extremely effective against ground targets as well. A short burst from a calliope could shred a combat car and turn its crew into cat's meat. . . .

Pritchard's full figure replaced the image of the calliope. "I'm not making light of the job you face," he said. "But I do want to emphasize that the Volunteers are *not* soldiers. Most of them have only small arms, they aren't disciplined, and they've never faced real firepower. If you hit them hard and fast they'll break, troopers. You'll break them to pieces."

"Calliopes cost money," Mitzi Trogon said. "More money than I'd expect from a bunch of hicks in the sticks."

Pritchard nodded again. "Whatever you think of the documents the Point security police found," he said with a grin, "we have evidence that the government of Solace is indeed supporting the Freedom Party."

Solace would be insane not to, Huber thought. Arming the internal enemies of a hostile government was about the cheapest way to reduce its threat.

In the street and sky, the citizens of Midway danced and sang. They were the rulers, the people who split among themselves the wealth and the status and the political power of the Point. They were right to fear Melinda Grayle, a demagogue who'd united the Moss rangers against the urban elite who lorded it over them.

Captain Sangrela rubbed the back of his neck. "We're going cross-country, I suppose?" he said. "There isn't much *but* cross-country on this bloody planet."

"Not exactly," Pritchard said as the image of a terrain map replaced that of his body. "The direct route'd take you through ancient forest. The trees are too thick and grow too densely for your vehicles to push through or maneuver through either one. We've plotted you a course down the valley of the River Fiorno. It won't be fast, but the vegetation there's thin enough that even the cars can break trail."

The red line of the planned course dotted its way along the solid blue of a watercourse. Not far from the coast, the red diverged straight northward for some fifty kilometers to reach Bulstrode Bay.

"The last part of the route, we'll clear for you with incendiary rounds. We estimate it'll take you nearly two days to reach the point you'll leave the Fiorno. The fire should've burned itself out by then, so you can make the last part of your run relatively quickly."

Pritchard smiled again. "The fire should also limit the risk of ambush," he said; then he sobered and added, "But that'll be a very real possibility while you're following the river. We'll do what we can from Base Alpha, but you'll have to proceed with scouts and a full sensor watch the same as you did on the way here."

Pritchard's image looked around the gathering. "Any questions?" he asked.

"I don't like to complain, Major . . ." said Sergeant Jellicoe, lacing her fingers in front of her. "But do you suppose after this, somebody else in the bloody regiment can get a little action too?"

Everybody laughed; but everybody, Pritchard included, knew that the comment hadn't entirely been a joke. "I'll see what I can do," he said.

On the fiddler's platform below, the woman dancing had stripped off her panties as well. Huber glanced down at her . . . and turned his head away.

He was going to need his rest. The next part of the operation sounded like it was going to be even rougher than what it'd taken to get Task Force Sangrela this far.

Huber called up a remote from *Flame Farter*, on the move with White Section for the past ten minutes. The Fiorno River was only thirty meters wide and almost shallow enough to wade where it curved around the north and east of Midway. The scouts' skimmers danced in rainbows of spray out in the channel to avoid the reeds along the margins; the combat car was chuffing down the bank, spewing mud and fragments of soft vegetation from beneath her skirts.

"Red Section, move out!" Captain Sangrela ordered. The main body with Jellicoe's *Floosie* in the lead was already lined up on the Axis north of the Assembly Building. Dust puffed beneath their skirts as they lifted from the gravel. One at a time, carefully because objects so powerful must move carefully if they're not to destroy themselves and everything around them, the seven vehicles of the main body started down the avenue. The doughnuts of dust spread into wakes on either side.

Sergeant Nagano glanced over from *Foghorn*'s fighting compartment; Huber was keeping his section on the Mound till the main body had cleared the road beneath. Huber gave Nagano a thumb's up. Nagano hadn't commanded a car before the operations against Northern Star, and he was doing a good job.

"How'd you make out last night, El-Tee?" Sergeant Deseau asked, stretching like a cat behind the forward gun.

"I slept like a baby," Huber said. "I never sleep that well on leave when I'm in a bed."

The Assembly had offered the Slammers any kind of billets they wanted, but Captain Sangrela had decided to keep his troopers beside their vehicles for the night. Nobody'd argued with him. The weather wasn't unpleasant, and chances were some Freedom Party supporters had stayed in Midway. The risks of going off by yourself were a lot greater than any benefit a bed in an unfamiliar room was going to bring.

"Not me," said Deseau, grinning even broader. "The people here are *real* grateful, let me tell you."

Learoyd looked around from his gun. Shyly he said, "The girls didn't charge nothing, El-Tee. I never been a place before that the girls didn't charge."

A Gendarmery aircar came up the Axis from the south, flying low and slow. Huber caught the motion in the corner of his eye, then cranked the image up to x32 as an inset on his faceshield. As he'd thought, Captain Orichos was in the passenger seat.

The fourth D company tank pulled out at the back of the main body, accelerating with the slow majesty that its mass demanded. *Floosie* was out of sight beyond the northern end of the Axis, into the mixture of forest and scattered houses that constituted the city's suburbs.

"Fox Three-six to Three-one," Huber said to Sergeant Nagano. "Move into the street. We'll follow you down and bring up the rear. Three-six out."

Foghorn lurched from its berth and ground through a hedge that'd survived Task Force Sangrela's arrival. *Whoever was driving for Nagano today must be keyed tighter than a lute string,* Huber thought; he grinned faintly. *Which showed the driver understands what we're about to get into.*

"Sir, shall I shift us now?" Sergeant Tranter prodded from the driver's compartment.

"Give me a moment, Tranter," Huber replied. "I think I've got a visitor."

"Hey, it's your girlfriend, El-Tee," Deseau said cheerfully. He waved at the aircar swinging in along *Fencing Master's* port side.

"Not *my* girlfriend," Huber said as he lifted himself out of the fighting compartment to stand on the plenum chamber. And probably not even a friend, to Arne Huber or to any member of the Slammers. Orichos had other priorities, and Huber had only the vaguest notion of what they might be.

As the aircar hovered beside them, the Gendarmery captain tossed Huber a satchel no larger than the personal kit of a trooper on active deployment. "I hope you don't mind, Lieutenant . . ." she called over the thrum of the aircar and the whine of *Fencing Master's* idled fans. "But I'm going to join you again."

Huber thrust the satchel behind him for Deseau to take.

He extended his right hand while his left anchored him to the fighting compartment's coaming.

"Welcome aboard, Captain," he said, swinging Orichos across to the combat car. She was surprisingly light; his subconscious expected the weight of a figure wearing body armor, of course.

Mauricia Orichos wasn't welcome, but she was part of Huber's job so he'd make the best of it. And he really had more important things on his mind just now. . . .

Huber heard a coarse *ripping* as three more rounds from batteries far to the south streaked overhead. To give the shells sufficient range from the Slammers' gun positions in the UC, a considerable part of what would normally be payload was given over to the booster rockets.

"What's that?" asked Mauricia Orichos, pointing upward. The shells' boron fluoride exhaust unrolled broad, poisonous ribbons at high altitude, spreading as she watched. *"Are we under attack?"*

"No, that's outgoing," Huber explained, mildly surprised that their passenger had picked up the sound of artillery over *Fencing Master*'s intake howl. Orichos noticed quite a lot, he realized, and she had the knack for absorbing what was normal in a new situation so that she could quickly identify change. "They're prepping the route for us."

He wasn't sure how much Orichos knew about the plan, and he wasn't going to be the one to tell her anything Base Alpha hadn't already explained. If it'd been up to Arne Huber, he'd have told the Point authorities an amount precisely equal to the part Point forces were taking in the reduction of Fort Freedom: zip.

He glanced up at the path the shells had taken northward. For this use, the reduced payloads didn't matter. The shells would spill their incendiary bomblets at very high altitude to get maximum dispersion. The target wasn't a single facility but rather a fifty-kilometer swathe of forest, and there was plenty of time for the widely-spread ignition points to grow together into a massive firestorm.

Which wasn't the sort of thing a local from Plattner's World, where the forest was preserved with almost religious fervor, could be expected to like. Colonel Hammer put his troopers' lives first, though, and Colonel Hammer was calling the shots on this one.

The vehicles ahead of *Fencing Master* had mown and gouged the riverbank into a muddy wasteland. Wherever possible the lead car had chosen a route that kept its skirts on solid ground, but occasionally an outcrop or a deep inlet forced the column partly into the water. Each *thrum!* as plenum-chamber pressure beat the river echoed for kilometers up and down the channel.

Huber grinned. Orichos misread his expression, for she smiled back ruefully and said, "*I suppose I do sound like a Nervous Nellie. Sorry.*"

"What?" said Huber. "Oh, not at all. I was just thinking that there's never been an armored column in human history that sneaked up on anybody, and this time isn't going to be the exception."

"*El-Tee?*" said Learoyd, staring dutifully into the holographic display. "*Take a look at this, will you?*"

Huber'd put his right wing gunner on the first sensor watch of the run because he hadn't expected anything to show up so early. He'd manually notched out *Fencing Master* and the other vehicles in the column during the run from Northern Star, so that they wouldn't hide the more distant, hostile, signals. Unlike a quicker mind, Learoyd's wouldn't be lulled into daydreams by the minute changes in pearly emptiness that was probably all that he'd see in the display, but Huber feared that Learoyd might not notice subtleties that really had meaning.

Except that the trooper'd done just that. Huber frowned at the display in dawning comprehension, then said, "Sierra Six, this is Fox Three-six. We've got an aircar, probably a small one, following us about a kilometer back. I figure if it was just civilian sightseers, they'd be, well, in sight. Over."

"*Roger, Three-six,*" Captain Sangrela said. "*We leave a broad enough track that the Volunteers figure they can follow us without coming so close we spot them. Good work, Huber. I'll drop off a fire team to take care of it. Six out.*"

"Three-six out," Huber said. "Break. Blue Section, some infantry's staying behind to clean off our tail. Don't run 'em over, and get ready to back 'em up when the music starts. Three-six out."

"We gonna get a chance to pop somebody, El-Tee?" Deseau asked, turning hopefully to meet Huber's eyes.

"Not a chance, Frenchie," Huber said. "But we're going to follow the drill anyway."

A thought struck him and he went on, "Captain Orichos? Is there any chance that a Gendarmery aircar is trailing the column? If there is, tell me now. You won't get a second chance."

Orichos frowned. *"One of ours?"* she said. *"Not unless somebody's disregarded my clear instructions. And if that's happened, Lieutenant—"*

She smiled. Frenchie Deseau couldn't have bettered the cruel surmise in her expression.

"—then the sort of lesson I assume you propose will bring the survivors to a better appreciation of the authority granted me by the Assembly."

Huber nodded and returned his attention to his tribarrel's sector forward. He didn't have a problem with ruthlessness, but he found disquieting the gusto with which people like the Gendarmery captain did what was necessary.

"Three-six, watch the pedestrians!" Nagano warned from *Foghorn* fifty meters ahead. Four infantrymen had hopped their skimmers off one of the maintenance vehicles; now they were positioning themselves behind treeboles where they'd have good fields of fire for their 2-cm weapons as soon as the aircar came in sight above the water. Huber nodded in salute, but the infantrymen were wholly focused on what was about to happen.

The ambush team had shut down their skimmers immediately upon hitting the ground. The Volunteers weren't likely to have sensors that'd pick up a skimmer's small fans more than a stone's throw away, but Regimental training emphasized that you didn't assume any more than you had to. Plenty of stuff that you couldn't control was going to go wrong, so you made doubly sure on the rest.

"How long, Lieutenant?" Orichos asked. Not what: how long. She was a sharp one, no mistake.

"About a minute and a half," Huber explained. "We're travelling at about forty kph in this salad—"

He gestured to the soft vegetation just outside the track, where the previous vehicles hadn't ground it to green slime.

"—and our Volunteer friends back there'll be holding to the same speed. The last thing they want's to fly up on our tail."

He smiled. Which was just what they were about to do.

Orichos nodded and turned to watch the route behind *Fencing Master*. There wasn't anything to see but mud and muddy water, of course. Sight distances close to the ground were at most a hundred meters in the few places the river flowed straight, and generally much less where vegetation arched over the curving banks.

Huber imported to the lower left quadrant of his faceshield the view from the sergeant commanding the ambush team; it wouldn't interfere with his sight picture in the unlikely event that *Fencing Master* ran into trouble. After a moment's hesitation, he touched Orichos' shoulder. When she turned, he linked their helmets as he had while *Floosie* raked incoming shells from the sky. Orichos nodded appreciatively.

It took ten seconds longer than Huber'd estimated before an open aircar with four men aboard loitered into sight. Sangrela had chosen the ambush site well: the car slowed, dipping beneath a branch draped with air plants which crossed the river only three meters above the purling surface.

The lift fans flung a rainbow of spray through the sunlight, momentarily blinding the two men in the front. As the car started to rise again, three cyan bolts hit the driver, vaporizing his torso, and a fourth took off the head of the gunman in the passenger seat.

The driver jerked the control yoke convulsively, throwing the car belly forward and spilling the remaining gunman off the stern. The sergeant shot the falling man before he hit the water; the three troopers blew the car's underside into fireballs of plastic paneling superheated into a mixture that exploded in the air.

"Blue Section, reverse!" Huber screamed. Sergeant Tranter was a trifle slower to spin *Fencing Master* than he should've been; Huber'd forgotten the driver didn't have reflexes ingrained by combat like the rest of them did. "Move it! Move it! Move it!"

The ambush team didn't need help. The aircar crashed edgewise onto a spine of rock sticking up from the water; it broke apart. The fourth Volunteer had been concentrating on detector apparatus feeding through a bulky helmet. He must've been strapped in; his arms flailed, but he didn't get out of the car even when the wreckage slipped off the rocks and started to sink.

The river geysered as at least four and maybe twice that many 2-cm bolts hit the man and the water nearby. A bolt hit an upthrust rock; it burst like a grenade, shredding foliage on the bank with sharp fragments.

I guess the poor bastard's not going to drown after all, Huber thought.

When *Fencing Master* reached the ambush site a few seconds later, the infantrymen had remounted their skimmers. Huber gestured them forward to put the combat car in drag position again.

"You were right, El-Tee," said Deseau regretfully. *"Not a bloody thing for us."*

One of the infantrymen waved back as he passed *Fencing Master.* He was now wearing a helical copper bracelet, its ends shaped like snakeheads.

Apparently the leader of the squad Huber shot it out with in Freedom Party headquarters hadn't learned from that experience. Huber smiled coldly. The Slammers didn't give anybody a third chance.

The alert signal brought Huber out of a doze; it was like swimming upward through hot sand. He'd jumped to his feet and had the tribarrel's grips in his hands, straining for a target in his faceshield's light-amplified imagery, before his conscious mind took over and he realized why he'd awakened.

Learoyd was driving. Sergeant Deseau was at the forward gun, as rested as anybody could be after eighteen hours of slogging through river-bottom vegetation. Huber wouldn't have been able to drop off if he hadn't been sure Frenchie was there to take up the slack. He'd needed the mental down-time badly, though. The shoot-out in Freedom Party headquarters had drained him more than he'd realized right after it happened.

But that was part of the past, a different world, and now the present was calling. "Fox Three-six acknowledging!" Huber said, and his helmet dropped him into the virtual meeting room with Colonel Hammer himself and the other officers of Task Force Sangrela. He'd been the last to arrive, but from the look of Mitzi Trogon—her mouth was half-open and her eyes looked like they were staring into oncoming headlights—she was in at least as bad a shape as he was.

"Troopers," Hammer said, acknowledging his four subordinates with a glance that swept the table. The imagery was sharper than it'd been in the forest south of Midway; the sky above the Fiorno was fairly open. "There's Volunteers setting up a blocking position on an island three hours ahead of you. There's about two hundred men with buzzbombs and six calliopes if they're not further reinforced."

Hammer's torso vanished into a slant view of a roughly oval island; it covered about as much of the river valley as the channels flowing to north and south of it. From the scale at the bottom of the image, the heavily wooded surface between the streams was on the order of a square kilometer.

"They've been flying in from Bulstrode Bay over the past hour," Hammer said with a disbelieving shake of his head. "They apparently don't realize that here at Base Alpha we can follow everything they're doing, right down to who had grits for breakfast."

Icons of red light marked hostile positions: calliopes on the forward curve of the island, and squads of infantry both on the island itself and on the north bank of the floodway. The Volunteers probably intended the mainland element to halt the task force in line along the shore where the calliopes could rake the Slammers from the flank.

Sangrela laughed in derision. "You want us to go through 'em or around 'em, sir?" he asked. "For choice we'll go through."

"Neither," said Hammer with a spreading smile. "I'm just telling you what the situation is. We're going to handle it from here with artillery."

"Why in hell would you want to do that?" Mitzi Trogon snarled. She must've heard her own tone; she snapped fully awake at last. "Ah, *sir*, that is," she added with a grimace of embarrassment.

Hammer looked at Trogon without expression for a moment, then lifted his chin minutely to show that the incident was closed—if not forgotten. "Right," he said with a mildness that deceived nobody. "This ambush isn't a problem, but Fort Freedom is likely to be more of one. Here the Volunteers have their calliopes tasked for ground use, waiting for your column to come into their killing zone. They aren't professional enough to redirect the guns for artillery defense in the amount of time they'll have. Follow?"

Because Huber understood and none of his fellow officers were in a hurry to speak after Mitzi'd stepped on her dick, he said, "When a salvo takes out the whole ambush party, Volunteer command is going to decide it's our shells they ought to be worrying about. When we get to Bulstrode Bay, their calliopes are going to be aimed up for artillery defense and we'll take 'em with direct fire."

"Roger that, troopers," Hammer said, his face minusculely softer than it'd been a moment before. "This won't be a milk run for you, there's no way it's going to be that. But I told you from the beginning that you'd have all the support we could give you. Any questions?"

"Support" this time didn't mean the artillery, not really, Huber realized. It was the planning, the misdirection; the thinking two steps ahead of his own troops and at least six steps ahead of the enemy, that the Colonel was providing here.

"What orders do you have for us, sir?" Captain Sangrela asked, the burr of warmth in his tone suggesting that he was thinking along the same lines as Huber was.

"Keep on with what you're doing, that's all," Hammer said. His grin spread. "Which is plenty, I know that. We'll time the stonk for thirty seconds before you come into sight of the target. Hit anybody that shows himself, but keep going as fast as you can. That'll make more of an impression on what passes for a Volunteer command group than we would by digging out a couple shell-shocked wogs and blasting them. Clear?"

"Clear," said Sangrela, nodding, and Huber added his

"Clear" to the muttered "Roger," and "Clear," from his fellow lieutenants.

That'd save gun bores for the real fight at Bulstrode Bay as well. Maintenance had replaced the barrels burned out at Northern Star, but there probably wouldn't be time for another refit before Sierra slammed into Fort Freedom and the Volunteer's main body. . . .

Hammer gave a crisp nod. "Let me stick it to the bastards this time, troopers," he said. "There'll be plenty of opportunity for you up north."

The Colonel's image dissolved, returning Huber to *Fencing Master*'s jouncing fighting compartment. His mind and senses were as sharp as they'd ever been in his life. To the watchful expressions of his troopers and Captain Orichos, he began, "In about three hours . . ."

What looked like a streak of sparse vegetation at right angles to the river was a dike of impermeable clay channeling water into the softer soil beyond. The scout section infantry slid across without being aware of the change, but *Fencing Master* came down on algae-covered soup instead of the expected solid ground. A gout of mud spewed higher than the armored sides, drenching Huber and the others in the fighting compartment.

Tranter boosted power and adjusted the nacelles vertical for maximum lift. *Fencing Master* pogoed back onto an even keel and wallowed slowly across the basin.

"Fox Three-six to Sierra," Huber warned. "There's quicksand here. The panzers had better swing wide or they'll sink to wherever the bottom turns out to be. Three-six out."

By rights, *Foghorn* would've been the leading car if they'd gone by the preplanned rotation. Sergeant Nagano hadn't been pleased when Huber exercised his command prerogative to put *Fencing Master* in the lead as the column prepared to run the Volunteer ambush, but Huber was doubly glad he'd done it now. Only a driver as able as Sergeant Tranter would've kept from bogging or simply sinking out of sight in this soft spot, and there were bloody few drivers that good.

"*Roger Three-six,*" Captain Sangrela said. "*Delta units, follow the contour lines north. Looks to me like two hundred meters will let you cross safely. Six out.*"

Fencing Master lifted itself with a jerk onto higher, harder ground. Tranter paused a moment before readjusting the fans, checking to be sure that mud and water plants hadn't choked any of the intake ducts. The combat car built up speed again, shedding weed and watery mud like a dog emerging from a pond.

Mauricia Orichos dabbed at the muck staining her uniform, managing only to spread the stain until she gave up the pointless exercise. She noticed Huber's glance and smiled faintly.

"I suppose it doesn't matter," she said. *"I'm used to thinking in . . . urban terms, I suppose."*

"It doesn't matter," Huber agreed. *Especially if we're all dead in the next thirty seconds*, but he didn't let that last thought reach his tongue.

He heard the incoming shells at first as a distant friction in the sky. With shocking suddenness their howl filled the whole world and still grew louder. Sergeant Deseau hunched over the forward gun, aware that it was friendly fire aimed to impact half a klick ahead of *Fencing Master*; aware also that mistakes happen, that even the most technologically advanced shells land short occasionally, and that no fire is friendly when it's coming in on your position.

The Gendarmery captain's face went blank; her eyes opened wide. For a moment Huber thought she was going to throw herself as close to flat as she could get in the crowded fighting compartment, but she recovered her composure when she noticed he wasn't taking any action.

"It's all right," he explained. "This is the prep that's—"

The shells burst directly overhead with four distinct pops. The opened casings spilled the separate white streaks of over a thousand bomblets toward the ground ahead of *Fencing Master*. They whistled like a symphony for chalk on blackboards.

"—going to land on the—"

The timing was slightly off: *Fencing Master* tore through the last screen of feather-fronded vegetation a second before instead of a few seconds after the bomblets struck the Volunteer positions. The mid-channel island was a green mass against the tannin-black water. Near the shore the foliage was the same sort of lush shrubbery that Task Force Sangrela had ground through on the route from Midway, but there were some sizeable trees a hundred meters back from the bank.

The landscape disintegrated in crackling white flashes, snarling and sparkling for almost five seconds. A pall of mud and shredded greenery lifted several meters high, then settled back on a barren wasteland. Only memory could say that eastern half of the island and the spit of riverbank to the north of it had been covered by dense vegetation a moment before.

A cyan flash blew a temporary crater in the mud: a calliope's ammunition had detonated. A wheel spun skyward, then fell back and splashed into the river.

The scout infantry had grounded their skimmers at the moment of impact. Now they lifted again and resumed their course, four fingers feeling Sierra's path across the trackless terrain. *Fencing Master* snorted a hundred meters behind, the iridium fist ready to punch if the infantry touched anything.

"Not a bloody thing for us, El-Tee," Deseau said. "Not a bloody *thing.*"

The firecracker rounds had left a haze of explosive residue and finely divided soil above the island, blurring its shape, but Huber knew there'd have been little more to see even without that blanket. The rolling blasts had pulped everything in the impact area. Except for the single wheel, there'd been no sign of two hundred enemy soldiers and their equipment.

His nose wrinkled. That wasn't quite true. Besides the prickle of ozone and the sickening sweetness of explosive, the air had a tinge of burned flesh.

Fencing Master bucked into the undisturbed vegetation beyond the line which shell fragments had scythed. When the professionals sat down to the table, war stopped being a game for street thugs wearing uniforms. The Volunteers at ground zero here hadn't had time to learn that, but the folks who'd given them their orders must be thinking hard about the future by now.

Because the prevailing winds were from the northwest, Huber had been smelling the fire for almost three hours before the infantry sergeant with the scouting section called over the command channel, *"Blood and Martyrs, Captain! This is Charlie One-three-four. Are we supposed to go through this on skimmers? Over."*

Huber switched a quadrant of his faceshield to the view from *Floosie*, the combat car attached to White Section at the moment. It was like looking into the maw of Hell.

Regimental rocket howitzers hundreds of kilometers to the south in United Cities' territory had seeded the forest with incendiaries. Each time-fuzed zirconium pellet was capable of burning though light armor. When one landed in old growth forest, the likelihood of it igniting even green timber was three out of five . . . and there were tens of thousands of pellets in the shells, raining down over hundreds of square kilometers. The myriad simultaneous fires had spread till they joined in a firestorm, a towering conflagration that drove its column of smoke through the stratosphere and sucked air to feed it from all sides in a torrent at hurricane velocities.

Everything combustible within the core of the blaze had burned, including the loam. Silica in the clay substrate ran liquid before cooling into slabs of glass colored like the rainbow by trace minerals.

Though the first flush of the fire had burned to a glowing shadow of itself, what remained still shimmered. The boles of the largest trees smoldered, stripped to pillars of carbonized heartwood. Monstrous pythons of smoke and ash eddied, the ghosts of a forest dancing among its bones.

"One-three-four, recover to your carrier vehicle," Sangrela responded without hesitation. *"ASAP, troopers, don't get into that! There won't be an ambush in that stuff, not from anything these Volunteers have available."*

He paused, then resumed, *"Break. Sierra, button up all hatches. Drivers switch to microwave radar, and exposed personnel lock down your faceshields. Make sure your filters are working before we get into it. We'll form an echelon perpendicular to the prevailing winds so—"*

A route map clicked as an imposed overlay on the lower right corner of Huber's faceshield. Every trooper in the task force had the same image.

"—that we're not all driving through the trash the leaders stir up. Six out."

Floosie must've entered the burned area just as Sangrela spoke, because a plume of ash shot skyward two kilometers ahead of *Fencing Master*. It was like watching the first puff of a volcano gathering its strength.

The fire'd been set to clear the forest between Fort Freedom and the Fiorno Valley at its closest approach, some twenty klicks west of where the river entered the Northern Sea. The tract was well-watered and the foliage was in the green lushness of late spring, so the fire had generally burned itself out to either side of the kilometer-wide swathe seeded with incendiaries. Nothing organic could've resisted that dense rain of exothermic metal.

Deseau was driving; Huber heard the hatch cover close over him. Learoyd checked his faceshield and filters with his left hand, then drew up the throat closure of his blouse to get the maximum protection possible without donning an environmental suit.

Tranter was curled up asleep under the forward gun; his head rested on his commo helmet. Huber shook him awake and leaned close to shout, "Get your gear on and locked down, Sarge. There's going to be a lot of ash and sparks for the next hour or so."

As Tranter slipped his helmet on with a grin of embarrassment, Huber turned to Captain Orichos. She'd been watching the troopers, but she wasn't on the Sierra net and didn't know what was happening. Her expression was neutral, with just enough quirk to the lips to prevent it from being grim.

"We're going to be going through a burned-out area," he explained to Orichos over the intercom. He mimed locking down his faceshield rather than touch hers, at present raised. "Your nose filters ought to come down automatically when we hit the smoke, but you might want to push this button here—"

He touched the hinge of his faceshield; the filters dropped over his nostrils.

"—and deploy them manually right now."

"*Burned area?*" Orichos said. Her hand stopped halfway to her faceshield, then finished the movement. "*Have those animals set the forest on fire?*"

All the vehicles of the main body were out of the floodway

now, striking north toward their goal. Eight separate ribbons of smoke and ash trailed downwind, spreading till they
merged into a broad miasma that settled slowly back to the
ravaged forest.

"Whatever happened," Huber said, "it's going to be hot
going till we reach the marshes this side of Bulstrode Bay.
Get your filters in place now, all right?"

Fencing Master had reached the point at which Sierra's
route left the river; Deseau boosted fan speed and adjusted
his nacelle angles. The previous vehicles, particularly the
tanks, had battered the bank into a slope of glistening mud.
Skirts had dragged chunks of buried quartz up with them
in deep gouges through the clay.

Fencing Master roared, bursting over the top of the bank
at over thirty kph. Huber realized what was about to happen in time to brace his left hand against the coaming and
clasp Orichos to his chest with the other arm. The Gendarmery officer didn't have the instincts to react correctly
even if he'd had a chance to warn her instead of acting.

The car's nose skirts spilled air and dropped, slamming
down onto the charred soil. Despite being prepared, Huber's
own weight and that of Captain Orichos threw him hard
against the coaming. The rigid clamshell armor spread the
shock, but he'd still have bruises along the side of his ribcage
by the morning.

If he was alive in the morning, of course. Well, civilians
could die at any moment too.

Deseau took them into the hell-lit wasteland. Smoke was
a gray pall; sometimes dense enough to seem solid, sometimes hiding objects that were solid in all truth. Huber tried
light-amplified viewing but decided the lack of depth perception would be too dangerous at their present high speed.
Infrared—thermal imaging—wasn't ideal at the ambient
temperatures of the burning forest, but the helmet AI had
enough discrimination to make it the choice.

"*Vandals!*" snarled Captain Orichos. "*Stupid vandal bastards! What did they think they'd accomplish by this destruction?*"

There was no point in telling her how the blaze had really
started. Not when she and Arne Huber shared a crowded
combat car on the verge of action with an entrenched enemy.

Hot spots—open flames and sparks the skirts plowed up from fires banked in the ashes—were white highlights in the faceshield. The AI coded cooler objects through the spectrum from violet to dark reds that verged on black, though little in this expanse was colored below green. A suited human would be visible in outline against the brighter background, but nobody expected to find Volunteers waiting *here* in ambush.

Fencing Master bumped and racketed across the landscape, scraping its skirts frequently and often hurling up gouts of fire. Deseau was being careful—too careful. He was trying to avoid every possible stump and cavity instead of taking a line and holding it till a major obstacle interposed. The combat car repeatedly sideswiped the skeletons of fallen trees, blasting them into sparks, or grounded when the skirts swayed over the edge of a pit left when a toppling giant had dragged its root ball out of the soil. Sergeant Tranter gripped the coaming to either side of his gun pintle with a set look on his face.

Huber touched Tranter's shoulder to get his attention, then leaned close to shout into his ear instead of using the intercom circuit and including Deseau: "Don't worry, Sarge— you and Frenchie will switch positions when we form up for the attack."

Tranter nodded gratefully. He might or might not understand that Huber was even more interested in getting Deseau behind the forward tribarrel than he was to have Tranter's expertise in the driver's compartment. Horses for courses . . .

"*Vandals!*" Mauricia Orichos repeated as she stared across the flame-ravaged bleakness. Sparks whirled from the skirts and spun down again into the fan intakes, dusting those in the fighting compartment. Slammers' uniforms were flame resistant, but Huber stuck his hands under the opposite armpits and wished he had gauntlets.

Did Orichos think that Colonel Hammer cared about trees when the lives of his troopers were at stake? And if there'd been a thousand civilians in the corridor before the incendiaries fell, that wouldn't have changed the Colonel's plan either.

This was war. If the government of the Point hadn't known

what it meant to hire the Slammers to do their fighting for them, then they were in the process of learning.

Fencing Master slowed, wobbled drunkenly, and finally came to rest on a south-facing backslope with her fans at idle. Deseau rotated the driver's hatch open; Tranter was already climbing off the right side of the fighting compartment.

Huber raised his faceshield, then lifted the commo helmet for a moment to scratch his scalp. He grinned at Captain Orichos and said, "We're getting ready for the final run-up, Captain. If there's anything you need to do while we're halted, do it now. We won't stop again until the shooting's over."

He smiled more broadly and added, "At least over for us, I mean."

Huber was keyed up, but it was in a good way. The drive had been physically and mentally fatiguing. It had blotted out the past and future, turning even his immediate surroundings into a gray blur. Now adrenaline coursed through him, bringing the fire-swept wasteland into bright focus and shuffling a series of possible outcomes through his mind.

Arne Huber was alive again. He might die in the next ten minutes, but a lot of people never *really* lived for even that short time.

"No, I'm ready," Orichos said. She rubbed her hands together, then wiped her palms on the breast of her jumpsuit. If she was trying to clean the ash and grit off them, she failed. "What do you want me to do? In the battle, that is."

Frenchie climbed into the fighting compartment past his tribarrel; Tranter was walking forward on the steel bulge of the plenum chamber. The thirty-degree slope was awkwardly steep for the exchange, but the relatively sparse vegetation here had left fewer smoldering remains than the flatter, better-watered stretches the task force had been crossing.

"Keep out of the way," Huber said. "Keep your head down unless one of us buys it. If that happens, take over his gun and try not to shoot friendlies."

He grinned, feeling a degree of genuine amusement to talk

about his own death in such a matter-of-fact way. He'd chosen the line of work, of course.

Huber really would've preferred to get the Gendarmery officer off his combat car, but that wasn't a practical solution in this landscape. Orichos was smart and quick both, so he could at least hope that she'd jump clear if he or a trooper needed one of the ammo boxes stacked behind her.

Frenchie slid behind his gun and spun the mechanism, ejecting the round from the loaded chamber in a spurt of liquid nitrogen. As he did so, Tranter spun the idling fans up one at a time so that he could listen to the note of each individually. Both men were veterans and experts; they didn't trust their tools to be the way they'd left them until they'd made sure for themselves.

Barely visible eighty meters eastward, *Foghorn*'s crew were giving their car and weapons a final check. Sierra's remaining six combat vehicles waited still further to the east, out of sight from *Fencing Master* behind undulations of the ground.

Despite hotspots in the terrain, the infantry had deployed from the wrenchmobiles; they'd advance on their skimmers to avoid the risk of losing two squads to a single lucky hit. Besides, the recovery vehicles might shortly be needed for their original purpose.

"*Central, this is Sierra Six,*" Captain Sangrela reported over the command channel. "*Sierra is in position. Over.*"

"*Roger, Sierra,*" Base Alpha replied. Despite the compression and stuttering created when the transmission bounced from one ionization track to another, Huber would've been willing to swear the voice was Major Pritchard's. "*Hold two, I repeat, figures two, minutes while we prepare things for you from this end. Central out.*"

Though the transmission closed, an icon on the corner of Huber's faceshield indicated there was view-only information available if he wanted to tap it. He did, tonguing the controller instead of voice-activating the helmet AI.

A crystalline, satellite-relayed voice announced, "*Freedom command, this is Solace Intelligence! Emergency! Emergency! Slammers artillery is launching a maximum effort barrage on your positions! We will relay shell trajectories to you as they leave the guns!*"

The voice transmission ended without a signoff. A data

feed which the AI courteously translated into a schematic of lines curving from south to north across the continent replaced it. The tracks shown as emanating from all three of the Regiment's six-gun batteries were initially blue but turned red at a rate scaled to 880 meters per second: the velocity of 200-mm shells launched from the Slammers' rocket howitzers.

Learoyd clicked the loading tube into his backup weapon, a sub-machine gun, and turned to Huber. "Are we just mopping up again, El-Tee?" he said.

"No, Learoyd," Huber said. He was explaining to Captain Orichos as well. Deseau'd been on the net and would've understood the implications of the way the artillery smashed the Volunteer ambush. Learoyd hadn't understood, and Orichos hadn't heard. "Central's broken into the Solace net to send a false transmission to make the Volunteers think our enemies are helping them. There isn't really any artillery—"

As he spoke, the Regiment's Signals Section followed the graph of "shell trajectories" with computer-generated images of Hogs firing at their maximum rate of ten rounds per minute. The gun carriages jounced from the backblast of each heavy rocket. Doughnuts of dust lifted around the self-propelled chassis and a bright spark of exhaust spiked skyward for the seven seconds before burnout. Real shells would ignite sustainer motors in the stratosphere to range from firebases in the UC to the northern tip of the Point, but there was no need to simulate that here.

"—but if the Volunteers think there is, they'll switch their calliopes to high-angle use. They won't be waiting to hit us when we come into sight."

"This's what we've been waiting for, Learoyd," Deseau said, murderously cheerful. "We get to blow away a bunch of civilians in uniform!"

"Oh," said Learoyd. He turned again and swung hi tribarrel stop to stop, just making sure it'd work when h needed it. Huber didn't recall ever hearing the trooper sour enthusiastic. "All right."

Herbert Learoyd wasn't the brightest trooper in the Re ment, but you could do worse than have him manning right wing gun of your combat car. In fact Huber was sure he could've done better.

It was time to be a platoon leader again. Huber cleared his faceshield and replaced the phony transmission with a fifty degree mask of the terrain map. It showed the planned routes that would take the four combat cars toward the outlying Volunteer positions and Fort Freedom itself. Colored bands connected each course to the segment of hostile terrain for which that car's guns were responsible.

"Fox Three-six to Fox," Huber said. "We'll be executing in a minute or less. If there's any questions, let's hear them now, troopers. Three-six over."

None of his vehicle commanders responded. He'd have been amazed if one had. Four green beads along the top of his faceshield indicated that the cars themselves were within field-service parameters. That could've meant they'd have been deadlined for maintenance on stand-down, but unless there'd been serious damage since the last halt Huber figured they'd all pass even rear-area inspection.

"*Central to Sierra Six,*" the command channel announced. "*You're clear to go. Out.*"

"*Sierra Six to Sierra,*" said Captain Sangrela. "*Execute, troopers!*"

"Go, Tranter!" Huber shouted, thinking that the former technician was waiting for his direct superior to relay the force commander's order.

Fencing Master was already moving. Tranter had fooled him by the skill with which he coaxed the nacelles into a smooth delivery of power, balancing acceleration against blade angle so perfectly that the speed of the eight fans didn't drop below optimum. *Fencing Master* lifted from the clay and climbed the hillside as slickly as a raindrop slides down a windowpane.

They shot over the brow of the hill. Bright verticals on Huber's faceshield framed the sector *Fencing Master* was responsible for, the left post on the western spur of the ancient cinder cone fifteen kilometers away.

To the right *Foghorn* blasted into view measurable seconds later, its bow skirts nearly a meter above the ground for the instant before gravity reasserted itself. *That'll rattle their back teeth*, Huber thought, but he had more immediate problems of his own.

A cyan bolt split the smoke-streaked gloom, whirling

helices of ash as it snapped toward the volcano. A gout of white-hot rock spurted from a cave mouth prepared as a firing position.

Two tanks were hanging back on overwatch while the infantry and the other six armored vehicles charged Fort Freedom at the best speed their fans could drive them. The second tank's bolt lit a secondary explosion, munitions detonating at the ravening touch of a 20-cm powergun. Even at this range, the main guns were capable of destroying anything short of another tank.

Fencing Master's path across the terrain was as smooth as a flowing river—not straight, but never diverging much from the line Tranter had chosen. The other cars and the two advancing tanks were plumes of ash streaking the sky to eastward; they were falling behind *Fencing Master,* though not by so much that Huber worried about it. Somebody had to lead the advance, after all, and he guessed that was what he was being paid for.

The tanks on overwatch, now well to the rear, continued firing, one and then the other. They could hit on the move, but they'd halted so that irregularities of terrain wouldn't mask their fire at some instant it was critically needed. Even the best soldiers and best equipment in the universe—and most of Hammer's troopers would say that meant the Slammers—couldn't keep things from going wrong in battle, but good planning limited the number of opportunities Fate got to screw things up.

Floosie raked the volcano's eastern margin with two tribarrels. The streams of 2-cm bolts interlaced like jets from a fountain—now crossing, now fanning apart. The impacts sparkled against the lava like dustmotes caught in a shaft of sunlight. At twelve kilometers' range the tribarrels weren't likely to be effective, but Jellicoe always claimed that keeping the other guy's head down was the first rule of survival.

The platoon sergeant was a twenty-year veteran so she must know something, but Huber didn't want to burn out his barrels now when in a matter of minutes he'd be at knife range with several thousand hostiles. There wasn't a right way to do it. If suppressing fire was the rabbit's foot Jellicoe used to get through hard times, Huber wasn't going to order her to stop.

Not that he thought she'd obey him anyway.

A geyser of cyan light—powergun ammunition gang-firing—lit the side of the volcano. Blast-gouged rock gleamed white, fading toward red in the instant before the shattered slope caved in to hide it. The tanks were first hitting positions which Central believed were occupied, though they'd shortly hammer the locations where the Volunteers planned to move their guns after the first exchange of fire.

The bloody *civilians* didn't understand that none of their guns would survive its first shot at the Slammers.

A calliope opened up, one of those dug so deep into the forward slope that Volunteer command couldn't retask it to air defense. Its dense volley of 30-mm bolts was probably aimed at *Flame Farter*, which'd already raced past the narrow window through which the calliope fired. The rounds instead came dangerously close to the infantry following. Calcium in the clay soil blazed white in the center of gouting ash; the skimmers maneuvered wildly to avoid the track of shots.

Two 20-cm bolts hit the firing slit in quick succession. The calliope might have been deep enough that neither tank had a direct line on the weapon itself, but the amount of energy the main guns liberated in the tunnel would be enough to cook the crew in a bath of gaseous rock. The hillside burped, then slumped as it rearranged itself.

Fort Freedom loomed above the plain five klicks ahead like a sullen monument. Where the eastern sun angled across ravines, shadows streaked the cinder cone. Speckles against the lava indicated a few Volunteers were firing their personal weapons. At this range the electromagnetic carbines were harmless; the slugs probably wouldn't carry to the oncoming Slammers. Though the attempt showed bad fire discipline, it also meant that not all—not quite all—of the enemy were cowed by the sight of the iridium hammers about to fall on them.

The ground rose slightly into a ridge paralleling the base of the cone and changed from clay to a friable soil that must have been mostly volcanic ash. The forest here had been of tall trees spaced more widely than those of the stretch the task force had just traversed, but the firestorm had reduced them to much the same litter of ash and cinders.

The two tanks accompanying the combat cars halted on the ridge; the wake of debris they'd raised during their passage continued to roll outward under its own inertia. They immediately began punching Volunteer positions with their main guns. The panzers now far to the rear began to advance, accelerating as quickly as their mass allowed. They'd each shot off the twenty round basic load in their ready magazines and couldn't use their main guns until a fresh supply had cycled up from storage in their bellies.

Mercenary artillery in Solace might weigh in at any time. The tanks' tribarrels were tasked to air defense. With the wide sight distances here, that should be a sufficient deterrent. If it wasn't, well, Huber had more pressing concerns right now.

His faceshield careted movement at the top of the cinder cone: the Volunteers were shifting calliopes from air defense sites in the interior of the ancient volcano to notches cut in the rim from which they could bear on the advancing armored vehicles. Huber adjusted his sight picture onto the leftmost caret, enlarging the central portion around the pipper while the surrounding field remained one-to-one so that he wouldn't be blindsided by an unglimpsed danger.

The gun crew had rolled their multi-barrel weapon into position and were depressing their eight muzzles at the mechanism's maximum rate. Huber locked his tribarrel's stabilizer on the glinting target and squeezed the trigger.

Huber's AI blacked out the 2-cm bolts from the magnified image to save his retinas. Instead of a smooth *Thump! Thump! Thump!* as the tribarrel cycled at 500 rounds per minute, it stuttered *Thump!* and a moment later *Thump! Thump!* again. The stabilizer adjusted the weapon within broad parameters, but *Fencing Master* was jolting over broken terrain with a violence beyond what the servos were meant to control. The software simply interrupted the burst until the gun bore again on its assigned target.

The calliope in the holographic sight picture—its iridium barrels gleaming against the frame of baked-finish steel and the taut-faced Volunteers crewing it—slumped like a sand castle in the tide. The impacts were smears of emptiness, but the image cleared in snapshots of destruction, headless bodies falling and white-glowing cavities eaten from the carriage and gun-tubes.

The target's magazines detonated. The flash scooped the square-bottomed firing notch into a crescent five meters across. A mushroom of vaporized rock lifted from the site. Nothing remained of the calliope and its crew.

Blasts and gouts of lava spurted from a dozen places on the crater's rim as combat cars raked the enemy with their tribarrels. Deseau and Learoyd both fired at the turret of an armored car which the Volunteers had held beneath the crater rim until the Slammers were within range of whatever weapon it mounted. Satellite imagery from Central cued the troopers' AIs, so they were waiting with their thumbs on their triggers at the instant the armored car's crew drove up a ramp into firing position.

The turret of high maraging steel blazed in a red inferno before its gun could swing on target. Internal explosions must have killed the whole crew, because they didn't attempt to back the vehicle or bail out of it.

Deseau and Learoyd continued firing, eating away the rock to get to the car's hull. They didn't have a better target— other tribarrels had cleared the rest of the Volunteer positions—and they saw no reason to stop shooting at something that might possibly be useful to the enemy. A fireball of exploding fuel finally ended their fun.

Fencing Master bucked onto humped, barren ridges of hard rock. Layers of ash blown from the vent had formed most of the nearby landscape, but here magma had rolled out of cracks in the base of the cone and solidified. The steel skirts clanged and squealed, scraping showers of red sparks.

Huber grabbed the coaming with his left hand. Captain Orichos shouted as the car bounced her forward into Deseau. Frenchie snarled a vivid curse, but he didn't lose his grip on the tribarrel.

"They're running!" somebody shouted over the general channel. From the voice and the way the AI let it cut through the chatter of a dozen or more excited soldiers, Huber figured it was Captain Sangrela. *"Get the bastards! Get 'em all!"*

The Volunteers had spent years building Fort Freedom. In addition to tunnels carved through the cone, they'd dug hundreds of bunkers on the volcano's outer face. The squads and fire teams placed there hadn't run earlier because there was no way out except up a bare slope; by the time they'd had a good enough look at what was coming toward them, they were more afraid to show themselves than they were to stay.

The shriek as combat cars crossed rock and the nearing intake howl of the fans changed the equation. First a few, then many scores of Militiamen clambered out of their holes to dash for the rim and what they hoped was safety. It was near suicide, but with the tanks continuing methodically to pulverize bunkers, running may still have been the better option even so.

The Volunteers' black uniforms would've blended well with the slopes of compacted ash, but the Slammers' helmets keyed on motion. A forest of translucent red carets lit on Huber's faceshield. All he had to do was swing his sight picture onto the thickest clumps and squeeze his trigger, letting *Fencing Master*'s movement hose the burst across running victims. Bodies and severed limbs bounced against the rock, shrouded in smoke from burning uniforms.

"Get the bastards before they grow their spines back!" Captain Sangrela screamed. *"Get 'em all!"*

Some Volunteers fired from their bunkers or turned to fight like cornered rats as cyan bolts slaughtered their comrades. A burst hit *Fencing Master*'s bow slope and ricocheted in dazzling violet streaks. The car's armor rang like a trip hammer working, but that was just a fact of life. Huber's skin prickled and his throat was as raw as if he'd drunk lye.

Fencing Master reached the cone. It was steep, forty degrees on average and occasionally almost vertical where weather had sheared the concreted ash. Tranter fought his controls, fishtailing the car so that they mounted the slope in a series of switchbacks instead of fighting gravity head on. The combat cars had a higher power to weight ratio than the massively armored tanks did so they could climb the cone, but it still took finesse to do it well.

A powergun bolt stabbed over the rim of the fighting compartment's armor, splashing the interior. The cyan brilliance blew a chunk of iridium into a white-hot bubble between Huber and Deseau.

The gas flung Huber backward, tearing his hands from the tribarrel. He felt as though he'd been slammed in the crotch by a medicine ball.

Heat penetrated a moment later. The fabric of his uniform was temperature resistant, but the metal resolidifying as a black crust over the khaki had vaporized at something over 4800 degrees. *I'll worry about it later. . . .*

Frenchie'd gone down also. He was still holding his tribarrel's left grip, but that was the way a drowning man clutches flotsam. Litter on the floor of the compartment had ignited, twigs and leaves which had whirled into the vehicle during the march as well as plastic wrappers and similar human trash.

Learoyd ripped short bursts toward what was now blank hillside above them: the Volunteer sniper had ducked into his foxhole after firing, and the slope itself concealed the opening. The shooter must've been lucky to hit a target he couldn't see till he showed himself, but he was also good. If he thought he was safe because he was out of sight again, though—

The rock Learoyd's 2-cm bolts was splashing into fist-sized divots of glass suddenly erupted as though the volcano had gone active again. Two tanks hit it, then doubled the initial impacts as soon as their main guns could cycle. Each bolt lifted a truck-sized volume of compacted ash which strinkled down again on the breeze.

There was no sign of the shooter. If his ammunition had gone off, its flash was lost in the immense violence of 20-cm bolts.

Huber's legs were splayed before him; his hands waved in the air. Captain Orichos caught his right wrist and bent close. "Should I take your gun?" she shouted. "Can you—"

"I'm all right," Huber said, forcing the words out. The shock had numbed his diaphragm; breathing was one agony among many. He braced his left arm against the side armor, then let the car's lurch help Orichos lift him to his feet again.

On his feet but not upright; he was still half doubled over and he was pretty sure that he'd vomit if he tried to straighten fully. Via! but he hurt.

Deseau's gun thumped a burst toward the top of the cone. Huber didn't see a target there; Frenchie was probably just proving to himself and others that he was alive and functioning . . . which is what Huber was doing, after all.

"I'm all right!" he repeated, forcefully and with more truth this time. He took his tribarrel's grips in his hands as *Fencing Master* lurched to the top of the ridge, the western battlements of the Volunteer fortress. Below was the interior of the partial cone, and beyond that the sea.

Aircars ranging from the big trucks that could haul twenty or more armed men to hoppers with one seat and room for a sack of groceries were mixed indiscriminately on the crater floor. The drivers had squeezed in wherever they'd seen a place to set down. The Volunteers had left Midway in a near panic; they probably hadn't landed here in much better emotional condition.

There wasn't room in the tunnels to conceal so many vehicles, so the calliopes had been the Volunteers' only means of protecting their hope of escape if things went wrong—as they were certainly going wrong now. Those calliopes were molten ruin, but there was no need to waste shells on the aircars. They were perfect targets for *Fencing Master*'s tribarrels.

A few minutes ago there'd have been only a handful of Volunteers in the open. The maze of tunnels would've seemed safety until those inside realized that the Slammers would with certainty penetrate the outer defenses and so control the tunnel entrances. Now several of the armored doors had swung back; black-uniformed figures were running for vehicles. Huber's view was like a child's of a stirred-up anthill.

A Volunteer drew a holstered powergun and fired in the direction of *Fencing Master* as he ran. One of the bolts snapped only twenty meters overhead, but that was dumb luck: nobody was that good, not with a pistol. Learoyd's short burst vaporized everything between the Volunteer's neck and his knees without any need for luck. He was an expert using a stabilized weapon with holographic sights. Learoyd could've put a round into his target's left nostril if he'd wanted to.

The accompanying infantry squads spaced out to either

side of *Fencing Master*, taking firing positions along the ridge. *Foghorn* still labored a hundred meters down the slope. Huber didn't have leisure to see how Jellicoe's section was doing on the eastern edge of the cone where a deep gully complicated the approach, but he knew she'd get them into action as quick as anybody could.

An aircar lifted. Huber fired as he tracked it, his bolts splashing behind the accelerating vehicle for a moment before three flashes walked up the fuselage from the back. The car, a luxury model, flipped over and crashed under power. Ruptured fuel cells sprayed their contents over a dozen other vehicles, some of which also started to burn.

"Cue aircar motors!" Huber shouted, shifting his AI to mark the electromagnetic rhythms of fan motors spinning. "Gunners—"

Going to intercom.

"—hit the moving cars, not the men!"

Three more vehicles tried to take off. One didn't have enough altitude and collided immediately with the truck parked ahead of it. As it tumbled, Learoyd's burst chopped the car's belly open.

The infantry were shooting at individual targets. Though their weapons were semi-automatic, a single 2-cm bolt was enough to disable an aircar—let alone kill the driver.

One and then both cars of Jellicoe's section opened fire from the other side of the crater. *Foghorn* finally not only mounted the rim but started down the steeper inner slope, wreathed in the grit its steel skirts rasped from the soft rock. Solid cyan streams lashed from its guns.

Deseau either didn't hear Huber's order or ignored it, instead laying his sights onto an entrance. He squeezed his trigger till a blast within spurted a cloud of smoke and yellow flame into the sunlight; the tunnel collapsed.

Three Volunteers rose together behind the bed of a truck, aiming at *Foghorn* for the split second before Huber shot them down. One's carbine fired skyward as his head exploded. Huber'd been swinging his gun onto the car behind the men; its driver leaped out and flattened on the ground. The empty vehicle started to loop before falling sideways and crashing.

Fuel fires and the foul black plumes of burning plastic

rose from dozens of vehicles. Nobody was coming out of the tunnels any more, and the Volunteers surviving on the crater floor either huddled beside cars—there was no "behind" to the crossfire from the rim—or raised their hands in surrender. Many of the latter had their eyes closed as if they were afraid they'd see death coming for them.

"*Sierra, cease fire!*" Captain Sangrela called. "*The enemy's radioed to surrender! Cease fire!*"

A carbine fired. The *whack* of the electromagnetic coils might've gone unnoticed in the chaos, but the *clang!* of the slug ricocheting from *Foghorn*'s armor was unmistakable. Some Volunteer hadn't gotten the word. . . .

Huber hadn't seen the shooter, but Deseau did: his tribarrel was one of five or six guns which spiked the closed cab of an aircar. That car and three more nearby erupted in fireballs. A body panel fluttered skyward, deforming in the heat of the blast that lifted it.

"*Cease fire!*" Sangrela repeated angrily. His jeep was so heavy with electronics that he hadn't been able to reach the rim, so he didn't know the reason for the additional gunfire. "*Cease fire!*"

The shooting stopped. Arne Huber took his hands from the tribarrel grips and flexed them cautiously, afraid they'd cramp. He might need to use them if things got hot again. The underside of his chin was as stiff and painful as if it'd been flayed. The skin there'd caught some of the iridium vaporized when the bolt hit inside the fighting compartment.

"*Cease fire!*" said Captain Sangrela, but nobody was firing any more.

"*Blood and Martyrs!*" Deseau wheezed, raising his faceshield. "*I'm as dry as that rock out there!*"

Huber'd had the same thought. In turning toward the cooler that still should have a few beers in it, he caught sight of Captain Orichos' expression: she looked as though she'd just been told she was Master of the Universe.

It shouldn't have disturbed Huber, but it did.

It'd been pouring rain. Now that the afternoon sun was out, the tents steamed and the clay had already started to bake to laterite. Ash lay as a slimy gray coating over ridges in the soil, but the sides of the rain-carved gullies were the color of rust. Dead tree trunks stood like tombstones for the forest that had once grown here.

"What a bloody fucking awful fucking place!" Deseau snarled, flipping up the front of his poncho without taking it off; the rain could resume any moment. "Learoyd, did you ever see such a bloody fucking awful fucking place?"

"Sure, Frenchie," Learoyd said, frowning as he tried to puzzle sense out of the question. "Remember Passacaglia, where the dust got in everything and we kept burning out drive fans? And that swamp the place before that? And where was it everybody got skin fungus if they didn't wear their gas suits all the time? Was that—"

"Yeah, well, this's still a crummy place," Deseau muttered. He saw Huber smiling and grimaced, turning his head away. Frenchie'd been around Learoyd long enough to know the trooper had too much trouble with the literal truth to make a good audience for a figure of speech—even a figure as simple as rhetorical exaggeration.

Looking eastward toward a dirigible unloading what seemed to be empty shipping containers, Deseau went on, "I wish to hell they'd let us go when the local cops arrived. They can handle anything that's left, can't they?"

Dirigibles full of Gendarmes and the supplies needed for an open-air prison had begun arriving within a few hours of the collapse of Volunteer resistance. Huber, *and* Captain Sangrela, *and* probably every other trooper in the task force, had thought Sierra would be released immediately. The optimists had even hoped they'd be sent back by way of Midway, with a few days of leave as a reward.

Surviving a major engagement like the one just completed made even level-headed troopers optimistic.

Central hadn't felt that way. Sierra had stayed where it was for the three days it took for a column from Base Alpha to reach them.

"It won't be long, Frenchie," Huber said. He quirked a smile. "It shouldn't be long, anyhow."

There were worse places, just as Learoyd said, but this was bad enough in all truth. The Slammers had snagged tents from the loads brought in to house the prisoners, but they didn't help much. You could keep the rain from falling on you, but the ditches the troopers dug around the tents hadn't been enough to stop streams of ash-clogged water from finding their way in from below and soaking everything.

Huber looked over at the POW camp which lay between Task Force Sangrela's defensive circle and the slopes of what had for a short time been Fort Freedom; it was now Mount Bulstrode again. The prisoners had it worse than the troopers did, of course. There wouldn't have been enough tents to go around even if the Slammers hadn't imposed their tax on defeat, but accommodations weren't what was probably worrying the former Volunteers. The Slammers knew they'd be leaving within a few days, maybe even a few hours. The prisoners weren't sure they'd be alive in a few hours.

"*Sierra,*" said Huber's commo helmet in the voice of the signals officer of the approaching column, "*this is Flamingo Six-three. We'll be in sight in figures two, I say again, two, minutes. Don't get anxious. Flamingo out.*"

"Stupid bitch," Deseau muttered. "The only thing I'm anxious about is getting away from this bloody place. And if they'd got the lead outa their pants, that could've happened yesterday."

Huber's opinion was similar enough that he didn't bother telling Frenchie to cool it. You never get relieved as quickly as you want to be. . . .

He wondered if Sierra would be allowed to pick its own route back through the unburned forest, or if in the interests of speed they'd have to return across the fire-swept wasteland. The downpour would've quenched the hotspots, but the filthy sludge the vehicles'd be kicking up in its place wouldn't be much of an improvement.

Huber chuckled. Deseau gave him a sour look.

"Don't mind me, Frenchie," he said. "I'm just thinking that I went into the wrong line of work if I wanted luxury travel arrangements."

"Guess they had to keep us," Learoyd said, nodding toward the waste of mud and tents and captured Volunteers. "I mean, if them guys tried to break out, what was the cops gonna do about it?"

Learoyd was right, as he usually was when he offered an opinion. Squads of Gendarmes patrolled the perimeter of the vast razor-ribbon cage. Six or eight strands of wire were strung on flimsy poles only two meters out of the ground; all things considered, it wasn't much of a barrier. The Point didn't have the resources to deal with the sudden influx of over five thousand prisoners.

The Gendarmes had carbines and pistols. If they'd hoped to supplement those with automatic weapons captured from the Volunteers, they were out of luck. Every crew-served weapon in Fort Freedom had been brought out to face the Slammers, and none of them had survived. For the most part, the sharp-shooting tanks had destroyed the emplacements before the Slammers were in range of the defenders' return fire.

If the prisoners, many of whom were rightly desperate, made a concerted rush on the fence, a few hundred Gendarmes weren't going to stop them. The Slammers' massed fire would, and the certainty the powerguns would hose the camp indiscriminately meant that prisoners who *didn't* want to try a breakout were going to be bloody determined to keep their wilder fellows in line also.

"Via, where's there to run to?" Deseau said. He spat toward the camp a hundred meters away, then started to shrug out of his poncho after all.

"Back into the tunnels, for one thing," Huber said. "There might be enough guns down there to equip a division. It won't be safe till the support column comes up with the gas cylinders."

"That what they're doing, El-Tee?" Deseau said, his tone bright with interest. "Pump the place full of gas?"

Huber shrugged. "Nobody's appointed me to the staff," he said, "but that'd be standard operating procedure: fill the tunnels with KD1 or another of the persistent agents and forget about 'em."

Sledges had been ringing on iron posts as prisoners constructed a narrow chute from the eastern end of the camp. An off-key *whang* indicated a hammer'd hit skew and broken the helve. A Gendarme shouted in a tone of anger tinged with fear, drawing the three troopers' attention.

"Naw, nothing," Deseau muttered, lifting the muzzles of his tribarrel a safe fifteen degrees again so that the weapon wouldn't hit anything in the vicinity if it fired accidentally.

"Them cops, they're ready to piss their pants they're so scared."

Twenty Gendarmes guarded a crew of no more than fifty prisoners driving posts and stringing the wire. They seemed nervous to Huber, also. Maybe they knew what was planned and were afraid of what would happen when the prisoners learned also.

"*Sierra, this is Flamingo Six-three,*" the voice said. "*We're coming into sight. Flamingo out.*"

The vehicles of the task force were bows-out in a defensive circle, though the formation was looser than it'd have been if there were a real likelihood of attack. Instead of turning his head, Huber switched the upper left quadrant of his faceshield to the view from *Floosie* at the opposite side of the formation.

A combat car slid over the ridgeline where Sierra had launched its assault on Fort Freedom. Three similar vehicles followed, then a dozen air-cushion trucks, and after them two wrenchmobiles modified to carry troops. The last vehicle in line was a command car.

"It's the White Mice," Deseau said. From the tone of his voice, Huber thought he might be about to spit. "You know, I was kinda hoping I wouldn't see them again for a while."

"If they're relieving us," Learoyd said, "I don't care who they are."

"Yeah, I guess that's right," Deseau said; but Huber wasn't sure he agreed.

Some prisoners drifted toward the south edge of their camp, interested in the column as a break in their miserable routine and probably also concerned about what it might mean. Huber noticed that others of the former Volunteers were disappearing into tents. He didn't know what they expected to gain by that, but he understood the impulse.

A dozen civilians had come in by aircar a few hours before. They wore hooded raincapes even now that the sun was out, but Huber had raised his faceshield's magnification until he was sure of what he'd suspected: one of the newcomers was Speaker Nestilrode, and he recognized two others as cabinet ministers he'd seen when he entered the Assembly with Captain Orichos.

Now they came out of Orichos' tent. She and the Speaker

shook hands; then the civilians strode quickly to their car without a backward glance.

Orichos sauntered toward the chute of razor ribbon. Perhaps she felt Huber's eyes on her because she turned her head and waved before she walked on.

Deseau snickered. "She fancies you, El-Tee," he said.

"Balls," Huber muttered. Orichos had been running the operation ever since enough Gendarmes had arrived to take primary responsibility from Task Force Sierra. The route march had been just as hard on her as on the Slammers, and so far as Huber'd seen she hadn't had a moment's downtime since. Despite that, Orichos looked as coolly fresh as she'd been the night a lifetime ago when Joachim Steuben introduced her at Northern Star.

Learoyd looked over his shoulder at Huber. "He's right, El-Tee," he said. "She does."

Huber shrugged rather than speaking. He didn't know what to say because he didn't know what he thought. He figured if he pretended not to care, they'd drop the subject.

There was motion in the near distance eastward. "Hey, what d'ye suppose that's all about?" Frenchie said, swinging his tribarrel both as a pointer and out of judicious concern.

Six dirigibles hovered a half kilometer east of the enclosure. Slung beneath them were bar-sided containers like those Huber had seen transporting livestock from the feedlots of Solace to the United Cities where they'd be slaughtered. The props of one of the big airships began to turn at a slightly faster rate than what was necessary to hold position against the breeze. It crawled closer to the camp, its empty containers bonging occasionally when they touched the ground.

Instead of halting to coordinate with Task Force Sangrela, the A Company combat cars drove past the defensive circle and continued around the east side of the prisoner cage. Their skirts squirted water and gray sludge in jets punctuated by the furrows in the soil. Prisoners putting the finishing touches on the chute dropped their tools and scuttled away from the spray.

"Fox Three-six to Sierra Six," Huber said. "Any word what we're supposed to be doing? Over."

The cars' passage splashed the guards as well. A Gendarme officer retrieved the hat that'd been blown into a puddle and shook his fist at the big vehicles. Deseau snickered and said, "Bad move. Could've been a *real* bad move if the dumb bastard'd decided to wave his gun instead."

"*Sierra, this is Six,*" Captain Sangrela said, replying to the whole unit. "*I've been told we're to hold ourselves in readiness to support Flamingo as required. If that sounds to you like, 'Go play, kiddies, while the big boys get on with business,' then you've got company thinking that. Six out!*"

The incoming infantry drove their skimmers off while the wrenchmobiles were still slowing. Huber noticed with some amusement that they didn't perform the operation as smoothly as Captain Sangrela's troopers had. The White Mice were real soldiers as well as being the Regiment's police and enforcers, but they didn't use skimmers nearly as much as the line infantry did.

The newcomers began to deploy along the southern length of the cage. There were only forty of them, so that meant almost ten meters between individuals. They carried 1-cm sub-machine guns rather than a mix of the automatic weapons with 2-cm shoulder weapons.

Deseau must've been thinking along the same lines as Huber was, because he said, "Blow apart the first man who moves with one a' these—"

He patted the receiver of the 2-cm weapon wedged muzzle-down beside his position between two ammo boxes and the armor.

"—and you quiet a mob a lot faster than spraying it with a buzz-gun."

Learoyd looked at him. "Did you ever do that, Frenchie?" he said. "To a mob?"

Huber kept his frown inside his head. You didn't generally ask another trooper about his past. Learoyd had an utter, undoubted innocence that allowed him to say things nobody else could get away with . . . and a lack of mental wattage that made it very likely he would.

Deseau said nothing for a moment, then shrugged. He nodded to Huber, explicitly including him, and said, "Naw, that was back on Helpmeet when I was a kid, Learoyd. I was on the other side of the powergun, you see. So when things quieted down, I joined the Regiment before they shipped out again."

The moving dirigible settled so that all three containers dragged, then detached them. The center box stuck momentarily. The airship bounced upward when the weight of the other two released, so the third clanged loudly to the ground when it finally dropped. It hit on a corner which bent upward, kinking the bars.

"Good thing it wasn't full of cattle," Huber muttered, frowning at the thought of broken legs and beasts bellowing in pain and terror. Now that he'd seen dirigibles in operation, he realized that they were about as unwieldy a form of transportation as humans had come up with. Useful here on Plattner's World, though.

"The cows're gonna be killed anyway, El-Tee," Deseau said. "It don't matter much, right?"

"Maybe not," Huber said; not agreeing, just ending a discussion that didn't have anywhere useful to go. Maybe nothing at all mattered, but on a good day Arne Huber didn't feel that way.

The command car pulled up alongside the chute, making a half turn so that its bow angled toward the camp proper. Though it was an hour short of sunset and the clouds had cleared, the driver switched on his headlights. In their beams the strands of razor ribbon glittered like jagged icicles. Two troopers with sub-machine guns got out of the vehicle and walked over to the wire.

"Prisoners of Hammer's Regiment!" a voice boomed through the command car's loudspeakers. "You will walk in line through the passage at the southeast corner of this camp. As you pass my vehicle—"

The whip antenna on top of the car glowed, becoming a wand of soft red light.

"—you will turn to face it. Then you will walk on to the containers in which you'll be transported to Midway. There you'll be released."

The words were being repeated on the north side of the POW encampment. It wasn't an echo from the volcano, as Huber thought for a moment. The A Company combat cars were relaying the speech through their public address systems.

"Who's that in the car?" Deseau said. From the way his eyes were narrowed, he already knew the answer to his question.

"It sounds like Major Steuben," Huber said. "As you'd expect."

A full company of Gendarmes stood by the shipping containers. Mauricia Orichos was among them, her hands linked behind her back. Huber had been watching her as Steuben spoke. Orichos hadn't been best pleased at the words, "Prisoners of Hammer's Regiment."

That was tough. She knew she'd been the only member of the Point forces present when Fort Freedom fell. The Slammers had taken these prisoners, and if the Gendarmery wanted to get snooty about it, the Slammers could take the prisoners away from their present guards any time they wanted to.

A prisoner bellowed something toward the car. Though he made a megaphone of his hands, Huber couldn't catch the word or brief phrase.

Steuben did, however. The loudspeakers boomed, "A gentleman has expressed doubt that you will actually be released. Let me assure you, mesdames and sirs, that if I wished to kill you all I would not bother with play acting. When you get to Midway, you will be told to sin no more and be released."

The trucks had unloaded their pallets of black-banded gas cylinders. Five of them shut down. The sixth lifted and lumbered past Task Force Sangrela to settle again beside the command car. The driver opened the cab door and stood on his mounting step, looking at the camp. Another squad of White Mice dismounted from the back and walked over to the chute.

"Very well," the PA system thundered. Amplification softened Steuben's clipped tones, making his words sound pompous. Huber found the contrast with the real man chilling. "Start coming through. The sooner you get moving, the sooner we can all get on to more congenial tasks."

A prisoner near the front looked around, then shambled into the chute. One of the White Mice reached an arm over the wire to halt the man in the headlights. His head rose in surprise and sudden fear.

"Keep going!" the amplified voice ordered.

The trooper's arm dropped; the prisoner jogged the rest of the way to where Gendarmes herded him into the first container. Several more prisoners followed, shuffling forward in a mixture of desperation and apathy.

"I suggest reconsideration on the part of anyone who thinks he'll remain in the tents," Steuben continued, the catlike humor of his tone coming through despite mechanical distortion. "We're going to destroy the entire site, starting at the north side. We can see you through cloth as surely as we'll be able to see you in the dead of night, so don't be foolish."

There was a hollow *boop,* then a second later a white flash and a shattering crash. A second *boop, Wham!* followed immediately. Troopers in the combat cars on the north side were firing grenade launchers into the tents.

Thermal viewing would show any holdouts, so there was no need for the grenades. Major Steuben was just making a point, to the Gendarmes as surely as to the captive Volunteers.

"*Sierra, this is Flamingo Six-three,*" said the A Company signals officer. "*Fox Three-six is to report to the command car ASAP. Out.*"

Deseau and Learoyd both looked at Huber. From the driver's compartment, Sergeant Tranter said over the intercom, "*El-Tee? What's going on?*"

Huber cued his intercom and said, "Curst if I know, Sarge. I'll tell you when I get back. Assuming."

He swung his left leg over the armor, then paused. He unclipped the sling of his 2-cm weapon from the epaulet and offered the big gun to Learoyd, saying, "Trade me, will you, Herbert?"

"Sure, sir," the trooper said. He took the 2-cm weapon and slapped the butt of his sub-machine gun into Huber's palm.

Deseau cackled like a demon. "Handier inside a car, eh, El-Tee?" he said.

Huber climbed the rest of the way out of the fighting compartment, then hopped from the plenum chamber to the ground. He started grinning also. You might as well see the humor in the screwed-up way things worked. It didn't change things; but then, nothing *did* change them.

He started toward the command car, his boots squelching and tossing mud up his pants leg with each stride. He didn't look over his shoulder to see the troopers of Task Force Sangrela watching him, but the Gendarmes watched and the driver of the big air-cushion truck stared down from the cab with a puzzled expression.

Grenades continued to crash on the north side of the camp. They'd started several fires; the sluggish flames gave off curls of black smoke.

Enough prisoners had passed through the chute that the cage meant for twenty cattle was what Huber would've called full. The Gendarmes seemed happy to pack more in. Well, if the former Volunteers had nothing worse in their future than an uncomfortable airship ride, they were luckier than they deserved to be.

"That one," the loudspeaker ordered crisply. A low-intensity laser stabbed from the mount of the command car's tribarrel. Its yellow dot quivered like a suppurating boil on the cheek of the bald-headed man nearing the end of the chute.

The fellow looked up in startled horror. One of the waiting troopers grabbed him left-handed by the shoulder, holding the sub-machine gun back like a pistol in his right where the prisoner couldn't reach it.

The trooper walked the fellow out of the chute. Instead of leaving him for the Gendarmes, he handed him over to another of the White Mice who led him in turn to the back of the air-cushion truck.

The prisoners had been moving with something like the docility of the cattle normally loaded into the shipping containers. Now they paused; the woman two places behind the fellow who'd been taken away tried to go back.

"Move it!" the other trooper at the chute snarled, waggling his weapon.

The woman resumed her way down the chute—and out the other end to the Gendarmes, ignored by the voice from the command car. A man who'd been waiting in the crowd turned and started to force his way back through his fellows.

"Halt!" called the trooper nearest to him along the fenceline as he leveled his sub-machine gun. The prisoner tried to run, pushing at others who were trying desperately to get out of the line of fire. The sub-machine gun stuttered a short burst into the man's legs, one bolt into the left calf and two more at the back of the right knee.

The prisoner fell, screaming with surprise. It was too soon yet for the pain to have reached him; though that'd come, it'd surely come. Only a tag of skin and one tendon connected his right thigh and lower leg.

"Two of you carry him through," ordered the loudspeaker. "Make sure to turn his face toward me."

The wounded man continued to scream. He tried to stand but slipped onto his right side.

From the command car, Joachim Steuben giggled. Amplified, the sound was even more gut-wrenching than it'd seemed when Huber heard it from across the major's desk.

The prisoners nearest the fallen man stood frozen till the trooper waggled the glowing muzzle of his sub-machine gun. Then they grabbed his arms convulsively and stumbled through the chute as he screamed even louder. One brushed the razor ribbon, leaving much of his sleeve on the wire and blood dripping from his torn arm. The wounded man's legs didn't bleed; the powergun bolts had cauterized the wounds.

"A moment of your time, Lieutenant Huber," said Captain Orichos. He jumped. She'd walked over to him while his attention was on the byplay in the camp.

"Ma'am?" he said. Without thinking about it, he stiffened to Parade Rest. "That is, Captain?"

"Mauricia, I hope," Orichos said. After the battle she'd resumed wearing her beret instead of a Slammers commo helmet. She took it off now and shook her short hair loose before replacing the cap. "I suppose you know your unit will be routed back with a stopover in Midway?"

"No ma'am," Huber said with a faint grin. "There were rumors, but we're line soldiers. Nobody tells us anything."

"Well, I'm telling you," Orichos said with a mixture of crispness and challenge. "I'll be flying back by car shortly; there are some things to clear up in in the capital now that the threat's been dealt with."

She cleared her throat and looked away. "What I'm saying, Arne, is that I hope when you arrive in Midway, you'll get in touch with me. I'll have some free time by then, and

I'd really like to repay you for all you've done for the Point and for me."

Orichos smiled. It softened and transformed her face to a remarkable degree.

"I think I can guarantee you a good time," she said. She touched the back of Huber's wrist, then turned and went back to her fellows.

Huber rubbed his wrist with the fingers of his other hand as he walked on, thinking about Orichos and about the shooting he'd just watched.

It'd taken skill to hit the running man and not nail a couple of the bystanders. Though it could as easily have been dumb luck: he didn't suppose either the trooper or Major Steuben would've cared if some of the other prisoners had lost limbs.

Huber reached the hatch in the rear of the command car. It opened before he rapped it with the barrel of his powergun. The two men inside had their backs to him as they watched a high-resolution image of prisoners moving steadily through the chute to the shipping containers.

Joachim Steuben was as dapper as if he'd spent the past three days in Base Alpha instead of making a thousand kilometer run over difficult terrain. His companion was blond and in his thirties; Grayle's chief civil aide, Huber recalled, the one who'd disappeared between the Assembly meeting and the time Captain Orichos found incriminating papers in the files that had been under the aide's control.

"That one!" the aide said. What was his name? Patronus; *that* was it. "He's Gerd Danilew. He was in charge of off-planet weapons purchases!"

"That one," Steuben said, his amplified voice damped to silence when the hatch closed behind Huber. The pipper of the cab-mounted tribarrel framed the face of the sallow, moustached prisoner walking nervously between the barriers of razor ribbon.

The man looked up. Instead of trying to run, he fell in a faint as limp as if the tribarrel had decapitated him—as the slightest additional pressure of Steueben's finger on the trigger control would've made it do.

"Well, carry him, then," Steuben ordered into the pickup for the external speakers. He looked over his shoulder at

Huber and raised an eyebrow in delighted amusement, then turned back and added, "Now!"

The procession resumed. Patronus kept his face rigidly forward as if he thought that by refusing to acknowledge Huber, he could deny what was going on.

Steuben rotated his full-function chair to smile at Huber. "So, Lieutenant," he said. "I thought I'd use this opportunity to see if you're still happy with a line command."

Instead of the slot in the White Mice that he offered me three weeks ago, Huber thought. He shrugged and said, "Yeah, I'm happy. We did a good job here."

He guessed he'd made that sound like a challenge, which wasn't the smartest sort of attitude to show when you were talking to a weasel like Joachim Steuben. Huber didn't care much at the moment.

"Indeed you did," Steuben said, nothing in his tone but mild approval. "Both the task force and you personally . . . which is why my offer is still open."

He cocked an eyebrow.

"I said I was happy!" Huber said. Via, he was going to have to watch himself. It'd be a hell of a note to come through a mission like this one and then be shot because he mouthed off to a stone killer like Joachim Steuben.

He smiled—at himself, but it was probably the right thing to do because the major giggled in response.

"That one!" Patronus said, pointing at the image. His hands were clean but he'd chewed his fingernails ragged.

Major Steuben's right hand moved minutely, then clicked the switch that controlled the laser marker. Huber didn't see him look around, not even a quick glance, but the pipper was centered on the forehead of the grim-looking man who'd brushed his full moustache in an attempt to cover the scar on his cheek. "That one," Steuben repeated into the PA system.

In a quick voice, bobbing his head to his words, Patronus continued, "That's Commander Halcleides, he took over after Commander Fewsett—that is, when he died."

"What happens next?" Huber asked. He didn't exactly care, but he knew Deseau'd ask when he got back to *Fencing Master* and he wanted to have an answer. "You'll shoot them?"

Patronus turned with a furious expression. "They're traitors!" he snarled. "They deserve to die!"

Steuben made a peremptory gesture with his left hand. His head didn't turn, but Huber saw his eyes flick toward the former aide.

"Master Patronus," Steuben said without raising his voice, "I'd appreciate it if you'd attend to your duties while the lieutenant and I speak like the gentlemen we are. I don't want the bother of replacing you."

He giggled again. To Huber he added, "Though shooting him would be no bother at all, eh, Lieutenant? For either of us, I suspect."

Patronus was on a seat that folded down from the sidewall. He turned again to face the screen across the front of the compartment, pointedly concentrating on the prisoners shambling through the identification parade. His face flushed, then went white.

Huber looked at the man who'd first planted evidence on his friends and now was fingering his closest colleagues for probable execution. In a good cause, of course: the Regiment's cause. But still . . .

"No, Major," Huber said. "It wouldn't be much bother."

"But to answer your question," Steuben continued, "no, we're not going to shoot them, Lieutenant. They'll be shipped off-planet to a detention center; an asteroid in the Nieuw Friesland system, as a matter of fact. The Colonel believes they'll be a useful . . . reminder, shall we say, to the government of the Point as to what might happen if it suddenly decided to back away from its support for the war with Solace."

"Th-the-there," Patronus said, pointing at the strikingly attractive woman going through the chute. His outstretched hand trembled. "Talia Mandrakora, she was in charge of propaganda."

"That one," Steuben said, highlighting the woman. To Huber he added, "Do you fancy her, Lieutenant? I dare say you could convince her that the only chance she has to survive would involve pleasing you."

Huber felt his lip curl. "No thanks," he said. "I don't have trouble finding company for the night."

"I'm sure that's true," Steuben said with a smirk. He

rotated his chair toward the screen again. His posture didn't change in any definable way, but he was no longer the man who'd been joking with catlike cruelty. "And now, I think, we have the personage we've been waiting for."

The prisoners waiting to walk through the chute parted, glancing over their shoulders and then lowering their faces as they pushed clear. Melinda Riker Grayle strode through the gap which fear rather than respect had opened for her. She was no longer the woman who'd cowed her colleagues in the Assembly. She wore a white uniform but the right sleeve had been singed and at least some of the stain on her trousers was blood. Nonetheless she walked with her back straight, glaring toward the command car.

"Invite Assemblyman Grayle to join her associates in our van, if you please, Sergeant Kuiper," Steuben said into the pickup.

Grayle walked alone into the chute. The trooper there hesitated, his arm raised but not fully extended.

"Keep your filthy hands off me!" Grayle said. Steuben must've switched on the external microphones, for the assemblyman's voice sounded as clear as if she'd been in the compartment with them.

She turned to face the car and shouted, "You in there, whoever you are! Hired killers! You know the election was rigged! And *you* know that you're charging ten times what the citizens think they're paying for your services! Tell them!"

"Take her away, Kuiper," Steuben said, sounding vaguely bored. "I'd rather you not shoot her in the legs so that she has to be carried, but do that if she won't come peaceably."

"You know it's true!" Grayle screamed. When the trooper reached for her shoulder she slapped his hand away, but instead of resisting further she marched down the chute and turned toward the truck where her aides were being held. Her head was high, and she didn't look around.

Steuben smirked at Huber. "She's right, you know," he said conversationally. "The election was rigged. The Freedom Party would've taken forty-four percent of the seats if your friend Captain Orichos hadn't manipulated the vote count."

Huber looked sharply at the smaller display above the big screen, a 360-degree panorama from the command car.

Mauricia Orichos stood watching the parade with three other Gendarmery officers, a few meters behind the White Mice who did the sorting. They followed Grayle with their eyes until she'd disappeared into the box of the truck.

"Orichos did that?" Huber said.

"She asked us for technical help so it could be done without detection," Steuben said, looking up at the panorama with a faint smile. "I provided someone from my signals section. It would've been extremely awkward if Grayle had become Speaker and tried to take the Point out of the war."

As Steuben spoke Patronus turned slowly toward him, like a rat hypnotized by the slowly waving hood of a cobra. Steuben focused his ice-colored eyes on the traitor and said, "I believe I told you—"

He broke off in the middle of the passionless threat for another giggle. "But then," he continued, "with Mistress Grayle in hand, we don't have to worry about other threats to hold over our friends, do we? I suppose we could just dismiss the rest of the prisoners . . . though I don't believe we will for the moment."

He gestured Patronus back to the screen and the line of prisoners resuming their procession through the chute. Patronus obeyed with the slow, jerky motion of an ill-made automaton.

"Was the rest of it true too?" Huber asked harshly. His throat hadn't recovered from the ozone he'd breathed during the battle, but he and the major both knew there was more to his tone than that. "About the costs being higher than they know?"

Steuben shrugged. "In a manner of speaking," he said. "The governments of the Outer States believe the Regiment's price is only about twenty percent of the real figure. . . . But don't worry: our fees *are* being paid, and line lieutenants don't have to worry about where the money comes from."

"I suppose not," Huber said. He tried to make his mind go blank, but he couldn't manage it. "Sir, if you don't have any further duties for me here . . . ?"

"You don't like our company?" Steuben said, his smile flashing on and off like a strobe light. "All right, Lieutenant. You're free to leave."

Major Steuben rotated his chair toward Huber again. His face, too pretty to be handsome in a man, was suddenly as hard as chilled steel. "The offer remains open, Lieutenant," he said. "You should feel flattered, you know."

"I appreciate your confidence, sir," Huber said. He turned to the hatch; it opened before he could touch the control plate.

Huber stepped into the gathering darkness. Grenade launchers continued to work, the choonk/*wham!* choonk/*wham!* punctuating the sound of drive fans and power tools. Troopers were pulling maintenance on their vehicles with spares the column had brought from Base Alpha. The white flashes of the bombs were quick speckles through the fabric of tents bulging outward before they collapsed.

Mauricia Orichos saw Huber come out of the command car. She stepped away from the group she was with and waved to him.

Huber looked at her, then slipped his faceshield down and quickened his stride in the direction of *Fencing Master*. As he'd told Major Steuben, he could find his own company. And he wasn't going to find it there.

NECK OR NOTHING

"Red Section, pull back two hundred meters!" Lieutenant Arne Huber ordered over the platoon channel. A laser from one of the hostile hovertanks touched a tree to the right, blasting a ten-meter strip off the trunk. Fragments of bark and sapwood stung Huber and the two gunners with him in the combat car's open fighting compartment. "Blue, we'll hold till Red's in position! Six out."

The artificial intelligence in Huber's commo helmet imposed a translucent red caret on his faceshield, warning of movement to the left. Huber was *Fencing Master*'s left wing gunner as well as commander of platoon F-3. At the moment, swinging his tribarrel onto the threat took precedence over controlling the platoon's other five cars.

The motion was the hull of a hovertank from a mercenary unit hired by Solace in its war with the Outer States. The vehicle was three hundred meters away, much farther than you could generally see in the forests of Plattner's World, and the tank's two crewmen probably weren't aware of *Fencing Master* as they drove across the battlefront hoping to take F-3 in the flank.

The target quivered in Huber's holographic sight picture. He settled his weapon and squeezed the butterfly trigger with both thumbs. The cluster of iridium barrels rotated as they fired, giving each tube a moment to cool after spewing a bolt of ionized copper downrange at the speed of light.

The narrow window didn't allow Huber to choose a particular spot on his target, but the energy a 2-cm powergun packed made most things vulnerable. The compartment holding the hovertank's crew was armored with ceramic layered in ablative sheets, proof against single bolts or even a short burst, but the skirts enclosing the plenum chamber were light plastic to keep the weight down. Huber raked the bulge where the two joined.

A fireball erupted from the tank's port side: the cyan plasma had converted the plastic into its constituent elements—which recombined explosively. The flash ignited even the loam of the forest floor.

"I can't see it!" screamed Frenchie Deseau at *Fencing Master*'s bow gun. "Padova, pull up, for Hell's sake! I can't see the target!"

The hostile was directly ahead of *Fencing Master*, so by rights it should've been Deseau's target while Huber watched the left flank the way Trooper Learoyd was doing the right from the other wing gun. It was a chance of visibility that made the tank Huber's prey while the trees concealed it from Deseau.

The tank rocked to the right, then slewed to a halt because Huber'd ripped its skirts wide open. The tank's gunner tried to rotate his roof-mounted laser, but Huber's tribarrel blew the weapon to fiery slag an instant before rupturing the crew compartment itself.

What mattered was that *some*body got the tank before it took F-3 from the rear; but if F-3 didn't fall back quickly, another tank or tanks *were* going to circle them. There were too many hostiles for a single platoon of combat cars to deal with for long. Where the bloody hell was Ander's Legion, the combined arms battalion that was supposed to follow when F-3 seized the knoll in the face of the advancing Solace column?

"*Three-six, this is Three-three!*" crackled the voice of Platoon Sergeant Jellicoe, commanding the three cars of Red Section. For this operation Huber would rather have operated in three two-car sections, but two of his vehicles were crewed with replacements. The newbies had been trained and may well have been veterans of other units before they joined Hammer's Slammers, but Huber didn't want to risk anybody operating alone until he'd personally seen how they held up in combat. "*We're in position! Over!*"

"Blue Section," Huber ordered, "pull—"

Fencing Master was already starting to reverse. Although she'd just been transferred to F-3, Padova'd already shown an ability to anticipate orders—sometimes the difference between life and death in combat. As the car grunted backward, Deseau and Learoyd fired simultaneously.

For an instant, saplings ranging from thumb-thick to thigh-thick blazed. When the blue-green bolts had sawn through the undergrowth, they flashed and cascaded from the sloping armor of the hovertank coming up from a swale less than twenty meters away.

"*Via!*" Huber shouted. The tank was well to starboard, but *Fencing Master* shimmied as Padova backed so there was a chance the stern would swing enough to give Huber a shot. He tried to bring his tribarrel to bear as he cursed himself for not keeping better tabs on the sensor readouts. Because Huber was the platoon leader, *Fencing Master* carried a Command and Control box whose holographic display would show the heat, noise, and radio-frequency signatures of a fifty-tonne tank charging to within stone's throw. He just hadn't taken—hadn't *had*—time to glance at it.

The tank's sloping armor reflected a portion of the bolts' energy as a haze of cyan light, searing the leaves from overhanging trees. The glare was so intense that Huber's faceshield blacked it out to save his eyesight.

Despite the hits, capacitors feeding the tank's laser screamed twice. The first pulse fried the air close enough overhead that Huber might've lost his hand if he'd raised it at the wrong time. That was probably a chance shot, though, because the second charge ripped empty forest twenty meters to the left, and then the tank's ceramic armor failed under the tribarrels' hammering.

At the temperature of copper plasma, almost everything burns. The gulp of orange flame from the tank's interior was partly plastic, partly fabric, and partly the flesh of the crew.

Padova kept backing away from the line of contact. Flat-screen displays provided a combat car's driver with just as good a view to the rear as forward, but driving through dense woodland in reverse required considerable skill. *Fencing Master*'s skirts struck only one tree too thick to shear off.

Even that was a glancing blow, though it threw the troopers hard against the fighting compartment's armor.

"Blue Section, pull back!" Huber said, completing the interrupted order as he checked his display. The other two cars were already retreating up the forested ridgeline; their commanders must have filled in the obvious if their drivers had needed the prodding. You didn't have to be a military genius to know that F-3's position wasn't survivable for long, when at least a company of hostile tanks was advancing and there was no bloody sign of Ander's Legion.

The woods were afire in a dozen places, ignited by energy weapons and the violent destruction of several vehicles— all of them hostile so far, the Lord be thanked, but that couldn't last forever. Besides the wall of trees, smoke obscured normal vision. That gave F-3 an advantage because the Slammers' sensors were better than those of their opponents, but in the confusion of battle there were too many inputs for anybody to use them all. Quick reactions, not technology, had saved *Fencing Master* when the hovertank roared up at them from less than pistol range.

Red Section waited hull-down over the reverse slope of the ridge from which F-3 had advanced twenty minutes before. Huber had expected to form a skirmish line while Ander's Legion dug in to ambush the oncoming Solace column. Ander hadn't come and the hostiles had—*very* aggressively.

Padova brought *Fencing Master* back to where they'd started their advance, in the shelter of smooth-barked trees whose foliage was a golden contrast to the deep green of most of the species around them. The economy of Plattner's World was based on gathering the so-called Moss, a fungus that parasitized the native trees and which could be processed into the anti-aging drug Thalderol. In normal times here, the wanton destruction of forest was a serious crime.

War imposed different standards. The recent engagement had turned a kilometer of woodland into a spreading blaze where munitions occasionally exploded. The hostiles, elements of the West Riding Yeomanry hired by Solace, had halted to regroup to the west of the fiery barrier. The tanks would come on in a moment, buttoned up and using their numbers to envelope the Slammers on both flanks even though Huber had stretched F-3 with forty meters between combat cars.

That was far too great an interval in forest where normal sight distance was only half that. *Foghorn*, immediately to the right of *Fencing Master*, was an occasional glint of iridium through the foliage. Skilled infantry could slip through the line to do all manner of damage before the troopers knew what was happening.

The long burst had heated *Fencing Master*'s right tribarrel till it jammed. A smear of the plastic matrix that held copper atoms in alignment in the chamber clogged the ejection port instead of spitting out cleanly. Learoyd was chipping at the mess with his knife while Deseau covered both front and starboard with quick jerks of his head and a tense expression.

"Fox Three," Huber ordered; it was time and past time to cut and run. "We'll withdraw in line behind Three-six on the plotted track."

As he spoke, he entered Execute on the manual controller of the C&C box, transmitting to all the troopers of his platoon the course the AI had chosen to his directions. They'd retreat parallel to the line on which they'd advanced, but not over the same track in case Solace forces had laid artillery on it in the interim.

"I'm going to start at forty kph and I'll raise our speed if I can," Huber continued. "If you've got trouble keeping interval let me know, but I don't want these bloody tanks up our ass. Over."

"*Three-six, this is Three-three!*" Jellicoe called from the north end of the line. "*I've got movement to my rear, El-Tee! D'ye suppose Ander's got his thumb outa his butt finally? Over.*"

"Fox Three," Huber ordered as he switched his display to give the readout from *Floosie*, Jellicoe's car. "Hold in place! Three-six out."

Everything takes time.... F-3 couldn't sit long on a hillside in the face of flames and a hostile armored column, but Huber *had* to process information before he made a decision on which turned a battle and the lives of all his troopers. Beside him, Learoyd spun his barrel cluster a third of a turn to charge the weapon. Deseau slewed his tribarrel to the left; the bearing squealed faintly. Now Frenchie was covering the port side while his lieutenant concentrated on sensor readouts.

For a moment Huber thought they might pull this off after all: Ander's Legion was late, but the delay would've convinced the hostiles that the Slammers had been left hanging. When F-3 pulled back, the Yeomanry were likely to follow without keeping a proper lookout. With any kind of luck, Ander's force could take them in the flank and hammer them good while Huber brought his cars around to block the Solace line of retreat.

Except—

"Bloody fucking Hell!" Huber shouted.

He didn't want it to be true, but there was no question in the world that it was. Sergeant Jellicoe wasn't at fault: all the cars carried the same sensor pack, but the additional sorting power in *Fencing Master*'s Command and Control box made the difference.

There was an armored column coming up fast from F-3's rear, all right, but it wasn't Ander's Legion which rode on *tracked* armored personnel carriers. These twenty-three vehicles, a mix of APCs and gun carriers, ran on six or eight wheels. The AI gave a 93 percent probability that they were a company of the Apex Dragoons, another of the units in Solace pay.

F-3 was trapped.

"Fox Three, this is Three-six," Huber said, his voice calm. He was speaking noticeably slower than he usually would have. Every syllable was precise, a reaction to stress rather than a conscious attempt to be clear in a crisis. "The vehicles approaching from the east are hostile also. We'll charge through them in line abreast instead of withdrawing to the southeast as planned."

As Huber spoke, his right hand laid out routes and targets in the C&C display for immediate transmission to the helmets of his troopers. There were more enemy vehicles than there were guns in F-3, almost four targets per car, so he had to overlap the assignments.

That was if everything went right, of course. As soon as F-3 started taking casualties, its suppressing firepower went down and with it everybody's chance of survival.

"Hit anything you see, troopers, but remember job one is to save our asses," Huber said. "Drivers, keep your foot in it. Don't slow for anything, get through and get out, that's the only way we're going to be around to talk about this afterwards."

Beneath Huber, Padova was rotating *Fencing Master* on its axis to align its bow for the coming attack. Huber was conscious of the change only as vibration and a blur in his peripheral vision; his focus was utterly on the holographic landscape of six blue dots and the hornet's nest of red hostiles through which F-3's commander had to lead them.

"We'll execute on the command," Huber said, giving the display a last searching glance as he prepared to exchange it for the view through his tribarrel's sights. "And the Lord help us, troopers, because there sure as hell isn't anybody else on our side today. Fox Three, *execute!*"

Padova had *Fencing Master*'s drive fans whining at full power. Instead of setting the blades to zero incidence, she'd chosen to cock the nacelles against one another in pairs so that they were already flowing maximum air and wouldn't have to accelerate against a fluid mass when it came time to move. *Fencing Master* pogoed minusculely as it slid downhill through the undergrowth. The Dragoons, approaching in line abreast, were within half a klick but still on the other side of rising ground.

Fencing Master's skirts crumbled a low overhang into a flat-bottomed swale. There must've been a watercourse here in season, but now the leaves the fans stirred were dust-dry. Huber watched his sector, his tribarrel slanted slightly upward to cover the crest of the ridge beyond the concealing undergrowth.

The soil on the slope must not have been as good as that in most of the region, because the trees were sparser and averaged twenty meters in height instead of the twenty-five or thirty normal for adult specimens of the same species elsewhere. More light reached the understory and low brush grew thicker.

Huber ignored the C&C display to focus on the portion of *Fencing Master*'s surroundings for which he was personally responsible. The Slammers' faceshields used sensor data to caret the most probable vectors from which targets might appear. He'd directed the AI to screen out hostiles to the rear. In the unlikely event the pursuing tanks caught up with F-3, Huber and his troopers were dead with absolute certainty: there was no point in worrying about what couldn't be changed.

The vehicles' electronics suites meant the Slammers had a huge amount of information. Unless they were careful, they could drown in information instead of making the instant decisions a battle demanded of anyone who hoped to survive.

Arne Huber wouldn't allow his mind to lose itself in data instead of action, but the sensors' warning had saved F-3 from stumbling unaware into a superior enemy. The Apex Dragoons were a respectable force, but they didn't have electronics of comparable discrimination and might not even know the combat cars were heading toward them. Though Huber couldn't kid himself that the Solace forces had mousetrapped his platoon by pure accident. . . .

"*Wait for it . . .*" Deseau warned over the intercom; talking to himself mostly, because they were all veterans and knew what was about to happen.

Padova tweaked her fan nacelles expertly, lifting *Fencing Master* over the crest on nearly an even keel. Below, zigzagging because their power-to-weight ratio didn't allow them to climb the steeper reverse slope straight on, were three armored personnel carriers with a pair of anti-tank missiles on a cupola mounting an automatic cannon. Far to *Fencing Master*'s right was a larger vehicle with a long electrochemical cannon in its turret. Huber squeezed his trigger as his tribarrel settled on the nearer of the two APCs on his side.

The APC's commander had his head out of the cupola hatch to conn his vehicle. He'd started to duck, but Huber's first bolt decapitated him in a cyan flash. The rest of the burst splashed on the cupola, setting off an anti-tank missile in a gushing yellow low-order explosion.

Huber'd pulled the APC's teeth by wrecking the turret. Without spending more rounds—*Fencing Master* would be through the Dragoons and gone before the infantry in the rear compartment could unass their vehicle and start shooting—he swung his gun toward the APC that he'd assigned both to himself and the car to the left, Sergeant Nagano's *Foghorn*. Deseau and Learoyd were firing, and the forest echoed with the snarling thump of powerguns punctuated by the blast of the Dragoons' weapons.

When Huber saw black exhaust puff from the far side of his target's cupola, he knew he'd been too late to keep the gunner from loosing a missile. Though the cupola hadn't rotated onto *Fencing Master* yet, as the missile came off the launch rails it made a hard angle toward the combat car on the thrust of its attitude jets.

"*Via!*" Huber screamed, knowing that now survival was in the hands of the Lord and *Fencing Master*'s Automatic Defensive System. A segment of the ADS tripped, blasting a charge of osmium pellets from the explosive-filled groove where the car's hull armor joined the plenum chamber skirts.

Fencing Master jumped and clanged. The pellets met the incoming missile, shoving it aside and tearing off pieces. The warhead didn't detonate—a good thing, because this close it still would've been dangerous—but a shred of tailfin slashed Huber's gunshield, leaving a bright scar across the oxidized surface.

Learoyd's target, a forty-tonne guncarrier, went off like a huge bomb. The concussion spun *Fencing Master* like a top, slamming Huber against the side of the fighting compartment. Despite the helmet's active shock cushioning, his vision shrank momentarily to a bright vertical line.

The guns of the Apex Dragoons used liquid propellant set off by a jolt of high current through tungsten wire. Besides adding electrical energy to the chemical charge, the method ignited the propellant instantly and maximized efficiency for any bore that could accept the pressures.

Learoyd's burst had detonated the reservoir holding the charges for perhaps a hundred main-gun rounds. The explosion left a crater where the vehicle had been and a cloud of smoke mushrooming hundreds of meters in the air.

Fencing Master grounded twice, sucked down when the wave of low pressure followed the shock front. Padova fought her controls straight, then tried to steer the car back in the original direction; they'd spun more than a full turn counterclockwise and were now headed well to the left of the planned course.

The shockwave rocked the Dragoon APC up on its three starboard wheels. The vehicle didn't spin because it was some distance farther from the blast and its tires provided more stability than the fluid coupling of pressurized air linking the combat car to the ground.

Huber's eyesight cleared; his tribarrel already bore on the APC's rear hull. He fired, working his burst forward while bolts from Deseau's weapon crossed his. Their plasma shattered the light aluminum/ceramic sandwich armoring the APC's side. The hatches blew open in geysers of black smoke which sucked in, then gushed as crimson flames.

Learoyd lay huddled on the floor of the fighting compartment. His left hand twitched, so at least he was alive. There was no time to worry about him now, not with all F-3 in danger.

Fencing Master drove between the two APCs, both oozing flames, and roared down the steep slope. Explosions thundered in the near distance. Huber glanced to his left as a ball of orange flame bubbled over the treetops. It had vanished some seconds before the ground rippled and the walls of the valley channeled a wave of dust and leaf litter past *Fencing Master* and on.

Huber pivoted his tribarrel to cover the rear. In shifting, he banged his right side on the coaming. The unexpected pain made him gasp. The blast had bruised him badly and maybe cracked some ribs.

Deseau took over the right wing gun. Learoyd had managed to get to his hands and knees, but it'd be a while before he was able to man his weapon again.

Or maybe it wouldn't, come to think. Bert Learoyd had the tenacity of an earthworm, though perhaps coupled with an earthworm's intellectual capacity.

Huber checked his C&C display. All six cars were still in action, though the icons for *Foghorn* and *Farsi's Fancy*—Car Three-seven in Jellicoe's section—showed they were reporting battle damage.

Even the Slammers' electronics couldn't discriminate between the signatures of vehicles with some systems running though the crews were dead, and those which were fully functional. Apart from the occasional catastrophic explosion like that of Learoyd's target, there was no way to be sure of how much of the hostile mechanized company remained dangerous. They'd taken a hammering, no mistake, but right now all Huber was concerned about was F-3's survival. Thanks to Ander's inaction, the Slammers had lost this battle before the first shot was fired.

The United Cities government had employed many small units of mercenaries instead of a few large formations, because noplace on the planet except Port Plattner in Solace could land a starship big enough to hold a battalion and its equipment. Hammer's Regiment was one of the the largest units in UC pay, and some of the others were only platoons.

There would've been coordination problems even at best, but the real trouble arose because neither the UC nor any of the other Outer States had a military staff capable of planning and executing a war on the present scale. Colonel Hammer and his team at Base Alpha had taken over the duties because there was no one else to do it, but that caused further delays and confusion. Everything had to be relayed through UC officers who often didn't understand the words they were parroting, and even so other mercenary captains dragged their feet on orders they knew were given by a peer.

Some UC units were incompetently led; that might well be the case with Ander's Legion. Their communications systems varied radically; Central at Base Alpha could communicate with all of them, but many couldn't talk to one another. And some mercenary captains, especially those who commanded only a company or platoon, were less concerned with winning wars than they were with protecting the soldiers who were their entire capital.

Those were staff problems, but they became the concern of line lieutenants like Arne Huber when they meant that his combat cars were left swinging in the breeze. Ander hadn't gotten the word, or he hadn't obeyed orders, or he was simply too bumbling to advance when he was supposed to.

There was an obvious risk of further Solace units following close behind the initial company of Dragoons, but despite that Huber had a bad feeling about continuing on his plotted course to the southeast. He'd already asked his AI to assess alternate routes, but before he got the answers the C&C

display threw sensor data across the terrain in a red emergency mask. It was worse than he'd feared.

"Three-six to Fox Three," Huber said in a tone from which previous crises had burned all emotion. "Hostile hovertanks have gotten around us to the south. Fox Three-three—" Sergeant Jellicoe in *Floosie* "—leads on the new course at nine-seven degrees true. Three-six out. Break—"

His voice caught. He thought for a moment that he was going to vomit over the inside of his faceshield, but the spasm passed. There'd been too much; too much stress and pain and stench, even for a veteran.

"—Padova, throttle back so that we stay on the crest after the rest are clear. We may need the sensor range."

The Solace commander had reacted fast by sending part of the Yeomanry around the Slammers' left flank at the same time as the mechanized company circled their right. Huber'd held F-3 too long as he waited for supports that never came, but there was still a chance. The crews of the hovertanks wouldn't be in a hurry to come to close quarters with the cars that had bloodied their vanguard so badly at the first shock.

Fencing Master growled onto the ridge line. The rise would separate the combat cars from the units they'd already engaged, though the tanks approaching from the south were in the same shallow valley. The forest was somewhat of a shield for F-3, maybe enough of one.

Learoyd was on the forward gun now, swaying as though the grips were all that kept him upright. Deseau scanned the trees to the right, the direction the tanks would come from. Undergrowth was sparse here, but the treeboles allowed only occasional glimpses of anything as much as a hundred meters away.

F-3 was in line with the flanks echeloned back. The four cars in the center were across the ridge and proceeding downslope, but Jellicoe had slowed *Floosie* also. The additional ten seconds of sensor data hadn't brought any new surprises, so Huber said, "Padova, goose it and—"

The clang of a slug penetrating iridium echoed through the forest. The icon for Fox Three-three went cross-hatched and stopped moving across the holographic terrain of the C&C display.

"Padova, get us to *Floosie* soonest!" Huber shouted. "Break! Fox Three, follow the plotted course. Three-one, you're in charge till I rejoin with the crew of Three-five! Three-six out!"

Huber hadn't thought, hadn't had time to think, but he knew as Padova jerked *Fencing Master* hard left that instinct had led him to the right decision. Though two other combat cars were nearer *Floosie* than *Fencing Master* was, they'd have to reverse and climb the slope to reach the disabled vehicle. Gravity was more of a handicap than an extra hundred meters on level ground when you were riding a thirty-tonne mass.

Sergeant Nagano—Fox Three-one—was a few months junior in grade to Three-seven's Sergeant Mullion, but Nagano'd been in F-3 when Huber took command a year ago while Mullion had been posted into the platoon only a few days before. Mullion might turn out to be a real crackerjack, and if so Huber would apologize to him at a suitable time. Right now there was enough else going wrong that Huber wasn't about to trust his troopers to an unknown quantity besides.

Fencing Master wove between the trunks of massive trees. Learoyd slid the fingers of his left hand under his helmet to rub his scalp and forehead, but his right never left the grip of his tribarrel. He seemed to be back to normal now, or anyway what passed as normal for a trooper in the middle of a firefight.

Chatter filled the platoon push, but none of it came from Jellicoe and her crew. Huber tuned out the empty noise—anybody was likely to babble in the stress of a battle, no matter how well-trained and experienced they might be—and concentrated on what wasn't there.

The icon for Three-three continued to pulse sullenly. Huber imported a remote image from Jellicoe's gunsight to the corner of his faceshield. He got only a motionless view of treetops, but at least that was better than the black emptiness of an open channel.

"*There's* Floosie!" Learoyd said. "*El-Tee, they been hit from your side!*"

Floosie was tilted against the west side of a huge tree, spun there by the first of the two rounds which'd hit her.

The slug had struck the back of the fighting compartment and penetrated cleanly, angling slightly left to right and exiting above the driver's hatch.

Floosie'd stalled at the impact. The second shot had slammed into the plenum chamber before the driver could restart his vehicle. That wasn't his fault: the combined shock of the slug and collision with a three-meter thick treebole was more any anybody could've shrugged off instantly, even protected by the automatic restraint system of the driver's compartment. The follow-up round had put paid to *Floosie*: there was a gaping hole in the skirts and at least half the fan nacelles would've been damaged or destroyed.

The tank had that knocked out the combat car was sited on the high ground a kilometer to the west. The hostile gunner had been lucky to get a sight line through the trees, but he'd been bloody good to react to the unexpected target and then to punch out a second round to finish the job. With so many shots ripping through the forest, one of them was bound to connect with something. . . .

"Padova, get us—" Huber said, but his driver was already slewing *Fencing Master* to the right, putting the tree and the bulk of the disabled car between them and the Solace gunner. The tank might've moved forward after it fired; but its commander just might have decided that he was better off where he was than he'd be if he came to close quarters with the Slammers' tribarrels.

Deseau braced himself against the coaming beside Huber, cursing a blue streak. He'd grabbed Learoyd's backup 1-cm sub-machine gun from its sling on a tie-down beside the right tribarrel. It wasn't much of a weapon to threaten tanks with, but at least Deseau could point it toward the probable dangers.

Fencing Master slewed around the tree and grounded hard, its port quarter almost in contact with *Floosie*'s damaged bow skirt. The ragged exit hole was bigger than an access port.

Jellicoe's driver climbed out of his hatch. He'd lost his helmet and his mouth hung open. A bitter haze of burned insulation lay over the fighting compartment, but as *Fencing Master* stopped, Huber saw a hand reach up to grip the coaming: Sergeant Jellicoe was still alive, if only just.

"Get aboard!" Huber screamed to the driver. As he spoke,

he lifted his right foot to the top of *Fencing Master*'s armor and leaped into the disabled car. If anybody'd asked him a moment before, he'd have said he was so exhausted he had trouble just breathing. Deseau, continuing to curse, took over the left wing gun.

Floosie's fighting compartment was an abattoir. The guns that hit her fired frangible shot that broke into a hypersonic spray on the other side of the penetration. Jellicoe had been manning the left wing gun and out of the direct blast, but the sleet of heavy-metal granules had splashed the thighs and torsos of her crewmen across the interior of the armor. Huber's boots slipped when they hit the floor.

He fell with a dizzying shock. He was up again in a moment, but his right side was numb.

He lifted Sergeant Jellicoe. She was a stocky woman, still wearing the body armor that'd saved her life. Huber didn't try to strip the ceramic clamshell off her now because he wasn't sure his fingers could manipulate the catches. He stepped back and bent, throwing Jellicoe's torso over his shoulders, then stumbled forward.

Learoyd and Deseau fired past Huber to either side; his faceshield blacked out the vivid cyan of their bolts. *Via!* there was no way in hell he was going to get aboard *Fencing Master*. He couldn't carry Jellicoe and he sure couldn't throw her into—

"*Gotcha, El-Tee!*" Frenchie said, bracing his left hand on the tribarrel's receiver as he prepared to cross to help. "*We're golden!*"

Huber didn't hear the shot that struck *Floosie*'s bow slope, but he felt the car buck upward in the middle of a white flash.

Then he felt nothing. Nothing at all.

. . . *he should be coming around very shortly . . .* some part of the cosmos said to some other part of the cosmos.

Awareness—not consciousness, not yet—returned with the awkward jerkiness of a butterfly opening its wings as it poises on the edge of its cocoon. *My name is Arne Huber. I'm—*

Huber's eyes opened. He saw three faces, anxious despite their hard features. Then the pain hit him and he blacked out.

He regained consciousness. The world was white, pulsing, and oven-hot—but he was alert, waiting for his vision to steady. He knew from experience that he hadn't been out long this time, but how long he'd been *here*, in the main infirmary at Base Alpha . . . He must've been hurt bad.

"How's Jellicoe?" he said. Huber'd heard rusty hinges with better tone than he had now, but he got the words out. "How's my platoon sergeant?"

The technician adjusted his controls, his attention on the display of his medical computer. He nodded in self-satisfaction. Huber felt a quivering numbness in all his nerve endings.

The other men in the room were Major Danny Pritchard and—Blood and Martyrs—Colonel Hammer himself.

"She didn't make it," Hammer said flatly. "If you hadn't had her over your back, you wouldn't have made it either. The shot that hit Three-three's bow slope splashed upward. The good part of it is that the impact pretty well threw you aboard your own car. Your people were able to bug out after the rest of the platoon with no further casualties."

"It was quick for her," said Major Pritchard. He smiled wryly. "This time that's the truth."

You always told civilian dependents that their trooper's death had been quick, even if you knew she'd been screaming in agony, unable to open a jammed hatch as her vehicle burned. You didn't lie to other troopers, though, because it was a waste of breath.

Huber nodded. Pain washed over him; he closed his eyes. The technician muttered and made adjustments. Huber felt the pain vanish as though a series of switches were being tripped in sequence.

The Slammers used pain drugs only as first aid. Once a trooper was removed to a central facility, direct neural stimulation provided analgesis without the negative side effects of chemicals. The Medicomp had kept Huber unconscious while he healed, exercising his muscles group by group to prevent atrophy and bed sores. He'd been awakened only when he should be able to walk on his own. The technician was smoothing out the vestiges of pain while Huber lay in a cocoon of induced inputs.

Huber opened his eyes. His brain was still collecting itself; direct neural stimulation tended to separate memory into discrete facets which reintegrated jarringly as consciousness returned. Part of Arne Huber understood it was remarkable that the Regiment's commander and deputy commander stood beside his pallet, but *everything* was new and remarkable to him now.

"How long's it been?" he said aloud, marvelling at the sound of his voice. "How long've I been out?"

"Four days," Danny Pritchard said. "Going on five if you count the time before we got you back to Base Alpha by aircar."

"Right," said Huber. "Well, I'm ready to go back to my platoon now. Are we still in the field?"

As he spoke, he braced his hands on the edges of the pallet and with careful determination began to lever his torso up from the mattress. A spasm knotted his muscles; his vision went briefly monochrome. The technician clicked his tongue.

"F-3 ought to be out of the line," Hammer said in a gravelly voice, "but we can't afford that luxury just now. We've assigned a car from Central Repair and personnel from the depot to bring them up to strength. I've put in a lieutenant named Algren as CO. He's green as grass, but he was top of his class at the Academy."

"I'm the fucking CO of F-3!" Huber said, swinging his legs over the side of the bed. "I can—"

He lurched to his feet. His knees buckled. Hammer caught him expertly and lifted him onto the pallet. Huber gasped, hoping he wouldn't vomit. There was nothing in his stomach, but acid boiled against the back of his throat while the technician's fingers danced on his keypad.

"No, you can't," Major Pritchard said. "We need the troopers we've got too badly to let you get a bunch of them killed to prove you're superman, which you're not. Besides, I want you in Operations."

"Right," said Hammer. "Bad as things are in the field, just now I need experienced officers on my staff worse than I do line commanders. I might transfer you to Operations even if you were fit to go back to F-3."

Huber glared at the Colonel, then let himself relax on the

pallet. "Yeah, well," he said. "I'm not fit, you've got that right. But . . ."

"But when you are," Hammer said, "then I guess you've earned your choice of assignments. You did a good job getting your people out of that ratfuck. I won't bother saying I'm sorry for the way you got left hanging, but sure—I owe you one."

"For now you can do the most good to F-3 and the whole Regiment just by helping ride herd on what passes for the military forces of the United Cities," Pritchard said. "If we don't get them working together, it's going to be . . ."

His voice trailed off. He shook his head, suddenly looking drawn and gray with despair.

"The first thing you can help with," said Hammer, "is coming up with a platoon sergeant. I don't want to bring in somebody new, not with a newbie CO. I offered the job to your blower captain, Sergeant Deseau, and he turned it down; the others aren't seasoned enough on paper, and I don't know any of them personally."

"Frenchie'd hate the job . . ." Huber said, his mind settling into professional mode instead of focusing on his body and its weakness. "He could do it, but . . ."

"I can put the arm on him," the Colonel said. "Tell him it's take the job or out—and I wouldn't be bluffing."

"No," said Huber. "There's a sergeant in Log Section now, Jack Tranter. He's worked with us before. He isn't a line trooper, but he's seen the elephant. He's got the rank and organizational skills, and he's got the judgment to balance some young fire-eater straight out of the Academy."

"I remember him," said Pritchard with a frown. "He's a good man, but he's missing his right leg."

"The way things are right at the moment, Danny," said the Colonel with a piercing look at his subordinate, "he could be stone blind and I'd give him a trial if Huber here vouched for him. We don't have a lot of margin, you know."

Pritchard nodded with a grim smile. "Yeah," he said. "There's that."

Hammer turned to Huber again. The movement was very slight, but his gaze had unexpected weight. Huber felt the sort of shock he would if he'd been playing soccer and caught a medicine ball instead.

"So, Lieutenant?" he said. "Are you going to do what I tell you, or are you going to keep telling me what *you'll* do?"

"Sir!" said Huber, sitting up. He didn't feel the waves of nausea and weakness that'd crumpled him moments before, but neither did he push his luck by swinging his feet over the side of the bed. "You're the Colonel. I'll do the best job I can wherever you put me."

Hammer nodded, a lift of his chin as tiny as the smile that touched his thin lips. Huber wondered vaguely what would've happened if he'd been too bullheaded to face reality. Hard to tell, but the chances were he'd be looking for a civilian job when he got out of the infirmary instead of arguing about where he belonged in the Regimental Table of Organization.

Danny Pritchard looked at the technician and said, "When'll he be able to move? Sit in front of a console in the Operations shop I mean, not humping through the boonies."

The technician shrugged. "I can have him over there by jeep in maybe three hours. It's not how brave you are or how many pushups you can do, it's just the neural pathways reconnecting. D'ye want me to requisition a uniform or did his own gear come in with him?"

All three men looked reflexively at Huber. Huber gulped out a laugh and felt better by an order of magnitude to have broken his own tension that way.

"Hey, when I came here the only thing I had on my mind was my hair," he said. "Draw me a medium/regular and I'll worry about my field kit later."

"Roger that," said Hammer, ending the discussion. His glance toward Huber was shrouded by layers of concerns that had nothing to do with the man on the bed. "You'll report to Operations as soon as you can, Lieutenant, and Major Pritchard'll bring you up to speed."

Hammer started out of the room. Pritchard put a hand on the Colonel's shoulder and said, "Sir? You might tell him about Ander."

Hammer looked from his Operations Officer to Huber. "Yeah," he said, "I might do that. Lieutenant, the UC government ordered General Ander's arrest after his failure to execute their lawful orders. While he was in a cell pending his hearing before the Bonding Authority representative, he committed suicide."

Huber frowned, trying to take in the information. "The UC arrested him?" he said. "Sir, how in hell did they do that? Ander's Legion may not be the best outfit on the planet, but the UC doesn't have anything more than a few forest guards with carbines."

"I suggested they deputize a platoon of the White Mice for the job," Hammer said. "I believe Major Steuben chose to lead the team himself."

"Ah," said Huber. He didn't say, "Why would Ander kill himself?" because obviously Ander hadn't killed himself. Huber'd turned down a chance to serve in the White Mice, the Regiment's field police and enforcers; but he understood why they existed, and this was one of the times he was *glad* they existed.

"Right," he said. "Ah . . . thank you, sir, though I hadn't been going to ask. I know we're in a complicated situation here on Plattner's World."

"You just think you know," said Pritchard over his shoulder as he followed the Colonel out of the room. "After a day in Operations, Lieutenant, you'll know bloody well."

Like every other line soldier throughout history, Arne Huber had cursed because his superiors expected him to follow orders without having a clue as to what was really going on. Transferred now to the operations staff, he found himself in a situation he liked even less: he knew the Big Picture, and the reality was much worse than he'd believed when he had only a platoon to worry about.

Even more frustrating, there was nothing he could do to change the situation. It was like trying to push spaghetti uphill.

Huber cut the present connection, watching the image of a dark-skinned officer in a rainbow turban shrink down to a bead and vanish. Colonel Sipaji swore that his troops were already in position outside Jonesburg, save for the few support units which were still en route from the spaceport at Rhodesville. Jonesburg's own spaceport had been closed because of the danger from Solace energy weapons. Like all the ports in the United Cities, it was only a dirigible landing field which small starships could use with care.

Sipaji commanded the Sons of Mangala, a battalion-sized infantry unit, not very mobile but potentially useful when dug in at the right place. Satellite imagery showed that not only were they not in Jonesburg, they were halted only two kilometers outside Rhodesville. The visuals were good enough that with a modicum of enhancement Huber had been able to see the cluster of officers outside the trailer that served as Colonel Sipaji's Tactical Operations Center. They were sitting on camp stools with their legs crossed, drinking from teacups.

And that knowledge didn't make the least bit of difference, because Colonel Sipaji was going to stick to his lie with the bland assurance of a man who knows what the truth ought to be and isn't affected by consensus reality. Sipaji wasn't a coward and if his battalion ever got into position it would be a very cost-effective way of protecting the northern approaches to Jonesburg; but it *wasn't* going to get there before Solace forces had closed the route from Rhodesville. Intent was reality to Sipaji, and he truly intended to go to Jonesburg . . . soon.

Huber stood. He was at one of a dozen consoles under a peaked roof of extruded plastic whose trusses were supported by posts along each of the long sides. This annex to the Regimental Operations Center was located in the parking lot of the Bureau of Public Works for the City of Benjamin, the administrative capital of the United Cities.

The portable toilet within the chain link fencing hadn't been emptied in too long, which was pretty much the way life had been going for Huber during the week since he got out of the infirmary. He turned, then swayed and had to catch himself by the back of the console's seat. He'd been planning to go inside the wood-frame Bureau HQ itself, but now he wasn't sure that he'd bother.

"Lieutenant Huber," said the officer who'd come down the aisle behind him. "Take a break. I don't want to see you for the rest of the day and I mean it."

Huber jumped in surprise. He'd been so lost in his frustration that he hadn't seen the section chief, Captain Dillard, coming toward him. Dillard was a spare man with one eye, one arm, and a uniform whose creases you could shave with. Huber respected the man, but he didn't imagine the captain had been anyone he could've warmed to even before the blast of a directional mine had ended Dillard's career as a line officer.

"Sir," said Huber, "I can't get the Sons of Mangala to move. I thought if I took an aircar to where they're camped, maybe—"

"Get out of here, Lieutenant," Dillard said in the tone he'd have used to a whining child. "If you went to see Colonel Sipaji, his troops still wouldn't move. I don't care to risk the chance that you'd shoot him. That'd cause an incident with the Bonding Authority and delay the deployment even longer. Get a meal, get some sleep, and don't return before ten hundred hours tomorrow."

"But—"

"I mean it!" Dillard snapped. "Get out of here or you'll leave under escort!"

"Yessir," Huber muttered. He was angry—at the order, at Sipaji, and at himself for behaving like a little boy on the verge of a tantrum.

The troopers at the occupied consoles pretended to be lost in their work. Three of the eight were on the disabled list like Huber; the remainder had been culled from other rear-echelon slots to fill the present need to coordinate the mercenary fragments of the UC forces. Text and graphics were more efficient ways to transfer data to the other units, but face-to-face contact had a better chance of getting a result on the other end of the line of communication.

Huber gurgled a laugh, surprising Captain Dillard more than the snarl he'd probably expected. Huber's stomach was fluttery—he did need food—and if he was letting anger run him like that, he needed rest besides.

"Captain," he said, "it looks to me like we're hosed on this one. The UC's hosed, I mean, so we ought to advise 'em to make peace with Solace on whatever terms they can get. Solace has columns moving on Simpliche and Jonesburg both. We can—the Regiment can—block either one, I guess, but I don't see any way Solace won't capture one place or the other unless the units we're operating with get their act together. And when the core cities of the UC start to fall—

it's over, the rest of Outer States'll cut off their financing, and then everybody goes home. Which we may as well do right now, hadn't we?"

"That's not my decision, Lieutenant," Dillard said impatiently, "nor yours either. Get some food and rest, report at ten hundred hours."

He made a brusque gesture with his hand. So far as Huber had been able to tell during his week's contact with Captain Dillard, the man genuinely didn't care whether or not what he was doing had any purpose. Maybe to Dillard, *nothing* had purpose . . . which wasn't a bad attitude for a professional soldier. Anyway, it didn't keep Dillard from being efficient at his present job.

Huber walked out of the lot and stumped up the stairs to the back of the HQ building. His quarters were in a barracks within the Central Repair compound in the warehouse district. It was walled and guarded by a platoon of combat cars, making security less of a problem than it would've been elsewhere in the city. There'd be an aircar driven by a contract employee, a UC citizen, in front of the Bureau HQ, or if there wasn't the receptionist in the entranceway would call one.

After he took a leak . . .

"Lieutenant Huber?" called the receptionist as he pushed open the door to the rest room. Huber ignored him. To his surprise, the door opened again as he settled himself before the urinal. The receptionist, a middle-aged warrant officer with signals flashes on his epaulets, had followed him in.

"Sir?" the fellow said. "There's a woman out front to see you. She's been waiting, but I told her nobody disturbed the personnel on duty."

"I've been disturbed ever since I was assigned here," Huber muttered, "but that's nothing new. Who is she and what's she want?"

His tension and frustration drained away as he emptied his bladder. Was it that simple? All the trouble in life was just a matter of physical discomfort?

No, there were still the Colonel Sipajis of this world. They might have no more value than a bladderful of urine, but they weren't as easy to void.

"Her name's Daphne Priamedes, sir," the receptionist said.

"I don't know what she's got in mind, but she's a looker, *that* I know."

She must be, to get a plump, balding veteran this excited. Well, the receptionist hadn't spent the past fourteen hours talking to the commanders of mercenary units who had an amazing number of variations on the theme of, "No, I think I should do something else instead."

"Never heard of her," Huber said. Right now the only thing that was going through his mind was that if he let her, she'd slow him down on his way back to the barracks and a bed. He didn't plan to let her. He turned, closing his fly. "There a car out front to take me home?"

"She's got a car, sir," the receptionist said. "A big one, brand new."

Huber started to swear and realized he didn't have the energy for it. The receptionist got out of the way as Huber lurched toward the doorway and down the hall.

Huber hadn't been able to find a comfortable position to sleep in, and being tired made his left leg drag worse than it would've anyway. Slivers of metal from both the frangible shot and the bits it'd gouged from *Floosie*'s bow armor had spattered him from knee to pelvis, and even the most expert nanosurgery did additional damage in removing the tiny missiles.

A striking black-haired woman stood between Huber and the outside door. She was within a centimeter of his height; her gaze was as direct as it could be without being hostile.

"Lieutenant Huber?" she said in a pleasant contralto. "I heard you tell Chief Warrant Leader Saskovich that you needed a ride. I have a car, and if you'll permit me I'll also buy you a better meal than you're likely to get on your own."

"Ma'am . . ." said Huber. He wondered if she was going to jump out of his way like the receptionist—Saskovich, apparently, and this woman had not only noticed the fellow's name but she'd gotten his rank right—or whether Huber would shoulder her aside on his way to the door. "The *only* bloody thing I know is that my job doesn't include talking to civilians. Find somebody in the public affairs section or talk to your own government; I don't have the time or the interest."

Through the glass front door of the building Huber could see a combat car on guard—there were no unit numbers stenciled on the skirts; it was an unassigned vehicle from Central Repair—and two aircars. One was a battered ten-place van with a Logistics Section logo on the side; a local contract employee chewing tobacco in the cab. The other was a luxury vehicle.

"*My* government is the Republic of Solace," the woman said. She stiff-armed open the swinging door and held it for him. "My father is Colonel Apollonio Priamedes. You saved his life at Northern Star Farms where he'd been in command when you attacked. I want to thank you in person before I accompany him back to Solace in tomorrow's prisoner exchange."

Huber's mouth opened, then closed as he realized that all the several things he'd started to say were a waste of breath. He remembered the Solace colonel limping out of the smoke to surrender, just as straight-backed as this woman who said she was his daughter.

Huber knew now what that erect posture had cost Priamedes. Because of that, and because Daphne Priamedes really *was* a stunner, he said, "'Ma'am, I don't want company for dinner. But if you'll run me back to my barracks down in the warehouse district, I'll buy you a drink on the way."

"Yes, of course, Lieutenant," the woman said. "And I'd appreciate it if you'd call me Daphne, but I understand that you may prefer a more formal posture. Perhaps you're uncomfortable with the attitude toward hostilities we have on Plattner's World."

She strode past and opened the limousine's passenger door for him. That was a little embarrassing, but there wasn't a lot Huber could do about it in his present condition. Walking upright was about as much as he could manage at the moment. He braced his hands on the door and side of the vehicle to swing himself onto the seat, noticing the inlays of wood and animal products on the interior panels.

"I'm not uncomfortable, ah, Daphne," he said, "since it's the same attitude we mercenaries have toward each other: we may be enemies today and fighting on the same side tomorrow, or the other way around. Either way the relationship's professional rather than emotional. But I didn't expect to see a Solace citizen travelling openly in the UC capital when there's a war on."

Daphne Priamedes got in behind the control yoke and brought the car live. The vehicle had six small drive fans on each side instead of the normal one at either end; it was noticeably quieter than others Huber had ridden in.

Aircars were uncommon on most planets, but special circumstances on Plattner's World made them the normal means of personal transportation. The per capita income here was high, the population dispersed, and the preservation of the forests so much a religion—the attitude went beyond awareness of the economic benefit—that people found the notion of cutting roadways through the trees profoundly offensive.

Only in the Solace highlands where trees were sparse and not parasitized by Moss was there a developed system of ground transportation. There a monorail network shifted bulky agricultural produce from the farms to collection centers from which dirigibles flew it to the Outer States and returned with containers of Moss.

"There's ten generations of intercourse between Solace and the Outer States," Priamedes said. "This trouble—this war—is only during the past six months. We *need* each other on Plattner's World."

Her eyes were on the holographic instrument display she'd called up when she started the motors; it blinked off when she was comfortable with the readouts. She twisted the throttle in a quick, precise movement.

As the car lifted, she glanced over at Huber and went on, "Besides, for the most part it's you mercenaries fighting—not citizens. We in Solace tried to fight with our own forces at the beginning, but we learned that wasn't a satisfactory idea."

She smiled. Her expression as bright and emotionless as the glint of cut crystal.

"War's a specialist job," Huber said, keeping his tone flat. The car was enclosed and its drive fans were only a hum through his bootsoles. "At least it is if you've got specialists on the other side. We are, the Slammers are, and the other merc units are too even if they don't necessarily have our hardware."

He paused, then added, "Or our skill level."

"As I said, we recognized that," Priamedes said. "A disaster like Northern Star Farms rather drives the point home, particularly since it was obvious that things could have gone very much worse than even they did. Instead we're mortgaging ten years of our future hiring off-planet professionals to do what the Solace Militia couldn't."

Huber didn't speak. He regretted getting into the car with this woman, but he regretted a lot of things in life. This wasn't his worst mistake by any means.

Northern Star was a collective farm that'd been turned into a firebase under Colonel Priamedes. He commanded an infantry battalion and an artillery battery from the Solace Militia, with a company of mercenaries whose high-power lasers were supposed to be the anti-armor component of the force.

Huber'd led the combat cars in the company-sized Slammers task force that had punctured the defenses like a bullet into a balloon. The Militia were brave enough and even well trained, but they weren't veterans. The cars' concentrated firepower had literally stunned them, and the mercenary lasers were too clumsy to stand a chance against 20-cm tank guns which had virtually unlimited range across flat cornfields.

In retrospect it hadn't been much of a battle, though it'd seemed real enough to Arne Huber as he watched scores of Militiamen rise from a trench and aim at his oncoming combat cars. And all it takes is one bullet in the wrong place and you're dead as dirt, no matter how great your side's victory looks to whoever writes the history books.

Priamedes shook her head in inward directed anger, then turned a genuinely warm smile toward Huber. "I'm sorry," she said. "The situation frustrates me, but that isn't your fault and it's not what I came to see you about. Will this place do for our drink? I like it myself."

She banked the car slightly and gestured through her window. On Plattner's World, there was forest even in the cities. She was pointing toward a three-story structure shaded by trees on all sides. On the roof were open-air tables, half empty at this hour, and a service kiosk in one corner with an outside elevator rising beside it. Above, a holographic sign, visible from any angle, read GUSTAV'S. The letters changed from dark to light green and back in slow waves.

"That's fine," Huber said. "Anywhere's fine. I don't know much about Benjamin."

He'd been on seven planets besides Nieuw Friesland where he was born, and he didn't know much about any of them. He remembered the way powergun bolts glinted among the ice walls on Humboldt and the way the whores on Dar es-Sharia dyed their breasts and genitalia blue; those things and scores of similar things, little anecdotes of existence with nothing connecting them but the fact they were fragments from the life of Lieutenant Arne Huber.

Priamedes brought them around in a tight reverse instead of angling the fans forward to slow them. The car dropped between the treetops to level out just above the gravel roadway. The elevator was descending with a pair of well-dressed men in the glass cage.

Dust puffed as Priamedes landed smoothly in a line of similar cars. City streets in the Outer States were for parking and delivery vehicles. They were almost never paved, because that would speed storm-water runoff and decrease the amount of water that penetrated the soil to nourish vegetation.

Huber reached for his door release; parts of his body decided to protest, cramping when they were directed to move. He gasped with pain, then tried to cover his weakness with a blistering curse.

"Wait, I'll—" Priamedes said.

Snarling under his breath, Huber shoved the door open before his hostess could get around the vehicle to help him. He hopped out, forcing his left leg to work even though it felt as if somebody had turned a blowtorch on the hip joint.

She paused, turning her head away politely, and waited for Huber to join her so that they could walk to the waiting elevator together. "My father was injured in the fighting before he was captured," she said in a neutral tone. "He got off crutches a few days ago and should make a full recovery."

Huber laughed as the cage rose. "So will I," he said, more cheerfully than he felt. "Look, mostly I'm just stiff from sitting at a console all day. I'm not used to desk duty, that's all."

That was part of why he was stumbling around, all right; and he was tense from frustration at the people he had to deal with, which was another part of the problem. But at the back of Huber's mind was the awareness that the fragments he'd caught when the shot struck might have done damage that even time and the best medical treatment couldn't quite repair. That he might never again be fit for a field command . . .

"Lieutenant?" the black-haired woman said in concern.

Via, what had his expression been like? "Sorry," Huber said, forcing a smile. "I was klicks away, just thinking of the work I've got to do in the morning."

He must have sounded convincing, because Priamedes' features softened with relief. To keep away from the subject of his health, Huber made his way to a table near the wickerwork railing and pulled out a chair for the woman. It was with considerable relief that he settled across from her, though.

A waitress approached with an expectant look. The dozen other customers were glancing covertly at them as well, their eyes probably drawn by Huber's uniform and possibly his limp. There were a lot of mercenaries in Benjamin now, but the Slammers' khaki and rampant lion patch were the trappings of nobility to those who were knowledgeable. On a planet as wealthy and interconnected as Plattner's World, that meant most people.

Because of that perfectly accurate perception and because of the perfectly normal human resentment it engendered in other mercenaries, the United Cities were going to lose the war. A single armored regiment couldn't defeat several divisions worth of enemies, many of whom were themselves highly sophisticated; and the other UC mercenaries weren't cooperating with the Slammers the way they'd need to do to win.

"Lieutenant?" said Daphne Priamedes, loudly enough to penetrate Huber's brown study. They were waiting for his order, of course. . . .

He swore in embarrassment. "Ah, there's corn whiskey? I don't remember the name for it here, but my sergeant when I was in Log Section . . . ?"

Priamedes nodded understanding and said to the waitress, "Zapotec—and water, I believe, unless . . . ?"

"That's fine," Huber said in reply to her raised eyebrow. "Anything's fine, really."

He didn't know whether Zapotec was generic or a brand name; if the latter, it was probably the best available unless he'd misjudged Daphne Priamedes. Huber suddenly realized that he knew very little about anything beyond what he needed to do his job well. He and his fellow troopers wouldn't have been nearly as effective if they hadn't focused so completely on their jobs, but when he thought about it he felt lonely.

The waitress trotted away. Priamedes glanced around the covered patio, slapping the eyes of the others back to their own proper concerns. When she and Huber were as private as one ever is in open air, she said, "My father told me what happened at Northern Star, Lieutenant. At the end, I mean. He said it would've been much easier for you to kill him and his men than to capture them, but you took a considerable risk to spare their lives."

The waitress came back with the drinks. Priamedes entered her credit chip in the reader before Huber even thought to take his out of its pouch. Via! Maybe it was a good thing he wasn't in the field right now, because he was dropping too bloody many stitches.

Though . . . in the field he knew what he was doing reflexively. This was civilian life, and that was another matter. Arne Huber hadn't been a civilian for a long time.

He took a swig of the liquor; it cleaned the gumminess from his mouth and tongue and focused his mind like a leap into cold water. "Ma'am," he said, "I guess I've done worse things than shooting civilians who didn't have sense enough to give up, but only by mistake or when I had to."

He drank again; too much. He'd supposed he'd made his opinion of the Solace Militia clearer than he should've to an officer's daughter. The whiskey was good but it was strong as well, even cut with water; the big slug made his throat spasm and he had to cough.

Covering his embarrassment, Huber went on, "Ma'am, I can give you policy reasons why my commanding officer didn't want to blow away your father's men when they made a break for it. The truth is, though, neither I nor Captain Sangrela really likes to kill people. I'm a soldier, not a sociopath."

"I see that," she said, smiling faintly. "And I still prefer Daphne, Lieutenant."

"It's the booze talking," Huber said, smiling back. It was warm in his stomach, though and it felt good. "Look, Daphne, I appreciate the drink, but I really need to get to a bunk."

"Very well," she said, tossing off the rest of the fizzy, light green concoction she was drinking over ice. "If I can't offer you dinner . . . ?"

"No ma—no *Daphne*," Huber said, rising more easily than he'd sat down. "I'll eat some rations, but right now I need sleep more than company—even company as nice as you."

"Then I'll just thank you again for sparing my father," she said, standing also. "And I hope we'll see one another again in the future when you're better rested—Arne?"

"Arne," Huber agreed. "And I hope that too."

"I'll expect your report in three hours, then, General Rubens," Huber said and broke the connection. He adjusted the little fan playing on him from the console as he thought about the next call he had to make. The day'd started out cool, but now by mid-morning it was unseasonably hot for Plattner's World.

Parts of Base Alpha were climate controlled, but mostly the Regiment's machines and personnel were expected to operate under whatever conditions nature offered. You weren't going to win many battles from inside a sealed room, and the Colonel tried to discourage people from thinking you could.

As a break from talking to people he didn't like and didn't trust—he knew they probably felt the same way—Huber called up the Solace Order of Battle. He wasn't sure he was really supposed to have the information, but he'd found that his retina pattern was on Central's validation list. A benefit of being assigned to Operations . . .

As he viewed the latest information, his gut told him that he'd have been better off staying ignorant. Sure, things could've gotten worse—things can always get worse—but he hadn't really expected them to go this bad. Daphne'd said Solace was mortgaging its next ten years to hire mercenaries. Huber knew now that she'd been understating the real costs.

He looked out through the fence, trying to settle his mind. An aircar with Log Section markings had landed in the street under the guns of the combat car on guard. The driver, one of the locals the Regiment had hired for non-combat work, waited in the cab. A tall civilian in an expensive-looking pearl gray outfit got out, stalked to the gate, and said, "I am Sigmund Lindeyar. Take me to Colonel Hammer at once!"

Instead of snapping to attention obediently, Captain Dillard turned his back to the furious man on the other side of the fence. He was frowning as he called Central on his commo helmet.

The fellow ought to be more thankful than he seemed. Dillard was treating him a lot better than some troopers would've done to a civilian who raised his voice to them.

Dillard grimaced minusculely as he signed off. When he focused again on his present surroundings, he caught Huber's eye. "Lieutenant Huber?" he called. "Will you join us, please?"

Huber cut the power to his console manually instead of trusting it to turn itself off when he rose from the attached seat. He didn't want anybody else to see what he'd just learned. *Blood and Martyrs, a brigade of armored cavalry in addition to what Solace was already fielding!*

"Sir?" said Huber crisply to Captain Dillard. He stood at parade rest, trying to look like what a civilian expected a professional soldier to be. He'd picked up from Dillard's expression that Central had confirmed the civilian's high self opinion, so a little theater was called for.

Huber's rumpled fatigues weren't what a rear-echelon soldier would've called "professional appearance," but Huber *wasn't* a rear-echelon soldier.

Huber'd thought Lindeyar was an old man; viewing him closely, he wasn't sure. The hair beneath the fellow's natty beret was pale blond, not white, and his face was unlined; despite that, his blue eyes had age in them as well as a present snapping fury.

"Lieutenant," Dillard said, turning to include both Huber and the civilian, "Mr. Lindeyar is the Nonesuch trade representative. His driver brought him here rather than to the Tactical Operations Center at Base Alpha, where he's to meet Colonel Hammer. I'd like you to escort Mr. Lindeyar to the correct location."

"Yessir!" Huber said, his back straight. He thought about saluting, but that'd come through as obvious caricature if Lindeyar knew *anything* about the way the Slammers operated. Besides, Huber was lousy at it.

"Mr. Lindeyar," Dillard said, shifting his eyes slightly, "Lieutenant Huber is my second in command. He'll see to it that there isn't a repetition of the error that brought you here in the first place."

"He'd better," said the civilian, his eyes flicking over Huber with the sort of attention one gives to a zoo animal. "Your colonel is expecting me. Expecting me before now!"

"We'll get you there, sir," Huber said as Dillard opened the gate. He was the only officer in the annex besides Dillard himself, but "second in command" was more theater. If one of the warrant officers or enlisted men had caught Dillard's eye at the moment he needed a warm body to cover somebody else's screwup, that trooper would have become "my most trusted subordinate" as sure as day dawns.

And screwup it'd been. The driver had a navigational pod, but he or it had chosen the coordinates for the operations annex instead of the TOC. A soldier wouldn't have made that mistake, but to the contract driver it was simply a destination. That probably wasn't the fault of anybody in the Regiment—and it certainly wasn't Captain Dillard's fault—but Lindeyar didn't seem like the sort of man who worried about justice when he was angry.

They walked toward the street together. The path was gravel and Huber's left knee didn't want to bend. He tensed his abdomen to keep from gasping in pain as he kept up with the long-legged civilian.

"I want you to drive," Lindeyar said as they reached the aircar—a ten-seat utility vehicle that'd seen a lot of use. "I don't trust this fool not to get lost again."

"Negative!" said the scruffy driver—who turned out to be female, though Huber couldn't imagine anyone to whom the difference would matter. "I own this truck and I'm not letting any soldier-boy play games with it!"

"No sir," said Huber, letting himself breathe now that he didn't have to match strides with Lindeyar, "I can't drive an aircar. We won't get lost."

He got into the cab, motioning the driver aside. She opened her mouth for another protest. "Shut up," Huber said, not loudly but not making any attempt to hide how he felt.

He was pissed at quite a number of things and people right at the moment, and the driver was somebody he could unload on safely if she pushed him just a hair farther. Huber didn't know how to drive an aircar, that was true; but he was in a mood to give himself some on-the-job training with this civilian prick along for the ride.

The driver shut her mouth. Huber switched on the dashboard navigational pod, synched it with his helmet AI, and downloaded the new destination. Lindeyar climbed into the back, looking tautly angry but keeping silent for now.

"All right," Huber said to the driver, more mildly than before. "I'll check as we go, but you shouldn't have any trouble now. Let's get going."

She nodded warily and fed power to her fans. The drive motors were in better shape than the truck's body, which was something. They lifted smoothly, sending back a billow of dust before they transitioned from ground effect to free flight.

Why did a trade representative figure he could give orders to the Slammers? And being pretty close to right in the assumption, given the way Captain Dillard had hopped to attention after checking with Central. Nonesuch bought half the Thalderol base which Plattner's World exported, but that was no concern of the Regiment's.

Except that it obviously was a concern, if Hammer himself took time to meet with the fellow while the war was going to hell in a handbasket. Huber chuckled.

"You find something funny in this, Lieutenant?" Lindeyar said in a voice that could've frozen a pond.

"I'd been thinking earlier this morning that things can always get worse, sir," Huber said calmly. When you've spent a significant fraction of your life with other people shooting at you, it's easy to stay calm in situations where the

potential downside doesn't include a bullet in your guts. ·
"I won't say I'm glad to've been right, but I guess I do find
it amusing, yes."

Lindeyar didn't reply, not so that he could be heard over
the fans at any rate. Huber'd called up a topo map as a
thirty percent mask on his faceshield. Base Alpha lay just
beyond the city's eastern outskirts. The driver was holding
them on a direct course toward it, the only variations being
those imposed by traffic regulations which were completely
opaque to an outsider like Huber.

As well as five dirigibles hauling heavy cargoes, there were
hundreds of aircars in sight. That in itself was a good reason
to leave the driving to a local.

Base Alpha was a scar on the landscape, a twelve-hectare
tract scraped bare of forest. There was nothing else like it
in the Outer States. Even the dirigible fields where starships
now landed were smaller. The soil had a yellow tinge and
was already baking to coarse limestone. A two-meter berm
of dirt stabilized with a plasticizer surrounded the perimeter; the TOC complex was a cruciform pattern dug in at
the center.

The clearing wasn't just to house the vehicles and temporary buildings required for the headquarters of an armored
regiment: Hammer also demanded sight distances for the
powerguns that defended the base against incoming aircraft
and artillery fire. The UC government had protested, but that
didn't matter. The Colonel didn't compromise on military
necessities; he and his troops were the sole judges of what
war made necessary.

One or more guns had been tracking the aircar ever since
it came over the horizon on a course for the base. An icon
quivered in the right corner of Huber's faceshield, indicating that his AI had received and replied to Central's authen-
tication signal.

A kilometer from the base, the driver slowed her vehicle
to a hover. Lindeyar leaned forward and said, "Why are we
stopping?" in a louder voice than the fan roar demanded.

Huber tapped the green light on top of the navigational
pod and said to the driver, "Go on in, we're cleared."

"No, I've got to call in," the driver said. "Otherwise they'll
shoot us out of the air. It's happened!"

"I told you, we're cleared!" Huber said. "Do as I tell you or I'll shoot you myself!"

Most of that was for Lindeyar's benefit—but he wasn't in a good mood, that was the bloody truth. Not that he'd have shot the woman while they were a hundred meters in the air and she was driving . . .

The driver obeyed with a desperate look, though they flew into the compound at a noticeably slower pace than they'd crossed Benjamin proper. The navigation pod directed her to a ten-by-ten meter square just outside the gate through the razor ribbon surrounding the TOC. The troopers on guard in a gun jeep watched with bored interest rather than concern, but their tribarrel tracked the car all the way in.

Huber hopped out immediately and offered Lindeyar his arm for support; the open truck didn't have doors in back, though the sidewalls weren't high. The civilian ignored the offer with the studied discourtesy that Huber'd expected.

A staff lieutenant—an aide, Huber supposed, but he didn't know the fellow—trotted up the ramp from the TOC entrance as Huber and the civilian got out of the aircar. The driver kept her fans spinning, so grit swirled around their ankles and made Huber blink. He didn't bother snarling at her.

"Mr. Lindeyar?" the aide called as he swung open the wire-wrapped gate. "Please step this way. The Colonel's waiting for you."

Well, I guess that's "mission accomplished" for me, Huber thought. He turned to get back into the aircar. His helmet filters slapped down as the driver took off without him in a spray of dust. Some of it got under his collar, sticking to the sweat and making the cloth feel like sandpaper when he moved.

Lindeyar and his new escort were already entering the TOC, four buried climate-controlled trailers. Corrugated planking roofed the hub, and there was a layer of dirt over the whole. It wouldn't do much against a direct hit by artillery, but the air defense tribarrels took care of that threat. A sniper with a 2-cm powergun could be dangerous from an aircar many kilometers away, though; burying the TOC avoided possible disruption.

Rather than call Log Section for another ride, Huber nodded to the troopers on guard and walked toward a

temporary building a few hundred meters away. He wasn't in a hurry to get back to the operations annex. The Lord knew, he'd always tried to do his job; but it was hard to see what good he was doing there, or what good he or anybody else *could* do in a ratfuck like Plattner's World was turning into.

A combat car drove slowly along the clearing outside the berm; Huber could see only the upper edge of the armor. The trooper in the fighting compartment was part of the training cadre, giving a newbie driver some practice. The car was either worn out or a vehicle straight from Central Repair, being tested before it was released to a field troop.

Either way, the car and both troopers were going to be in combat very shortly—unless the UC faced reality and surrendered. The Colonel'd have to throw everything in to stop the Solace juggernaut, and it wouldn't be enough.

The building's open window had screens whose static charge repelled dust. The door with the stenciled sign SIG-NALS 2 wasn't screened, so Huber stepped inside quickly and closed it behind him. Three troopers looked at him through the displays of their specialized consoles.

"Is Lieutenant Basime here?" Huber asked. "I was told—"

Doll Basime stepped out of a side office, looking elfin although she wore issue fatigues without the tailoring some rear-echelon officers affected. "Arne! Come on in. Yeah, I've been at Central the past three weeks. Are you okay, because from what I'd heard . . . ?"

"Hey, I'm walking around," Huber said with a laugh. "That'll do for now."

Doll's office was really a cubicle, but it had a door as a concession to her rank. She closed it behind Huber and motioned him to the chair behind the console, taking the flip-down seat on the wall for herself.

"You're going to be a remf like me from now on, Arne?" she asked, smiling but obviously concerned. She and Huber had been good friends at the Academy, a relationship sim-plified by the fact that neither had any sexual interest in men.

"Just for now," he said as he sat down carefully. "I'm getting movement back day by day, and it doesn't hurt much any more."

He shrugged, wishing he could truthfully say more. It felt *really* good to take the weight off his left leg, and that scared him. "A trade representative arrived from Nonesuch for a meeting with the Colonel and wound up in the wrong place. I got to bring him back here."

Doll's face went grim. "Do you know anything about what's going on, Arne?" she asked. She patted her console. "Because I wasn't about to eavesdrop on the Colonel's private meetings."

"Could you?" Huber said, interested.

She grinned, a more familiar expression. "Yeah," she said, "but I couldn't do it without leaving a trail that the counterintelligence people could follow. I don't want to discuss that with Joachim Steuben."

"It'd be a short discussion," Huber said, also with a smile of sorts. Major Steuben was as *pretty* as Doll herself. Frequently his duties involved killing somebody, a task at which Steuben was remarkably good. Inhumanly good, you might say.

"I don't know anything about Lindeyar except he seemed to expect a red carpet and wasn't best pleased not to have one," Huber said. He rubbed his neck; Doll gestured to the box of tissues on the console.

"Doll?" he went on, meeting her eyes. "Do you know how bad it is out there?"

She shrugged in turn. "I know it's not good," she said. "My section's job is to keep up the links with friendly units, so I see all the traffic whether I want to or not."

"Solace is pushing us everywhere," Huber said. He was glad to talk to somebody. Misery wanting company, he supposed, and he knew he could trust Doll. "We're just trying to block their advances."

He shrugged again and went on, "The Waldheim Dragoons are landing at Port Plattner in a day's time. They're mechanized and brigade strength, maybe a thousand combat vehicles. They've got powerguns and there's three 5-cm cannon in each platoon. Those'll take out a tank at short range, and a combat car's toast any time they hit it."

Doll made a moue and patted her tight black hair with her fingertips as she absorbed the information. "I can tell you," she said, staring toward the bulldozed wasteland past

the slanting louvers, "that the UC isn't expecting the arrival of any significant reinforcements in the next ten days. I'd have been warned to make sure there'd be circuits clear."

"It wouldn't matter," Huber explained. "Solace is landing the Dragoons in a single lift. In a week or less they'll be organized and move out. It'd take a month to unload a brigade in what passes for spaceports in the UC, and it'd take longer than that to put the dribs and drabs together as a fighting force. Via, what we've got *now* isn't a coherent force except for the Regiment!"

"Could Nonesuch do anything?" Doll asked. "They're the major player in this arm of the galaxy."

"Lindeyar isn't somebody whose good will I'd want to depend on," Huber said. He chuckled at the thought. "But I sure don't see a better hope."

He was still wearing his commo helmet out of habit. The faceshield was raised, so the attention signal chimed in his ear instead of being a flashing icon. At the same time Doll's switched-off console lit under Central's control.

Colonel Hammer's face coalesced out of pearly light. He looked grim, though that was normal for the few times Huber had seen the Colonel make a Regiment-wide announcement.

"Listen up, troopers," Hammer said. Huber and Basime stared at the display. Hammer's hard gray eyes were locked with theirs, despite the varied angles, and with those of everyone else who viewed the transmitted image. "Orders'll be coming down in two hours. Be ready to move with your field kit. This means *everybody*. There'll be reassignments of rear echelon personnel to line slots where they need to be filled."

The Colonel rubbed his forehead; for a moment he looked very tired. His expression hardened again and he went on, "You've been the best soldiers every place you've fought. It's no different here. Do your jobs, troopers; and if I do mine as well as you've always done yours, we're going to pull this off yet!"

The image shrank and vanished; the memory of the Colonel's words hung a moment longer in the small office. Huber got to his feet.

"Going to get your kit together, Arne?" Doll said as she squeezed aside to let him past.

"That's next," Huber said. "First I'm going to see the Colonel."

He grinned at Doll as he opened the door. He felt numb, and there was a glowing wall in his mind that blocked off all the future except the next five minutes or so.

"First . . ." Huber said as he stepped into the outer office. "I've got to make sure I'm going back to the line!"

Huber strode toward the TOC entrance, his left leg stiff but not slowing him up a bit. He didn't know how he was going to bluff his way through the guards, but as it chanced he didn't have to. They'd heard the Colonel also, and they knew a lot of people were going to be moving fast on Regiment business.

Half a dozen figures came up the ramp from the TOC at the same time as Huber reached the wire going the other way. He unhooked the gate and pulled it open, then closed it behind him when they'd passed.

The last one through was the civilian, Lindeyar. He reached back and caught Huber's arm over the wire. "You, Lieutenant!" he cried. "There's to be a vehicle to carry me to Benjamin!"

Huber hooked the wire loop to the gate's frame. He pulled his arm away, suppressing a momentary desire to slap the civilian back on his haunches with the same movement. He nodded to the guards and shuffled down the ramp, keeping to the right side as three more officers came out of the buried trailers with set expressions. They were on their way to duties that weren't limited to staring at a display as other people fought a war. . . .

Huber grabbed the door before it closed; the air puffing from the interior was cool. The man coming out *now* was Colonel Hammer himself, with Major Kreutzer—the S-4, Personnel Officer—just behind him. Kreutzer's arm was raised; he was in an agony of wishing he dared to physically restrain his commanding officer.

"Sir!" said Huber, stepping in front of Hammer.

"Not bloody now!" the Colonel snarled. He looked as though he might bull past. Huber braced himself, but there was no contact.

"Sir, you said you owe me," Huber said, pitching his voice loudly enough to be heard over the sound of vehicles spinning up all around the base. "I'm collecting now. I want to go back to the field."

Behind Kreutzer were three other officers, trying to catch Hammer before he went off without answering their questions. Warrant officers sat at consoles to either side of the narrow aisle, immersed in their displays.

"Huber?" Hammer said. His face thawed like ice breaking up on the surface of a river. "Via, yeah, you're going back if you're able to walk."

He looked over his shoulder at the personnel officer. "Kreutzer, you wanted a CO for L Company?" he said. "All right, put Huber in the slot. And brevet him captain when you get a chance."

"No sir!" Huber said. He'd expected the fury in Hammer's expression, so it didn't slow him down as he continued, "Sir, I've never commanded infantry and this is no time for on-the-job training. Send me back to F-3."

"You only get away with crossing me if you're right, Lieutenant!" Hammer said; and smiled again, minusculely. "Which you are this time. Kreutzer, got any suggestions?"

"Yancy in L-2's senior enough," Kreutzer said. He shrugged. "We'll see if she can handle it. There's not a lot of choice, not now."

"Not a bloody lot," Hammer agreed. "All right, and we'll transfer—Algren, isn't it? The newbie we put in F-3 to L-2. Get on with it."

He pushed past Huber. The S-4 locked down his faceshield and passed the orders on, his voice muffled by his helmet's sonic cancellation field. Huber fell in behind the Colonel, heading back to the surface and an aircar to take him to wherever platoon F-3 was while the movement orders were being cut.

Lieutenant Arne Huber was going home.

Huber could've held a virtual meeting, but for his first contact with F-3 since his medevac he preferred face-to-face. The platoon could still scramble in thirty seconds if they had to; as they well *might* have to. . . .

Fox Three-eight was straight out of Central Repair and

hadn't been named yet. Until this moment Huber hadn't seen either the vehicle or its crew, three newbies commanded by a former tank driver named Gabinus who'd just been promoted to sergeant.

Its forward tribarrel, tasked to sector air defense, ripped a burst skyward. One of the newbies jumped.

"Relax, trooper," Sergeant Deseau said, making a point of being the blasé veteran. "They're just sending over a round every couple hours to keep us honest. If one ever gets through, then they'll start shelling us for real."

Nothing would get through while elements of the Slammers were stiffening the defenses of Benjamin. This shell popped above the northern horizon, leaving behind a flag of dirty black smoke. The sun was low above the trees, though it'd be three hours before full dark. Three hours before the start of the mission.

"For those of you who don't know me . . ." Huber said. Because Three-three had been knocked out in his absence, eight of the wary faces were new to him. "I've been at Central for the past three weeks, and I'm glad to be back with F-3 where I belong."

"And we're bloody lucky to have you back, El-Tee," Deseau muttered. "It's going to be tough enough as it is."

It's going to be tougher than that, Frenchie, Huber thought, but aloud he said, "We're part of Task Force Highball—" the whole Regiment had been broken up into task forces for this operation; Captain Holcott of M Company was leading Task Force Hotel "—with F-2, Battery Alpha, and the infantry of G-1 riding the Hogs and ammo haulers. We'll have a tank recovery vehicle, but it'll be carrying a heavy excavator. If a car's hit or breaks down so it can't be fixed ASAP, we combat loss it and proceed with the mission. Got that?"

A couple of the veterans swore under their breath; they got it, all right. An operation important enough that damaged vehicles were blown in place instead of being guarded for repair meant the personnel involved couldn't expect a lot of attention if they were hit, either.

"I'm in command of the task force," Huber continued. "Lieutenant Messeman of F-2 is XO. We've got six cars running, they've got four. There'll be six Hogs—" self-propelled 200-mm rocket howitzers "—and eleven ammo vehicles in the battery, and G-1 has thirty-five troops under Sergeant Marano."

"Thirty-five?" Sergeant Tranter said. "I'd heard they were down to two squads after the holding action at Beecher's Creek."

"Sergeant Marano got a draft from Base Alpha an hour ago," Huber said grimly. "They've all had combat training even if they've been punching keys for the past while. They're Slammers, they'll do all right."

"So what's the mission, El-Tee?" Deseau said. "We're going to hit the hostiles that're pushing Benjamin?"

"Come full dark, we're going to break through the Solace positions around Benjamin," Huber said. "Other units will continue to defend the city. When we're clear, we'll strike north as fast as we can run."

"What d'ye mean, 'north'?" asked a sergeant Huber didn't know. He was a grizzled veteran with a limp, probably transferred back to a line slot under the same spur of necessity that had returned Huber to F-3. "How far north?"

"All the way to the middle of Solace," Huber said flatly. "We're going to take Port Plattner before Solace gets its latest hires into action. We'll cut all Solace forces off from their base and leave them without a prayer of resupply."

"Blood and Martyrs," the sergeant said; Deseau was one of several who muttered some version of, "Amen to that!"

"That's what we're going to do, troopers," Huber said. The left side of his body was trembling with adrenaline and weakness. The future spun in a montage of bright shards, no single one pausing long enough to be called a hope or a nightmare.

"That's what we're going to do," he repeated, "or we'll die trying."

He laughed, and half the veterans around him joined in the laughter.

A battalion of UC militia held the portion of the Benjamin defenses a klick to F-3's southwest. From there scores of automatic carbines snarled unrestrainedly. The electromagnetic weapons used by all the Outer States fired with a sharper, more spiteful sound than chemical propellants; the fusillade sounded like a pack of Chihuahuas trying to pull down an elephant. Occasionally a ricochet bounced skyward, a tiny red spark among the gathering stars.

"*What've they got to shoot at?*" asked Padova from the driver's compartment. Rita Padova had proved solid when it came down to cases, but she didn't like twiddling her thumbs and waiting for the green light. "*Did somebody jump the gun, d'ye think?*"

"They're nervous, they're shooting at shadows," Huber said. "Keep the channel clear, trooper."

He frowned to hear himself. If he hadn't been wound too tight also, he wouldn't have jumped on Padova that way. With careful calm, Huber went on, "Wait for it, troopers, because it ought to be happening right about—"

The sky flickered soundlessly to the northwest: not heat lightning but a 20-cm bolt from one of the tanks holding high ground at Wanchese, thirty kilometers from Benjamin. A moment later there was an even fainter shimmer from far to the east. The panzers were shooting Solace reconnaissance and communication satellites out of orbit. Until now the warring parties hadn't touched the satellites, a mutual decision to allow the enemy benefits that friendly forces were unwilling to surrender.

The Slammers had just changed the rules. The war was no longer between Solace and the Outer States but rather between Hammer's Slammers and the rest of the planet. If the disruption from Solace's certain retaliation caused problems for the UC, that was too bloody bad. To pull this off, the Slammers had to hide what they were doing for as long as possible.

An instant after the big powerguns fired, the rocket howitzers of Battery Alpha cut loose with three rounds per tube from their position near Central Repair in the heart of Benjamin. Backblast reflected briefly orange from wispy clouds in mid-sky before the bright sparks of rocket exhaust pierced them and vanished in the direction of Simpliche.

"Blue element," Huber said, "the batteries in Jonesburg and Simpliche'll be scratching our backs in about eighty seconds. You've all got the plan, you all know your jobs. In and out, shake 'em up but *don't* stick around, then reform on at grid Yankee-Tango-Four-four-three, Two-one-four where the Red element will be waiting."

Red element was Messeman with F-2 and the artillery. The guns couldn't move till they'd fired the salvo that would rip the Solace units which threatened Simpliche.

Besides the Slammers' Battery Alpha, there were ten mercenary batteries in Benjamin. It would've been simpler to delegate the preparatory barrage to the others so that Battery Alpha could move instantly, but there was the risk the orders would be intercepted—or ignored.

Central chose to add a minute and a half delay to the Red element rather than chance much worse problems. Huber's combat cars would be delayed much longer than that while they shot up the firebase that anchored the Solace forces facing Benjamin.

"On the word," Huber said, "we'll—"

The sky to the east and west popped minusculely. If Huber had been looking in just the right direction, he might have seen tiny red flashes as bursting charges opened cargo shells several kilometers short of their targets. Calliopes, multi-barreled powerguns, began to raven from the Solace positions. They directed their cyan lightning toward the sub-munitions incoming from both Jonesburg and Simpliche.

The initial shells were packed with jammers—chaff and active transmitters across the electro-optical spectrum. The second and third salvos burst much closer, spewing thousands of anti-personnel bomblets with contact fuses and a time back-up to explode duds three minutes after they left the cargo shell.

"Blue element, execute!" Huber ordered, feeling *Fencing Master* lift beneath him as Padova anticipated the order by an eyelash.

The six combat cars reversed out of the semi-circular berms protecting them from direct fire and advanced through the open woodland in line abreast. Solace troops weren't in contact with the Benjamin defenses anywhere that the Slammers stiffened the line. Hostiles couldn't conceal themselves from the Regiment's sensors, and anybody who could be seen vanished in a fireball in the time it took a trooper to squeeze the thumb trigger of his tribarrel.

Nevertheless Learoyd fired as *Fencing Master* rounded its fighting position, his blue-green bolts raking trees and leaf-litter forty meters from the car. Flames blazed yellow-orange from a shattered treetrunk. If anybody else had shot, Huber would've thought they were jumpy; Learoyd was as unlikely to be jumpy as he was to start lecturing on quantum mechanics.

The artillery impact zone was out of Huber's sight, but the sky flickered white with reflected hellfire. At least one round of the second salvo escaped the calliopes' desperate attempt to sweep the cargo shells out of the sky before they opened. The calliopes stopped firing when the glass-fiber shrapnel scythed down the gunners who hadn't thrown themselves under cover.

As the crackling snarl of the single previous round reached Huber, all six shells of the third salvo burst over the target. The sky beyond the branches was bright as daylight, and the blast remained louder than the car's intake howl for nearly a minute.

The bomblets were anti-personnel, but several must have hit fuel or munitions. Secondary explosions, red and orange and once the cyan dazzle of ionized copper, punctuated the ongoing white glare.

Huber swore softly. He knew he should've felt pleased. The firecracker rounds were landing on the enemy, clearing a path so that Task Force Huber had a chance of surviving the next ten minutes. Sometimes, though, Huber found it hard to forget that the hostiles were human beings also, soldiers very like his own troopers.

And maybe Huber wasn't alone in his reaction. Frenchie Deseau, nobody's choice for Mr. Sensitive, pounded the coaming with the edge of his left hand. His right was still on the grip of his tribarrel, though.

Stray bomblets had lit scores of small fires outside the main impact area. That and the continuing roar had confused the troops in the ring of Solace bunkers outside the firebase berm. Huber's faceshield alerted him for the oncoming target for thirty seconds before *Fencing Master* wheeled around a giant tree and got a clear view of a low log-covered bunker some sixty meters away. The defenders had cut three firing lanes through the undergrowth to give them several hundred meters of range along those axes, but Padova had split a pair of them and *Foghorn* to *Fencing Master*'s right had done the same.

Huber aimed at the bunker's firing slit. The car's jouncing advance through the forest made perfect accuracy impossible but he didn't need perfection, not with the amount
of energy in a 2-cm bolt.

Cyan flashes caved in the bunker's thick face and shattered the collapsing roof despite the layers of sandbags
overhead. Ammunition inside blew the wreckage into the
air a moment later. The shockwave shoved Huber hard
against the side of the fighting compartment and slewed
Fencing Master against a treebole.

Padova recovered with a savage thrust of her fan nacelles.
Fencing Master charged through the line of trees into the
hundred-meter clearing around the Solace perimeter.

There were bunkers built into the berm, but the troops
within them still had their heads down when F-3 roared into
the open. The bunker roofs were proof against the anti-
personnel bomblets which had carpeted the firebase, but the
thunder of multiple explosions was literally stunning. The
main blast had ended, but duds continued to go off with
occasional vicious *cracks* that were almost equally nerve-
shattering.

Huber's helmet picked targets for him, coordinating its
choices with the AIs of the platoon's other gunners. *Fencing Master* was on the left of the line, so Huber raked a
sandbagged watchtower several meters above the western
curve of the berm. The wooden roof—a shelter, not ballistic protection—already smoldered where a bomblet had hit
it. Huber's burst was low, but his bolts blew apart two of
the support posts. The structure twisted and collapsed under
the weight of its armor, spilling sandbags, weapons, and
several screaming soldiers.

The night sizzled with the blue-green glare of tribarrels.
Every gun in the platoon was firing as the combat cars
charged the firebase. Huber switched his point of aim to a
bunker and held his trigger down for three seconds. A red
flash lifted the roof before dropping it back into the blast-
scoured interior.

Coils of barbed wire crisscrossed the cleared area. *Fencing Master* hit a post and slid over it, dragging the
tangles of wire under the skirts. If Padova had gotten the
wrong angle, the wire would've scraped up the bow slope

and decapitated any gunner who hadn't ducked quickly enough.

The pressure of the air in the plenum chamber was enough to detonate anti-personnel mines even when the skirts didn't touch the ground. Several went off in quick succession, *Whang! Whang! Whang!* like hammers striking the car's underside. Huber jumped at each blast though his conscious mind knew the worst harm a few ounces of high explosive beneath *Fencing Master* could do was maybe fling stones into a fan blade.

Padova canted the rear nacelles, swinging *Fencing Master*'s stern out to starboard without changing the car's direction of movement. They bumped down into the shallow ditch where Solace engineers had scraped up dirt to raise the two-meter berm. The earth wasn't compacted; it lay at the angle of repose, about forty-five degrees.

Padova shoved the throttles to their gates, giving the fans as much power as they could take without overheating. *Fencing Master* mounted the berm at a slant, wallowing but never bogging. Soft dirt sprayed in all directions. She reversed the cant of her nacelles; the combat car roared down the other side and into the Solace firebase.

A heavy electromagnetic slugthrower opened up just as the combat car tipped downslope. The gun was only thirty meters away, mounted on the cab of the tracked prime mover parked beside the nearest of the dug-in howitzers. Heavy-metal slugs spurted dirt to starboard, then clanged into *Fencing Master*'s skirts and hull as the gunner walked his burst onto them.

Learoyd's tribarrel tore apart the cab; the metal shutters on the windows flopped open a moment before the plastics and fabric of the interior gushed red flame. The vehicle's light armor had shrugged off shrapnel, but it wasn't meant for trading shots point blank with a combat car.

There was a line of tents along the inside of the berm. Bomblets had torn and flattened many of them, but Huber raked his tribarrel across the row anyway. Treated canvas burst into ugly red flames with billows of smoke, a good way to confuse and disrupt the defenders. Midway through Huber's burst, a crate of flares erupted in red, green and magnesium white sprays, setting alight tents that the tribarrel hadn't reached yet.

Everything was shouting and chaos. *Fencing Master* drove between gunpits, firing with all three tribarrels. Huber aimed down at a howitzer, hitting the recoil mechanism. Hydraulic fluid sprayed, then exploded as the car swept past.

It was impossible to pick targets but there was no need to choose: every bolt served F-3's purpose, to throw the Solace forces off-balance so that they'd be unable to react as the thin-skinned, highly-vulnerable vehicles of Battery Alpha drove through the siege lines, blacked-out and at moderate speed. If Lieutenant Messeman's escorting combat cars had to shoot, then the plan had failed. All F-3's gunners had to worry about was not hitting friendly vehicles, and their helmet AIs kept them from doing that.

Deseau's tribarrel jammed. Instead of clearing the sludge of melted matrix material from the ejection port, he grabbed his backup 2-cm shoulder weapon and slammed aimed shots at men running in terror.

"Blue section, withdraw!" Huber shouted, hosing a group of trailers around a latticework communications mast. Their light-metal sheathing burned when the plasma lashed it. "All units, withdraw!"

An orange flash lit the base of the clouds. Huber ducked instinctively, but the shockwave followed only a heartbeat later. The blast shoved *Fencing Master* forward in a leap, then grounded them hard. The skirts plowed a broad ditch till the car stalled. The gunners bounced against the forward coaming, and the shock curtains in the driver's compartment must've deployed around Padova.

A red-hot ball shot skyward and had just started to curve back when it exploded as a coda to the greater blast that'd flung it into the heavens. Somebody'd hit an ammo truck or a dump of artillery shells offloaded for use.

Huber hadn't been trying to keep control of his platoon in the middle of a point-blank firefight, but now one of the five green dots along the top of his faceshield pulsed red. At the same instant a voice cried, *"Somebody help us! This is Three-seven and our skirts are clean fucking gone! Get us out!"*

The man shouting on the emergency channel was

Three-seven's commander, Sergeant Bielsky—the retread with the limp—but he was squeaking his words an octave higher than Huber had heard from him in the past.

"*Fox, this is Three-five!*" Sergeant Tranter said, his transmission stepping on Bielsky's. "*We've got them, we're getting them out, but cover us!*"

Padova had lifted *Fencing Master* and started to turn clockwise to take them back over the berm where they'd entered: if they left the firebase by the opposite side, the north-facing bunkers might rip them as they crossed the cleared stretch. Now instead of continuing her turn, the driver straightened again and accelerated to where Three-seven lay disabled in the center of the compound. Huber fired short bursts into a line of shelters that the huge explosion had knocked down. Hostiles might be hiding in the piles of debris, clutching weapons that they'd use if they thought it was safe to.

Another orange flash erupted, this time near the eastern edge of the compound. It wasn't as loud, especially to senses numbed by the previous explosion, but two more blasts stuttered upward at intervals of a few seconds.

Fencing Master rounded a line of wrecked trucks, several of them burning fitfully. Car Three-seven lay canted on its starboard side beyond. Bielsky hadn't been exaggerating: the blast that shook *Fencing Master* had torn the port half of Three-seven's plenum chamber wide open. The gunners were clambering aboard Tranter's *Fancy Pants* as that car sawed the darkness. It was a wonder that they'd survived; they must've had enough warning to flatten themselves on the floor of the fighting compartment.

Huber's faceshield warned him of motion to his left rear. He pivoted the tribarrel. A pair of Solace soldiers knelt on a ramp slanting up from an underground bunker Huber hadn't noticed until that moment. The muzzles of their submachine guns quivered with witchlight, light-metal driving bands ionized by the dense magnetic flux that accelerated slugs down the bore. Three-seven's armor sparkled and one of the escaping crewmen flung his arms up with a cry.

Huber blew the men apart with a dozen rounds before *Fencing Master*'s motion carried him beyond the bunker entrance. Something flew over Huber's head and bounced down the ramp, then exploded: Frenchie'd emptied his powergun and was throwing grenades.

"*Three-five clear!*" Tranter shouted as *Fancy Pants* shifted away from the wrecked vehicle, accelerating as fast as fans could push its thirty tonnes. Ropes of 2-cm bolts snapped past *Fencing Master* to either side, other cars keeping the defenders' heads down.

"Blue element, withdraw!" Huber shouted as he raked the camp. "Go! Go! Go!"

Padova fell in behind *Fancy Pants*; Deseau'd reloaded and was leaning out the back of the fighting compartment, punching the night dead astern. The tunnel mouth burped a red fireball. It hung in the air for measurable seconds before sucking in as the bunker collapsed.

Fancy Pants drove through a waste of shelters destroyed when F-3 entered the camp; the car's fans whirled smoldering canvas and scantlings into a sea of flame. Preceding vehicles had scraped the berm to a low hump for which Tranter's driver didn't bother to slow. *Fancy Pants* lifted, then vanished into the night with *Fencing Master* close behind her.

Huber took his thumbs off the trigger as they crossed the berm. Shooting now would call attention to the escaping cars for any of the defenders who'd kept their composure.

That wasn't a serious danger. Huber took a last view of the firebase as *Fencing Master* returned to the forest's concealment. Scores of fires within the compound silhouetted the furrowed berm. Another explosion flung sparks a hundred meters into the sky.

Huber took a deep breath and almost choked. Struggling not to vomit in reaction to the adrenaline that had burned through his body for the past several minutes, he said, "Red element, this is Highball Six. Blue element will rendezvous as planned in—"

His AI prompted him with a time display on the upper left quadrant of his faceshield.

"—three, that's figures three, minutes. Six out."

Deseau had his tribarrel's receiver open to chip at the buildup of matrix material. It was a wonder that Huber's gun hadn't jammed also: its iridium barrels still glowed yellow. They'd been white hot when *Fencing Master* crossed the berm.

Frenchie glanced back. *"Not bad, El-Tee,"* he said over the intercom. *"About time we showed 'em who's boss!"*

Another explosion rocked the night. Solace forces around Benjamin weren't going to be worrying any time soon about the breakout from the city.

But there was a long road still ahead, for the Slammers and especially for Task Force Huber. . . .

Sergeant Nagano in *Foghorn* led the column. Huber'd decided to run without a scouting element a kilometer in the lead. He was more afraid that Solace units would stumble onto Task Force Huber by accident than he was of driving into hostiles with their signatures masked against the Slammers' sensors.

Even with the drivers trying to keep minimum separations, the line of twenty-seven vehicles stretched nearly half a klick back through the forest. A single aircar flying between Solace positions could see the column and end the secrecy that was their greatest protection.

Deseau slept curled up on the floor of the fighting compartment. The surest mark of a veteran was that he could sleep any time, any place. On Estoril Huber had awakened one night only when the level of cold rainwater in his bunker had risen to his nose and he started to drown. Soldiering was a hell of a life, a *Hell* of a life, and Arne Huber and every other trooper in the Regiment was a volunteer.

Learoyd braced his right boot on an ammo box to raise his crotch over the coaming of the fighting compartment, then emptied his bladder into the night. He stepped down again, sealing his fly, and said, "Is Frenchie going to take the next shift driving, El-Tee, or d'ye want me to do it?"

He'd spoken directly instead of using the intercom that might've awakened Deseau. *Fencing Master* was driving between the massive trees at a steady, moderate pace, and experienced troopers could hear one another over the intake noise.

Bert Learoyd sometimes made Huber think of a social insect: he seemed to have almost no intellectual capacity, but through rote learning alone he'd become capable of quite complex activities. It was bad to wake up your buddies unnecessarily, so Learoyd didn't do that.

"I'll put Deseau in next," Huber said aloud. Frenchie was too active to be a good driver; he kept overcorrecting, second-guessing himself. Learoyd didn't have Padova's genius for anticipating the terrain, but his stolid temperament was well suited to controlling a thirty-tonne vehicle in tight quarters. "He'll be all right on this stretch; it's pretty open."

Pretty open compared to much of the forest on Plattner's World, but light amplification didn't make driving a combat car at night through the woods a piece of cake. Huber'd been hoping to raise the column's speed to forty kph, but that didn't seem likely now that the whole task force was assembled. The combat cars might be able to make it, but the Hogs' high center of gravity made them dangerously unstable while running cross-country. As for the recovery vehicle, it was a full meter wider than the cars whose drivers were choosing the route.

Another thought struck Huber. "Learoyd?" he said. "Have you seen Padova manning a gun? In action, I mean—I know she's checked out in training."

Learoyd shrugged. "She's okay," he said, flicking regular glances toward his side of the car just in case there was something besides treeboles there. "She was on nightwatch when them wog sappers tried to creep up on us a couple weeks ago. She didn't freeze up or something."

Good enough. On this run there'd be no halts except to change drivers. There was no way of telling who'd be in the fighting compartment if the task force ran into hostiles— as they surely would, later if not sooner. The best driver in the Regiment was a liability if she panicked when she needed to be shooting.

"El-Tee?" Learoyd said. He was talkative tonight; by his standards, that is. "What's going to happen back at Benjamin when we're not there? The wogs'll waltz right in, won't they?"

"There's enough other mercs in the garrison to hold the place," Huber said. "The Poplar Regiment and Bartel's Armor, they're troops as good as anything Solace has close by."

He grimaced. Benjamin was all right, sure, but Solace hadn't been making a real effort on the UC administrative capital yet. Jonesburg and Simpliche were in serious danger even before the Slammers there abandoned the defenses they'd been stiffening to run north at the same time Task Force Huber did.

"Look, Learoyd, we've got to hope for the best," he said. "Chances are the Solace command's going to take a while to figure out what's going on. With luck they still think we withdrew back into Benjamin instead of breaking out."

Learoyd shrugged. "I just wondered, El-Tee," he said. "I don't think them other lots're worth much, but if you do . . ."

The trouble was, Huber didn't.

He suddenly laughed and clapped Learoyd on the shoulder. "What *I* think, trooper," he said, "is that everybody in Task Force Huber does his job as well as you've always done yours, then we're going to come through this just fine. The other guys, they have to take care of themselves."

He realized as he spoke that he was more or less echoing Colonel Hammer. Well, he didn't guess the Colonel had lied to the Regiment, and the Lord knew Huber wasn't lying to Learoyd either.

And because of that, just maybe the Slammers were going to pull this off after all.

According to the topo display, the Salamanca River was shallow at present though it regularly flooded its valley when the rains came in autumn. Huber hadn't expected much difficulty in crossing it until Lieutenant Messeman—F-2 was in front for the moment—radioed, *"Six, this is Fox Two-six. Take a look at these sensor inputs from—"*

Huber was already bringing up the data transmitted from Messeman's lead car.

"—my Two-five unit. Over."

"This is Six!" Huber said. He couldn't fully understand the data without a little time to digest it, but it was *bloody* obvious that Task Force Huber wasn't crossing at the ford Central had picked for its planned route. "All Highball units, halt in place!"

Learoyd obeyed the orders literally: instead of canting all eight nacelles forward for dynamic braking, he feathered the fan blades to drop their thrust to zero. Gravity slammed *Fencing Master* down, chopping the skirts into the soil like a giant cookie cutter.

The car hopped forward, grounded again, and skidded to a complete stop in a cascade of dust and grit. They'd halted within five meters of the point Learoyd got the order.

Huber'd braced himself on his gun pintle when he realized what was about to happen. He swore viciously and he glanced astern to see if *Flame Farter*, the next car back, was going to slam into them. It didn't, partly from the driver's skill and partly because he angled his bow into a stand of saplings growing up in place of a giant tree that'd fallen a few years previous.

I'm *the bloody fool who said "Halt in place,"* Huber thought. *It's nobody's fault but my own.*

"Highball," he resumed aloud, "keep a low profile. There's an enemy battalion on the other side of the bluffs across the river we were going to cross. They don't act like they know we're here—this is just bad luck. We'll head southwest, that's upstream—"

His hand controller drew a line on the terrain display of his Command and Control box, transmitting it automatically to the helmets of his troopers

"—and cross—"

The C&C box provided Huber with both a graphic and a tabular description of the hostiles arriving on the other side of the river. The database identified them as an elite unit of the Solace Militia, the 1st Cavalry Squadron, fully professional and equipped with nearly a hundred air-cushion armored vehicles mounting powerguns.

Instead of driving overland, Solace command had airlifted the squadron to a landing zone in the valley paralleling the Salamanca to the northwest. The terrain made the location safe from sniping by the Slammers' tanks, and it was as close to the fighting as a dirigible could approach.

"—seven klicks down, there's another ford there, and we're on our way again. Fox Three-zero leads until further notice. Six out."

If Task Force Huber had arrived six hours sooner, they'd have been past before the Solace squadron landed; two hours later they'd have fought a meeting engagement as the hostile vehicles—which mounted twin 3-cm powerguns as well as carrying an infantry fire team in the rear compartment—came over the bluffs on the south side of the river. As it was, it just meant the Slammers had to detour and add an hour or so to their travel time.

Flame Farter lifted and started to reverse in its own length. Deseau—who was blower captain, commanding *Fencing Master* while Huber's duties were for the whole task force—said over the intercom, *"Turn us around, Learoyd. We're following Three-zero up the river, now."*

Padova slapped the receiver of the right wing gun in frustration. She was a slight, dark woman and smart enough to be an officer some day if she learned to curb her impatience. Padova thought Learoyd should've understood Huber's unit order as meaning he should rotate *Fencing Master* . . . and so he should've, but—

Before Huber could speak, Deseau took Padova by the arm and turned her so they were facing. Both were short, but Frenchie had an hourglass figure and the shoulders of a wrestler.

"I'll tell you, Padova . . ." he said, shouting over the howl as the fans accelerated under load instead of using the intercom. "When you can make headshots every time at five klicks downrange, then maybe you'll be ready to give Bert lessons on being a soldier. Got it, trooper?"

Padova glanced at Huber, perhaps expecting support. Huber gave the driver a hard grin and said, "Saves me telling you the same thing. You're good at your job, but you're still the newbie in this car."

Padova forced a smile and turned her palms up; Frenchie nodded and let her go. *A first-rate driver, and apparently smart enough to learn . . .*

Huber went back to the display as the combat car shifted beneath him. *Fencing Master* was another world, one he didn't have to worry about right at the moment.

He had plenty of other worries. Reversing the order of march put three ammunition haulers immediately behind the two combat cars in the lead. He'd interspersed F-3's remaining three cars among the artillery vehicles, with all of F-2 in the lead to deal with trouble in the most likely direction. He could reorganize the order of march, but first they had to get away from the Solace cavalry.

The problem wasn't anybody's fault. This Solace deployment must've been planned weeks in the past, but the

dirigibles wouldn't've lifted off until after the reconnaissance satellites went down at the start of the breakout.
Central couldn't have extrapolated the appearance of an
armored cavalry squadron across Task Force Huber's line
of march. It'd been close, but close only counts in horse-
shoes—

"Bloody hell, Six!" Lieutenant Messeman shouted over the
command channel. *"There's a couple aircars coming over!
They're going to spot us sure!"*

—and hand grenades.

Huber opened his mouth to order the task force to hold
its fire; the Slammers' discipline was good enough that his
troops would probably have obeyed, though the gunners with
a clear shot at the aircars would've cursed him.

But secrecy was screwed regardless. Unless the Solace
scouts were stone blind, they weren't going to miss a
company's worth of thirty- and forty-tonne armored vehicles
on the route they'd been sent to reconnoiter.

"All Highball elements!" Huber ordered. "Slap 'em down
as soon as you can get both at the same time! All Fox units,
form below the ridgeline—"

His controller drew another line across the terrain map.

"—in line abreast, five meter intervals between cars, and
wait for the command to attack. Fox Two-six has the right
flank. India elements—"

The infantry platoon under Sergeant Marano, and Lord
help them if the influx of rear-echelon troopers weren't up
to the job.

"—on your skimmers and prepare to follow the cars over
the ridge."

Fencing Master grounded again, not as hard because they
weren't scrubbing off the inertia of thirty kph this time.
Huber was barely aware they'd halted, but from the corner of his eye he saw Padova climb out of the fighting
compartment. A moment later Learoyd clambered in and
seized the grips of his tribarrel. Frenchie was giving the
orders Huber would've wanted if he'd had time to think
about Car Three-six at this juncture.

Tribarrels, at least a dozen of them, snarled from the head
of the column. Huber couldn't see the targets from where
he was, but an orange flash briefly filled interstices in the

foliage to the north. The aircars were chemically powered, and the multiple plasma bolts had atomized their fuel cells into bombs.

The C&C box had converted Huber's orders to a graphic of routes and positions for the nine combat cars. Huber could've overruled the computer but there was no reason to. He'd planned to put *Fencing Master* on the left end of the line, but that would mean changing position with *Flame Farter* when there wasn't much room or time either one. Sergeant Coolidge and his crew could handle the flank.

Fencing Master was moving again without the bobbling usual when a combat car lifted from the ground. That was good, but having Learoyd on the right wing was better yet. . . .

"X-Ray elements—"

The vehicles seconded to the task force from Regimental command: the artillery, transport, maintenance, and engineers that the line elements were escorting.

"—hold what you got, we'll be back for you."

Huber drew a deep breath and raised his head from the holographic display. *Fencing Master* was passing to the left of an ammo hauler with about the thickness of the paint to spare. Huber would've liked more clearance, but he wasn't going to second-guess Padova.

"Troopers," Huber resumed, his eyes on the trees jolting past, "on the command the combat cars are going over the hill to shoot up all the hostiles we can in thirty seconds. We're going to make it look like we're trying to force the crossing, but we'll pull back, I repeat, pull back in thirty seconds. The infantry follows the cars over the ridge line ten seconds later but grounds and conceals itself on the downslope instead of withdrawing."

Lord, Lord. . . . He was counting on the hostiles being fooled by a fake withdrawal, counting on them not spotting the infantry ambush, counting on not losing every car in the task force in the initial attack which *had* to look real if this had a prayer of working.

And there was no choice.

"When the wogs're moving up from the river," Huber continued aloud, "the bypassed India elements will hit their flanks and rear, then Fox comes back over the hill and finishes the job. It'll be a turkey shoot, troopers! Six out."

Huber rubbed his face with both hands. The trouble was that these turkeys would be shooting back.

The combat cars were just below the crest of the reverse slope but still out of sight from across the river. The Solace sensors weren't good enough to pin-point them, although the Slammers weren't making any real effort to suppress their signatures. They couldn't, not and balance on a twenty-degree slope.

Mercenaries wouldn't've tried to use aircars to scout against the Slammers, but the Solace Militia hadn't yet come to terms with what it meant when the other side had powerguns and sensors good enough to tell them exactly when you were going to come in sight. The Solace scout crossed the river three klicks upstream, then rose above the forested hills to see what Task Force Huber was doing.

Flame Farter's forward tribarrel snarled out six shots, every one of them a hit. The scout disintegrated like sugar dropped into flashing cyan water. It didn't explode in the air, but a fiery mushroom rose over the trees where the wreckage landed.

Frenchie muttered something, to himself or Learoyd. Solace gunners across the Salamanca opened fire, raking the ridgeline and the tops of the trees growing on the southern side. A pair of 3-cm bolts hit the thick trunk to *Fencing Master*'s immediate right, shearing it ten meters above the ground. The blasts showered flaming splinters which drew smoke trails behind them. The Solace vehicles mounted high-intensity weapons, slow-firing compared to the Slammers' tribarrels but round for round far more powerful.

The upper three-quarters of the treebole toppled downslope and hit with a crash, igniting the undergrowth. Despite recent rains, there'd be a major forest fire on this side of the river shortly. That didn't matter to Huber, because shortly he and his troopers would either be well north of here or dead.

Learoyd took one hand from his tribarrel's grips and brushed burning debris from the other arm and shoulder. His face had no more expression than a Buddha's.

"Fox elements . . ." said Huber, his eyes on the C&C display. Three Solace armored cars started down the slope toward the river, moving cautiously instead of trying to outrace the bolts that might come slashing toward them. A dozen similar vehicles were settled on the ridge behind them to overwatch. Their twin guns ripped and snarled, blasting only trees and rocky soil because the Slammers were still sheltered by the high ground.

All the troopers in the task force could watch the situation map on their helmet displays if they wanted to. Most of them wouldn't, avoiding distractions that didn't have much to do with their jobs. Knowing too much is a handicap when instant decisions mean life or death. Their AIs would pick targets for them and they'd hose those targets with their tribarrels; that's all that would matter in the next minute and a half.

"The wogs 've taken the bait," Huber went on, speaking calmly and distinctly as he timed his words with the order to come. "We'll go over in thirty, that's three-zero, seconds. Six out."

Huber shut down the C&C display and straightened behind his tribarrel. The simple choices made by Huber's eye and trigger finger would be a relief after the sorts of imponderables he'd been balancing for way too long. . . .

A haze of dust and leaf litter swirled about *Fencing Master* and the other cars spaced along the forested slope. Their fans were spinning at high output, wasting their energy beneath their raised skirts. When the drivers tilted their nacelles forward, the cars would drop into ground effect and lurch into action on the thrust of those fans.

Infantrymen hunched on their skimmers in groups of three and four a little below the big vehicles. Their nose filters were down so that they could breathe despite the fan blast and the smoke from the scores of fires lit by the Solace powerguns. They must be miserably uncomfortable, but they were still better off than they'd be in the next few seconds. That was a risk that came with the uniform.

"Fox units, execute!" Huber shouted. "In and out, troopers! In and out!"

Fencing Master roared up the remaining slope, moving against gravity with glacial deliberation though their fans spun on overload power. Padova angled the car to the right where an instant before a pair of 3-cm bolts had grazed the crest, spraying fans of molten rock and organic material southward.

Huber swung his sight picture onto the opposite ridgeline. Deseau fired a heartbeat before the two wing gunners. Huber thumbed his trigger, sending a rope of cyan bolts into the humped shape of a Solace armored car. Its twin guns were mounted on top of the hull in an unmanned barbette. The muzzles already glowed white from firing before the Slammers gave them a target. They fired again, a quick SLAM/SLAM of bolts so fiercely powerful that the slope to Huber's left erupted like a volcano under their released energy.

Padova had allowed for the fact the Solace car was traversing its weapons as it raked the hill. By lifting over the crest where bolts had just struck, *Fencing Master* survived when the gunner twitched his trigger reflexively instead of swinging back to where his target really was.

Huber's burst struck the car's bow slope, the first bolt or two splashing reflected radiance before the thin armor ruptured. The forward compartment bulged; then the fuel tanks on the underside of the hull exploded, sending fiery debris in all directions. The twin powerguns lifted toward the river, tumbling over and over.

The Salamanca Valley was shallow and a kilometer wide from crest to crest, but frequent floods had scoured all but scrub vegetation from its slopes. The foliage was almost maroon rather than the vivid green of the forests elsewhere in the lowlands.

The world to Huber's left flashed white as *Flame Farter* took a direct hit. The high-intensity bolt vaporized the right side of the bow armor, swinging the car counterclockwise in reaction.

Flame Farter staggered forward, out of control though its running gear was still whole. Two figures rolled out of the fighting compartment as more bolts struck the vehicle broadside. The spray of molten iridium ignited the coarse shrubs in a ten-meter semi-circle below the destroyed vehicle.

Huber's bolts merged with those from Deseau's gun, raking the Solace car that had fired. Powergun ammunition detonated in an intense blue flash devoured the target.

The Slammers infantry had come over the crest and vanished downslope as planned. The brush grew three meters high; it would've seemed sparse from directly above, but its knitted branches provided good cover from eyes at the height of an armored car's viewslits.

Huber shifted his sights onto another Solace vehicle. It exploded before he could squeeze the trigger. Flames and black, roiling smoke marked the opposite ridgeline, each the pyre of an armored car and most of its crew.

A car of the advance party near the river was still firing, its bolts gouging the hillside; the panicked gunner was shooting low. His bad aim had kept him from being an immediate threat—and therefore target—but now half a dozen tribarrels converged on the car. The rear hatch flew open. Three black-clad Solace Militiamen sprang out, throwing themselves into the brush to hide as their vehicle sank into a sea of fire behind them.

For a moment Huber thought they were going to survive, at least for now, but one of Messeman's gunners switched to thermal imaging that let him see through the thin brush. The third man ran into the open after short bursts incinerated his companions; the single shot that decapitated him was bragging.

"Fox units withdraw!" Huber ordered. "All units withdraw at speed!"

It was war; those three desperate Militiamen were enemies who'd wanted to kill Huber and his troopers. But Huber'd still just as soon they'd been allowed to hide. . . .

Fencing Master shuddered as Padova cranked the nacelles forward. Once *Fencing Master*'d gotten over the crest, she'd let inertia and gravity take them downslope with the fans vertical, supplying lift but no thrust. It was time to get the hell out; in a firefight that meant backing so that the thicker bow armor and all three tribarrels continued to face the enemy.

Their skirts touched, a jar but not a disorienting crash. Padova got control again and *Fencing Master* began to slide backwards up the hill again.

Huber fired a short burst over the opposite crest. He didn't have a target at the moment, but his faceshield indicated a Solace armored car was driving up the reverse slope. He wanted the hostile driver to hesitate until the Slammers were back under cover.

There were vehicles advancing behind the whole length of the opposite ridge. At least fifty Solace armored cars were in line, and there were others forming behind to replace casualties. The Solace commander might not have a subtle grasp of tactics, but there was nothing to fault in his courage or that of his troops. And with odds of ten to one in favor of the Militia, they'd win a slugging match against eight surviving combat cars if Huber were dumb enough to try one.

Fencing Master snorted and scraped, reaching the ridgeline and then dropping with more enthusiasm than control onto the reverse slope. Huber checked his icons; all the cars had made it back except Three-zero, *Flame Farter*. He'd seen two men bail out. The driver was surely dead, but maybe the fourth crewman—

Reality returned, smothering hope like clouds covering the moon. The fourth crewman was dead also, dead when the follow-up bolts had vaporized the fighting compartment even if the initial hit hadn't killed him. The survivors must've gone to ground with the infantry. For now that was a better choice than trying to scramble back over the crest while a lot of very angry Solace gunners were looking for targets.

Learoyd was unfastening his clamshell armor, moving awkwardly because his right arm didn't seem to be working. Deseau turned to help. What in hell had happened to Learoyd?

But that was a problem for later; first Huber had to make sure there'd *be* a later. A storm of 3-cm bolts ripped from the other side of the river, blasting trees twenty meters above the concealed combat cars. The Solace commander had decided to take no chances whatever: his gunners started shooting before they could see the crest, let alone the Slammers below it.

"All Highball units," Huber ordered. He'd have liked to transmit in clear so that the Militia commander might hear him, but that would be too obviously phony to risk. "Withdraw to the southwest along the plotted course. X-Ray elements lead, Fox elements follow as rear guard in present order. Six out!"

The forest was already burning fiercely. There were fires in the Salamanca Valley also, but the brush was green and the flood-swept slopes weren't covered with leaf litter and humus to get a real blaze going in the next half hour. The smoke and sluggish flames would help conceal the infantry in ambush; or at least Huber prayed they would.

Crossing at an upstream ford wasn't a real option now that the Solace forces knew the location of Task Force Huber. By the time the Slammers could grind seven kilometers through forest and rough terrain, the enemy would've flown in at least a platoon of infantry. The availability of aircars here on Plattner's World meant that light forces could be shifted very quickly; light forces with buzzbombs and 2-cm powerguns were quite sufficient to turn a truckload of artillery ammunition into an explosion that'd clear everything in a half-klick radius.

The withdrawal would *look* real, though; a maneuver forced by desperation on Slammers who had to cross the river and who'd failed to shoot their way through at their first attempt. The Solace commander would certainly have sent a report and request for support back to his superiors, but he'd also be looking for revenge. The 1st Armored Cavalry would follow the retreating Slammers— cautiously, because the Militiamen had learned how dangerous the combat cars could be—in hopes of closing the door behind them when other Solace troops had blocked the way forward.

Of course for Huber's plan to work, the Solace commander had to know what the Slammers appeared to be doing.

"All Highball units," Huber said. "When enemy scouts appear, shoot to miss, I repeat, *miss* them. We want the wogs to know that we've cut and run. Six out."

His helmet buzzed with a series of callsigns followed by "Roger." The ball was in the Solace court. Huber could only hope his opposite number would act sooner rather than later; which was a pretty fair likelihood, given the way he'd responded to the initial exchange.

The artillery vehicles were taking longer to get turned around than they would've done if this had been a real change of plan, but the delays and seeming clumsiness were perfectly believable. The Hogs were bloody awkward under the best conditions, and the ammunition haulers rarely operated very far off a road. The maintenance vehicle was larger and heavier still, but its driver was used to maneuvering anywhere a combat vehicle could go—and become disabled.

Huber brought up the C&C display again to check the location of his vehicles. "Padova," Huber ordered, "get us moving but not fast."

The X-Ray portion of the task force was half a klick south and west of the combat cars. The last Hog in line wasn't moving yet, but it would be before *Fencing Master* closed up. The forest fire was getting serious enough to pose a danger, especially to Lieutenant Messeman's cars at the end of the line.

Padova eased *Fencing Master* into motion, picking a line close to the crest. The fire was bloody serious, but more so downslope where Solace bolts had flung most of the flaming debris.

Huber looked at his gunners again. Learoyd's body armor lay on the ammo boxes at the back of the compartment. Deseau'd sliced off Learoyd's sleeve with his belt knife and was covering the shoulder with bright pink SpraySeal, a combination of replacement skin with antiseptic and topical anesthetic. Learoyd tried to watch, but because of the angle his eyes couldn't both focus on something so close.

"Bert's all right!" Frenchie said over the intake noise. He gestured with the can of SpraySeal. "Make a fist, Bert! Show him!"

Learoyd obediently clenched his right fist. His thumb didn't double over the way it should have. Frowning, he bent it into place with his left hand.

"A chunk of *Flame Farter* spattered him," Deseau explained. "It was still a bit hot, but Bert's just fine. A little bad luck is all."

Learoyd opened his hand again. This time the thumb worked on its own, pretty well. The molten iridium had hit mostly on the back of his clamshell, but some splashed his upper arm where nothing but a tunic sleeve protected the flesh.

Frenchie *needed* to believe Learoyd wasn't seriously injured. Learoyd being who he was, that was probably true:

another man who'd been slammed by a quarter-kilo of liquid metal might well have gone into shock, but apart from stiffness and the fact his shoulder was swelling, Learoyd seemed to be about what he always was.

"Learoyd," Huber asked. He nodded toward the clamshell behind him. "Can you get your armor back on over that?"

"I guess," Learoyd said. He worked his fist again; the thumb still didn't want to close. Doubtfully he went on, "Frenchie, will you help me?"

"Sure, Bert, sure!" Deseau said, his voice as brittle as chipped glass.

He snatched up the armor, holding the halves apart for Learoyd to fit his torso into. The fabric covering the right shoulder flare had been melted down to the ceramic core; in its place was a wash of rainbow-hued iridium, finally cool after flying from *Flame Farter*'s hull to strike Learoyd thirty meters away.

"Good," said Huber as he turned deliberately back to the C&C display. "Because we've still got work to do today, and I want you dressed for it."

That blob of white-hot metal could as easily have hit Huber himself between helmet and body armor, burning through his neck . . . or it could've missed *Fencing Master* and her crew entirely. You never knew till it was over.

Task Force Huber was moving at last. Padova held *Fencing Master* twenty meters off the stern of the last Hog in line. More debris flew from beneath the skirts of a self-propelled howitzer than even a combat car threw up.

Huber grinned. It could be worse: following a tank closely was a good way to get your bow slope sandblasted to a high sheen. Of course if Huber had a platoon of tanks with him right now, he'd be dealing with the Solace cavalry squadron in a quicker fashion. . . .

The C&C display warned of new movement on the Solace side of the river. "Fox elements!" Huber said. "Four wog aircars are lifting; it looks like they're going to swing around us to east and west in pairs. Remember, shoot to miss."

A thought struck him, almost too late, and he added, "And make sure your guns aren't in Air Defense Mode! Put your guns on manual, for the Lord's sake! Six out."

The cars' gunnery computers couldn't be programmed to miss. If a gun was on air defense—and one on each combat car normally would be while the column was in march order—then the Solace scouts were going to vanish as quickly as they appeared. That'd almost certainly be before they could report back.

Frenchie and Learoyd lifted the muzzles of their tribarrels, tracking blips on the inside of their faceshields. *Fencing Master* was now weaving through forest that hadn't been cleared by plasma bolts and the fires they ignited. The gunners were tracking on the basis of sensor data because the low-flying aircars were screened by bluffs and undamaged treeboles. When metal finally showed through a gap in the foliage, they were going to be ready.

The Hog immediately ahead wobbled through the forest, moving at about twenty kph but seeming even slower than that. The leading vehicles had rubbed the bark to either side of the route, leaving white blazes a meter high on the treetrunks. Often their skirts had gouged brushes of splinters from deep into the sapwood.

Tribarrels volleyed from the tail of the column; an instant later Deseau and Learoyd fired together, their guns startling Huber out of his concentration on the display of sensor data overlaid on a terrain map. He jerked his head up as the upper half of a tree thirty meters toward the northwest burst into red-orange flames. The blasts of plasma had shattered the trunk, blowing it into spheres of superheated organic fragments which exploded when they mixed with oxygen-rich air a few meters distant.

In the sky a kilometer away, a diving aircar flashed its belly toward the column. Deseau sent another burst into empty sky; some of the artillerymen were firing sub-machine guns from the cabs of their Hogs.

Huber checked his display again. Three of the scouts had flattened themselves close to the Salamanca's surface. The fourth—

"*Six, this is Two-six,*" Lieutenant Messeman reported in a clipped, cold voice. "*I regret to report that we hit one of the aircars. The other should've gotten a good look at us before it escaped, though. Two-six over.*"

"Roger, Two-six," Huber said. "Proceed as planned."

This was even better than if all the scouts had gotten away: it made the Slammers' response look real. Messeman would be talking to the shooter when things had quieted down, though. Hitting the car had been a screw-up, and a battle at these odds was dangerous enough even when all your people executed perfectly.

Huber's gunners had blown apart a tree in order not to hit their pretended target. It now finished toppling to the ground with a crash and ball of flaming debris. Undergrowth ignited immediately, reminding Huber that his cars would be driving back through a full-fledged forest fire. That couldn't be helped.

And a forest fire was a hell of a lot less dangerous than what came next, anyway.

"All Highball elements," Huber said, "reverse and hold until ordered to take assault positions."

He'd have liked to put his cars under the hillcrest right now, but he didn't dare do so with the fire so bad on the slope where they'd have to wait. It was one thing to drive through the inferno at speed, trusting nose filters and the temperature-stable fabric of the Slammers' uniforms. Those weren't enough protection that troopers could twiddle their thumbs in Hell and still be ready for action, though.

"And troopers?" he added. "Those scouts had their only free pass. If they come back for another look at us, shoot fast and shoot to kill! Six out."

Fencing Master slowed to a halt, then rotated deliberately on its axis without touching the ground. Huber wasn't sure whether Padova was showing off or if she was simply so good that she executed the difficult maneuver without thinking about it.

"*Six, this is Two-six!*" Lieutenant Messeman said excitedly on the command channel. "*They took the bait! They're coming, it looks like four waves! Two-six over!*"

Messeman's *Fandancer* was a half kilometer closer to the enemy than *Fencing Master*, so its sensors provided a sharper picture than Huber's of what was going on across the river. The Command and Control unit synthesized inputs from every vehicle in the task force, though, so Messeman's report—while proper—wasn't news to Highball Six.

"Roger," Huber said, feeling a familiar curtain fall between him and his present surroundings. His hands were trembling, but that'd stop as soon as he placed them back on his tribarrel's grips. "Break. All Highball units, reduce speed to ten kay-pee-aitch but continue on the plotted course. The wogs must have *some* kind of sensors, and I want any data they get to show we're still moving southwest for as long as possible."

He took a deep breath and continued, "They're coming, troopers. India elements, we're depending on you—but you can count on the rest of us to help as soon as you stick it to them. Six out."

He grimaced and rubbed his palms on his body armor. He wanted to grab the tribarrel, but it wasn't time yet. Lord! he was keyed up.

"Hey El-Tee," Deseau said over the intercom. *"Learoyd and me got a bet on who gets the most wogs this time. You want a piece of it? A case of beer to the winner."*

"Hell, yes!" Huber said, grinning with the release of tension. "Though one case isn't going to cut the thirst I'm working up on this run."

He turned his gaze back on the C&C display. Nineteen armored cars had driven down the slope and were crossing the Salamanca, in some confusion because the ford wasn't wide enough to take them all in a single passage.

Huber'd expected the Solace hovercraft to be able to skitter across the water's surface, but though they weighed much less than his combat cars, their power-to-weight ratio wasn't as high either. They needed to be able to touch their skirts to the bottom. When two on the upstream end had gotten deeper than that, they'd stalled.

A second line of twenty-three armored cars had just pulled over the crest to follow. The remainder of the squadron, forty vehicles—a mixture of armored cars and headquarters vehicles—lined the far ridgeline with only a meter or two between their bulging skirts.

Under other circumstances Huber would've kept his combat cars where they were and delightedly called in artillery, but the target was too close for Battery Alpha and Central's movement orders had made it clear that every task force was on its own. The operation was more important than the problems of any individual element.

The first wave of armored cars started up the southern slope. For the most part they advanced at the speed of a walking man, but several of the drivers seemed to think speed was protection and drew ahead. They were wrong, of course, but their timid fellows weren't going to survive the morning either if things went the way Huber planned.

"All Fox units," he ordered, "reverse course and take up attack positions. X-Ray units, reverse but hold in place till ordered. Execute. Six out!"

Fencing Master rotated smoothly. Padova dipped the skirts to the ground this time so that she wouldn't run *Fencing Master* up the stern of *Foghorn* whose driver had bobbled the maneuver.

Huber wrung his hands together, wishing he had real-time imagery from the other side of the ridge. Red beads moving on a landscape of green contour lines didn't give him the feel of big vehicles shouldering their way through the scrub, their fans whirling sluggish fires to new life as their paired 3-cm cannon probed the crest above them. The Solace gunners would be ready to shoot if a cloud blew across their sight picture; they'd remember the way a dozen cars like their own had been reduced to flaming wreckage a few minutes before.

Fencing Master began to accelerate, holding interval. Both platoons were returning to the positions they'd held on the reverse slope before the initial skirmish. *Foghorn* roared through what had been a burning treetop before the six cars ahead had driven over it. Now it was a swirl of sparks, eddying out from beneath her skirts and curling back through the intakes into the plenum chamber again. Sergeant Nagano and his crew hunched over their guns, their hands clamped into their armpits for protection.

Fencing Master followed into a surge of heat with occasional prickles where sparks found bare skin. It was like being in a swamp full of biting insects, frustrating and unpleasant but not life-threatening, not unless you let it drive the real dangers out of your mind. Beyond the first obstacle was what had been a glade and now was so many vertical pillars of flame; they drove through that also. In another thirty seconds, it would be time.

Huber kept his attention on the C&C display, pretending

to ignore the distortions that flying debris threw across the holographic imagery. The Solace headquarters group, twelve vehicles armed with only light weapons, left the slope. The second wave was mostly across the Salamanca, and the first was nearing—

The flicker of a plasma bolt through gaps in the blazing forest could've been overlooked, but the *zzt!* of RF interference through the commo helmet was familiar to any veteran. A moment later a column of burning hydrocarbon fuel mushroomed from the other side of the ridge, vividly orange and much brighter than the smoky red flames of the well-watered forest.

One of the Slammers infantry had fired his 2-cm weapon into an armored car, picking his spot. At point blank range the powerful bolt had burst the car's fuel tank and turned the vehicle into a firebomb. Huber hoped the shooter hadn't been caught in his own secondary explosion, but he had more important concerns just now.

"Fox elements, do not engage!" he shouted. "Hold in your attack positions! Do not—"

Though the combat cars weren't back to their start positions, Huber was afraid that one or more of his vehicle commanders would react to the shooting across the crest by piling into it instantly. That was a good general response for any trooper in the Regiment, but right now timing would be the difference between survival and not.

"—cross the ridgeline!"

At least a hundred 3-cm powerguns fired at or over the quarter kilometer of hillcrest which was already scarred and glazed by previous bolts. The lighter *crack!* of infantry weapons was lost in the roar of cannons volleying at where the gunners thought the enemy must be. Another fuel tank detonated, lifting ten square meters of glass-cored aluminum armor with it; the magazine explosion a heartbeat later burned so vividly cyan that the light seemed to seep through solid rock.

Fencing Master reached its start position and rotated ninety degrees counterclockwise, putting its bow to the ridgeline and the enemy. Flames licked up behind and beside the car, but the trees close by had been burned and blasted into a bed of coals rather than towers that might topple.

The Solace cavalrymen were shouting over at least six channels. Huber'd set his C&C box to give him a graph of the number of Solace transmissions. He could've listened to them as well—most of the hostiles were too panicked to bother with encryption—but Huber already knew what they'd be saying: *"Help!"* and *"Where?"* and *"You're shooting at us, you idiots! Cease fire!"*

Especially *"Cease fire!"* from the armored cars on the south slope who *knew* there was nobody on the ridge immediately above them. Therefore the shots that'd destroyed their fellows had to be bolts misaimed by the cars blazing away from across the river.

The storm of bolts fired at empty rock slowed, then ceased. Apart from anything else, the Solace cars must've exhausted their ready magazines and heated their guns dangerously hot by sustained fire. The squadron commander would be starting to reassert control; in a moment somebody would realize how the leading wave had been ambushed.

"Fox elements . . ." ordered Arne Huber as his hands settled on his tribarrel's familiar grips. "Charge! Take 'em out, troopers!"

Fencing Master lifted with the ease of a balloon slipping its tether. By judicious adjustment of nacelle angles Padova kept the hull nearly horizontal despite the slope, so that all three tribarrels came over the ridge together.

Huber squeezed his trigger as his muzzles aligned with an armored car on the opposite ridgeline, its twin guns glowing white. Huber's burst walked down the barbette and blew the glacis plate inward. Fire and black smoke burst from the car's seams; the hull settled into the plenum chamber and began to burn.

Huber's faceshield careted his next target, also an overwatching armored car, but before he could fire it blew up on the skewer of Learoyd's gun. There'd been more Solace vehicles on the far ridge than there were tribarrels in Huber's two understrength platoons, but the combat cars had destroyed both their primary and secondary targets without taking a single additional casualty. Some of the Solace cannon had burst in vivid rainbows even before Huber counterattacked; they'd been fired so fast and so often that the overheated bores finally gave way.

The timing worked the way Huber'd hoped and prayed. The Solace gunners, confused and half-disarmed by the number of rounds they'd fired into emptiness, couldn't react to the sudden appearance of real targets; and the Slammers didn't miss.

Fencing Master continued forward and over the hill. An armored car was stalled ten meters ahead, its guns traversed to the right. The gunner had tried to reply to the pair of troopers with shoulder weapons lying belly-down on the slope as they blew holes in the thin-walled plenum chamber. The vehicle's cannon couldn't depress low enough to hit them, and the five Solace infantrymen who'd leaped out of the rear compartment lay in a bloody tangle just beyond the hatch. This close, a 2-cm bolt vaporized a human torso and flung the head and limbs in separate parabolas.

Huber put a three-round burst into the car's barbette; 3-cm ammunition in the loading tray gang-fired, devouring the breeches and mountings.

The cannon barrels tilted down. He didn't bother firing into the hull. The Solace driver and gunner might well be unharmed, but they were no longer a danger to the task force.

Arne Huber didn't kill people for pleasure: that was simply an aspect of his business.

His faceshield careted the smoke-shrouded net of air roots supporting a copse of thin trunks. He didn't see a target— maybe he would've in infrared—but he mashed his trigger with both thumbs. His chain of cyan bolts reached out, spinning eddies in the white haze. A Solace armored car drove out, its hatches blown open and spewing oily black smoke. Huber's nose filters were in place, but he nonetheless smelled cooking flesh as *Fencing Master* passed downwind of the target.

The smoke grew thicker. He switched from normal optics to thermal imaging.

An armored car stood broadside and motionless; had its crew already bailed out, hoping to be ignored and to survive? The AI called the vehicle a target, so Huber's bolts punched at the forward compartment until something shorted and the car started to burn.

A man in a black Solace uniform ran in front of *Fencing*

Master. Huber didn't shoot him but somebody did, a single bolt; probably an infantryman who didn't see any reason to quit just because the combat cars had joined the fight. Vehicles blew up, some of them so violently that the smoke now covering the valley surged and rippled like a pond in a hailstorm.

Fencing Master reached the river, its bank broken down by the armored cars which had recently crossed. At least a dozen were burning in the water or just beyond it. Huber's faceshield cued the far slope. He elevated his tribarrel, noticing that the muzzles glowed white though he'd been trying to keep his bursts short.

Some of the Solace command vehicles were trying to escape. They couldn't be allowed to. This battle had been a victory for Task Force Huber by anybody's standards, but the fragments of the Solace squadron were still sufficient to do serious damage to the artillery vehicles if anybody got them organized.

Fencing Master plunged into the Salamanca, bucking forward in a rainbow of mist. Even drops of water could dissipate a powergun's jet of plasma. Huber waited for the car to lift, concurrently flattening the curtain of spray, before he squeezed the trigger.

His burst struck the squared rear end of a communications van. The plating was so thin that the second round ignited the interior through the hole the first had blown; the three bolts that followed were probably overkill.

There was still shooting, some of it probably at real targets, but Huber's faceshield didn't highlight anything for his gun. Strung out to the right of the commo van, other headquarters vehicles belched smoke and flame. Tribarrels had ripped them open even more easily than they did the armored cars.

Via! That one was an ambulance. Well, worse things happen in wartime. . . .

"X-Ray elements, proceed across the ford at your best speed," Huber ordered. He was panting and for a moment his vision blurred. "Fox Three elements, take overwatch positions on the north ridge. Fox Two elements, wait on the south side and escort X-Ray. India elements, recover to the X-Ray vehicles and mount up. You did a hell of a job."

Fencing Master swerved right, then left, to avoid a pair

of burning vehicles. Something *whump*ed inside one; a crimson geyser blew debris out of the driver's hatch. It would've been attractive in its way if Huber hadn't realized the tumbling object was a shriveled human hand.

"Via, troopers . . ." he said, looking back across the valley as his combat car swung into position on the crest. Despite the filters, his eyes watered and the back of his throat felt raw. "We *all* did a hell of a job! Six out."

Smoke, gray and becoming black, blanketed the ford. In some places it bubbled above a particular vehicle, but for the most part it hung silently. Because Huber's faceshield was still set for thermal imaging, he could see through the pall to the wreckage littering the valley. The smoke would make a good screen against sniping by Solace survivors, in the unlikely event that any of those survivors wanted to continue the battle.

The tank recovery vehicle carrying the excavator in its bed grunted over the south crest and drove slowly into the smoke. It was the first of the X-Ray units, but a Hog was close behind and then two ammo haulers. Infantry swung aboard the big vehicles, dragging their skimmers up behind them.

Tribarrels continued to snarl, and once Huber thought he heard the sharp hiss of a Solace rocket gun. The ford wasn't perfectly safe, but this was a war and nothing was perfect. Better to run the noncombat vehicles through immediately than wait to completely clear the area and give the enemy time to respond.

Huber eyed the flame-shot wasteland again. "A hell of a job," he repeated.

And a job of Hell.

"*Six, this is Three-five,*" reported Sergeant Tranter; he was pulling drag on this leg of the run, while *Fencing Master* was in the center of the column between a pair of ammo haulers. "*We've got three aircars incoming just like planned, all copacetic. Three-five over.*"

Huber examined the data from *Fancy Pants* on his C&C box. Three-five's sensors had picked up the aircars while they were still over the southern horizon. Their identification transponders indicated they were the resupply mission which Central's transmission had said to expect, and they were within ninety seconds—early—of the estimated time of arrival, but still . . .

"Highball elements," Huber said, "we'll laager for ammo resupply for ten minutes at point—"

The AI threw up an option, a knob half a klick ahead and close to the planned route. It wasn't quite bald, but the trees there were stunted and would allow the tribarrels enough range for air defense.

"—Victor Tango Four-one-two, Five-five-one. Take your guns off automatic but keep alert. The wogs could've captured aircars with the IFF transponders and they might just've gotten lucky on the timing. Six out."

Fencing Master bumped a tree hard enough to throw those in the fighting compartment forward. Padova'd gotten over the reflex of growling every time the driver—Deseau was in front at the moment—didn't meet her standards, but this one made her wince.

"It'll be good to stand on the ground again," Padova said, bending forward to massage her calf muscles. She looked up at Huber in concern. *"Ah—we will be dismounting, won't we?"*

"We'll have to," Huber said, forcing himself to grin. "Those ammo boxes aren't going to fly out of the aircars. We'll be humping 'em."

He was bone tired, but he wasn't going to take another popper just now. Task Force Huber had a long way to go, and he'd need the stimulant worse later on.

The C&C box projected halt locations in the temporary laager to all the drivers. *Fencing Master* growled up the slight rise, then pulled into scrub forest which the bigger X-Ray vehicles ahead in the column were scraping clear. The place the AI had chosen for *Fencing Master* was across the circle of outward-facing vehicles. They brushed the massive wrenchmobile closer than Huber would've liked, but it was all right. Frenchie wasn't a great driver and it was near the end of his two-hour stint anyway. They hadn't collided, and this wasn't a day Arne Huber needed to borrow trouble.

Deseau set them down and almost immediately climbed out the driver's hatch. He wasn't under any illusions about his driving, though he didn't complain about the duty. Learoyd ought to take the next session, but . . .

Huber looked at Padova. "You up for another shift?" he asked. "It's not your turn, I know."

"You bet I am," she said, nodding briskly. "You bet your ass!"

"*Highball, we're coming in,*" an unfamiliar female voice said. "*Three aircars at vector one-one-nine degrees to your position. Action Four-two out.*"

"Roger, Action," Huber said. "Highball elements, hold your fire. Six out."

He knew he was frowning. He'd expected the resupply to be carried out by Log Section, maybe even UC civilians under contract to the Regiment. "Action" was a callsign of the White Mice.

The recovery vehicle had ground the brush in the center of the laager to matchsticks, then shoved the debris into a crude berm. The aircars came low over the treetops, circled a moment to pick locations, and landed. All showed bullet scars. They each carried two troopers, but the guard on one lay across the ammo boxes amidships, either dead or drugged comatose.

"*Fox elements,*" ordered Sergeant Tranter, acting as first sergeant for the task force, "*each car send two men to pick up your requirements. India elements, two men per squad. Also we'll transfer the dead and wounded to the aircars. Three-five out.*"

"Frenchie," Huber said, "hold the fort. I'm going to learn what's going on back at Base Alpha."

He swung his legs over the coaming, paused on the bulge of the plenum chamber, and slid to the ground. He almost crumpled under the weight of his clamshell when he landed. Via! he was woozy.

The troopers in the aircars were loosing the cargo nets over their loads; they looked as tired as Huber and his personnel. The woman with sergeant's pips on her collar was working one-handed because the other arm was in a sling.

"Tough run?" Huber asked, sliding out a case of 2-cm ammo for Learoyd, who took it left-handed. There were spare barrels too, thank the Lord and the foresight of somebody back at Central.

"Tough enough," she said, not quite curt enough to be called hostile.

"How are things at Base Alpha?" Huber asked, passing the next case to Padova. He didn't know who was defending the base with so many of the combat-fit Slammers running north. He was sure it wasn't a situation anybody was happy about.

"We'll worry about fucking Base Alpha," the sergeant snarled. She met his eyes; she looked like an animal in a trap, desperate and furious. "You worry about your job, all right?"

"Roger that," Huber said evenly, taking a case of twelve 2-cm gunbarrels to empty the belly of the car. "Good luck, Sergeant."

"Yeah," the woman said. "Yeah, same to you, Lieutenant."

The three dead infantrymen and the incapacitated—three more infantry and *Flame Farter*'s left wing gunner—had been placed in the aircars. *Flame Farter*'s driver and commander were ash in the remains of their vehicle.

The sergeant settled back behind the controls and muttered something on her unit push, the words muffled by circuitry in her commo helmet. Nodding, she and the other drivers brought their fans up to flying speed again.

"*Action Four-two outbound*," crackled her voice through Huber's commo helmet. The White Mice took off again, their vector fifteen degrees east of the way they'd arrived. Their approach might've been tracked, so they weren't taking a chance on overflying an ambush prepared in the interim.

"Bitch," said Padova, who'd been close enough to hear the exchange.

Huber stepped to *Fencing Master* and paused before swinging the spare barrels to Deseau waiting on the plenum chamber. The case of fat iridium cylinders was heavy enough in all truth; in Huber's present shape, it felt as if he were trying to lift a whole combat car.

"Got it, El-Tee," Learoyd said, taking the barrels one-handed before Huber had a chance to protest. He shoved them up to his partner in a movement that was closer to shot-putting than weight lifting.

Huber stretched, then quirked a grin to Padova. "I guess

even the White Mice are human," he said, grinning more broadly. "We all do the best we can. Some days—"

He held his right arm out straight so that she could see he was trembling with fatigue.

"—that's not as good as we'd like."

"*Mount up, troopers,*" Sergeant Tranter ordered. He gave Huber a thumb's up from *Fancy Pants'* fighting compartment. "*Fox Three leads on this leg.*"

Padova scrambled down the driver's hatch. Huber climbed the curve of the skirts and lifted himself into the fighting compartment without Deseau's offered hand. He seemed to have gotten his second wind.

As the fans lifted *Fencing Master* in preparation to resume the march, Deseau said, "Glad they brought the barrels, El-Tee. We were down to two sets after what we replaced after that last fracas. I don't guess that's the last shooting we'll do this operation."

"I don't guess so either, Frenchie," Huber said. For a moment he tried to visualize the future, but all his mind would let him see was forest and stabbing cyan plasma discharges.

"Hey El-Tee?" Learoyd said. Huber looked at the diffidently waiting trooper and nodded.

"What about the panzers, El-Tee?" Learoyd asked. "Aircars can't carry the barrel for a main gun, and even if they could it takes three hours and the presses on a wrenchmobile to switch barrels on a tank."

"I don't know, Learoyd," Huber said. *Fencing Master* reentered the unbroken forest, the second vehicle in the column this leg. "I guess they'll just make do like the rest of us."

Or not, of course; but he didn't say that aloud.

The trees in this stretch had thick trunks and wide-spread branches. That made the driving easier, especially now in deep darkness. Of course if a car hit one of them squarely, it wasn't going to be the tree that was smashed to bits.

A red bead pulsing twice in the center of Huber's faceshield gave him a minimal warning before Central crashed the task force net with, "*Highball, this is Chaser Three-one. You will halt for an artillery fire mission in figures three-zero seconds. Mission data is being downloaded now. You will resume your march after firing a battery three. Chaser Three-one over."*

The voice on the other end of the transmission was broken and attenuated to the verge of being inaudible. Central was bouncing the message in micropackets off cosmic ray ionization tracks, the Regiment's normal expedient on planets where security was the first priority or there weren't communications satellites. Even so—and despite interference from the foliage overhead, a screen if not a solid ceiling—the transmission would normally have been crisper than this.

What the hell was going on at Base Alpha?

But like the A Company sergeant said, it wasn't Arne Huber's job to worry about Base Alpha. Nor to ask questions when Central's orders were brusque because there was no time to give any other kind.

"Roger, Chaser Three-one," Huber said. "Highball Six out."

"Chaser Three-one out," the voice said, fading to nothingness in the middle of the final syllable.

"Highball, this is Six," Huber said. Deseau had turned to look at him. "Halt at Michael Foxtrot Four-one-six, Five-one-four. Fox elements will provide security while Rocker elements—"

The artillery.

"—carry out their fire mission. Break. Rocker One-six, I want to be moving again as soon as possible. Copy? Six over."

"Roger, Highball Six," Lieutenant Basingstoke replied crisply. He had more time in grade as well as more time in the Regiment than Huber. Huber suspected that Basingstoke thought he should've been task force commander in Huber's place, which was just another piece of evidence as to why a redleg lieutenant didn't have sufficient judgment to command a mobile force. *"You don't want us to reload the gun vehicles before proceeding, then? Rocker One-six over."*

"Negative!" Huber responded. He bit off the words, "You bloody fool!" but he suspected his tone implied them, which was just fine with him. "Rocker, I don't want to be halted in enemy-controlled territory an instant longer than we have to be, especially after we've been shooting artillery so they know *exactly* where we are. Six out."

Learoyd pulled *Fencing Master* into the halt location the AI had chosen for them. Huber looked up, frowning. The patches of sky overhead weren't sufficient for the Automatic Air Defense system to burst incoming shells a safe distance away. So long as the task force kept moving they were probably all right, but now, halted—

Well, Central knew the score; and anyway, the Regiment wasn't a democracy. *Ours not to reason why . . .*

The Hogs swung into position, their turrets rotating and launch tubes rising while the vehicles were still in motion. The ammunition haulers pulled off to either side of the guns. The F-2 combat cars tried to keep outside the scattered trucks, but this wasn't a defensive position in any sense of the term. The Lord save Highball's souls if any Solace forces were close enough to take advantage of the situation.

"Lieutenant?" said Padova, leaning close to shout over the idling fans. "I didn't think we were going to hear anything from Central on this run. That we were on our own?"

Huber shrugged. His shoulders ached from the weight of his armor, but that was nothing new. "The operation was pretty spur of the moment, Rita," he said. "I guess they're flying it by the seat of their pants, just like we are."

The howitzers fired, rippling with a half second between discharges so that the shockwaves from the shells didn't interfere with other rounds in the salvo. The nearest gun was within ten meters of *Fencing Master*. Huber's helmet damped the blasts so they didn't break his eardrums, but the pressure of 200-mm shells tearing skyward squeezed his whole body like loads of sand.

The Hogs weighed forty tonnes apiece, and the steel skirts of their plenum chambers stabilized them better than conventional trails and recoil spades could do. Despite that the big vehicles jounced so hard when they fired that puffs of dirt and leaf litter spurted out of their fan intakes.

The rounds didn't reach terminal velocity for seven seconds, but the *crack!* of each going supersonic stabbed through the deeper, world-filling snarl of the rocket motors. Overhead, branches whipped and shredded leaves swirled in roaring eddies.

Huber'd wondered how the guns would fire through dense

foliage, but that obviously wasn't a problem. The shells could course correct if they had to, but the disparity between the massive projectiles and the leaves made Huber grimace at the foolishness of his concern.

The first howitzer launched a second round immediately after Gun Six fired its first; the third followed three seconds later. As the launch tube sank back to its travel position, the Hog's driver began spinning up his fans: they'd been shut down while the gun was firing lest the blades whip into their housings and wreck the nacelle.

"*Highball Six!*" Lieutenant Basingstoke said, his voice crackling with the effort of Huber's commo helmet to make it audible over the thunderous conclusion of the fire mission. "*Rocker elements are ready to move. Rock—*"

Gun Six fired its third and final round. The shriek of the shells arching southward seemed like silence after the cacophony of the preceding seconds.

"*—er One-six over.*"

"All Highball units," Huber said. The whole operation had taken less time than switching drivers; a minute at the outside. "Resume march order. Six out."

He grinned wryly. While he didn't suppose Lieutenant Basingstoke was going to become a bosom buddy, at least he knew his job.

And because he was thinking that, Huber said, "Rocker One-six, this Highball Six. It's a pleasure to serve with real professionals, Lieutenant. Please convey my congratulations to your troopers. Six over."

Foghorn slid out of sight among the trees. Learoyd brought *Fencing Master* up, following thirty meters behind the lead car. That was a greater interval than they'd maintain when the task force had reached a constant speed.

"*Highball Six, this is Rocker One-six,*" Basingstoke said. "*I've passed on your congratulations to my gunners.*" After a pause he added, "*I'm glad we were able to perform to the standard the infantry and your combat car crews have demonstrated in order to get us this far. Rocker One-six out.*"

Huber looked up at branches whipping past against a dark sky. He grinned faintly. "Thank you, Rocker One-six," he said. "Six out."

He wondered how much farther Task Force Huber was going to get. *Who knows? Maybe all the way.*

And then what? Huber added to himself; but that was a problem for another day.

Huber awakened from a doze. He'd been hunched into the back corner of the fighting compartment, held upright by ammo boxes and a carton of rations. Fields of dark green soybeans rolled to either horizon beyond the iridium walls, punctuated by stretches of native vegetation.

According to the briefing cubes, Solace was several times as populous as all the Outer States put together. Those people were heavily concentrated in the center of the country around Bezant and Port Plattner, however, with the remainder of the country given over to the collective farms which produced food for the entire planet.

Huber frowned as he thought about the rations. He'd swallowed a tube of something a little after dawn as they negotiated the foothills of the Solace Highlands, but he'd had nothing since. He didn't feel hungry but supposed he ought to eat something.

It was an effort to get anything down because he was so fatigued by the constant vibration. Besides, the poppers made food taste like it'd been scraped from the bottom of a latrine. That wasn't much of a change from what ration tubes ordinarily tasted like, of course.

He jolted alert, suddenly aware of why he'd awakened. Padova'd been on duty with the C&C display while he rested. She was trained but she didn't have the sixth sense for what wasn't *right* that'd come with a year or two of combat operations.

"I've got the watch," Huber said. He took the controller from Padova's hand as he spoke, lurching upright. She jumped aside, startled and maybe a little snappish at the lack of ceremony. The reaction passed before it got to her tongue, which was just as well.

As Huber adjusted the display to make explicit what instinct already told him, he said, "Highball, we're going to have to adjust course to the left by thirty degrees. There's a monorail line eighteen klicks ahead, and if we continue as planned we'll be spotted by a train headed southward. We'll—"

He stopped because he'd caught the fine overtone to the sensor data, the descant he'd ignored for the moment while he focused on the electronic signature of a six-car train heading south at 120 kph. Task Force Huber could avoid observation from a train at ground level, but—

"Bloody Hell!" Huber snarled, interrupting himself. "This is going to take a moment, troopers. There's aircars scouting for the train and they'll spot us sure!"

"*Six, this is Two-six,*" Lieutenant Messeman said on the command channel. "*I suggest it's a troop train and the aircars are escorts. Over.*"

"Roger," said Huber, because it couldn't be anything else once Messeman had stated the obvious. He shook his head angrily. He must still be waking up. He couldn't afford to miss cues; he couldn't, and the troopers who were his responsibility couldn't afford him missing them either.

"Roger," Huber repeated, but with a note of decision. There was nothing wrong with his tactical appreciation once he got his mind in gear. "Highball, we can't avoid them so we'll engage and keep moving. Fox will attack on a company front—"

That was a bit of an overstatement, given that the Fox elements under Huber's command were two understrength platoons, but it'd do.

"—from point Echo Michael Four-two, Six-one. X-Ray elements continue in march order. Fox elements form to the right on Three-six in line abreast with five, I repeat five, meter intervals. Execute! Six out."

Padova looked at him wonderingly. It was too bad Learoyd wasn't on the right gun, but the newbie was going to have to get her feet wet some time. This was probably as safe a place to do it as any.

"Crew," Huber said, switching his helmet to intercom. *Foghorn* was moving up on their right with the other cars of F-3 slanted farther back as they drove through the soybeans to their stations. Lieutenant Messeman's platoon would take longer to join from the middle and rear of the column, but it'd be in line by the time it needed to be. "Frenchie, set our guns to take out the scouts when we're sure of getting them both."

The aircars were keeping station to either side of the track, five hundred meters up and a kilometer ahead of the train. They were looking for trouble on the line rather than scouting more generally, but even so from their altitude they were bound to notice the Slammers' vehicles.

Deseau keyed the command into the pad on his tribarrel's receiver. Instead of executing immediately he said, *"You don't think it'll warn them, El-Tee?"*

"It's a train," Huber snapped. "They're not going to turn around, they won't even be able to slow down."

Deseau grimaced and pushed EXECUTE. *Fencing Master*'s tribarrels slewed to the right and elevated under the control of the gunnery computer.

"The C&C box'll divide our fire so that the whole train's covered," Huber continued, deliberately speaking to his whole crew over the intercom rather than embarrassing Padova by singling her out for the explanation. "We'll shoot it up on the fly, not because that'll damage the enemy but—"

Fencing Master's tribarrels fired, six-round bursts from the paired wing guns and about ten from Deseau's as it destroyed an aircar by itself. Padova jumped, instinct telling her that the gun'd gone off by accident. She blushed and scowled when she realized what had happened.

Above the horizon to the north, a cottony puff bloomed and threw out glittering sparks. The flash of the explosion had been lost in the distance, even to Huber who'd been looking for it.

"—because if we don't, we'll have whatever military force is aboard that train chasing us," Huber continued, giving no sign that he'd noticed Padova's mistake. "We're going to have enough to do worrying about what's in front without somebody catching us from behind."

The gunnery computer returned the tribarrels to their previous alignment. Huber and Deseau touched their grips, swiveling their weapons slightly to make sure that a circuitry glitch hadn't locked them; Padova quickly copied the veterans. *Yeah, she'll do.*

A column of black smoke twisted skyward near where the white puff had appeared in the sky. The second Solace scout hadn't blown up in the air, but its wreckage had ignited the brush when it hit the ground.

"Six, this is Two-six," Messeman said. *"I'll take my*

Two-zero car out of central control to cut the rail in front of the train. All right? Over."

"Roger, Two-six," Huber said. He thought Messeman was being overcautious, but that still left seven combat cars to deal with a six-car train.

Sunlight gleamed on the elevated rail and the line of pylons supporting it across the dark green fields. The train itself wasn't in sight yet, but at their closing speed it wouldn't be long. Huber settled behind his gun, staring into the holographic sight picture.

Fencing Master came over a rise too slight to notice on a contour map but all the difference in the world when you were using line-of-sight weapons. The train, a jointed tube of plastic and light metal, shimmered into view, slung beneath the elevated track.

"Open fire," Huber said calmly. His thumbs squeezed the butterfly trigger.

Padova's bolts were high—meters high, well above even the rail—but Huber and Deseau were both dead on the final car from their first rounds. Huber traversed his gun clockwise from the back of the target forward. Frenchie simply let the train's own forward motion carry it through his three-second burst so that his bolts crossed with his lieutenant's in the middle of the target. By that time Padova corrected her aim by sawing her muzzles downward.

The car fell apart, metal frame and thermoplastic paneling alike blazing at the touch of fifty separate hits, each a torch of plasma. The Solace mercenaries on the train carried grenades and ammunition, but those sparkling secondary explosions did little to increase the destruction which the powerguns had caused directly.

The second car back had something more impressive in it, perhaps a pallet of anti-armor missiles. When it detonated, the shockwave destroyed the whole front half of the train in a red flash so vivid that even daylight blanched. The low pressure that followed the initial wave front sucked topsoil into a dense black mushroom through which the rear cars cascaded as blazing debris.

"Cease fire!" Huber ordered. "Don't waste ammo, troopers, we've worked ourselves out of a job."

He took a deep breath; his nose filters released now that

the air was fit to breathe again. Plasma bolts burned oxygen to ozone, and the matrix holding the copper atoms in alignment broke down into unpleasant compounds when the energy was released. Huber's faceshield had blocked the direct intensity of the bolts to save his retinas, but enough cyan light had reflected into the corners of his eyes that shimmers of purple and orange filtered his vision.

"Reform in march order," Huber concluded hoarsely. "Six out."

"They didn't have a chance," Padova said. She sounded as though she was on the verge of collapse. *"They couldn't shoot back, they were helpless!"*

"It's better when they don't shoot back," Learoyd said from the front compartment. He'd buttoned up before they went into action; now the hatch opened and the driver's seat rose on its hydraulic jack, lifting his head back into the open. *"They might've got lucky, even at this range."*

"Some a' them caught us with our pants down when we landed here," Frenchie Deseau said harshly. *"We weren't so fucking helpless! Ain't that so, El-Tee?"*

Huber flipped up his faceshield and rubbed his eyes, remembering unwillingly the ratfuck when a Solace commando ambushed F-3 disembarking from the starship that had just brought them to Plattner's World. *A buzzbomb trailing gray exhaust smoke as it curved for Arne Huber's head . . .*

And afterwards, the windrow of bodies scythed down by a touch of Huber's thumb to the close-in defense system.

"No," he said in a husky whisper. "We weren't helpless. We're Hammer's Slammers."

Task Force Huber continued to slice its way north, moving at an even hundred kph across the treeless fields.

"Highball Six, this is Flasher Six," the voice said faintly. The signal wobbled and was so attenuated that Huber could barely make out the words. *"Do you copy, over?"*

Ionization track transmissions could carry video under the proper circumstances, but communications between moving vehicles were another matter. Huber would've said it was impossible without a precise location for the recipient, but apparently that wasn't quite true.

"Flasher Six, this is Highball Six," he said, shutting his mind to the present circumstances though his eyes remained open. Deseau and Learoyd glanced over when he replied to the transmission, then returned to their guns with the extra alertness of men who know something unseen is likely to affect them. "Go ahead, over."

Huber had no idea of who Flasher Six was nor what he commanded. The AI could probably tell him, but right now Huber had too little brain to clutter it up with needless detail.

Fencing Master's sending unit had the reference signal from the original transmission to go on, so Huber could reasonably expect his reply to get through. It must have done so, because a moment later the much clearer voice responded, *"Highball, you're in position to anchor a Solace artillery regiment. I need you to adjust your course to follow the Masterton River, a few degrees east of the original plot. I'm downloading the course data—"*

A pause. An icon blinked in the lower left corner of Huber's faceshield, then became solid green when the AI determined that the transmission was complete and intelligible.

"—now. Central delegated control to me because they haven't been able to get through to you directly. Flasher over."

Task Force Huber was winding through slopes too steep and rocky to be easily cultivated. Shrubs and twisted trees with small leaves were the only vegetation they'd seen for ten kilometers. That was why they'd been routed this way, of course: the chance of somebody accurately reporting their location and course to Solace Command was very slight.

Huber was behind schedule, and the notion of further delay irritated him more than it might've done if he hadn't been so tired. He glared at the transmitted course he'd projected onto a terrain overlay and said, "Flasher, what is it that you want us to do? We're to attack an artillery *regiment*? Highball over."

"Negative, Highball, negative!" Flasher Six snapped. *"These are the Firelords! There's an eight-gun battery of calliopes with each battalion and they'd cut you to pieces. Your revised course will take you through a town with a guardpost that'll alert Solace Command. That'll give the Firelords enough warning to block the head of the valley with their calliopes*

and take you under fire with their rockets. We'll handle it from there. Over."

Huber called up the Firelords from *Fencing Master's* data bank; his frown grew deeper. They were one of several regiments fielded from the Hackabe Cluster. Their truck-mounted bombardment rockets were relatively unsophisticated and short ranged but they could put down a huge volume of fire in a short time.

"Flasher," Huber said, switching his faceshield back to the course display, "the Firelords'll be able to saturate our defenses if they try hard enough. I'll have to put all my tribarrels on air defense, and even then it's going to be close. Are you sure about this? Over."

"Roger, Highball!" Flasher said in a tone of obvious irritation. *"Your infantry component will have to handle local security. Are you able to comply, over?"*

"Roger, Flasher," Huber said. It wasn't the first time he'd gotten orders he didn't like. It wouldn't be the last, either—if he survived this one. "Highball Six out."

He paused a moment to collect his mind. The AI was laying out courses and plotting fields of fire; doing its job, as happy as a machine could be. And Arne Huber was a soldier, so he'd do his job also. If it didn't make him happy, sometimes, he and all the other troopers in the Regiment had decided—if only by default—that it made them happier than other lines of work.

"Trouble, El-Tee?" Deseau asked without looking up from his sight picture. He'd been covering the left front while Huber was getting their orders.

"Hey, we're alive, Frenchie," Huber said. "That's something, right?"

He looked at the new plot on the C&C display, took a deep breath, and said over the briefing channel, "Highball, this is Six. There's been a change of plan. We're to proceed up the valley of the Masterton River, through a place called Millhouse Crossing. There's a Militia guardpost there."

In briefing mode, the unit commanders could respond directly and lower-ranking personnel could caret Huber's display for permission to speak. Nobody said anything for the moment.

He continued, "We'll shoot up the post on the move, but

be aware that they may shoot back. We'll continue another fifteen klicks to where the road drops down into the plains around Hundred Hectare Lake. We'll halt short of there because an artillery regiment is set up beside the lake, the Firelords. We're to keep their attention while a friendly unit takes care of them. Any questions? Over."

"*If they're so fucking friendly,*" Deseau said over *Fencing Master*'s intercom, "*then let them draw fire and we'll shoot up the redlegs. How about that?*"

There was a pause as the rest of the task force stared at the transmitted map; at least the unit commanders would also check out the Firelords. The first response was from Lieutenant Basingstoke, saying, "*Highball Six, this is Rocker One-six. The Firelords can launch nearly fifteen hundred fifteen-centimeter rockets within five seconds. You can't—the task force cannot, I believe—defend against a barrage like that. Over.*"

Huber sighed, though he supposed it was just as well that somebody'd raised the point directly. "One-six," he said, "I agree with your calculations, but we have our orders. We're going to do our best and hope that the Firelords don't think it's worth emptying their racks all in one go. Over."

Somebody swore softly. It could've been any of the platoon leaders. Blood and Martyrs, it could've been Huber himself muttering the words that were dancing through his mind.

"All right, troopers," Huber said to the fraught silence. "You've got your orders. We've all got our orders. Car Three-six leads from here till we're through this. Highball Six out."

Padova obediently increased speed by five kph, pulling around *Foghorn* as Sergeant Nagano's driver swung to the left in obedience to the directions from the C&C box. As soon as they were into the broader part of the valley, they'd form with the combat cars in line abreast by platoons at the front and rear of the task force. The X-Ray vehicles would crowd as tightly together between the cars as movement safety would allow.

Bombardment rockets had a wide footprint but they weren't individually accurate, so reducing the target made the tribarrels' task of defense easier. Not easy, but an old soldier was one who'd learned to take every advantage there was.

Padova took them up a swale cutting into the ridge to the right. Deseau looked at the landscape. By crossing the ridge, they'd enter a better-watered valley where the data bank said the locals grew crops on terraces.

"*Ever want to be a farmer, Bert?*" Deseau asked.

"*No, Frenchie,*" Learoyd said.

Deseau shrugged. "*Yeah, me neither,*" he said. "*Besides, I like shooting people.*"

He laughed, but Huber wasn't sure he was joking.

Fencing Master nosed through the spike-leafed trees straggling along the crest. They were similar to giants Huber'd seen in the lowland forests, but here the tallest were only ten meters high and their leaves had a grayish cast.

Limestone scraped beneath *Fencing Master*'s skirts as they started down the eastern slope. The landscape immediately became greener, and after less than a minute they'd snorted out of wasteland into a peanut field.

A man—no, a woman—was cultivating the far end of the field with a capacitor-powered tractor. The farmer saw *Fencing Master* and stood up on her seat. As *Foghorn* slid out of the scrub with the rest of the column following, she leaped into the field and began crawling away while the tractor continued its original course. The peanut bushes wobbled, marking her course. Deseau laughed.

"*It's like a different planet,*" Padova said, taking them down the path to the next terrace, a meter lower. *Fencing Master* was wider than the farm machinery, so they jolted as their skirts plowed the retaining wall and upper terrace into a broader ramp. The valley opened into more fields interspersed with the roofs of houses and sheds. "*All green and pretty.*"

An aircar heading south a kilometer away suddenly turned in the air and started back the way it'd come. Learoyd and Deseau fired. Half the vehicle including the rear fan disintegrated. The forward portion spun into the ground and erupted in flames.

"*Just wait a bit, Rita,*" Frenchie said with a chuckle.

The Solace Militia used civilian vehicles with no markings that'd show at a quick glimpse through a gunsight. That aircar might've been a farm couple coming home with all their children, but Huber would've fired also if he hadn't been concentrating on other business. He had to cover the sensor readouts as well as the position of his task force.

Killing civilians—maybe civilians—wasn't a part of the work that Huber much cared for, but you'd go crazy if you let yourself worry about the things you couldn't change. Go crazy or shoot yourself.

In the interests of command, *Fencing Master* should've been farther back in the column with *Foghorn* or *Fancy Pants* leading . . . but Huber was making the choice, and he knew that afterwards the CO had less to explain to the survivors if he'd been leading from the front. He had less to explain to himself, too, if he was one of those survivors.

Padova increased speed, crossing the fields at forty kph and using the extra inertia to help break down the retaining walls before accelerating again. Huber frowned, but the rest of the column kept station. Since *Fencing Master* was widening the ramps, the following vehicles didn't have to slow as much to negotiate the terraces.

The valley's lower levels were planted in rice, a green much brighter than the leaves of the peanut bushes. The paddies were flooded; showers of spray, muck, and young plants erupted as the Slammers drove through. Upper fields began to drain as the column's passage opened the dikes.

Occasionally someone stepped out of a wood-framed dwelling or glanced up in a field to see what the noise was. Some continued to stare as the column howled by, perhaps thinking they were mercenaries under contract to the Solace government.

Twice an aircar appeared in the far distance. A tribarrel in air defense mode ripped each out of the sky.

The Masterton River here was twenty meters wide, too narrow to rate as a river back on Friesland. Even so, it carried more tumbling water than Huber'd have wanted to take his combat cars over without being sure of a ford.

No need to cross, of course. There was plenty of room on the broad bottom terrace to form on a platoon front. *Foghorn* came up on the right of *Fencing Master*, with Gabinus' Three-eight and *Fancy Pants* falling in alongside.

Funnel-mouthed fish weirs lined both banks. The small boys tipping them up to check the catch turned and to watch the passing armored vehicles. *Fencing Master* still set the pace. Padova continued to accelerate now that they were no longer descending the slope.

The town, Millhouse Crossing, was two rows of buildings which began as a straggle of shacks with board walls and roofs of corrugated plastic. Further on the houses were masonry and two or three stories high. The road was barely wide enough for the recovery vehicle, and even the combat cars would have to go through one at a time.

A black-and-yellow Solace flag flew over the cupola of a building in the center of town. All the F-3 vehicles fired as soon as the guardpost came in view, shattering the stuccoed limestone in dazzles of cyan and white.

Chickens were running in nervous circles in the street. A cart and small tractor stood forlorn beside a roofed marketplace on the inland side. The cart was half-loaded, but its owner and every other human in Millhouse Crossing was trying to hide.

"Highball, form on Three-six in line ahead," Huber said. "We'll go back to platoon front on the—"

As *Fencing Master* drew ahead again, Deseau decided he had a fair shot at the facade of the guardpost—and took it. He was more right than not, placing most of his ten-round burst in the ground floor of the government building, though a pair of 2-cm bolts blew in the arched entryway of the private house next door.

"—other side of town. Six out."

Huber swiveled his gun so that it covered building fronts a hundred meters ahead on his side. Padova brushed a pair of shacks that'd been built closer to the road than most of the row, knocking them to scrap. A sheet of plywood flipped outward and slapped down over a screened intake on *Fencing Master*'s port side; it clung there, partially blocking the duct, till Padova deliberately swerved through another shack and swept the debris off. A brief snowstorm of chicken feathers sprayed from beneath the skirts.

They howled past a house painted pale green. In the corner of his eye Huber saw a white face staring from the interior. The spectator was no threat, and besides Huber's attention was focused on the magnified image of buildings well in the distance. A sniper directly alongside would be for *Foghorn*'s gunners to deal with.

Learoyd's gun hammered, the bolts' intense cyan reflecting from the soft pastels of the building fronts. His burst fanned the interior of the government building which Deseau's gun had already set alight. As *Fencing Master* passed, orange flame *whuff*ed! from the window openings, a gas stove adding its note to the ongoing destruction.

Fencing Master hit the cart in the roadway, flinging its contents into the air, and bunted the tractor through the lightly framed market stalls. Huber flinched reflexively as cans of meat bounced off the armor beside him. Civilians scrambled out of the wreckage running in circles much as the chickens had moments before.

The rest of the way was clear. Padova kept *Fencing Master* on the raised roadbed through the village, then dropped into the lefthand paddy at a slant to let the rest of the platoon fall in beside them. High-pressure air squirting from beneath the plenum chambers excavated furrows twice the width of the vehicles themselves, gouging out the young rice.

The crop could be replanted; the damaged buildings could be repaired. In a few years, people in Millhouse Crossing would no longer talk about the day Hammer's Slammers roared through. Nothing really matters but life itself, and death.

The village was twelve kilometers from the mouth of the valley. According to the terrain display, the Masterton River dropped twenty meters in the next five hundred, boiling over a series of cataracts that closed it to navigation, and from there meandered another eight klicks to Hundred Hectare Lake.

In the geologic past the lake had been of twice its present area. When the water drained, the original shoreline remained as a limestone escarpment on the south and western margins. Though never more than a few meters high, it was sufficient to cover an artillery regiment against powerguns firing from the Masterton Valley.

Under other circumstances, Huber might've considered taking his combat cars in a balls-to-the-wall charge across the farmland south of the lake. The Firelords' calliopes, emplaced on the escarpment and manned by professionals, made that notion suicide.

Another option—the one Huber would've picked—was to

have halted well beyond the twenty-kilometer range of the Firelords' bombardment rockets and let Battery Alpha clear the problem. Again the calliopes were the difficulty. Saturating the Firelords' air defenses would require much of the ammunition the battery was carrying, and there wouldn't be any resupply until after—and if—the Regiment captured Port Plattner.

Which left the third option, Flasher Six dealing with the Firelords in his own good time and fashion, while Task Force Huber took whatever was thrown at them. Maybe next time his troopers'd be dishing it out while somebody else drew fire. . . .

The sensor display gave Huber the warning: not movement but a radio signal from the hills overlooking the broad pass to the north. A Solace lookout was signaling back to headquarters near the lakeside.

"Highball!" Huber called. He didn't aim his own gun; he had other duties. "Tar—"

Deseau must've expected an outpost and set his AI to caret RF sources. Most civilians would be using land lines, but a mercenary unit would generally depend on its own communications system. While Huber was still speaking, Frenchie acted. A three-round ranging burst hiss/*CRACK*ed from his tribarrel, vivid even in sunlight.

"—get at vector zero-seven degrees, radio trans—"

Nobody was good enough to hit a target ten kilometers away with his first shot. Deseau adjusted his aim, dialed up the magnification on his holographic sights, and engaged the gun's stabilizer. Learoyd leaned over his own gun, importing the target information from Deseau's weapon instead of duplicating the effort.

"—mitter. Fire at—"

Deseau and Learoyd fired together. Their tribarrels spat streams in near parallel, merging optically as they snapped through the sunlight ahead of the task force.

"—will!"

The distant slope winked—cyan from the impacting plasma, red and gushing gray steam where brush burned explosively. There was a burp of orange and the radio signal cut off.

"Got 'em!" Deseau shouted as he and Learoyd took their

thumbs from their triggers. He wasn't on intercom, but Huber could easily hear his excited voice. "Got the bastards!"

Fancy Pants and Three-eight ripped ropes of blue-green hellfire toward the pass. A stretch of hillside where the vegetation was dry began to burn with some enthusiasm. Another gun, this one from F-2 aiming past the X-Ray vehicles, joined in.

"Cease fire!" Huber ordered. "Six to Highball, cease fire! Save your gunbarrels, troopers, because we're going to need them bad. Out!"

"*Here it comes,*" Deseau said, reading the flicker of saffron from beyond the mouth of the valley. "*For what we are about to receive, the Lord make us thankful.*"

The sensor suite analyzed the sound some ten seconds after Frenchie had correctly identified the exhaust flashes reflected from clouds of dust: rocket motors igniting, sixty of them rippling in groups of six every second. A Firelord battery had just launched half the rockets on its six trucks.

"Fox elements," Huber said, "put all your guns, I repeat *all* your guns in air defense mode. Have your backup weapons ready to deal with ground threats."

He pressed his hands against his armored chest to keep from balling them into fists till they cramped.

"Troopers," he went on, "this is going to be hard but we're going to do it. Hold station on Three-six, watch for problems on the ground, and let our gunnery computers do their job. They can handle it if anything can. Six out. Break."

The armored vehicles bucked through the muck of the paddies, throwing up curtains of spray to the rear and sides. The mid-afternoon sun struck it into rainbows, dazzlingly beautiful over the bright green rice plants.

"Padova," Huber continued, "keep picking up the pace as long as the rest of Highball can stay with us. Don't let 'em string out, but the Firelords may not have us under direct observation. I'd like to be somewhere other than they calculate. Out."

"*Roger,*" the driver said. She sounded focused but not concerned. Huber couldn't tell without checking whether *Fencing Master*'s speed increased, but he figured he'd delegated the decision to the person best able to make it.

Deseau set the tribarrels on air defense; the guns lifted

their triple muzzles toward the northern sky like hounds casting for a distant scent. He took his 2-cm weapon out of the clip that held it to his gun's pintle; Learoyd held his sub-machine gun in his right hand as he snapped the loading tube out of the receiver, then in again to make sure it had locked home. Huber grinned tightly and drew his own 2-cm weapon from its muzzle-down nest between ammo boxes at the rear of the compartment.

All the tribarrels in the task force opened fire, their barrel clusters rotating as they slashed the northern sky. The Command and Control box coordinated the cars' individual AIs so that all the incoming missiles were hit without duplication. Red flashes and soot-black smoke filled the air beyond the mouth of the valley. A rocket, gutted but not destroyed, spun in a vertical helix and plunged back the way it had come.

The guns fell silent; then Deseau's weapon stuttered another four-round burst. A final rocket exploded, much closer than the smoky graveyard of its fellows. The tribarrel originally tasked with that target must have jammed before it finished the job, so Frenchie's gun was covering.

"Hold for a jolt!" Padova called, her voice rising.

The sky ahead flashed yellow-gray again, silhouetting the hills. For a moment Huber, focused on the C&C display, thought the driver also meant the next inbound salvo.

Fencing Master's bow lifted, spilling pressure. The combat car hurtled onward on inertia, its skirts skimming but not slamming straight into the cross dike which had just appeared at the end of the paddy.

Fencing Master came down like a dropped plate. The Lord's *Blood*! but they hit. Padova'd executed the maneuver perfectly, but there was no way you could sail thirty tonnes of iridium into watery muck and the passengers have a good time. Huber had the coaming in his left hand and his tribarrel's gunshield in his right; otherwise he'd have hurtled out of the compartment.

"Padova, slow down!" Huber bellowed, though the driver had already cut back on the car's speed by bringing the fan nacelles closer to vertical. "Highball, watch for the fucking dike here! Six out!"

He glanced to the right to see how the other cars of the

platoon had handled the obstruction. Three-eight's driver had negotiated it flawlessly and was still parallel to *Fencing Master*. Sergeant Tranter must've seen the dike coming and warned his driver, because *Fancy Pants* had slowed to climb it in rulebook fashion and was now lurching down the other side.

Foghorn had tried to plow straight through. The dike was only a hand's breadth above the water and some forty centimeters down to the floor of the paddy. It was a meter thick, though, and over the width of a combat car's skirts even mud weighed several tonnes. The crew in the fighting compartment were all down, though the left wing gunner was trying to lift himself with a hand on the coaming. The car wallowed; the driver'd lost control when the shock curtains deployed automatically to save his life.

All the tribarrels fired again, those mounted on *Foghorn* along with the rest; the impact hadn't affected the gunnery computer. That was a good thing, because this time the Firelords had launched 240 rounds, a battalion half-emptying its racks.

Plasma bolts stabbed home. Flame and dirty smoke spread across the sky in a solid mass, replacing the dispersing rags of the previous salvo.

"Sir, I didn't see the wall!" Padova said. *"Via, sir, I'm sorry!"*

"Roger that," Huber said. F-3 had gotten straightened out and was cautiously accelerating across the second paddy. Nagano and both his wing gunners were on their feet again, though *Foghorn*'s guns pecked the sky in short bursts regardless of what the crew was doing. The X-Ray element had reached the dike and was crossing in good order, in part because of the holes the combat cars had torn. "Drive on."

The crackling roar of the first salvo's destruction rolled over Task Force Huber as the second flashed and spurted a little nearer. The tribarrels continued to fire, switching from target to fresh target as the rockets curved downward. The math was easy—two hundred and forty incoming projectiles, twenty-four guns to sweep them out of the sky—

Or not.

The left wing gun spun and stopped. It was properly

Huber's weapon, but Deseau was at it before Huber could react. Without even a pause to check the gun's diagnostics, Deseau snatched open the feed trough and used his knifeblade to lever out the disk that'd kinked and jammed. Grinning at Huber, he charged the gun and stepped back as it resumed blasting cyan bolts through barrels already white hot.

Huber tensed, waiting for the third salvo; possibly more than a thousand rockets, launched against combat cars whose guns were dangerously hot from dealing with the previous hundreds of projectiles. Instead, cyan light flickered behind the hills. Moments later, rolling orange fireballs mushroomed in response.

"*Highball, this is Flasher Six,*" the unfamiliar voice called. The tone of crowing triumph was evident despite the compressed and tenuous transmission. "*Thanks for your help, troopers. We've got it from now. Flasher out.*"

"*The hell he says!*" Deseau snarled, turning a furious face toward Huber. "*El-Tee, are you going to let them tankers have all the fun? We're not, are we?*"

Another volley of 20-cm bolts speared into the plains from higher ground somewhere to the northeast. Again whole truckloads of bombardment rockets exploded, the fuel and warheads going off in split seconds. Flasher Six commanded at least a company of tanks; their main guns were raking the Firelords, probably from beyond the distance an unaided human eye could see.

Tribarrels didn't have that range . . . but the combat cars weren't nearly that far away, either. Huber checked the terrain display and made an instant decision. *Like Frenchie says, why should the tankers have all the fun?*

"Highball, this is Six," he said. He might get in trouble for this in the after-action debriefing, but that would be a long time coming—if he survived. "X-Ray elements will halt inside the valley at point Delta Michael Four-one, Three-seven. India elements will dismount to provide security. Fox elements will take hull-down positions in the valley mouth—"

The C&C display obligingly detailed firing positions west of the river for each of the eight combat cars.

"—and engage the enemy. Hit the calliopes first, troopers, and any vehicles that aren't running—but my guess is that with the panzers shooting them up they're going to have forgotten about us till we give 'em reason to remember. Six out."

Padova tilted her fans for greater forward thrust. Lieutenant Messeman's cars were passing through the X-Ray element, slewing from side to side in the wakes of the big vehicles. The terraces narrowed on the steeper slopes above the cataracts; the C&C box had set their course along the road in line ahead now that air defense was no longer the primary concern.

Huber hadn't taken the guns out of air defense mode, though, because there was still a chance that the Firelords would try to carry their enemies with them to Hell. A slim chance. They were all mercenaries; their war was a business, not a holy crusade.

Sensor suites gave the task force few details of what to expect in the plains below. At this distance electronic and sonic signatures couldn't pinpoint targets, and the cars didn't have a line of sight. Obviously Flasher had the enemy under direct observation, but the link between the tank unit and Highball was too marginal for complex data transmission.

There shouldn't be a big problem. The artillerymen were so busy getting out of the frying pan that they weren't going to worry about the fire.

Because of the angle, F-2's cars were in position before *Fencing Master* tore through the stunted nut trees on the upper slope. Messeman's gunners opened fire while Deseau screamed angry curses at Padova. She ignored him, swinging them with necessary caution around a spur of rock into the position the AI had chosen. Here they'd be sheltered from possible snipers higher up the hill.

The plains beyond were full of targets. After a volley into their rocket-laden trucks had put the Firelords off-balance, Flasher concentrated on the calliopes in firing positions on the lip of the escarpment. The multi-barreled 3-cm powerguns could be dangerous even to tanks at long range. Main gun bolts had blown all of the calliopes to shimmering vapor before the combat cars nosed over the rise, but there were enough other things to shoot at.

Huber swung his tribarrel onto a ten-wheeled truck trying to flee through a field of sorghum. He squeezed and

watched his plasma snap in cyan brilliance across the bed
loaded with bombardment rockets in five forward-slanting
racks. Before the third bolt hit, the vehicle erupted into
rolling orange fury, searing a black circle from the crops.

The Firelords had set up between the ridge and the
lakeside, shielded from the task force. When the tanks began
to rake them from the flank and rear, some of the hundreds
of vehicles—not just rocket trucks but also the command,
service, and transportation vehicles that an artillery regiment
requires—tried to escape west along the lake's margin.
Others—the truck Huber hit was one—had climbed out of
the bowl and spread out across the fields.

Another volley of 20-cm bolts lashed the milling chaos,
setting off further secondary explosions. The billowing flames
and blast-flung debris curtained the survivors to some degree
from the tanks fifty, eighty—maybe over a hundred kilometers
distant, but the combat cars had good visibility.

Huber ripped a tank truck. It turned out to be a water
purification vehicle, not a fuel tanker, but it gushed steam
and began to burn anyway.

Three white flares burst over the center of the encampment. A man jumped onto the TOC, a cluster of sandbagged
trailers, waving a towel—beige, but Huber understood—over
his head. All around him was blazing wreckage, but apart
from a few hits by 2-cm bolts the TOC had been spared.
The Slammers had concentrated on targets that'd give the
greatest value in terms of secondary explosions, and there
was no lack of those in an artillery regiment.

"Enemy commander!" said a hoarse voice. Huber's AI
noted that the fellow was broadcasting on several frequencies,
desperately hoping that one would get through to the gunners
shooting his troops like ducks in a barrel. *"The Firelords
surrender on standard terms. I repeat, we surrender on terms.
Cease fire! Cease fire!"*

"Highball, cease fire!" Huber repeated, and as he did so
another volley of tank bolts lanced into the lakeside with
fresh mushroomings of flame. Flasher couldn't pick up the
radio signal—a truckload of exploding rockets had knocked
down the transmitter masts—and the white flares could be
easily overlooked in the general fiery destruction.

"Flasher Six!" Huber shouted, the AI switching his

transmission to the ionization track system. "Cease fire! All Flasher units, cease fire! They're surrendering!"

Explosions continued to rumble in the plains below, but the ice-pick sharpness of plasma bolts no longer added to it. Even before they got Huber's warning, the Flasher gunners would've noticed that Highball had stopped firing. A blast had knocked the officer with the towel to his knees, but he kept his hand high and waving.

"Firelords, this is Slammers command," Huber said, responding on the highest of the frequencies the Firelords had used. He *wasn't* in command, of course, Flasher Six was, but the tanker couldn't communicate with the poor bastards down below. "We accept your parole. Hold in place until my superiors can make arrangements for your exchange. Ah, that may be several days. We will not, I repeat not, be halting at this location. Slammers over."

"Roger, Slammers," the enemy commander said, relief and weariness both evident in his voice. "We've got enough to occupy us here for longer than a few fucking days. Can you spare us medical personnel? Over."

"Negative, Firelords," Huber said. "I hope your next contract works out better for you. Slammers out."

He lifted off his commo helmet and closed his eyes, letting reaction wash over him. He was exhausted, not from physical exertion—though there'd been plenty of that, jolting around in the fighting compartment during the run—but from the adrenaline blazing in him as shells rained down and he could do nothing but watch and pray his equipment worked.

He settled the helmet back in place and said, "Booster," to activate the C&C box, "plot our course north from this location."

On the plains below, fuel and munitions continued to erupt. It didn't make Huber feel much better to realize that the destruction would've been just as bad if those rockets had landed on Task Force Huber instead of going off in their racks.

It was an hour short of full darkness, but stars showed around the eastern horizon; stars, and perhaps one or more of the planet's seven small moons. Sunset silhouetted the

three grain elevators a kilometer to the west where monorail lines merged at a railhead. Timers had turned on the
mercury vapor lights attached to the service catwalks as the
task force arrived, but there was no sign of life in the huge
structures or the houses at their base.

"Suppose we oughta do a little reconnaissance by fire, El-
Tee?" Deseau said hopefully. He patted his tribarrel's receiver.

Padova and Learoyd slept on the ground beside *Fencing
Master*. They hadn't strung the tarp, just spread it over the
stubble as a ground cloth. The car's idling drive fans
whispered a trooper's lullaby.

"Do I think you should use up another set of barrels just
because you like to see things burn, Frenchie?" Huber said,
smiling faintly. "No, I don't. We'll have plenty to shoot at
for real in a few hours, don't worry."

A tribarrel across the perimeter snarled a short burst.
Huber jerked his head around, following the line of fire to
a flash in the distant sky.

"*Highball, Fox Two-six,*" Lieutenant Messeman reported.
"*Air defense splashed an aircar, that's all. Out.*"

Probably civilians who hadn't gotten the word that a
Slammers task force had driven into the heart of their
country. Huber'd lost count of the number of aircars they'd
shot down on this run; thirty-odd, he thought, but poppers
always washed the past out of his mind. He needed the
stimulant a lot more than he needed to remember what was
over and done with, that was for sure.

The tracked excavator whined thunderously as it dug in
the second of the six Hogs. The note of its cutting head
dopplered up and down, its speed depending on the depth
of the cut and the number of rocks in the soil.

The task force was carrying minimal supplies, so the
excavator didn't have plasticizer to add to the earth it spewed
in an arc forward of the cut. The berm would still stop small
arms and shell fragments. If Battery Alpha needed more than
that, the Colonel had lost his gamble and the troopers of
Task Force Huber were probably dead meat.

Lieutenant Basingstoke, half a dozen of his people, and
three techs from the recovery vehicle, stood beside the Hog
whose starboard fans had cut out twice during the run.
Sergeant Tranter had joined them. He wasn't in Maintenance

any more, but neither was he a man to ignore a problem he could help with just because it'd stopped being his job.

Huber looked westward. Lights were on in the spaceport seven klicks away, backlighting the smooth hillcrest between it and Task Force Huber.

He could imagine the panic at Port Plattner, military and civilians reacting to the unexpected threat in as many ways as there were officials involved. They'd be trying to black out the facilities, not that it would make much difference to the Slammers' optics, but they hadn't yet succeeded. The port was designed to be illuminated for round-the-clock ship landings. Nobody'd planned for what to do when a hostile armored regiment drove a thousand kilometers to attack from all sides.

The sky continued to darken. Huber always felt particularly lonely at night; in daytime he could pretend almost any landscape was a part of Nieuw Friesland that he just hadn't seen before, but the stars were inescapably alien.

Grinning wryly at himself, he said, "Frenchie, hold the fort till I'm back. I'm going to talk to the redlegs."

Another thought struck him and he said, "Fox Two-six, this is Six. Join me and Rocker One-six. Out."

He lifted himself from the fighting compartment as Messeman responded with a laconic, *"Roger."*

The cutting head hummed to idle as the excavator backed up the ramp from the gun position it'd just dug. Waddling like a bulldog, it followed the sergeant from the engineer section as he walked backwards to guide it to the next pit. A Hog drove into the just-completed gun position and shut down its fans. The hull was below the original surface level, and the howitzer's barrel slanted up at twenty degrees to clear the berm.

Huber nodded to the munitions trucks loaded with 200-mm rockets. He said to Lieutenant Basingstoke, "I hope the engineers have time to dig those in too, Lieutenant. After watching what happened to the Firelords when their ammo started going off."

"If we begin firing at maximum rate . . ." Basingstoke said. He was a tall, hollow-cheeked man. His pale blond hair made him look older than he was, but Huber suspected he'd never really been young. "We'll expend all the ammunition we've carried in less than ten minutes. No doubt that will reduce the risk."

He smiled like a skull. Huber smiled back when he realized that the artillery officer had made a joke.

Lieutenant Messeman trotted over, looking back toward his cars and speaking into his commo helmet on the F-2 frequency. He turned and glared at Huber, not really angry but the sort of little man who generally sounded as though he was.

"Any word on when we'll be moving?" he demanded. "We *are* moving, aren't we? We're not going to have to nurse-maid the artillery while the rest of the Regiment attacks?"

Basingstoke stiffened. Before he could speak—and they were all tired, but Blood and Martyrs, didn't Messeman have any sense at all?—Huber snapped, "We're going to leave the two combat cars which I determine to be sufficient for air defense, Lieutenant. That's one from each platoon. Personally, I expect to be thankful for all the artillery support we can get when we attack."

Messeman grimaced but shrugged. "Yeah, I'll leave Two-four. The patch we put on the plenum chamber after the breakout's starting to crack. They can use the time to weld it properly."

"Seven kilometers," Basingstoke said, glancing to the west. The crest showed up more sharply against the port light-ing as the sky darkened. "That's closer to the target than I care to be, but—"

He gave the other officers another skull smile.

"—I've been glad to have the combat cars' company for as long as possible, and I realize that means following you to your attack positions."

Tranter crawled out of an access hatch in the Hog's ple-num chamber. He was a big, red-haired man who moved so gracefully that you generally forgot that his right leg was a biomechanical replacement for the one severed when a tank fell off a jack.

"Got it, Lieutenant!" he called cheerfully to Basingstoke. "They pinched a cable when they replaced your Starboard Three, so when the nacelles're canted hard right you get a short. The wrenches'll have it rerouted in ten minutes."

"Three-eight'll be staying here with the Hogs, Sergeant,"

Huber said, looking over his shoulder. The combat cars faced outward around the artillery vehicles. The circuit was too open for defense against serious ground attack but admirably suited to stop incoming shells and possible Solace infiltrators. If the Waldheim Dragoons and the scattering of Militiamen and other mercenaries in Port Plattner mounted an attack before the Regiment was ready to strike, the cars' sensor suites would give Huber sufficient warning to change his dispositions.

"Roger," Tranter said, nodding. "Ah, El-Tee? Can I swap out Chisum on Three-eight for Stoddard on my car? Stoddard pukes every time he takes a popper, so he's pretty washed out after this run."

"Right, the cars here'll be in air defense mode unless a lot of wheels fall off," Huber said, frowning to hear that Stoddard couldn't take stimulants. That didn't handicap a trooper quite as badly as blindness would, but it wasn't something a platoon leader wanted to hear about a useful man. "Want me to . . . ?"

"I'll tell him," Tranter said, throwing Huber a brilliant smile again as he strode off to inform Chisum and Gabinus, Three-eight's commander. Tranter wore a slip-over shoe on his right foot to raise it to the height of the boot on his left, giving his leg movements an unbalanced look.

The excavator started on a fifth gun pit. Messeman watched a Hog slide into the one just completed with the delicacy required by tight quarters. He said, "Ah, Six? Will we be getting a view of the target before we go in?"

"What I've been told," Huber said, "is that they'll launch a commo and observation constellation just before we drop the hammer. They're estimating that the new satellites will survive two minutes, certainly no more than five. That's why they're saving it till everything's ready."

Messeman sighed. "Sure, makes sense," he said. "I like to tell my people what we're getting into, that's all."

"Tell them there's nobody on the planet as good as they are, Lieutenant," Huber said. His glance took in Lieutenant Basingstoke as well. "We proved that getting here. Tell them one more push and we'll be able to stand down."

Messeman and Basingstoke nodded agreement; Huber gave them a thumbs-up and headed back to *Fencing Master*.

It was true, as far as it went: one push and a stand-down.
If they survived.
And until the next time.

Automatic weapons had been firing from the port area
at intervals ever since sunset three hours ago. Occasional
tracers ricocheted high enough to be seen over the hills.
Less often, a tribarrel flickered across the cloud bases like
distant cyan lightning. That'd be another task force splashing
an aircar or something equally insignificant . . . except for
the poor bastards on the receiving end.

The alert signal at the upper left corner of Huber's
faceshield was the first message he'd gotten from Central
since the fire mission before they'd reached the Solace
Highlands. He let out his breath in a gasp.

There might not have been a Central any more. Base Alpha
might have fallen and the Solace forces begun mopping up
the Slammers task force by task force, bringing to bear as
much weight as they needed to crush each hard nut. Huber'd
kept his fear below the surface of his mind, but it'd been
there nonetheless.

"*All units, prepare to receive orders and target informa-*
tion," said a voice as emotionless as the surf on a rocky
shore. "*Don't get ahead of your start times, and once you*
commit don't, I repeat do not, stop shooting until you're told
to. Regiment One out."

The data dump started at once, progressing for thirty
seconds instead of concluding instantaneously. Satellite
reconnaissance was updating the information at the same
time those satellites transmitted it to the Regiment's scattered elements. Port Plattner, an oval five kilometers by
three, expanded on the Command and Control display.
There'd been six warehouse complexes spaced about the
perimeter when the satellites shut down thirty-six hours
before; now there was a seventh beside the huge starship
on northwest edge, twelve large temporary buildings with
more under construction.

"*Regiment One? That's Major Steuben,*" Deseau muttered,
unusually worried for him. "*Is he in fucking charge now?*"

"Shut up, Frenchie," Huber snapped as he scrolled through
the download. He was more irritated than he'd have been

if a newbie like Padova had made the comment. Deseau should've known they didn't have enough data to guess what was going on. Steuben might be in command of Base Alpha because his White Mice were defending it, but that didn't mean the Colonel and Major Pritchard were casualties.

It didn't mean they *weren't* casualties, either.

"Right!" Huber muttered when he had the situation clear. At least it was clear enough that he knew staring at it longer wasn't going to change anything in a good way. "Red and Blue elements—"

F-2 and F-3 respectively, each with a squad of infantry in support.

"—will proceed to designated positions on the reverse slope—"

The download from Central set out the east side of the terminal building as the general objective for Highball's action elements, but Central hadn't known what strength Huber would have available for the attack. Huber's C&C box had broken the assignment into individual targets. Losing two cars and six infantry was probably better than Operations had calculated, though under normal circumstances twenty percent was a horrendous casualty rate.

"—and hold there till two-two-three-seven hours, when—"

Battery Alpha opened fire, loosing thunder and the long crackling lightning of sustainer motors as the missiles streaked west so low that they barely cleared the ridgeline. The Hogs rocked from the backblasts, slamming their skirts against the hard clay substrate.

"—we'll cross the crest and attack our objectives at forty kph. White element under Sergeant Marano—"

The remaining two combat cars and eleven infantry—some of whom were walking wounded only if they didn't have to walk very far.

"—remains here to provide security for the X-Ray element. Any questions? Over."

"*Let's do it, El-Tee,*" Sergeant Nagano said. He raised his gauntleted left hand from *Foghorn*, the thumb up.

"Roger that," Huber said, after a ten-second pause to be sure that nobody had anything substantive to add. "Move out, troopers. Keep it slow till we're in position, and nobody crosses the start line till it's time. Six out."

Fencing Master started forward, barely ambling. The other cars—particularly Messeman's trio from the east arc of the circle—had farther to go to get into position. Padova wasn't letting eagerness make her screw up.

The bone-shaking roar of the rocket howitzers paused on a long snarl as the last of the six rounds in the ready magazines streaked westward. Another battery took up the bombardment as Basingstoke's Hogs cycled missiles from their storage magazines in the rear hull into their turrets to resume firing.

The Hogs were launching firecracker rounds, anti-personnel cargo shells designed to dump thousands of bomblets each. Powerguns from the port's air defenses stabbed the sky for several seconds, bursting all the incoming rounds before they could open over the target. Then one got through.

Huber knew what it was like on the ground—and what it would've been like for Task Force Huber if the Firelords had gotten lucky with their less-sophisticated equivalents. When the bomblets swept over the defenses as a sea of white fire, shrapnel would kill the crews and disable gun mechanisms. Then the next round—and the next twenty rounds—would get through.

The cars aligned themselves to the right of *Fencing Master* at twenty-meter intervals. The eighteen infantrymen were twenty meters behind, their skimmers bobbling in the wake of the cars. They looked hopelessly vulnerable to Huber, but he knew from conversations that most infantrymen regarded combat cars as big targets, and tanks as bigger targets yet. They'd come in handy for clearing the terminal building, if they got that far.

Padova raised her speed to ten kph but didn't accelerate further. Huber frowned with instinctive impatience, then understood. "Highball," he said, "we're timing—"

Padova was timing.

"—our approach so we'll reach our attack positions at exactly the time to go over the crest. That way we'll already have forward inertia instead of lifting from a halt. Six out, break."

His frown deepened as he continued, "Trooper Padova, using initiative is fine, but don't play games or you'll be playing them in another unit. Tell me what you're planning the next time, all right?"

"*Sorry, sir,*" the driver said, sounding like she meant it. "*I wasn't . . . sorry, it won't happen again.*"

The cars and skimmers passed to the south of the grain elevators and their clustered dwellings. Deseau looked back over his shoulder, his hand resting lightly on the butt of his 2-cm weapon. If a sniper or Solace artillery observer appeared among the buildings now, the forward tribarrel wouldn't bear on it.

Huber smiled wryly. Frenchie was an optimistic man, in his way.

A line of posts supported plastic netting and a top strand of barbed wire, fencing to keep pastured cattle from straying into the railhead. All six cars hit it within an eyeblink of one another, smashing the fence down with no more trouble than they took with the spiky bushes which dotted the cropped grassland on the other side. Huber had been ready to duck if the wire flew toward him, but instead it curled around the next post to the left.

Learoyd was singing, mostly under his breath so it didn't trip the intercom. Occasional phrases buzzed in Huber's ears: " *. . . and best . . . lost sinners was slain. . . .*"

Fencing Master accelerated smoothly despite the increasing slope. The fans were biting deeper, but their note didn't change because Padova matched her blade incidence flawlessly against the increased power she was dialing in. The cars were nearing the crest. On the other side, sparkling explosions backlit stubble and the thicket of brush which grew from exposed rocks where mowers couldn't reach.

A salvo from Battery Alpha shrieked overhead, so deafeningly close that *Fencing Master* shimmied. Huber's exposed skin prickled and he heard an abrasive snarl against his helmet. He didn't know whether he was feeling debris from the exhaust or grit swept up from the ground by the shells' passage. Deseau shouted in angry surprise, though there was no real harm done.

It would've been a bad time to cross the ridge ahead of orders, though. A really bad time.

"Highball . . ." Huber said, judging the time by *Fencing*

Master's speed, not the clock he could call onto his faceshield if he wanted to.

"Execute!"

Battery Alpha's salvo of cargo shells opened just on the other side of the ridge. This close, the red flashes of the charges that expelled the contents were startlingly visible. The bomblets scattered on separate ballistic courses toward the terminal, detonating like so many thousand grenades just as the combat cars came over the rise. From where Huber watched, three kilometers away, the sea of glittering white radiance was beautiful.

His helmet gave him targets, first a calliope dug into the ground at the edge of the meters-thick concrete pad which supported starships as they landed and lifted off. Huber put a burst into it, his plasma glancing from the iridium gunbarrels but vaporizing the steel frame and trunnion. The gun was silent, its barrels already cooled to red heat: bomblets had killed its crew or driven it to cover.

Powerguns slashed the port's flat concrete expanse from all directions, tribarrels and the tanks' 20-cm main guns. Buildings, vehicles, and stacks of cargo on the immense concrete pad were burning.

There were over twenty starships on the pad. They weren't deliberate targets, but bolts splashed them with cyan highlights.

As Huber switched his aim to a wheeled vehicle racing away from the terminal, a last salvo struck the temporary buildings being erected next to the starship in the northwest. Nothing happened for a moment because instead of bomblets the rounds carried fuel-air warheads.

The delayed blast spilled air from *Fencing Master*'s plenum chamber and slammed the car down hard. Huber shouted, instinctively afraid that he'd been flung out of the fighting compartment. He bashed his chest into the grips of his tribarrel. The clamshell armor saved his ribs, but he'd have bruises in the morning.

Padova got them under weigh again, straightening their course; the blast had slewed the car a quarter-turn clockwise while shock curtains deployed around the driver. A column of kinked black smoke rose from where the shells had landed.

The pad wasn't cratered: the explosive had spread in a thin smooth sheet before it went off, and concrete has great compression strength. The structures which had covered more than a thousand square meters of the pad were gone except for twisted fragments which had fallen back after the blast blew everything skyward. The starship, thick-hulled and weighing over 150,000 tonnes, appeared undamaged. The valves had been wrenched off the two open cargo hatches, however.

Huber found the truck he'd been aiming at; the shockwave had shoved it into the loading dock which extended from the back of the terminal building. He gave it a three-round burst from reflex, watching it burst into flames as his AI found him something more useful to shoot at.

Deseau and Learoyd were firing at gun positions on the roof of the terminal, though nothing moved there except the haze of smoke from the anti-personnel bomblets which had gone off seconds before. Instead of a nearby target, Huber's helmet targeted a line of vehicles on the northern edge of the pad. At least a company of the Waldheim Dragoons were using blast deflectors as breastworks against the Slammers attacking from that side. Tribarrels on the Waldheim APCs and 10-cm powerguns on their tanks stabbed the distant hills.

The walls now raised from the pad were meant to deflect a giant starship's full takeoff thrust skyward so it wouldn't knock down everything within a kilometer. The structures were sufficient to stop even a 20-cm bolt, but the cars approaching from southeast had a clear shot at the sheltering vehicles.

Huber set the target and brought up his sight's magnification. He was using light amplication rather than thermal viewing; the many fires dotting the port's flat expanse provided more than enough illumination. When his pipper centered on a tank's turret ring, he thumbed the trigger and let the stabilizer hold his bolts on target. The tank's own ammunition blew it up in a cyan flash.

Huber shifted to the next target over, an APC rocking in the shockwave of the tank's destruction. Before he could fire, a 20-cm bolt hit the lightly armored vehicle and sprayed molten blobs of it a hundred meters away.

Fencing Master continued to advance. The ten-story

terminal building blocked Huber's line of sight to the Dragoons; his faceshield careted windows instead. He squeezed, slewing the tribarrel to help the car's forward motion draw his burst across the seventh floor from left to right. The rooms were dark till the bolts hit, but gulps of orange flame followed each cyan flash as plasma ignited the furnishings.

An equipment park on the southwest side of the pad had taken a pasting from incendiaries. Hundreds of vehicles were alight. Every so often one erupted with greater enthusiasm like a bubble rising in a caldera to scatter blazing rock high in the air. Eight combat cars skirted the park to the south, moving fast. Their tribarrels raked the back side of the terminal building.

At the beginning of the war, Solace had started building concrete-roofed dugouts at intervals around the perimeter of Port Plattner. The work had stopped when Solace command realized that the Outer States were barely capable of defense, and even those completed—three of them in the sector Central had assigned to Huber's troops—appeared to be unmanned.

Deseau and Learoyd had burned the firing slit of the southernmost to twice its original size. Now as *Fencing Master* swept around the squat structure, Learoyd depressed his tribarrel and fired a long burst down the entrance ramp at the back. The steel door gushed red sparks and ruptured inward, but there was no secondary explosion.

White flares popped from the roof of the terminal building. More flares followed from a dozen points across Port Plattner, including the northern perimeter where the Waldheim Dragoons had been fighting. "*UC forces, we surrender!*" a woman's voice cried. "*Terminal control surrenders, by the Lord's mercy we surrender!*"

She must have been using the port's starship communications system because her high-output transmission blanketed all frequencies. Every floor of the terminal building was ablaze, but those were merely administrative offices. The actual control room was in a sub-basement, armored against the chance of a starship crash.

Fencing Master turned left, away from the base of the terminal. Padova dropped the car twice onto the sodded lawn to scrub off inertia that wanted to carry them into the

burning building. The other Highball cars were braking in
roostertails of red sparks as their skirts skidded on concrete.
The terminal was a tower of flame, lashing the ground with
pulses of heat.

"*Sir, what should I do!*" Padova said. They were moving
slowly south along the face of the building, crushing ornamental shrubs under their skirts. *Foghorn* and *Fancy Pants*
followed, while Lieutenant Messeman's cars had halted on
the other side of a wing-shaped entrance marquee which
extended twenty meters from the front entrance.

"*All Slammers units,*" a familiar voice growled. "*This is
Regiment Six, troopers. Cease fire unless you're fired on. Under
no circumstances fire on the starships that'll start landing
shortly. Hammer out.*"

Deseau tracked a man running across the pad to the left.
He didn't shoot, but he was touching the trigger. Huber
hooked a thumb to back him off, then said, "Highball, we'll
laager a hundred meters back the way we came. Infantry
in the center of the circle."

He looked at the plot the C&C box suggested, approved
it, and concluded, "Six out."

That was far enough from the terminal building that they
wouldn't broil, though Huber wanted to keep Highball
reasonably close to its objective until somebody got around
to ordering them to move. The Lord knew when that'd be,
given what the Colonel and his staff had on their plate right
now.

The eight vehicles crossing the pad from the west slowed
as they approached the terminal. Huber's eyes narrowed:
one was a command car, a high-sided box built on the
chassis of a combat car to hold far more communications
and display options than could be fitted into a C&C box.
Mostly they were staff vehicles, though Huber knew a couple
of line company commanders preferred them to combat cars.

The shooting had probably stopped, though it was hard
to say because munitions continued to explode. That
wouldn't end for days, not with the number of fires burning across the huge port. You could get killed just as dead
when a truck blew up as you could by somebody aiming
at you. . . .

That reminded Huber of casualties. He checked the readout

on his faceshield and saw to his pleased surprise that all the personnel were green—infantry included—except for a cross-hatched icon on *Foghorn*. "Three-one, what's your casualty?" he said.

"*Six, the right gun blew back and burned Quincy both arms*," Sergeant Nagano replied. "*We got him sedated and covered in SpraySeal. He'll be all right, I guess, but he won't be much good in the field for a few months. Over.*"

"*Highball Six,*" broke in another voice before Huber could reply, "*this is Regiment Six. We're joining your laager but leaving you in local control. Out.*"

Huber felt a momentary jolt, but that was ingrained reflex; his conscious mind was far too exhausted to be concerned. "Roger, Six," he said. "Break. Highball, spread the laager to accommodate eight more cars. The command group's joining us. Highball Six out."

The eight vehicles with Colonel Hammer, five of them from K Company, idled toward Highball. The cars of Huber's original command reformed as the eastern half of circle instead of the complete circuit. Instead of steering *Fencing Master* straight to its new location and rotating the bow out, Padova drove the car sideways. She was bragging, but Huber was too wrung out to call her down for it.

"*Guess they didn't have a walkover like we did,*" Deseau said as he gave the newcomers a professional once-over. Three of the combat cars had holes in their plenum chambers; one was shot up badly enough that its skirts dragged. It probably couldn't have kept up with the rest of the unit if they hadn't been crossing such a smooth, hard surface. "*Nobody even shot at us that I saw.*"

"*They shot at us, Frenchie,*" Learoyd said. He tapped the bulkhead beside him with the knife he was using to scrape his ejection port.

Huber leaned forward to look past the trooper. Three projectiles, each separated from the next by a hand's-breadth, had dimpled the iridium inward. The third was deep enough that the armor had started to crack.

"*From the bunker when we got close,*" Learoyd explained; he sounded apologetic. "*I guess I shouldn't've quit shooting when something blew up inside.*"

The impacts must've been audible in the next county,

but Huber hadn't been aware of them, nor Deseau either it seemed. Aloud Huber said, "No harm done, Learoyd. Nobody'd guess their compartmentalization was that good, and it's not like there wasn't anything else needing attention."

The laager was complete with two meters between adjacent cars: tight, but giving them room to maneuver fast if something unexpected happened. The right wing gunner of the car next to *Fencing Master* raised his faceshield and shouted over the idling fans, "How's your leg, Lieutenant?"

"Sir!" Huber said. He'd expected Colonel Hammer to be in the command car. "Sir, my leg's fine, I guess, but I haven't been using it much except to stand on."

Huber's left leg ached like a wall was leaning on it, but the rest of his body wasn't much better. His skin itched and the slickness where his clamshell rubbed over his hipbones was either popped blisters or blood. In the morning, that might matter; right now, Arne Huber was alive and that was good enough.

Huber's AI pulsed a warning on his faceshield. The task force was still under combat conditions, and a pair of aircars were approaching from the northeast a thousand meters up. The cars' tribarrels weren't on air defense, and the AI thought maybe they ought to be.

"*They got running lights on, El-Tee,*" Deseau said, swinging his gun onto the aircars manually. "*They're not trying to sneak up on us, but maybe they're just too smart to try what wouldn't work.*"

"Put that gun on safe, trooper!" Colonel Hammer roared. Then he snapped his faceshield down and continued, "*All Slammers units, do not shoot. Under no circumstances harm the incoming aircars. They're bringing Solace representatives to treat with us! Six out.*"

The aircars hovered a kilometer from the perimeter of Port Plattner. Hammer continued an animated conversation with someone on a push that didn't include Highball Six. After nearly a minute's discussion, the aircars mushed toward the laager together. The command car's rear door opened; Major Pritchard stepped out of the vehicle.

Colonel Hammer nodded approval and swung his legs over

the coaming of his fighting compartment to stand on the plenum chamber. He looked at Huber, grinned, and said, "Come along with me, Lieutenant. We're going to take the surrender of the Republic of Solace.

The two squads of infantry tilted their skimmers on end and stacked them in groups of three between the combat cars of Highball section. Sergeant Tranter swung down a cooler from *Fancy Pants* since the infantry's supports were back with the Hogs.

The troopers looked more concerned with the Colonel and his operations officer in the center of the circle than they were with the crackling destruction that covered most of the near distance. They'd seen destruction more often than they'd been this close to the Colonel, after all.

The aircars hovered for a moment, then landed a hundred meters out from the laager. Hammer grimaced and snapped to Pritchard, "Get 'em in here, Major. Do they think we're going to walk over to them?"

Huber wasn't sure he *could* walk that far. His left leg had been numb till he dropped from the plenum chamber to the ground. That shock had seemed to drive a hot steel rod straight up from his heel to the hip joint. His knee didn't want to bend, and every time he moved the rod burned hotter.

Pritchard spoke into his commo helmet. He must have had a link to the aircars through his command vehicle, because after a moment they lifted and crawled toward the laager in ground effect. He smiled tightly to Hammer and Huber, saying, "The gentleman from Nonesuch was concerned that the terminal might fall in this direction. I assured him that the shell of a ferroconcrete building will remain standing after it's burned itself out."

His grin grew even harder. "I've got a lot of experience with that, of course. We all have."

"Right," said Hammer. "That's why they hire us." He glanced at Huber and added, "You've met Mister Lindeyar already, haven't you, Lieutenant?"

"Him?" said Huber, shocked out of his torpor. He wasn't sure he'd heard right; or if he had, that his brain hadn't taken a shock during the battle that was making him remember things that'd never happened. "There was a Lindeyar at Benjamin, but what's that got to do with Solace?"

A starship was dropping slowly. It was still at high altitude but the effort of supporting its mass in a controlled descent made it pulsingly noticeable. Hammer'd mentioned ships landing, so Huber supposed it part of the plan. Somebody's plan, and no concern for a line lieutenant.

"Sigmund Lindeyar is the Nonesuch representative for all of Plattner's World, not just to the United Cities," Major Pritchard said, sounding detached. "Quite an important man back home, I gather."

Hammer spat on the dirt at his feet. "Yeah," he said, releasing the catches on the right side of his clamshell. "And if you don't believe us, just ask Lindeyar himself."

The aircars landed again, this time a few meters short of the bows of the combat cars. The slick-finished limousines reflected the surging firelight like pools of oil; by contrast, *Foghorn* and *Fancy Pants* were hulking gray boulders, scarred by the ages.

The starship continued to drop, balanced on the repulsion of two self-generated electromagnetic fields. Violet corona discharges danced across the heavens, crackling and roaring. Huber glanced at it, then frowned as he looked higher in the sky. A second starship was descending, and he thought a third waited above the second.

"El-Tee, there's a couple more aircars coming up from the south," Deseau said over *Fencing Master*'s intercom. *"I don't guess there's a problem—they're responding with Regimental IFF—but I figured I'd mention it."*

Huber nodded to Deseau. Learoyd had the receiver cover of the left wing tribarrel raised to adjust the feed mechanism. The crew of a CO's vehicle caught a lot of extra work, which bothered Huber. Neither Deseau nor Learoyd seemed to notice, let alone care.

And it wasn't like either one of them wanted to be platoon leader.

A group of military and civilian personnel were getting out of one of the aircars. Among them was an attractive—

Via! The attractive young woman was Daphne Priamedes, and the senior officer whom she'd bent to help to exit was her father, Colonel Apollonio Priamedes. Huber'd never expected to see either one of them again.

Lindeyar had arrived in the other vehicle, alone except for three bodyguards. Huber looked at him and smiled wryly. *How many people have I killed in the last two days? And not one of them anybody I knew, let alone disliked.*

"Colonel?" Huber said aloud. "There's two more aircars coming from the south. I guess you've already got that under control, but—"

"But you thought you'd make sure I had the information," Hammer said with an approving nod. "Right, I do."

He gestured to the southern sky. "That's the UC delegation," he said. "They're our principals on this contract so they need to be here."

The first starship settled onto the far end of the pad, close by the ship that had brought the Waldheim Dragoons. The new vessel was about the size of the one that had held an entire brigade of armored cavalry. Its sizzling discharge ceased, but the concrete continued to vibrate at a dense bass note.

Lindeyar straightened the fall of his jacket and strode into the laager past the combat cars. His bodyguards waited beyond the circle.

The civilians who'd arrived in the other vehicle huddled for a moment. The old man wearing a fur stole and cap of office directed a question at Colonel Priamedes with a peevish expression.

Priamedes snapped a reply and walked after Lindeyar, his daughter at his side. Daphne kept her face blank, but Huber could see from the way she held herself that she was ready to grab her father if his body failed him. Exchanging looks of indignation, the four civilians followed.

The two aircars coming from the south landed with a brusque lack of finesse; one even bounced. Huber leaned back slightly to get a better look between two vehicles of Lieutenant Messeman's platoon. He'd been right about what he thought he'd seen: the four civilians getting out of the aircars were members of the UC Senate whom he'd seen before when he was assigned to duties in Benjamin, but White Mice were driving and guarding them. Their battledress was as ragged as Huber's own, and one trooper's plastron had been seared down to the ceramic core.

The man in the fur cap glared at Hammer. "You sir!" he said. "I'm President Rihorta. Colonel Priamedes tells me you're the chief of these hirelings. May I ask why it's necessary to hold these discussions in such a, such a—"

At a loss for words, he waved a hand toward the chaos beyond. His sleeves were fur-trimmed also. As if on cue, a fuel tank in the vehicle park exploded, sending a bubble of orange fire skyward.

"—a place?"

"Well, Mr. President . . ." Hammer said, putting a hand under his breastplate to take some of its chafing weight off his shoulders. "If I needed a better reason than that I felt like it, I'd say because it'll convince you that you don't have any choice. I could burn all of Bezant down around your ears even easier than I took the spaceport that your survival depends on."

"Bezant is a civilian center, not a proper target of military operations," Colonel Priamedes said in a tight voice.

"Is it?" Hammer snapped at the Solace officer. "I could say the same about Benjamin, couldn't I?"

He waved his hand curtly. "But we're not here to discuss, gentlemen," he went on. "We already did all the discussing we needed to with those—"

He pointed to the bullet-gouged hull of the combat car he'd arrived in.

"—and with the Hogs. We're here to dictate the end of the war on such terms as seem good to our principals."

The UC senators walked between the combat cars with as much hesitation as the Solace delegation had shown. One of them was coughing. The air reeked of smoke and ozone, so familiar to Huber that he hadn't thought about it till he watched the civilians' grimaces and shallow breaths.

A woman of thirty wearing battledress of an unfamiliar pattern entered the laager with the UC civilians. She nodded to Hammer, then stood at Parade Rest and watched the by-play with eyes that were never still.

"Masters and mistresses," Hammer said. His tone was even, but Huber noticed he gripped his breastplate fiercely enough to mottle his knuckles. "You politicians probably know each other—"

The delegations exchanged wary glances, even faint nods.

They had more in common with one another than they did with the soldiers and war material surrounding them.

"—and you know Mister Lindeyar—"

The Nonesuch official looked around the gathering, his face without expression.

"—but you may not know Mistress Dozier, who's the Bonding Authority representative with responsibilities for the contracts here on Plattner's World."

The woman in battledress said, "Good day. I'm here solely as an observer, of course. My organization has no interest in the negotiations between principals except to see that all parties adhere to the contracts which we oversee."

The second starship was in its final approach. Hammer raised his hand in bar. President Rihorta started speaking anyway, but the overwhelming *CRACKLE CRACKLE CRACKLE* penetrated even his self-absorption after a moment.

When the sound and dazzling corona died away, Sigmund Lindeyar said, "Rather than draw these proceedings out unnecessarily, I'm going to take charge now. Nonesuch has been subsidizing the mercenaries which the Outer States have hired for this conflict. In fact some eighty percent of the charges have come from our coffers—"

"What!" said President Rihorta. "But you've been insisting we raise port duties to upgrade the facilities!"

"You traitorous scum," Colonel Priamedes said in a quiet voice, stepping toward Lindeyar. Daphne tried to stop him. Huber placed himself in front of the Solace officer and held till weakness and Daphne's efforts forced Priamedes back.

His knees started to buckle. Huber caught him and shifted around to his right side, continuing to support Priamedes while Daphne held her father's other arm.

"I'm scarcely a traitor, Colonel," Lindeyar said with a chuckle. He fluffed the lapel of his jacket. "I've been quite successful in advancing the interests of my nation . . . which is Nonesuch, you will recall."

The UC delegates were whispering among themselves. Lindeyar fixed them with his cold eyes and said, "Now as for you gentlemen—"

The word was a sneer.

"—the first thing you need to know is that my government

has withdrawn its financial support. I've already informed the Bonding Authority—"

Mistress Dozier nodded agreement.

"—that as of this moment, Nonesuch will no longer pay the wages of the mercenaries employed on Plattner's World. Therefore unless the UC and its local partners are capable of paying those charges by themselves, the war is over and all the mercenaries will go home immediately. Can you pay, gentlemen?"

The four UC senators gaped at Lindeyar. Senator Graciano said, "Good Lord, man, of course we can't. But why would we want to? We've won. This is what we've been hoping for all along!"

"Mister Lindeyar," Major Pritchard said, "there was discussion about transferring the contract of Hammer's Regiment to Nonesuch directly."

Lindeyar met the unspoken question with a wintry smile. "Was there?" he said. "Perhaps there was. In the event, however, my government has decided to depend on its national forces for defense of its new concession here on Plattner's World."

The third starship landed near the two which had arrived minutes before. Huber couldn't see the ships from where he stood, but while everyone waited for the roar to quiet he shifted the upper right quadrant of his faceshield to the view from an H Company tank on the north side of Port Plattner.

Hatches on the first ship began to open as soon as the third touched down. The crew had been waiting till that moment. As close as the vessels were to one another, there might have been danger if the first-landed had begun disembarking previously.

The first personnel out were ship's crewmen, adjusting the ramps with hydraulic jacks. Starship personnel were used to the agonizing disorientation of interstellar travel. They had the same splitting headaches, the same blurred vision, and the same nausea as those who travelled less often, but they'd learned to work through the pain.

The noise died away. As Huber cut his remote to return to Lindeyar's response, he saw huge tanks on caterpillar treads starting to roll out of the starship.

"That's right, you've won, gentlemen," Lindeyar said with dripping disdain. "Go home and tell your people about your victory. Celebrate!"

He swung his blond, handsome head about the circle like a wolf surveying the henhouse he's just entered. "As for you, Mister President and *your* fellows, our terms are simple: Port Plattner is now an extraterritorial division of the Polity of Nonesuch. Port controls and fees are no longer your concern. If you choose to argue the matter, then we'll take over the administration of all Solace."

He pointed his left arm to the north, fingers outstretched, though he didn't turn his head away from the Solace delegation. "There's a division of the Nonesuch National Guard on the ground already. We can bring more troops in if we have to, but given the condition of your forces that obviously won't be necessary. And if you're thinking of mercenaries—I'm afraid you've overextended your off-planet credit already. Now that you no longer hold Port Plattner, Solace is bankrupt. The money you've placed with the Bonding Authority will just cover repatriation of the units already contracted to you, and the Authority won't approve any further hires."

All eyes turned to Mistress Dozier. She shrugged and said without emphasis, "The Authority isn't in the business of making moral judgments. We're employed—"

Her face hardened.

"—by all parties, let me remind you, to enforce contracts, nothing more. Mister Lindeyar has correctly stated the situation insofar as the Bonding Authority is concerned."

Colonel Priamedes' head lolled on Huber's shoulder. "Papa?" Daphne whispered urgently.

Huber touched the colonel's throat with an index and middle finger; his pulse was strong. Priamedes hadn't recovered from the knocks he'd taken at Northern Star Farms, and the present events were simply more than his system could handle without shutting down.

Huber's leg didn't hurt any more; the adrenaline surging through him was the best medicine for pain. He didn't know how long he could keep this up, but for the time being he could do his job—whatever that job turned out to be. He eyed Sigmund Lindeyar without expression.

"I don't have to explain this to Colonel Hammer," Lindeyar said, "but for the rest of you I'll point out that any mercenary unit which works without a paid contract becomes an outlaw in the eyes of the Bonding Authority. Civilization can't survive with bands of mad dogs roving from planet to planet without rules."

Hammer began to laugh so hard that his loose breastplate flapped back and forth. He said, "Oh, what a principled gentleman you are, Master Lindeyar!" and then bent over again in another spasm of mirth.

"On behalf of the Colonel," Major Pritchard said as the delegates of both sides stared at Hammer in disbelief, "I can assure you that Hammer's Regiment is scrupulously careful to operate within the constraints of the Bonding Authority. We aren't vigilantes who imagine that it's our duty to impose justice. . . ."

Pritchard swept the politicians with a gaze as contemptuous as that of Lindeyar a few moments earlier. He went on, "And if we were, we'd be hard put to find an employer who could meet our standards, wouldn't we?"

Lindeyar seemed more disconcerted by Hammer's laughter than he might have been by anger. He looked at the bodyguards standing by the aircar he'd arrived in: all three had their hands in plain sight. When he followed their gaze back, he saw Deseau's tribarrel aimed at them. Frenchie grinned down and pointed his right index finger at Lindeyar's face like a pistol.

In a careful voice, Lindeyar said, "Of course, Colonel Hammer, your troops' performance on Plattner's World won't go unnoticed, particularly the brilliant stroke by which you captured the port here. I'm sure you'll have no difficulty finding employment in the near future."

Hammer straightened. The laughter was gone; he gave Lindeyar a look of cold appraisal.

"I worry about a lot of things, Mr. Lindeyar," he said. "It's my job to worry; I'm in charge. But I've never had to worry about somebody hiring us. My Slammers are the best there is, and the whole universe knew it before we came here to Plattner's World."

Lindeyar nodded, licking his lips. "Yes, of course," he said. He cleared his throat before going on, "Since there's no need to conclude the formalities at this moment, I'll be off to other matters which require my attention. President Rihorta, I'll be in touch with you regarding the wording of your government's concession of Port Plattner."

He backed away from the circle, smiling fitfully each time his eyes met those of one of the Slammers. His hip bumped *Foghorn*'s skirt; he turned with a shocked expression, then walked at an increasing pace to his aircar.

Colonel Priamedes was able to support his own weight again. Huber released him and stepped aside, though Daphne kept hold of her father's other arm.

"I guess you people have things you'd better be about as well," Hammer said, surveying the delegations. All the civilians seemed to be on the verge of collapse; Priamedes, whose difficulties were merely physical, had gotten his color back and now stood straight. "Go on and do them."

He focused on Senator Graciano. "You and I'll talk regarding financial arrangements tomorrow. Mistress Dozier, you'll be present?"

"Yes, of course," the Bonding Authority representative said.

Lindeyar's aircar lifted and curved toward the ships disgorging a Nonesuch armored division. Huber'd left his 2-cm weapon in *Fencing Master*, so all he had was the pistol on his equipment belt. He'd never been much good with a pistol; but if he fired in the direction of the aircar, Frenchie would swat it out of the air in blazing fragments.

That'd be a violation of the contract, of course. The Colonel would have him executed immediately as the only way to prevent the Regiment from being outlawed and disbanded.

We're not in the business of dispensing justice. . . .

The delegations started moving away toward their own vehicles. Daphne Priamedes said, "It's over for us, now— Solace and the Outer States as well now that Nonesuch has the port. 'Woe to the conquered.' That's how it's always been."

Arne Huber thought about Sergeant Jellicoe, about *Flame Farter*'s two crewmen and all the other troopers he'd lost here on Plattner's World. He watched the aircar landing among the disembarking Nonesuch soldiers and said aloud, "Yeah, I suppose. But it's not just to the conquered, sometimes."

✧   ✧   ✧

Arne Huber stood on the berm against which *Fencing Master* nestled bow-on, surveying the landscape. It'd been a field of spring wheat before the engineers gouged Firebase One out of it two days ago and moved a third of the Regiment's combat elements into it.

Huber hadn't been a farmer; he'd seen no magic in the original flat expanse of green shoots stretching to the hills ten kilometers away. He was willing to grant that it'd been more attractive than this scraped yellow wasteland, though.

Deseau crawled carefully out of the plenum chamber. He was a small man, but battle and the hard run had left him stiff. You could hurt yourself on sharp, rusty metal when your muscles don't work the way you expect them to. He stepped away from the access port before he dusted his trousers with his hands; Padova followed him out. He grinned at Huber and said, "Funny to be on Plattner's World and not be skating in mud, ain't it, El-Tee?"

A dirigible slinging three pallets of howitzer ammunition was crawling upwind to the cargo pad. The big airships didn't overfly the firebase: they dropped their loads outside the berm, from where trucks with troopers driving hauled the material the short remainder of the way.

"Hadn't really thought about it, Frenchie," Huber said. His eyes were on the dirigible, but he wasn't really thinking about that either. "I can't say I like the dust here in the highlands a lot better."

"Hey, Learoyd?" Deseau called to the trooper in the fighting compartment. "Slide into the front, will you, and run up Port Two?"

Learoyd didn't work in the plenum chamber unless he had to. He was too big for the hatches even when he was fit, and now his right arm was in a surface cast to keep him from rubbing off the medication that the Medicomp had applied when things settled down enough for the support equipment and personnel to arrive from Base Alpha. A fresh set of barrels for the 2-cm automatics had arrived, so Learoyd was working on the tribarrels while the other crewmen realigned the nacelle that'd taken a knock from the dense rootball of a tree *Fencing Master* had driven over.

"I'll do it," said Padova, mounting the bow with a hop

and a grab for the first handhold on the hull proper. Rita'd settled in during the run and the three days of quiet following Port Plattner; now she was a member of *Fencing Master*'s crew, not just a skilled driver.

"Any word about when we might be moving out, El-Tee?" Deseau asked, shielding his eyes with his hand as he looked up at Huber. "I mean, we're off the clock, right? Paying for our own time."

A dotted line of dirigibles stretched to the southern horizon: Huber could see at least a dozen airships at once. There'd been a solid stream of airships transferring supplies and material from the UC ever since the Regiment pulled twenty kilometers back and set up three firebases equidistant from Port Plattner. They'd leave in a single giant transport from Port Plattner rather than in dribs and drabs from makeshift starports in the UC, so Huber supposed it made sense. Not that anybody cared what he thought.

"So far as anybody's told me, Frenchie," he said, "we're going to stay here till we've all grown long white beards. I don't expect that's what'll happen, but your guess is as good as mine."

Padova switched on the portside fans and ran them up together. Huber cocked his head, listening with a critical ear for any imbalance in the harmonics. So far as he could tell, the nacelles were tuned as sweetly as if they'd just been blueprinted in the factory.

"El-Tee?" called Learoyd. He pointed to *Fencing Master*'s port wing gun, slewing incrementally under the control of gunnery computer. "There's something coming."

Huber looked south again, noticing this time that two enclosed aircars were approaching fast below the dirigibles. His eyes narrowed: the cars' IFF must have been responding correctly or else the tribarrels on air defense would've shot them out of the sky a minute ago, but the drivers were taking a chance anyway. Even with the war over . . .

"Hey, what d'ye have?" Deseau said. He couldn't see what was happening from ground level, but he'd noticed Learoyd's and Huber's interest. Instead of immediately jumping onto the plenum chamber to see for himself, he first latched the access port closed so that *Fencing Master* would be able to maneuver again.

The aircars came over the berm twenty meters up, braking to a hover with a slickness that showed the drivers were expert. They set down in front of the TOC, between two of Battery Alpha's dug-in howitzers; dust skittered, dancing away to the west.

Huber jumped from the berm to the plenum chamber, his boots clanging. He climbed into the fighting compartment just as Deseau did; both men reflexively checked their tribarrels. Learoyd locked down the third barrel on his gun and slipped the adjustment wrench into its pouch on his belt.

"What d'ye think, El-Tee?" Deseau asked. "Did that bastard Lindeyar have second thoughts about terminating our contract?"

"None of them are Lindeyar," Learoyd said. "They're the other politicians' cars."

Fencing Master's tribarrels couldn't bear on the aircars because they were straight behind them, and anyway you didn't point a gun across a firebase unless you wanted to lose your rank. Frenchie was holding his 2-cm weapon in the crook of his arm, and Learoyd unclipped his sub-machine gun from the bracket on the inside of the armor.

The limousines' doors opened. Huber recognized Senator Graciano and his three colleagues, and the woman in battledress getting out of the front was Mistress Dozier. From the other aircar came President Rihorta and another member of the Solace delegation. The man accompanying those two was a stranger.

Aloud Huber said, "I don't know who the tall guy is. He's off-planet, that's for sure. I've never seen a hat like that—"

It was more of a turban; the stranger donned and adjusted it carefully before proceeding with the others toward the ramp down to the TOC.

"—on Plattner's World before."

"That's the Colonel waiting in the entrance for 'em," Deseau said. "I swear it is!"

"What do we do now, El-Tee?" Learoyd said. He knew the situation'd changed. He wasn't worried, just looking for direction from somebody smarter than he was.

"We wait for orders, trooper," Huber said. He pursed his

lips, then added, "And while we're waiting, I think we've got room here to stow another case of tribarrel ammo. Let's see if the quartermaster can help us out."

Huber's mind registered motion—a streak of light across the purple-black sky. He opened his mouth to shout a warning over the squadron net, then realized it was a shooting star rather than incoming artillery.

Padova stood on the plenum chamber where she could quickly slide down the driver's hatch. She looked into the fighting compartment and shook her head. "How can Frenchie sleep?" she muttered.

"I'm on watch, Rita," Learoyd said. "Why shouldn't he sleep? The El-Tee's awake too."

He blinked. "And you."

"Frenchie's been here a lot of times, Rita," Huber said, using that formation instead of, "Frenchie's a veteran," which the driver might find insulting. "As soon as there's a reason, he'll be up and doing his job."

He grinned with a kind of affection he felt only because he and Deseau were part of the same family. "Besides, if the job's killing, Frenchie could do that without waking up."

Padova'd seen the elephant by now, that was for sure; but there was a difference between one hard run punctuated by firefights and the bone-deep awareness that this might be the last chance to sleep for days or longer. Frenchie's *body* understood that sleeping curled up on the floor of the fighting compartment was best present use of his time.

"You think it's going to be fighting again, don't you?" Padova said angrily. "But who? The only people who could hire us is Nonesuch, and who would they need us to fight? They've got a fucking division on the ground, we saw them land it!"

"We're going to fight Nonesuch, Rita," Learoyd said calmly. He withdrew the loading tube from his back-up sub-machine gun, wiped it with an oily cloth, and clicked it home in the receiver again. "We're going to take the port back."

"And who the bloody hell is *paying* us to attack Nonesuch!" the driver snarled, balling her fists in frustration. "Are we going outlaw, is that what you mean?"

"I don't know who's paying us," Learoyd said, bending to check the bearing in the pintle supporting his tribarrel. "But there's nobody else to fight here, so we're fighting Nonesuch."

He shrugged. "The El-Tee knows we're getting ready to fight, we all know that. So it has to be Nonesuch."

Huber looked at Learoyd's round, placid face; as calm as a custard, reddened as usual by sun and wind. None of them understood how the Regiment could be going into battle again on Plattner's World. Learoyd was the only one who wasn't bothered by ignorance: he didn't expect to understand things.

"Yeah, Bert's right," Huber said. "Curst if I know how or why, but I can't say I'm sorry. I didn't like Lindeyar when I first met him, and he hasn't improved with time."

Padova hugged herself in frustration. "If we're really going to fight," she said, looking in the direction of the TOC, "why hasn't Central signaled us to stand to?"

"Do you see anybody in the base who isn't at his action station?" Huber said. "An alert might warn other people. Everybody's waiting for it, even Frenchie. Especially Frenchie."

He brought up the F-3 stats again on the C&C display. They were still at four cars. Sergeant Bielsky was bringing a repaired vehicle up from Benjamin, but he wouldn't arrive for thirty hours. The four cars of the present complement had shaken down during the run and attack, even Gabinus' Three-eight—which now had *Flamingo Girl* painted in fluorescent blue on both sides of the fighting compartment. All the guns had been rebarreled, all the fans were running within seventy percent of optimum, and each car had a full crew.

He glanced at Learoyd, his right arm in a stiff bend though the hand was free to grip with. Replacements had flown up from the UC in aircars, but there was no way in hell that Deseau—the car commander—or Huber wanted to go into battle with a trooper they didn't know in place of Learoyd with one arm. There were a couple more wounded crewmen in F-3 for the same reason; it wasn't ideal, but . . .

Huber chuckled.

"Sir?" Padova said, frowning at what she didn't understand.

"Kind of an old joke," he said. "If everything was ideal, nobody'd be hiring mercenaries, would they?"

He chuckled again; and as he did so, the alert signal pulsed red. Sergeant Deseau was on his feet, reaching for his tribarrel's grips before his eyes could focus.

Colonel Hammer's voice rasped in their commo helmets, *"Troopers, the United Cities and Republic of Solace in combination have hired us to wrest control of Port Plattner from the foreign invaders now holding it. Normally I don't discuss the financial details of the Regiment's contracts, but in this particular case I'll mention that our payment is guaranteed by a consortium of planets which in the past have purchased about half the Thalderol base produced on Plattner's World. They seem to feel it wouldn't be to their benefit if Nonesuch controlled access to the product."*

Deseau whooped and clapped his hands. Padova had already dropped into the driver's compartment. Huber switched the C&C box to display the download that would shortly arrive from Central.

"Your assignments are on the way," Hammer continued. *"Artillery prep will begin in three minutes, and the action elements will begin moving out of the firebases at the same time. Don't get overeager—we want plenty of time for the shells to soften 'em up. For this operation we won't enable the lockout on our guns. I'd rather take the risk of being shot by a friendly than having a software glitch keep me from nailing a hostile because there's a friendly on the other side of him. But remember, the terrain is dead flat and your gun'll shoot any bloody thing that you aim at."*

The Hogs of Battery Alpha elevated their launch tubes. They faced outward in a clock pattern centered on the TOC; now their turrets rotated so that the whole battery was aligned to the northwest, the direction of Port Plattner.

"I don't want any of you to think this'll be easy," Hammer continued. *"They've got a hundred and fifty tanks and their other vehicles mount tribarrels too. It doesn't matter how slow and clumsy they are, because they aren't coming to us—we have to go to them. But troopers—we've faced worse. Get out there now and help me show people what happens when you try to cheat the Slammers! Six out."*

The satellites were up again; some satellites, anyhow. The

download had full real-time coverage of the port. Approaches, lines of sight, threats and targets—the initial targets being the threats, of course—shimmered onto the holographic display in standard color overlays, as familiar to Huber as the grips of his tribarrel.

Four Nonesuch tanks moved in echelon to join the twelve parked in front of the smoldering terminal building. Each was built around a centerline 25-cm powergun. Though the big weapons could only be adjusted a few degrees in azimuth, their bolts were powerful enough to penetrate even the thick plating of a starship.

A line of dun-colored space-frame tents, sandbagged to the concrete, stood beside the vehicles. More tents—thousands of them—dotted the edges of the pad, most of them serving the infantry riding APCs. The latter, tracked like the tanks, had iridium armor and mounted a tribarrel in a one-man cupola.

Nonesuch fatigue parties worked on the perimeter bunkers without heavy equipment. Soldiers were mixing concrete in hand troughs. Huber wondered whether Lindeyar and his cronies had tried to buy construction mixers from Solace and been refused, or if this was merely a stopgap until dedicated support units arrived aboard later vessels.

Three ships, even such large ones, were barely enough to carry a division; the Nonesuch planners had concentrated wholly on combat personnel and equipment, accepting discomfort and inefficiency in order to frighten their possible opponents into quiescence. So far as the Solace Militia went, that may have been a good plan. . . .

"*Fox, this is Fox Six,*" Captain Gillig said. Her voice had a pleasant alto lilt even when she was giving battle orders. "*Fox Three will trail on the approach, but we'll attack with all platoons in line. There's a tank company in our sector, but the panzers'll deal with it while we hit targets of opportunity. With a division to choose from, there shouldn't be any lack of those.*"

Deseau turned to Huber and said, "*Hey, El-Tee? I couldn't believe that bastard Lindeyar was going to get away with shafting us. Could you?*"

Huber thought for a moment. Given the delays in star

travel, this coalition must have taken weeks or even months to put together. Hammer must have started planning it almost as soon as the Regiment arrived on Plattner's World.

"I did believe it, Frenchie," he said. "But that's all right— I'm just a line lieutenant. So long as I do my job, I can leave the rest to the Colonel."

The Hogs lit the night with flaring backblasts, beginning to shower 200-mm missiles on the enemy. The roar shook the ground. Moving as smoothly as water swirling down a drain, 1st Squadron's tanks and combat cars slid from the firebase, advancing toward Port Plattner twenty klicks away.

"Target!" said a machine voice in Huber's ear as *Fencing Master* led the rest of F-3 out of the angled passage through the berm. His faceshield gave him a vector.

So far as Huber could tell, the careted point on the crest ten kilometers distant was a few meters of brush and low trees, no different from everything for a klick to either side, but you didn't argue when Central told you to shoot. He laid his tribarrel on, careful not to overcorrect as the stabilizer fought with the combat car's motion, and dialed up magnification as the sight picture slewed toward the target. Huber was using a false-color infrared display, so the caret was a black wedge thrusting down from the top of the image.

He actually saw them in the instant his thumbs squeezed: three soldiers wearing drapes that almost erased their thermal signature, pointing a passive observation device toward Firebase One. They'd remained hidden till now, so they must have just attempted to send information back to Port Plattner.

Huber grinned with fierce pride that the *hiss/CRACK!* of his tribarrel's first round preceded the sound of *Fencing Master's* other two guns by a fraction of a second. He didn't often beat Frenchie and Learoyd to the punch, and neither did anybody else.

The eleven tanks of D Company—two more, deadlined for repairs but able to shoot, remained behind in the firebase for defense—had been first through the berm and were deploying across the wheat in line abreast. Colonel Hammer's combat car and that of the S-3—Huber wondered whether Major Pritchard was in it, as he certainly would choose to be, or if he'd been forced to remain in the TOC to coordinate the attack—followed, taking the right of the tanks along with two five-car platoons of G Company; the remaining platoon and the command cars of Regimental HQ Section remained behind as base defense. Captain Gillig and the sergeant major were next out, followed by F-1, F-2, and finally F-3.

The engineers had sited the firebase on a low rise, so *Fencing Master* in the entrance was slightly above the vehicles already spreading out to the northwest. Central tasked Huber and his crew because they had the best line on the target. Huber'd chafed to wait for everybody else to get under weigh before his cars did, but it'd worked out after all.

There's a lot of chance in life and especially in battle. Arne Huber just happened to be in the right place at the right time to send a burst of plasma bolts snapping straight as a plumb line into what till that instant was three enemy soldiers. His faceshield blocked their cyan core, but dazzle reflecting from the landscape quivered across his retinas.

Huber's first round hit the observation device, probably a high-resolution thermal imager. It contained enough metal to erupt into a blaze of white and green sparks. After that it was hard to say who hit what, because the three tribarrels put ten or a dozen rounds apiece into the target.

Huber switched his gunsight back to its normal seven-point-five-degree field. The freshly-lit fire on the ridgeline was only a quiver at this distance. In the magnified image Huber had seen an arm fly from an exploding torso and white-hot fragments blasted from the granite outcrop behind the scouts.

His gunbarrels shimmered, sinking back from yellow heat. The cluster continued to spin, pulling air through the open breeches to cool the bores.

Padova followed the course Captain Gillig's C&C box had programed. She didn't ask about the shooting. Huber supposed she was scared—as the good Lord knew he was himself—but she'd shaken down just fine. She'd be driving *Fencing Master* until she got a promotion, which at the rate she was going wouldn't be long.

F-3 followed two hundred meters behind the first and second platoons on the left flank, a reserve not only for Fox Company but for the whole squadron. Despite satellite coverage and the Regiment's sensor suites, there was always risk of an attack from some direction other than straight ahead. Huber's cars stayed back to deal with it.

"*Good to burn in our guns like that,*" Deseau said as his cluster stopped rotating. "*A few rounds to make sure the barrels're seated and there's no cracks in the castings.*"

Cyan bolts streaked up from the northwest horizon, ending in yellow flashes made ragged by the smoke of the explosions. Despite the decoy missiles of the first salvos, the Nonesuch defenses—over eight hundred tribarrels on the APCs and tanks—were shooting down the firecracker rounds that followed. The Nonesuch command hadn't been caught napping, more's the pity. . . .

The lead combat cars began firing. Flashes and the sparkling detonations of sub-munitions bloomed on the other side of the high ground separating 1st Squadron from the port. At least one Nonesuch artillery battery was firing on the attackers, a *much* faster response than Huber had expected from planetary forces which probably had no experience of real warfare. The shells didn't get through, but if the Nonesuch tankers were as good as their artillerymen this was going to be a very long night for the Slammers.

A long night, or a short one.

Much brighter cyan flashes lit the night: the tanks of Dog Company punched the ridgeline five klicks away with their main guns. Their thunder echoed across the fields.

Huber checked the C&C display, then said, "Fox Three, there was a Nonesuch infantry company picketed on the reverse slope. They moved into position and the panzers are taking care of them. Three-six out."

One of the eight Nonesuch APCs opened fire before it had reached the crest. The bolts of its tribarrels streaked five hundred meters over the Slammers in a rising slant. When the APC advanced high enough that its gun might have been able to bear on the attackers, the tank which had been waiting for a target fired. A brilliant secondary explosion lifted skyward a divot of soil and wood-chips.

Moments later, a *bum! bum! bum!* directly overhead made Huber twist to look up. Cargo shells from Battery Alpha had opened at low altitude, sending fingers of smoke toward the ridgeline. Their thousands of anti-personnel bomblets hit to carpet the target with lingering white flashes, scouring the hasty positions of Nonesuch infantry who'd dismounted before their APCs tried to engage.

Dirty smoke hung over half a kilometer of the hilltop. Huber could penetrate it with thermal imaging, but there was nothing to see except bare rock and the pulped remnants of the trees and shrubs that had grown there moments before. The enemy troops and their equipment had vanished except for the continuing sizzle of a battery pack shorting through commo gear, forming a hotspot on the image.

"Nothing for us there," Deseau said cheerfully. He patted his tribarrel's receiver. *"Well, we'll have our chance yet tonight, I figure."*

"Fox Three, this is Fox Six," Captain Gillig ordered. *"Move up on the left flank of Fox One, keeping ten meter intervals between vehicles. We'll take firing positions below the crest. Six out."*

Huber tensed as his faceshield flashed warnings. Chuckling, he relaxed. The squadron had torn through the fence separating the wheatfield from the pasture on the rougher terrain to the north. Wire flew up in springy coils around the vehicles, and the tug jerked the posts out of the ground in front of F-3. The motion was the same quick flicker men would make leaping to cover.

The northern sky quivered as with heat lightning. *"Hooboy!"* Deseau said. *"Some a' them firecracker rounds are landing where they ought to. I tell you, with a division of 'em down there, I don't mind a bit a' help from the cannon cockers."*

"We get paid the same if we get shot at or if we don't, Frenchie," Padova said. Her voice sounded artificially bright, but *Fencing Master* slid as if on rails to where it belonged on the left flank of the Squadron. *"I'd just as soon get easy money."*

Deseau laughed. Huber glanced at him, then looked away. Frenchie wasn't suicidal: he figured the risks that came with the job were plenty bad enough without doing crazy stuff. But when Frenchie had a chance to kill, the fact he might die didn't concern him.

Fencing Master started up the final rise, tearing through

three-meter shrubs with as little difficulty as it'd had with the wheat. Huber glanced back. Plenum chamber pressures compressed and deformed the loose earth of the plowed fields. Each of the vehicles had left a trench the full width of its skirts with a mound of soil and young shoots to either side.

Huber kept most of his attention on the Command and Control display. His cars were in the same condition as when they left the firebase, fully ready for battle if not for a rear-area inspection. The rest of the squadron was in similar shape, though a Golf Company car had lost a pair of fans and lagged behind on the slope. Sometimes bad luck was the only kind of luck there was; but if the car had been in Huber's platoon, tomorrow its sergeant/commander would be proving the problem wasn't because of a maintenance failure.

If the sergeant/commander survived, of course. And if Huber did.

Three shells from the Nonesuch battery burst several klicks back, sending spouts of black earth into the sky. Air defense hadn't bothered with them since they were no more danger to the Slammers than they were to the guns which'd fired them.

"Fox Three, this is Three-six," Huber said, glad to have good news to point out to his troopers a few seconds before they jumped into a tough one. "The hostiles are shooting where we used to be, so they don't have us under direct observation. When we reach our firing positions, we're going to get the first shot. If we can't kick their asses then, Via! we don't belong in this line of work! Six—"

Because of the way the ridge curved, *Fencing Master* pushed through the brush into a clear view of Port Plattner a heartbeat before the rest of the squadron did. Huber already had his tribarrel aimed at a predicted location even before his faceshield gave him real targets.

He squeezed the butterfly trigger as he shouted, "—out!" to his platoon.

A company of ten Nonesuch APCs had left the pad and was driving toward the ridge at the best speed turbine engines could move their caterpillar tracks. Their side armor, though thinner than that of the combat cars, was iridium, but hatches on the roofs of their troop compartments were thrown back so that the infantry in back could use their personal weapons.

Huber depressed his tribarrel and raked the hatches. Nonesuch troops carried powerguns; the blue-green flash of their stored ammunition melted the APC's frame from the inside so that the bow tilted upward. Fuel cells on the underside blew a circle of orange flames around the glowing wreckage.

Tanks and combat cars were firing all along the ridgeline. Though Huber couldn't have seen most of the Slammers' vehicles even if he'd taken the time to look to his side, streams of cyan plasma from their tribarrels and the tanks' stunning, world-searing flashes stabbed downward into easily visible targets.

The tanks were in hull-down positions where the firecracker rounds had scraped and sculpted the ground in erasing the Nonesuch picket. They shot as quickly as their gunners could work the foot-trips of their main guns, aiming at the company of Nonesuch tanks below. A 20-cm bolt hit massive frontal armor, rocking the target back on its treads in blinding coruscance.

To Huber's half-conscious horror, the centerline 25-cm gun shot back despite the Slammer's direct hit. The bolt gouged the hillside at least fifty meters from the nearest target, but the fact the tank fired at all was amazing.

A second bolt from the same Slammers tank struck where the armor glowed pulsingly white from the first. This time the glacis failed. The 25-cm magazine detonated, scooping the hull empty. The thick shell remained as a white-hot monument.

Huber swung his gun onto a company of buttoned-up APCs moving slantwise left to right in two echelons. They were several kilometers away, still on the concrete, when Huber hit the nearest vehicle in the lead row. Its side armor blew inward under the hammer of his 2-cm bolts. As the rest of the line drew ahead, Huber shifted his aim slightly onto the next APC and slashed it open the same way.

Huber steadied on the third APC, but as he did so the four second echelon vehicles opened fire on *Fencing Master* with their cupola tribarrels. One of them walked his burst up the sod, then splashed two bolts on *Fencing Master*'s bow slope and a third into the armor of the fighting compartment.

The combat car rocked at each impact. Huber's helmet deadened the clangs, but the jolts transmitted through the floor of the compartment buckled his knees. Before the Nonesuch gunner could finish the job, Deseau raked the APCs' cupolas, dismounting their tribarrels in rainbow brilliance.

Huber's third target exploded in a mushroom of crimson flame. As he hammered through the cab of the fourth and last, he saw Deseau's and Learoyd's guns crossing his burst to slaughter the soldiers bailing out of the vehicles Frenchie had disarmed.

The infantry weren't much of a threat now even if they got clear, but Huber shifted his own fire onto a car that his troopers hadn't hit yet. Body parts flew up at his lash before a secondary explosion finished the job in a saffron fireball.

Despite the filters over Huber's nostrils, *Fencing Master* stank of ozone and the vile slickness of burned metal. Vaporized iridium had burned the side of his neck, and his seared left sleeve stuck to his elbow. *Blood and Martyrs, that was close!*

Fencing Master jumped again. *We're hit!* but it wasn't incoming: a strip of the automatic defense array at the top of the skirts had gone off, sending a load of small osmium slugs out toward the left front. They met the anti-tank missile homing on the combat car.

The warhead detonated partially in a red flash. Bits of the debris sprayed *Fencing Master.* The concussion staggered Huber and a chunk of the rocket motor whanged the hull, but that was a cheap price. If the round'd hit squarely, the jet from its shaped charge would've gutted *Fencing Master* like a trout.

A 25-cm bolt hit close by, vaporizing a combat car forward of the rear bulkhead. A cloud of glowing iridium shimmered through all the colors of the spectrum, turning the ridgeline as bright as noon in Hell.

"*Shall I back up? Shall I back us up?*" Padova shouted into the intercom. *Fencing Master* lifted, quivering on plenum chamber pressure instead of resting its skirts firmly on the ground.

"Set us down!" Huber shouted, swinging his gun onto the pair of Nonesuch tanks sheltering at the side of a starship like tortoises in the lee of a high cliff. His tribarrel floated on a frictionless magnetic bearing, but inertia made slewing it a deliberate business. "Give us a solid—"

He had his target, not the glacis that could resist a tank's main gun nor the treads which a tribarrel could weld, immobilizing the huge vehicle without affecting its firepower. Huber aimed at the bore of the main gun, the 25-cm tunnel glowing from the bolt with which it had turned a combat car and its crew into fiery gases.

"—platform!"

Fencing Master thudded back to the ground as Huber's thumbs squeezed, but the stabilizer was locked on. His stream of blue-green bolts flared and sparkled against the tank's muzzle, its gun tube, and the mantle which covered the glacis opening.

A 25-cm bolt put such stresses on the bore that the guns' rate of fire was necessarily low, no more than two rounds per minute. Huber'd laid his tribarrel on the first tank nonetheless because that gunner'd proved he had the Slammers' elevation. Even the centerline gun's limited traverse would be sufficient to sweep six or eight vehicles to either side of the one it'd destroyed.

It was a calculated gamble, though, because the other tank was able to fire *now*. When a vivid cyan flash enveloped it, instinct told Huber this was a bolt which might blast *Fencing Master* and its crew to dissociated atoms.

The Nonesuch tank hadn't fired. A pair of 20-cm bolts had hit it simultaneously, lighting the concrete field with a rainbow bubble similar to what the combat car had become a moment before. Huber's faceshield blacked out almost totally. He kept his thumbs on the trigger, burning out his bores as he slashed his own massive target.

His faceshield cleared except for the streams from *Fencing Master*'s three tribarrels and the smudge of reflection where they hammered together into the Nonesuch tank. Then the tank and the world vanished again.

The protective black curtain cleared seconds later as the shockwave reached the ridgeline. The roof of the tank's fighting compartment toppled back toward the chassis which had been cleaned of its contents like a raccoon-licked clamshell. The tank's gunner had chambered another round. 2-cm bolts glancing down the bore from *Fencing Master* had detonated it before the breech was fully locked.

Focused on his gunsight, Huber hadn't heard the freight-train roar of 200-mm rockets passing low overhead, nor the *plop plop plop* of small charges ejecting sub-munitions from the carrier shells. The Nonesuch air defenses had been able to stop most of the incoming while it was simply them against the Hogs, but when the Slammers' vehicles appeared on the ridgeline the Nonesuch tribarrels were switched to direct fire. There was nothing to stop salvos from the batteries surrounding Port Plattner.

Each shell's twelve sub-munitions went off between twenty and forty meters above the ground, a yellow flash and a rag of smoke as the explosive charge forged a plate of uranium into a white-hot spike and drove it downward toward the Nonesuch vehicle its sensors had chosen. The Hogs were firing anti-tank shells, not firecracker rounds that barely scratched the paint of armored vehicles.

The self-forging fragments shattered the Nonesuch defenses already bruised by powerguns firing from the high ground surrounding the port. They punched through roof plating, relatively thin even on the tanks. Inside, the friction-heated uranium turned into balls of flame enveloping everything in the penetrated compartment. Hundreds of Nonesuch vehicles vanished into simultaneous blow-torch flames: fuel, flesh and munitions, all pulverized, all burning at the temperature of a star's surface.

Two more salvos popped in the air and raged on the ground. The thunderclaps of detonations died away, though some of the burning vehicles screamed as they lit the night with jets of fire.

Huber's gun had jammed, but nobody in 1st Squadron was shooting any more. There were cyan flickers on the pad's northern perimeter, but that might have been guns continuing to fire as they melted into the vehicles on which they were mounted.

"Cease fire!" Colonel Hammer rasped. *"All Slammers units, cease fire! Nonesuch representatives on the starships have offered their surrender. Cease fire, troopers, it's over!"*

Huber took his hands from the grips of his weapon. The barrel cluster continued to spin, a white blur that made the air throb as it threw off heat. Huber had a multi-tool in his belt pouch, but when he reached for it to clear the jam he realized that his fingers didn't want to close properly.

Deseau's tribarrel had jammed also. He held his backup 2-cm weapon, but he wasn't shooting into the thousands of helpless human targets sprawling and staggering on the concrete below. The hell-strewn carnage was enough even for Frenchie.

Learoyd took off his commo helmet to rub his bald scalp with his left hand. The skin of his chin and throat below the faceshield's protection was black where iridium vaporized from his gun bores had redeposited itself. He looked older than Huber had ever seen him before.

"Fox Three-six to Fox Three," Huber said in a voice that caught at every syllable. "Good work, troopers. Nobody ever commanded a better unit than I did tonight."

He swallowed and added the words that almost hadn't gotten past his swollen throat. "Three-six out."

Then, because his head throbbed and any constriction was an agony he couldn't bear for the moment, Huber took off his helmet. He regretted the decision immediately with the first breath he took of the unfiltered atmosphere.

He turned and vomited over the side of the fighting compartment. No matter how often he encountered it, the smell of burned human flesh always turned Arne Huber's stomach.

"Hey El-Tee!" said Deseau, standing with Padova on the plenum chamber to brace the replacement plate while Learoyd applied the cold weld. "That black-haired piece you met the first time the wogs threw in the towel? She's coming to see you."

"He's not an el-tee any more, Frenchie," Learoyd said, laying his bead along the seam as evenly as the fully-mechanized factory operation which put *Fencing Master* together to begin with. "He's a captain now."

Huber looked over his shoulder in the direction of Frenchie's gaze. He wasn't sure how Daphne Priamedes would take to being called a "black-haired piece," but it was accurate given Deseau's frame of reference. The other part, though . . .

Huber got up from the empty ten-liter coolant drum he was using as a seat while he worked at the Command and Control box. He wiped his hands on his utility blouse—newly-issued three days before and still clean enough—and said quietly, "I met her in Benjamin, Frenchie, back when I was in Operations."

"Captain Huber?" Daphne called from the ground. "I hope you don't mind my coming to offer you lunch. The orderly said that you have an office but that you usually worked in your combat car."

Huber shut down the display. "Glad to see you, Daphne," he said as he swung himself, left leg first, over the side of the fighting compartment. "I could use a break, but I don't know about lunch. Maybe . . ."

He paused as he slid to the ground, careful to take the shock on his right boot. He'd been going to say, " . . . the canteen," but the facilities here at Base Beta consisted of a plastic prefab with extruded furniture and dispensers for a basic range of products. Bezant was only twelve klicks away, so there was no need for the Regiment itself to provide off-duty troops with anything impressive.

Daphne flashed a smile of cool triumph. "I thought you might say that," she said, "so I've brought a cooler in the car. I thought we'd fly to a grove where we could find some quiet."

Huber looked down at his uniform. He hadn't been doing much manual labor—well, *much*—but he'd have wanted to change before an interview with Hammer; or with Joachim Steuben, now that he thought about it.

Daphne repeated the cool smile. "Come along, Arne," she said. "The trees won't care any more than I do. I left my aircar by the TOC."

She crooked her elbow for him to take and started off. Base Beta was an expansion of Firebase One, no prettier than it'd been before Engineer Section trebled its area to hold all three squadrons. As he passed *Fancy Pants*, Huber saw Tranter looking out of an access port and said, "Hold the fort for an hour, Sarge. If anybody really needs me, I've got my commo helmet."

"Roger that, sir," Tranter said cheerfully. He was holding a multi-tool and a pair of pliers, doing technician's work and pleased at the chance.

"Hey El-Tee?" Deseau shouted from *Fencing Master*, loudly enough that half the camp could hear him. "If there's any left that you don't need, remember me'n Learoyd."

Daphne appeared not to notice the comment, unless the faint smile was her response.

Huber cleared his throat, taking stock of the situation. Daphne was wearing a pants suit, simply cut and of sturdy— but probably expensive—material. It would've been proper garb if Huber'd decided to put on his dress uniform and take her to one of the top restaurants in Bezant, but it wasn't out of place in a firebase either.

Well, he'd never doubted that she was smart.

A starship lifted, its corona shiveringly bright even in broad daylight. The rumble of shoving such a mass skyward trembled through Huber's bootsoles, though the airborne sound was distance-muted and slow to arrive.

Huber nodded toward the rising vessel and said, "This time they're repatriating the other mercenary units before they terminate our contract. It'll probably take a while to find so much shipping."

"Yes, but the amount of trade Port Plattner carried before the war is simplifying the problem," Daphne said. They'd reached her car, parked on the concertina-wired pad under the guns of an A Company combat car. The Colonel and the staff he'd brought with him on the run north were sharing space in the trailers with the squadron commanders. That must've been tight, though Huber had his own problems. Tents beside the buried trailers provided overflow for activities that nobody would care about if the shooting started again.

"As for continuing to pay your hire until all the other forces are off-planet . . ." Daphne continued in a wry, possibly amused, tone. "That was a condition Colonel Hammer set on agreeing to allow us to employ the Slammers. Though I think that after seeing the mistake Nonesuch made, we would have decided to find the money whether or not it was a contract term."

The sergeant in charge of the White Mice at the aircar pad spoke to one of her troopers, who swung open the bar wrapped in razor ribbon. Huber noticed the sergeant's arm was in a surface cast, then recognized her as the commander of the resupply aircars. He nodded and said, "I'm glad you came through all right, Sergeant."

"Same to you, Captain," she said, surprised and obviously pleased at his notice. "And congratulations on your promotion."

They stepped into the fenced area. Daphne's limousine was as much of a contrast to the battered utility vehicles as she herself was to the several contract drivers resting in what shade they could find.

"I haven't congratulated you on your promotion, Arne," she said. She opened the door, then bent to touch the switch which slid the hardtop in three sections down into the seatback. "I'm very glad things worked out for you."

Does she know what she's saying? Huber wondered; but maybe she did. Various things Daphne'd said showed that she was far enough up in the government of Solace that she could probably learn anything she wanted to.

"Yeah," he said, getting into the front passenger seat. "The Colonel offered me an infantry company before we headed north, but I wouldn't have known what I was doing. I'm glad I waited."

Waited for a 25-cm bolt to turn Captain Gillig, a good officer and a first-rate bridge player, into a cloud of dissociated atoms. A bolt that could just as easily have hit fifty meters south and done the same thing to Lieutenant Arne Huber and his crew. There were religious people—some of them troopers—who believed everything happened by plan, and maybe they were right. Huber himself, though, couldn't imagine a plan that balanced details so minute and decided that tonight a particular lieutenant would be promoted instead of being ionized. . . .

Daphne ran her fans up to speed, then adjusted blade angle to lift the car off the ground in a jackrabbit start. Huber remembered that on pavement she'd been more sedate; she was outrunning the cloud of dust her fans raised from the scraped, sun-burned, clay.

"To be honest," she said, her attention apparently focused on her instruments and the eastern horizon, "I thought you might already have looked me up now that the war's over."

Huber didn't speak for a moment. He *had* thought about it. He'd decided that she wouldn't be interested; that she wouldn't have time; and that anyway, he flat didn't have the energy to get involved in anything more than a business transaction which cost about three Frisian thalers at the going rate of exchange.

Aloud he said, "Daphne, I just got promoted to command of Fox Company. I'm trying to integrate new personnel and equipment as well as repair what we can."

What remained of Captain Gillig's *Fantom Lady* would stand, probably forever, on the crest where it'd been hit. The eight fan nacelles hadn't been damaged, so Maintenance had stripped them off the hulk.

Relatives of the crew would be told their loved ones were buried on Plattner's World. That was mostly true, except for the atoms that other 1st Squadron troopers had inhaled.

Huber laughed. "No rest for the wicked, you know."

Daphne looked at him with unexpected sharpness. "Don't say that," she said. "You're not wicked. You saved our planet. Saved us from ourselves, if you want to know the truth!"

Did you have friends working in the terminal building when I shot it up, honey? Did you have a cousin paying his vehicle taxes when we blasted the police post at Millhouse Crossing? Other people did!

"Ma'am," said Huber, speaking very slowly and distinctly because this mattered to him. "I appreciate what you're saying, but don't kid yourself. If there's such a thing as wicked, then some of what I do qualifies. Some of what I've done on Plattner's World."

"I don't think you appreciate how true that is of other people too, Arne," Daphne said. She looked at him steadily, then put a hand on his thigh and squeezed before returning her attention to the horizon and steering yoke.

Well, that answered a question which, despite Deseau's certainty, had remained open in Huber's mind. Frenchie didn't have much to do with women like Daphne Priamedes.

He grinned. Neither did Arne Huber, if it came to that.

"The alliance of nations on Plattner's World which hired your Regiment," Daphne said, switching subjects with the grace of a mirror trick, "will continue to operate the port as a common facility rather than a part of Solace. We'll be raising the price of Moss and of Thalderol base to pay for port renovations."

She looked at Huber and grinned coldly.

"Which will be extensive, as you might imagine."

"Yeah," Huber said, "I can."

Just clearing wrecked equipment would be a bitch of a job: the melted hull of a two-hundred-tonne tank wasn't going to move easily, and thousands of plasma bolts had not only scarred the surface but also shattered the concrete deep into the pad's interior. The terminal building was gone, and the guidance pods which humped at regular intervals across the pad were scarred by shrapnel from the firecracker rounds if they hadn't been blasted by stray powergun bolts.

"Your backers are agreeing to the price rise?" Huber said. "The planets who funded us the second time, I mean."

"Their rates will go up ten percent," Daphne said primly. "They're quite comfortable with that. The rate to Nonesuch will go up thirty percent."

She looked at Huber and added, "I suppose you're surprised that we don't refuse to sell Thalderol base to Nonesuch regardless of the price?"

"No ma'am," Huber said, fighting to control his grin. What a question to ask a mercenary soldier! "I'm not surprised. I'd say it was a good plan to keep Nonesuch from getting so desperate that they'd try a rematch despite all."

Daphne smiled wryly. "Yes," she said, "I suppose it is at that, though I don't believe anyone was thinking in those terms when we came to the decision. We just wanted to set the rate at the maximum we thought they'd pay. We need the money rather badly, you see."

They both laughed; the tension of moments before was gone and nothing was hiding in the background so far as Huber could tell. Well, no conflict, anyway.

The aircar was five hundred meters above the ground, mushing along at about eighty kph. They'd flown beyond the wheat fields; below was pasture in which large roan cattle wandered in loose herds. Brush and small trees grew in swales, green against the rusty color of the grass at this season. Fencelines occasionally glinted from one horizon to the other, but there were kilometers between tracts.

Huber took off his commo helmet and set it in the compartment behind him. He probably wasn't going to be back in the hour he'd told Tranter, and that was all right too.

"A nice day," he said, stretching in his seat before he put an arm over Daphne's shoulders.

"Yes," she said, setting the aircar's autopilot as she leaned toward Huber. "A nice day for normal things instead of with guns and destruction."

They kissed, wriggling closer in their bucket seats.

In his mind, Port Plattner blazed with plasma bolts and the rich, red light of burning tents. *But for me,* Huber thought as he raised his hand to her breast, *guns and destruction* are *what's normal.*

ML

DRAKE   Drake, David.

           Paying the piper.

DATE			

BAKER & TAYLOR